C

HER BROODING ITALIAN SURGEON

BY
FIONA LOWE

A FATHER FOR BABY ROSE

BY
MARGARET BARKER

GW00601276

MILLS & BOON

HER BROODING ITALIAN SURGEON

BY
FIONA LOWE

MILLS & BOON

All the characters in this book have no existence outside the imagination of the author, and have no relation whatsoever to anyone bearing the same name or names. They are not even distantly inspired by any individual known or unknown to the author, and all the incidents are pure invention.

First published in Great Britain 2010
Harlequin Mills & Boon Limited,
Eton House, 18-24 Paradise Road, Richmond, Surrey TW9 1SR

© Fiona Lowe 2010

ISBN: 978 0 263 87903 2

Harlequin Mills & Boon policy is to use papers that are natural, renewable and recyclable products and made from wood grown in sustainable forests. The logging and manufacturing process conform to the legal environmental regulations of the country of origin.

Printed and bound in Spain
by Litografia Rosés, S.A., Barcelona

Always an avid reader, **Fiona Lowe** decided to combine her love of romance with her interest in all things medical, so writing Medical™ Romance was an obvious choice! She lives in a seaside town in southern Australia, where she juggles writing, reading, working and raising two gorgeous sons with the support of her own real-life hero! You can visit Fiona's website at www.fionalowe.com

Recent titles by the same author:

MIRACLE: TWIN BABIES
THE SURGEON'S SPECIAL DELIVERY
THE DOCTOR CLAIMS HIS BRIDE
THE PLAYBOY DOCTOR'S MARRIAGE PROPOSAL

In memory of Chris; a caring neighbour
who took great pleasure in sponge cakes,
Mr. Lincoln Roses and thoroughly enjoyed reading
Mills and Boon Romance. She'd always cross the
road to tell me, 'It's your best one yet, dear.'

Vale, Chris.

Special thanks to Josie and Serena
for their advice on all things Italian.

CHAPTER ONE

BRIGHT white lights radiated heat and sweat poured down Dr Abbie McFarlane's forehead as she gritted her teeth in concentration. A stray strand of hair escaped from her cap but she resisted the urge to wipe her forehead on her sleeve, the sterile law of the operating theatre drilled into her long and hard over many years. Her mouth framed the word 'sponge' but she quickly swallowed it, stealing it back before it tripped over her lips.

Squinting, she tried again. Her nimble hands, which usually deftly and ably sewed fine stitches, seemed at a loss as they plunged yet again down into the sticky mass and stalled.

'*Dottore*, do not stab it. *Il pane*, he needs you to be more gentle.'

Abbie sighed. 'Maria, the dough's just sticking to my fingers and I can't do anything with it.'

'You must use plenty of flour.' Maria's old, gnarled hands quickly scattered more flour on the workbench and expertly kneaded Abbie's sticky mess into a stretchy and elastic dough, before pulling it into a ciabatta roll.

Abbie immediately covered it with a fresh white tea towel. 'I think I'm a lost cause.'

The old woman grinned and shook her scarf-covered head. 'I do this for seventy years. You come again and try.'

Abbie played her only bargaining card in this unusual doctor-patient scenario. 'Only if you promise me you'll rest. Your blood pressure's a bit high and your family's worried about you. It's going to take the new medication a few days to start working, so you have to take it easy.'

'Pfft. I feel fine.' She patted her chest with her fist. 'My heart is strong.'

Abbie frowned and injected a stern tone into her voice. 'If you don't rest I'll put you in hospital.'

Maria sat down fast. 'You sound like my grandson.'

'He must be a wise man, then,' Abbie quipped as she washed her hands in preparation to head back to the clinic.

The eighty-year-old *nonna* rolled her eyes and jabbed the air with her finger. 'He is alone like you.'

'Well, I hope he's as happy as I am.' Abbie smiled and quickly laid the hand towel over the rail. Twelve months in Bandarra and she'd quickly learned every diversion tactic in the book to avoid being introduced to all and sundry's brothers, sons, cousins and grandsons. She'd even let the 'gay' rumour run wild until one patient had tried to set her up on a date with her daughter. Ironically, no one had made the connection to one of the reasons why she donated so much of her time to the women's shelter—it was the one place no one tried to match her up with anyone. If life had taught her anything, it was that she chose the wrong man every time so staying single was the safe choice. Nothing or no one was going to change that. Ever.

Abbie picked up the keys to her four-wheel drive. 'So, you're going to lie down for an hour until your daughter's back from the vineyard?'

Maria unexpectedly capitulated. 'Yes, *dottore*, I will do as you say.'

'Excellent. I'll call by tomorrow.'

'And I show you how to make bruschetta.'

Abbie laughed. 'Give up now, Maria. I can't cook.'

But the old woman just smiled.

'Karen, *cara*, my angel of the operating theatre, you can't be serious?' Leo Costa held his overwhelming frustration in check by a bare millimetre, knowing that yelling would work once but flattery worked for ever. Ignoring the pinching of his mobile phone against his ear, he poured on the charm. 'We organised this last week over lunch. I even filled in the paperwork as a special favour to you, so don't break my heart and tell me it's double-booked and I can't have the slot.'

A tiny silence ensued before Karen spoke. 'I guess I could ask Mr Trewellan to reschedule, seeing that we gave him an extra slot last week.'

'I like the way you're thinking, *cara*. Call me back as soon as it's sorted.' He snapped his phone shut without waiting for the theatre administrator's farewell and checked his watch. Damn it, but he was late for rounds and he hated starting the day on the back foot, especially when he had a full appointment list this morning in his Collins Street rooms.

He strode towards the bank of lifts and hit the up button, tapping his foot on the polished linoleum floor of Melbourne City Hospital. He'd had scant sleep last night, having operated on a road trauma case, and it hardly seemed any time at all since he'd left the hospital, and now he was back again. There'd only been enough time to catch a three-hour nap before a quick shower and shave and a much needed shot of espresso before arriving back at work.

As the light above the lift glowed red and the heralding 'ping' sounded, his phone vibrated in his pocket. Hopefully, it was good news about the theatre mess. He flicked his phone open. 'Leo Costa.'

'Oh, thank God, you're not scrubbed.' The unexpected but familiar voice of one of his many sisters came down the line.

'Anna?' He rubbed his hand through his hair. Usually at this time of morning she was knee-deep in children, the school run and juggling calls from restaurant suppliers. 'What's up?'

A half sigh, half cry came down the line. 'It's Nonna, Leo. This time you *have* to come back to Bandarra.'

Abbie stifled a yawn as she swung her red dust-covered boots from her four-by-four onto the hospital car park's sticky asphalt. The hot summer sun had finally fallen below the horizon and Venus twinkled at her as if to say, *Isn't life wonderful*. But she didn't feel twinkly today. The day had thrown everything at her, including an emergency evacuation from the Aboriginal settlement a hundred kilometres away. Now she longed to crawl out of the clothes she'd been wearing for seventeen hours, ached for a shower to wash the ingrained grit of the outback dust from her skin, and wanted nothing more than to snuggle into soft cotton sheets.

The automatic hospital doors opened and she walked into air-conditioned cool, a blissful respite from the outside summer heat that not even nightfall could cool. She paused, her ears and eyes alert, and then she smiled, letting out a long, slow breath. Calm.

Tonight, the small hospital had the air of quiet, drama-free purpose which, given her day, was exactly what she needed. She'd do a quick check on Maria, consult with the nursing staff about her other two inpatients and then head home and somehow convince Murphy, her Border collie, that he didn't want a walk tonight.

The nursing station was empty, but the charts had been gathered for the ease of the night shift and sorted into alphabetical order. She quickly rifled through them until she found the group labelled 'Rossi'.

'Page her doctor again.' A rich baritone voice, threaded with startling steel, travelled down the corridor, followed a beat later by, 'I'd really appreciate it, Erin.' The steel in the voice had vanished, replaced by a deep mellow sound reminiscent of a luxurious velvet cloak that wrapped enticingly around a person and caressed with beguiling softness.

Abbie knew all about velvet hiding steel. She'd grown up with it in many guises and it had chased her through a disastrous relationship. Charm so often hid threatening control.

'Of course, Mr Costa, I'll try again for you.' Erin Bryant, the immensely capable no-nonsense night-duty nurse who always did things her way, had just been vanquished with Charm 101. The fact that a relative was even in the hospital at this time of night was testament to that.

Holding the multicoloured charts, Abbie grinned, knowing that for the first time today the fates had actually come down on her side. She didn't have a Costa in hospital and Justin, her most recent locum who'd been gleefully counting down the days until he left for his cross-Asia trek back to his home town of London, would have to deal with this determined relative as one of his last obligations. Being British, he did polite much better than she did. Humming to herself, she walked down the corridor to Maria's room, turned into the doorway and stopped dead.

A man stood just inside the door, his presence filling the room with vibrating energy that swirled and eddied like a tornado, pulling at everything and everyone in its path.

An involuntary shiver shot through Abbie, immediately chased by a foreign flicker of heat. Heat that hadn't glowed in a very long time.

No way, not possible. But her hand instinctively tightened around the charts.

Erin's face beamed with a high-wattage smile. 'This is Dr McFarlane, Mr Costa, and I'll go and get you that coffee I promised.' Still smiling, she backed towards the door.

'*Grazie*, Erin.' His head tilted and his lips curved into a smile that travelled along black-stubble cheeks, and for a fraction of a second it lit up his eyes like the bright-white light of Venus.

Abbie took in a deep breath just as Maria's unknown visitor turned his unrelenting gaze to her. A gaze that shot from eyes as black as the night sky but was now minus the twinkle. One bold dark brow lifted as he took in her dust-streaked shorts, her crumpled and stained polo shirt and her uncontrollable mass of chaotic curls. Judging by the expression in the depths of his onyx eyes, he found everything about her eminently lacking.

Abbie needed to lift her chin to meet his scrutiny and if he, a patient's relative, had the temerity to openly give her the once-over, then *right back at you, pal*. But that was when irony socked her hard like a sucker-punch to the gut.

A strong, straight nose centred his Roman face and high cheekbones defined it as striking, but it was his well-shaped lips that told the truth – gorgeous and well aware of it. Despite the fatigue that played around his eyes and hovered near a jagged white scar on his square jaw, the man could have modelled for fashion week, although she sensed he'd have taken no nonsense and would have probably given the orga-nisers a very hard time.

He was urban chic from his glossy indigo hair down to

his Italian leather loafers. A black V-necked light cotton sweater clung to, and curved around, broad square shoulders, toned pecs and a flat stomach, boldly advertising the buff goods that nestled below. Soft and cool dune-coloured linen trousers caressed long, long legs unsullied by any hint of outback red earth or heat-induced perspiration. If she wasn't standing in front of him breathing in his scent of mint mixed with orange, she would have dismissed him as a mythical being that no mere mortal could ever hope to emulate.

She dropped her gaze and frantically gathered her scattered thoughts, focusing on the fact that she was the doctor and he was her patient's relative. She was therefore the one in charge. Dealing with relatives was something she prided herself on. She understood their occasional outbursts as a projection of fear and feelings of powerlessness in a foreign environment and, after all, hospitals were strange and frightening places for the general public. But absolutely nothing about this man looked uncertain or unsure, or powerless.

His firm stance of controlled casualness rippled with panther-like readiness and he spoke before Abbie could introduce herself. 'You're Nonna's doctor?' Incredulity mixed with a hint of censure rode on the words.

A shaft of determination straightened her spine. So what that she was dirty and grimy and he was 'Mr Ultra-Clean and well-kempt from the city'; he hadn't just spent the afternoon in the middle of nowhere keeping a young boy alive until the Flying Doctors had arrived. Given those neatly trimmed, dirt-free nails, he was probably an accountant and the closest he got to life and death was a wobbly row of figures.

It was hard to peer imperiously down her nose when he towered over her five foot two inches, so instead she extended her hand with crisp efficiency. 'Abbie McFarlane, GP, and you would be?'

He suddenly smiled, dimples spiralling into the inky stubble as his hand gripped hers. 'Leo Costa, Maria's grandson.'

Unambiguous sexual electricity zapped her so hard she saw stars. She pulled her hand back fast and somehow managed a garbled, 'Oh, right, yes, she mentioned you when I saw her yesterday', while trying to rein her wanton body back under the tight control she'd held it in for three years. Not an easy task after being broadsided by the explosive combination of his touch and smile. A smile that should come complete with a classification warning.

She caught a glance of the sleeping Maria, which immediately centred her, and she instinctively stepped back out into the corridor. 'Let's not wake your grandmother.'

Like a giant cat, Leo Costa moved forward with rippling fluidity, stepping into the space she'd just vacated, his energy ramming into her, setting up more unwanted and inappropriate tingling.

'How long have you been my grandmother's doctor?' The casual question, asked in a conversational tone, was at odds with the tension hovering across his shoulders and narrowing his eyes.

She thought about how long she'd actually known Maria and the time it had taken to convince her to accept an examination. 'A few weeks–'

'And you saw her yesterday?' The conversational tone slipped slightly.

Abbie nodded. 'I did. She was trying to teach me how to bake bread but–'

'A sick woman was teaching you to bake bread at a time when you should have been admitting her to hospital.'

His words were a shot across the bow, in stark contrast to the captivating smile. Warning bells rang loud in her head. 'I beg your pardon?'

He spoke quietly but every word reverberated like the strike against a bell. 'If you'd admitted my grandmother to hospital yesterday and monitored her more closely, she wouldn't have had a stroke.'

She sucked in a breath, hearing it whistle between her teeth. *Stay calm.* 'Mr Costa, I understand you're upset, as am I. Your grandmother is a very special woman but she didn't have malignant hypertension, which is extremely high blood pressure. Although her blood pressure was elevated, based on her observations yesterday, there was no need to admit her.'

He casually crossed his arms over his chest but she caught a silver flash of steel in his black eyes. 'You prescribed medication?'

She pursed her lips. 'Yes, she was commenced on medication to lower her blood pressure and she was instructed to rest.'

The corner of his mouth seemed at war with the twitching muscle in his jaw but the attempted smile lost out and the charm he'd used with Erin, and half-tried with her, totally vanished. 'And I put it to you that the medication was too strong and brought her BP down too fast, causing a focal cerebral ischemia.'

Focal cerebral ischemia? O-K. Maria's grandson definitely wasn't an accountant. His commanding control of the room suddenly made sense, although it struck her as odd that Maria hadn't mentioned her grandson was a doctor. That aside, his grandmother was *her* patient, not his and Maria's medical care had been textbook.

'Mr Costa—' she emphasised his title '—I'm assuming your expertise is in a branch of surgery not geriatrics.'

Dark eyes flashed before a tight smile stretched his mouth.

'I'm a trauma surgeon at Melbourne City with a private practice of general surgery. I don't believe you're a geriatrician either.'

Touché. The bald statement carried power and credence and told of a man used to getting his own way. She had a pretty good idea how he usually got what he wanted—with effortless charm and good looks—and, if that failed, he used a bulldozer.

Well, she wasn't about to be bulldozed. Not this time.

'Your grandmother hasn't seen a doctor in over two years and it took me a few weeks to convince her to let me examine her. I diagnosed her hypertension a few days ago. Although there's a slight chance that perhaps the medication lowered her blood pressure too quickly, it's far more probable that the stroke was caused by longstanding hypertension. She has a slight weakness on her right side but I'm very confident that with rehabilitation and time, it will resolve.'

'I'm glad you're confident.'

The disapproval in the quietly spoken words plunged deep like the cut of cold steel. She matched his black gaze. 'I'm very confident.'

He shrugged his broad shoulders and stared down at her, his eyes filled with condescension and backlit with righteous resolve. 'Look, I'm sure you've done *your* best but I know you'll understand when I say I want my *nonna*'s care transferred to another doctor.'

I know you'll understand. Outrage poured through Abbie and she clenched her hands by her sides to stop herself from lunging at his gorgeous but arrogant throat. Greg had used the very same words. So had her father just before he'd left. Somehow through clenched teeth she managed to speak. 'That's surely up to Maria.'

His head moved almost imperceptibly, the light catching

his hair, the sheen so bright it dazzled. 'Nonna usually takes my advice.'

It was a statement of fact spoken by a successful man. A man raised in the heart of a loving Italian family where education and experience were honoured and family was everything. The polar opposite of her own family.

She'd been left with no doubt that Leo Costa would advise his grandmother against her and she knew she had scant chance against the power of his recommendation, no matter how wrong she believed it to be. He had both the money and contacts to pull strings. 'Perhaps she might surprise you.'

Unfathomable dark eyes stared at her. 'I doubt that.'

Abbie forced herself to smile and to behave in the proper way a doctor should—putting her patient's needs first, irrespective of her own feelings. 'As Maria's asleep and her health and welfare are my paramount concerns, the decision will rest until morning.' She extended her arm towards the exit with an in-charge sweep. 'Good night, Mr Costa.'

He gave her a slight nod of acquiescence along with a wry smile, as if he'd just glimpsed something completely unexpected. 'Until the morning then, Abbie.'

He turned on his heel and somehow she forced her wobbly legs to hold her up until the doors opened and he was swallowed up by the night. She sank against the wall, hating the butterflies in her stomach that floated on a current of heat, trailing through her and upending every resolution she'd made three years ago.

Leo Costa with his effortless charm, devastating good looks and single-minded purpose was her worst nightmare and she was determined not to relive bad dreams. She gulped in air and her tattered resolve slowly wove itself back together.

Warrior Abbie stood firm and spoke sternly. *You'll miss Maria but you don't need him anywhere near you.*

And she couldn't argue with that.

CHAPTER TWO

'HAVE you lost your mind?' Anna slid a hot and frothy breakfast cappuccino towards Leo across the large wooden kitchen table.

'It was an unwise thing for you to do.' Rosa, his mother, quietly rebuked him as she passed a plate of fluffy light pastries and pushed two onto his plate.

Leo clung to his temper by a thread. Coming back to Bandarra always set him on edge but if he just breathed slowly, let them have their say, then he could move forward with the day doing things his way. He'd organise Nonna's care and then catch the afternoon flight back to the sanctuary of Melbourne. Breaking open the brioche, he slathered it with home-made raspberry jam, the sweet breakfast in stark contrast to the muesli he always ate in his Melbourne apartment. But the kitchen in Bandarra was a world away from Melbourne, despite the fact there was only a six-hundred-kilometre distance between the two places.

Rosa carefully stirred sugar into her coffee. 'I wish you'd come home rather than going direct from the airport to the hospital, and then all this could have been avoided.'

For the second time in twenty-four hours his usual sanguine approach slipped and his voice rose sharply. 'This is Nonna we're talking about! Of course I went straight to the hospital, especially as I'd had both you and Anna sobbing on the phone, not to mention Bianca and Chiara's texts.'

His gut clenched as a ripple of fear spread its dread again, just as it had last night when he'd stood at the end of the narrow hospital bed watching his amazing Nonna, always such a powerhouse of energy, looking so frail and tiny under crisp white sheets. He hated that feeling, that powerlessness and the way it dragged him back into the past. Back to the waterhole, back to failing Dom so badly. He abruptly rubbed his chin. 'I wasn't leaving until I'd spoken with her doctor, which is what I thought you wanted.'

His mother threw him a rueful smile. 'Considering how stubborn Nonna can be, Abbie McFarlane's been a saint. I told her how worried I was about your grandmother and she put up with all of Nonna's tricks and made home visits until Nonna finally let her examine her.'

Anna laughed. 'True, but not even Nonna has been able to teach Abbie to cook—she's hopeless.'

Leo frowned against the recurring and unwanted image of tangled and tumbling cinnamon-sprinkled caramel curls framing rainforest-green eyes. Eyes that hadn't flickered with the keen appreciation he was used to seeing when he met women's gazes. The vision had interrupted his sleep and increased his irritation. Women like Abbie McFarlane never got picked up by his radar, let alone landed a starring role in his dreams. With the exception of his ill-conceived marriage, where he'd been faithful to Christina, he'd always had his pick of women, and all his choices came with statuesque height, haute couture and heavenly features.

Name one that has really interested you in the last year.

Not wanting to go there, he pulled his mind back to the conversation. 'Well, I don't care about her cooking, or the fact she doesn't even look like a doctor. *I* wasn't impressed by her medicine.'

Anna raised both of her neatly shaped brows, taking in his crisp outfit of navy knee-length shorts teamed with a short-sleeved chambray shirt. 'Big brother, you've turned into a big city fashion snob. Abbie might dress like a female version of a crocodile hunter but her medicine's spot on. She's done more for this community in twelve months than old Doctor Renton did in his twelve years.'

Annoyance fizzed in his veins. 'That isn't saying much then, is it?'

His father, Stefano, who'd been silent behind the most recent edition of *Vintners' Monthly*, lowered the magazine. Wise molasses-coloured eyes stared back at Leo from behind rimless lenses. 'Your mistake is you've forgotten Bandarra isn't Melbourne and the choice of doctors here is seriously limited.'

Rosa sighed. 'Your *nonna*'s getting old, *figlio mio*.'

No. He wanted to put his hands over his ears like he'd done as a little child when he didn't want to hear. Right now he didn't want to hear or think about Nonna and death. Nonna was such a special part of his life. She featured in every child-hood memory—always there giving hugs while his parents had been busy establishing the vineyard, clipping him around the ear when he got too cheeky and always feeding him like he was a king.

Holding him so tightly after the accident.

Right then his exasperation with his family peaked. Enough! He'd let everyone have their say and now it was his turn. 'I'm the qualified medical practitioner in this conversa-tion and I've made a decision which I intend to follow through on.' He pushed back his chair, the red-gum scraping loud against the polished boards.

'You go and be the doctor but Nonna doesn't just need that.' Stefano rose to his feet and his quiet but determined voice stalled Leo's departure. 'Most of all she needs you to be a grandson and to give of your time. In fact, all of your family needs your time.'

Leo's throat tightened and every part of him tensed, all primed and ready to flee. For years he'd flown in and flown out of Bandarra, only ever staying forty-eight hours, often less. 'Papà, I can't. Work is busy.'

'Work is always busy.' His father downed the last of his coffee. 'You managed to arrange things so you could be here for Nonna. I'm certain you can arrange to stay longer if you choose. You haven't been home for a vintage since you were eighteen and we've never asked you to come, but you're here now. This time you need to stay for Nonna, your mother and the rest of us.' His hand settled on Rosa's shoulder and he gave her a gentle squeeze.

Leo's breath stuck in his chest as he tried to think of a way out, a way to avoid having to stay. Excuses rose to his lips but his father's implacable stance and knowing expression silenced them. His father would see them for what they were—excuses. The ties of family tightened around him, pulling him back to a place he didn't want to be.

Anna winked at him. 'Come on, big brother, stay a while. It'll be just like the old days, lots of fun.'

But fun was the last thing a holiday in Bandarra could ever be.

Bubbling frustration tinged with fury ate at Leo as he shifted in the car seat, unable to get comfortable. Bandarra Car Rentals didn't run to a Ferrari Spider and he was stuck in a small car which wasn't designed for men who were five foot six, let alone six foot one.

Although not even nine a.m., heat poured through the untinted windows, declaring that the day would be a scorcher. He pulled on his aviator sunglasses and slammed down the visor. His father hadn't pulled rank like that in seventeen years. On top of that, he couldn't get over his family's attitude towards Nonna's medical care. Didn't they want the best for her?

Perhaps she already has the best with Abbie McFarlane.

No, he couldn't believe that. The woman had disaster written all over her, from the rent in her khaki trousers to the burnt-red ochre smear on her freckle-dusted cheeks. Smooth, soft cheeks. He shook away the image and focused on his concerns. She looked about twenty-one, although he knew she had to be older than that, but still, she had the chaotic look of someone who could hardly look after herself, let alone patients. Nonna needed someone with solid experience—years and years of experience. Not someone with the bare basics of a couple of intern years, who still held a textbook in one hand and a prayer in the other.

It was well known that the further a person lived from a major capital city the more their health was compromised by their lack of access to state-of-the-art health care. That was a given in Bandarra, but at least it still had a small hospital which meant it attracted more doctors than other outback towns. He intended to talk to the senior practice partner—that was the doctor who should be looking after Nonna, not the trainee GP.

Vineyards and orchards flashed past as he headed into town, the rich red loamy river soil contrasting intensely with the grape-green foliage of the 'close-to-harvest' vines. The familiar clutch of unease tightened another notch and his chest hurt the way it always did when he found himself back under Bandarra's endless outback sky. His fingers whitened as he gripped the steering wheel overly hard and he concentrated on forcing away the demons that threatened to suffocate him. Pulling hard left, he deliberately avoided the river road, taking a longer route, a route that he could navigate with his eyes closed despite the fact he'd lived in Melbourne a very long time. Avoiding the river was the only way he was going to survive three to four weeks in Bandarra.

Visitors to the district were always amazed at how the pioneers had harnessed the power of the great Murray River and turned what should have been an arid and harsh land into the luxuriant and premier fruit basket of Australia. But back then the river had run with a lot more water and the current irrigators now faced a new set of problems that the pioneers had probably never envisaged.

Ten minutes later, Leo walked into the hospital and caught sight of the broad back of a male standing at the nurses' station. He was wearing a white coat. Leo smiled—now that was more like it.

'Excuse me.'

The doctor raised his head from the chart and turned his shirt-and-tie-covered torso towards him. 'May I help you?'

The English accent surprised Leo but this doctor had a gravitas that Abbie McFarlane lacked, despite the *Star Trek* tie. He extended his hand. 'Leo Costa, surgeon. Are you the Senior Medical Officer?'

'No, but I'd be happy to introduce you.' He shot out his hand. 'Justin Willoughby. It's brilliant that you're going to be working here.'

'*No!*' Hell would freeze over before he'd work in Bandarra.

Justin started with surprise at his emphatic tone and Leo sucked in a calming breath. In Melbourne he was known for high standards but with an easy-going approach. He wouldn't let a short time in Bandarra steal that from him. 'Sorry, what

I meant to say is, I'm Maria Rossi's grandson and I'm just up here for a few weeks until things are sorted out with my grandmother. Then it's *straight* back to Melbourne.'

'Ah.' Justin nodded but his expression remained disappointed. 'Pity. Bandarra could do with a visiting surgeon. The SMO's caught up in ED. This way.' He inclined his head and started walking down the corridor.

Leo fell into step with Justin and followed him through double perspex doors into a compact emergency department. Screens were drawn around cubicles and a pretty nurse walked towards them.

'Where's the boss, Lisa?' Justin asked.

'Not far away.'

'Leo, you stay here and I'll bring the boss to you. Back in a mo.'

Justin disappeared, leaving Leo with the nurse, who gave him a none too subtle look of curiosity which finished with smouldering interest. 'Hello. New to Bandarra?'

'I grew up here.' The words came out stark and brusque and he immediately forced himself to return her friendly look with a flash of his trademark smile. A smile he used many times a day without even thinking because it was never wise to burn bridges. His smile had gained him all sorts of things and had got him out of a few nasty situations. *Except for yesterday*.

Yesterday had been an aberration. His cool had slipped slightly with Abbie McFarlane and he'd chalked it up to his shock about Nonna and being back in a town he tried very hard to avoid. But everyone made mistakes and thankfully no real harm had been done.

'Were you a blockie?' Lisa used the local term to describe people who grew fruit on land with irrigation rights.

'My grandfather was.'

'Oh, are you related to the Italians out by Wadjera billabong?'

The name plunged into Leo like a knife to the heart and he stiffened. Thankfully, Justin's return ended the conversation.

'Leo, I'd like to introduce you to our SMO.'

Leo turned with a welcoming smile on his face. A pair of questioning moss-green eyes hit him with a clear and uncompromising gaze. Eyes that slanted seductively at the corners. A burst of unexpected heat fired low in his belly, disconcerting him for a second before reality crashed in, wiping out all other feeling. *Our SMO.* Damn it, how could she possibly be the senior doctor?

You've forgotten Bandarra isn't Melbourne. His father's voice rang loud in his head and the full ramifications of what he'd done last night hit him like a king punch. He'd let the Bandarra demons get to him and had made an ill-judged call.

He pulled himself together and, with aching cheeks, smiled. 'Abbie.'

Her mouth flattened. 'Leo.'

A startled expression crossed Justin's face. 'So you two have met before?'

'We met last night.' Abbie tugged at the edges of a clean starched white coat which covered a plain round-neck T-shirt and a straight no-frills navy skirt. The hiking boots had been replaced by flat utilitarian sandals of nondescript brown.

Not a trace of make-up touched her face but, despite that, her lips had a luminous sheen that pulled Leo's gaze and held it fast. What the hell was wrong with him? But he didn't have time to second-guess his reaction—the moment had come for damage control. He forced a self-deprecating quirk to his lips and gave a European shrug of his shoulders. 'I didn't realise Abbie was the SMO. A major error on my part.'

Justin laughed, giving his boss a cheeky grin. 'Poor Abs,

if you were a bloke you could grow a beard to look older.' He winked at Leo. 'She might forgive you in time.'

Going by the implacable set of her face and the tight pull of skin over her cheekbones, Leo wasn't so sure. Still, that didn't matter because he'd pull in a favour and ask the doctor from Naroopna to take over. 'May we speak in private?'

She matched his shrug and rolled her hands palm up. 'Is there anything left to say? You made your position quite clear last night.' Turning on her heel, she headed towards the perspex doors and thumped them open.

Ignoring the intrigued looks of the other staff, he walked with her. 'I do have something to say.'

'You surprise me.' Her sarcasm radiated from her like heat haze. She unexpectedly turned left into an empty ward and then spun back, crossing her arms hard against her chest, pushing her breasts upward. 'Look, Leo, I don't have time for this; I have patients waiting. Are you flying in a private doctor or transferring Maria to Mildura or Melbourne?'

He found it hard to resist sneaking a look at her surprising cleavage. 'Neither one of those options is my choice.' No matter how persuasive he knew he could be, there was no way he'd be able to convince Nonna to leave Bandarra. She'd lived here since arriving as a bride from Italy back in the fifties. Perhaps there'd been times in the past when she might have toyed with the idea of leaving but, since the accident, she'd refused even visits to Melbourne. She wouldn't leave Dominico. Leo alone had been the one to run.

He rubbed his chin and hauled his thoughts back to the here and now. 'You can hand over her care to David Martin.'

A deep V formed at the bridge of her nose. 'So you're transferring her to Adelaide?'

What? 'No, she's staying here.' He tilted his head slightly and met her gaze. 'Abbie.' He paused for the briefest moment, the beat lending credence to his upcoming words. 'Thank you for your care. This isn't personal; it's just that David's experience is what Nonna needs.'

For the first time since he'd met her, a smile pulled her generous mouth upwards. It danced along her cheeks and into her eyes, making them sparkle like the rainforest after rain. And then she laughed. A laugh tinged with incredulity and yet grounded with a known truth, as if she'd heard a similar story before. As if she saw straight through him.

A flicker of unease stirred his normally unshakeable confidence.

'It's been a while since you last visited Bandarra, hasn't it?'

And, just like that, he felt the power shift. 'What makes you say that?'

'David Martin moved to Adelaide ten months ago and the practice at Naroopna is vacant. As is the one at Budjerree. Right now, Bandarra is the only township within two hundred kilometres with medical staff. Come Wednesday, when Justin leaves, it's just me and the nursing staff.'

His breakfast turned to stone in his gut. All he'd wanted was the best for Nonna. Instead, he'd let fatigue and fear of the past interfere with his usual clear-thinking and now he'd backed himself into a corner.

The urgent bleep of her pager suddenly blared between them and she checked the liquid display. Without a word, she sprinted past him and out of the room, leaving behind only a lingering and delectable scent of strawberries and liquorice.

He hated that he instinctively took in a deeper breath.

Abbie raced into a chaotic ED, shedding all of her disconcerting and unsuitable thoughts about the infuriating and ridiculously gorgeous Leo Costa. There should be a law against men being that handsome, and a statute that stopped her even noticing. The piercing siren of an ambulance screamed in the distance, instantly focusing her with its howling volume that increased with every moment. An intense sound that never brought good news.

People were everywhere. Two teenagers sat pale and silent holding each other's hands, an elderly man supported a woman to a chair and a young woman clutching a baby called out, 'Help me,' and still people poured through the doors, many bloodied and hurt.

Lisa and Jason were murmuring platitudes mixed in with firm instructions as they tried to examine a hysterical woman with blood streaming down her face. Her shrieks of anguish bounced off the walls, telling a story of terror and pain.

The area looked like a war zone. 'What's happened and why haven't emergency services notified us?'

Justin grimaced. 'Apparently a bus hit a truck. Those who could, walked here.'

Triage. Years of training swung into action. 'Lisa, you're on walking wounded. Get a nurse from the floor to help you stat, and get someone to ring all the nursing staff and tell them to come in. I want a list of all names and all injuries. Prioritise, treat and be aware of anyone who blacked out. Any concerns, consult me or Jason.'

'Will do.' The experienced nurse headed to the chairs as Abbie grabbed the emergency radio.

'Bandarra Base Hospital to Bandarra Police, over.'

Daniel Ruston's voice crackled down the line. 'Abbie, a bus and a truck collided. The paramedics are on their way with the first of the seriously injured passengers. It's not pretty.'

'How many are there?'

'Two at least, probably more.'

'Thanks, over and out.' She headed straight into the resuss room, which was technically always set up ready for any emergency but she always liked to double-check. She glanced at the brand-new Virtual Trauma and Critical Care Service – a video conferencing screen on wheels. With its camera that used superfast broadband technology to transfer images from the country to the city, GPs in small towns could teleconference with specialists if need be. It was an extra medical lifeline in the tyranny of distance. Everything was ready. She didn't have to wait long.

The paramedics barrelled through the doors, their stretchers bringing in two patients, both wearing oxygen masks. Paul, the senior paramedic, his face grim, started talking. 'First patient is Jenny, a thirty-year-old woman, conscious with pneumothorax and suspected abdominal internal injuries. Chest tube and IV inserted in the field but BP continuing to drop. Second patient is Emma, a seventeen-year-old female with suspected spinal injuries, currently on spinal board and immobilised with a collar. Complaining of not feeling legs. IV inserted in the field and observations stable.'

Abbie bit her lip. 'What else is coming?'

Paul looked sombre. 'There's a forty-five-year-old male with a fractured pelvis and multiple lacerations, and a sixty-year-old woman whose leg has gone into the wall of the bus. Jaws of life are on hand.'

Adrenaline poured through her, making her shake. She had at least four seriously ill patients, a minimum of thirty walking wounded and only four staff until the other nurses arrived. The ratio of staff to patients totally sucked.

'It hurts.' Jenny's muffled sob came from behind the oxygen mask.

Abbie put her hand reassuringly on the woman's shoulder as the trolley was wheeled into the resuss room. 'I'm Abbie McFarlane and I'll give you something for pain as soon as I've examined you.'

Justin appeared. 'Lisa's got it under control out there and I've given the hysterical woman a sedative and will stitch her forehead later. If you're right here, I'll examine the other stretcher patient.'

'Great. Thanks.' Abbie wrapped the automatic blood pressure cuff around Jenny's arm and attached the electrodes to the ECG dots that the paramedics had applied. The reassuring beat of a regular heart rate traced across the screen.

The blood pressure machine beeped. Eighty on fifty.

Not good. 'I just have to feel your tummy, Jenny.'

'Will it hurt?' Fear lit the woman's eyes.

'It might.' Abbie gently palpated the woman's abdomen and her fingers met a rigid and guarded upper left quadrant.

Jenny flinched. 'Do you have to do that?'

'I'm sorry.' *She's bleeding somewhere.*

'What do you need? Catheter, plasma expander, abdominal ultrasound?' Erin walked into the room, lack-of-sleep-induced black smudges under her eyes but as competent as ever.

'All of the above, Erin.' *And more.*

Despite what Leo Costa thought of her, Abbie knew her medicine, knew her strengths and was well aware of her shortcomings. She was a bloody good GP but she wasn't a surgeon.

A patient with internal bleeding needed a surgeon.

She glanced hopefully at the Virtual Trauma and Critical Care Service but knew in her heart that this time a 'virtual' surgeon wasn't going to meet her needs. She needed a real live hands-on surgeon and she had one down the hall.

One who thought she was incompetent. One she wanted

to avoid at all costs, not work with side by side. But her breath shuddered out of her lungs, the sound telling. No matter how much she wanted to avoid the charismatic and opinionated Leo Costa, patients' needs and lives came first.

The BP machine screamed incessantly, telling its undeniable message in no uncertain terms. Jenny was bleeding into her abdominal cavity. It was just a matter of time before she had more blood there than in her arteries.

She grabbed the plasma expander and plunged the sharp tip of the IV into it, piercing the seal, and then hung the bag onto the hook, opening the flow to full bore. Her choice was no choice at all. Jenny needed surgery and Abbie had to ask for help.

'Erin, find Leo Costa and get him in here. Now!'

CHAPTER THREE

ABBIE had just finished catheterising Jenny when Leo strode into the room, instantly filling it with vibrating energy and command.

'You want me?'

His onyx eyes held hers with a hypnotic gaze and a sharp pang akin to hunger shook her so hard her fingers almost dropped the forceps. It had been years since she'd experienced anything like it. She cleared her throat, finding her in-charge voice. 'Jenny sustained a blunt trauma to the abdomen, is haemodynamically unstable and transfer to Melbourne at this point is risky. She needs a surgeon.' She pulled the ultrasound machine in close and turned it on, handing the transducer to him as Erin returned with a set of charts.

Leo put his hand gently on the terrified patient's arm and, using the velvet tone she'd heard him use with everyone except herself, he reassured their patient.

'Jenny, I'm Leo Costa and I'm a surgeon. Dr McFarlane's pretty concerned about you so I'm just going to see what's going on using the ultrasound.'

'OK.' Jenny gazed up at Leo as if he'd mesmerised her and all the resistance she'd used with Abbie melted away.

Abbie's jaw clenched as memories of her father and Greg swamped her but she reminded herself it didn't matter a jot if Leo Costa charmed every woman he ever met as long as he saved Jenny in a professional manner.

'It will feel cold.' He squirted the gel onto her abdomen and gently moved it across her distended belly. Black and white flickered on the screen until the image came into focus. He let out a low grunt. 'Good catch.'

Abbie followed the trace of his finger against the screen, making out the black mass that was darker than intact liver and splenic tissue. It was everywhere – between the left kidney and the spleen, behind the spleen and ultimately pooling in the pelvis, the blood having travelled via the paracolic gutter. Her diagnosis was correct, not that it made her feel at all happy because Jenny wasn't out of the woods yet.

Leo wiped the transducer and stowed it in its holder on the machine and returned his undivided attention to the patient. 'Jenny, I'm fairly certain the impact of the accident has ruptured your spleen and I'm going to have to operate.'

The already pale woman blanched even more, a tremble of fear on her lips. 'You're good at this, aren't you?'

Leo grinned, his smile streaking across his clean-shaven cheeks. 'Jenny, I'm more than good; I'm one of the best.' Then, as impossible as it was to imagine, his voice suddenly dropped even deeper, its timbre completely sincere. 'Most importantly for you, I've done this operation many times in Melbourne. Erin's going to get you ready for Theatre and I'll see you there very soon.'

Abbie knew at that moment if she'd been the patient she would have followed him to the ends of the earth. Thank goodness she wasn't. She was a wise and experienced woman and she didn't follow any man anywhere. Not any more.

Leo tilted his head towards the door, code for, *We need to talk*, and then strode towards it. Abbie followed him out into the corridor.

Without preliminaries, he cut to the chase. 'Can you anaesthetise?'

She nodded. 'I can and Erin can assist but that's all the staff I can spare because Justin and the nursing staff are needed down here.'

'Abbie—' Justin hurried towards them '—I'm evacuating the spinal injury to Melbourne by air ambulance.'

'What about the elderly woman?'

'She hasn't arrived yet; they're still trying to get her out but Paul's worried about a crush injury and possible risk of amputation.'

Abbie groaned. 'Man, I wish I could clone us. We've still got the fractured pelvis to assess. Get the paramedics to help you when they bring in the next two patients and—'

'Abbie.' Her name came out on a low growl as Leo slid his arm under her elbow in an attempt to propel her forward. 'We need to get to Theatre now.'

His urgency roared through her, along with a tremor of something else she refused to name. 'Justin if you—'

'He'll ring us in Theatre if he needs to consult. Come on.' Leo marched her back into the resuss room. 'Erin, *cara*, let's move.' He started to push the trolley through the door.

Then he swung back to Abbie, his well-shaped lips twitching with an unexpected smile tinged with cheeky humour as if he'd just realised something funny. 'Er… Abbie, exactly where is the operating theatre?'

Her already adrenaline-induced limbs liquefied. She could resist his *getting my own way* smile, knowing it was manufactured, but this smile was vastly different—it was one hundred per cent genuine and completely devastating. Somehow she forced her boneless legs to start moving. 'This way; follow me.'

'It's a mess in here.' Dealing with the pulped spleen made Leo frown in concentration as he carefully separated it from its anchoring ligaments. Every part of him operated on high-alert, not just because all emergency surgery meant the unknown but because added into this combination was working with today's less experienced staff. Still, he couldn't fault either of them. Abbie McFarlane had run the emergency as well as any of his veteran colleagues in Melbourne and right now she was coping with a tricky anaesthetic and acting as scout.

'Suction please, Erin.' The amount of blood in the field had him extremely worried. 'Abbie, how's her pressure?'

Remarkably calm green eyes peered from behind a surgical mask. 'Holding, but only just. I'll be happier when you've zapped the sucker.'

He grimaced behind his mask. 'You and me both.' He moved the probe into position and, using his foot, activated the diathermy. The zap sounded loud in the relatively quiet theatre, in stark contrast to Melbourne City where his favourite music was always piped in.

Erin's hand hovered, holding the suction over the clean site, and he counted slowly. By the time he got to four, blood bubbled up again, filling the space. 'Damn it.' He packed in more gauze.

'Pressure's still dropping.' A fray in Abbie's calm unravelled in her voice. 'She's lost three litres of blood and this is our last packed cell until the helicopter arrives.'

'It will be OK.' He said it as much for himself as to reassure Abbie and Erin. Closing out the sound of the beeping machines, he carefully examined the entire operation site millimetre by millimetre, looking for the culprit.

'O2 sats are dropping.' Stark urgency rang in Abbie's voice.

The gurgling sound of the suction roared around him as Jenny's life-force squirted into the large bottle under the operating table almost as fast as Abbie could pump it in. A flash of memory suddenly exploded in his head. Him. Raised voices. Christina's screams. Dom. Life ebbing away.

His heart raced and he dragged in a steadying breath. He hadn't known how to save Dom and he'd failed Christina but he was saving this woman.

Look harder. He caught a glimpse of something and immediately fritzed it with the diathermy. Still the blood gurgled back at him. He held out his hand. 'Four-zero.'

'She's about one minute away from arresting.' Abbie hung up the last unit of blood, her forehead creased in anxiety.

'I'm on it.' Sending all his concentration down his fingers, he carefully looped the silk around the bleeding vessel and made a tie. Then he counted.

This time the site stayed miraculously clear. His chest relaxed, releasing the breath he hadn't been aware he was holding.

'Pressure's rising, O2 sats are rising.' Relief poured through Abbie's voice as she raised her no-nonsense gaze to his. 'You had me worried.'

Despite her words, he caught a fleeting glimpse of approbation in the shimmering depths of green. 'Hey, I'm Italian— we always go for the big dramatic finish.'

Abbie blinked, her long brown lashes touching the top of her mask, and then she laughed. A full-bodied, joyous laugh that rippled through her, lighting up her eyes, dancing across her forehead and jostling the stray curl that had sneaked out from under her unflattering theatre cap.

And you thought she was plain? He frowned at the unwelcome question as he started to close the muscle layers.

Abbie administered pethidine for pain relief through a pump. 'Well, we Anglo-Saxons prefer the quiet life.'

'Speak for yourself. I'm not averse to a bit of drama and flair. It makes life interesting.' Erin fluttered her pretty lashes at him over her surgical mask, an open sign of *if you're interested, then I'm definitely in.*

The day his divorce had been finalised fifteen years ago, he'd committed to dating beautiful women and dating often—a strategy that served him well. He loved women and enjoyed their company—he just didn't want to commit to one woman. The emotional fallout of his marriage had put paid to that. Now he focused on work, saving lives and enjoying himself. It was a good plan because it left him very little time to think about anything else.

Usually when he was given such an open invitation as the attractive Erin had just bestowed, he smiled, called her *cara mia*, took her out to dinner and then spent a fun few weeks before the next pretty nurse caught his eye or he caught the glimpse of marriage and babies in her eyes.

But recently that game had got tired.

The theatre phone rang and Abbie took the call. 'Leo, Justin wants an opinion on the crushed leg so a decision can be made to either evacuate or operate first.'

'Tell him I'm five minutes away.'

When Abbie finished the call he continued. 'Whether I should operate or not might be semantics. Evacuation might be the only option due to staffing issues.'

Her shoulders squared, pulling her baggy scrubs across her chest and she rose on her toes. 'If the patient requires surgery before evacuation then Bandarra Base will make it possible.

You worry about the surgery and let me worry about the staffing issue; that's my job.'

Her professionalism eddied around him—her sound medical judgement, the composed and ordered way she'd run the entire emergency and the undeniable fact she'd stayed calm and focused even when she'd been pushed way out of her comfort zone by the emergency anaesthetic.

The fact she put her patient's needs first and asked you for help, despite how you treated her.

A streak of shame assailed him. Abbie McFarlane was a damn good doctor. How the hell had he missed that last night?

Abbie's legs ached with heaviness as she sank onto the saggy couch in the staff lounge. She slipped off her shoes and swung her legs upwards, breaking the rule of no feet on the coffee table. Today had been one hell of a day but, despite her fatigue, a glow of pride warmed her. Bandarra Base had coped with a full-on emergency and, although two of their patients were in a critical and serious condition, the fact they were still alive lay at the feet of her team.

And Leo Costa. The opinionated, charismatic and brilliant surgeon.

Last night she'd wanted to hate him, this morning she'd just wanted him to go as far away from her as possible but obviously that was far too simple a request. If the fates knew in advance she would need a surgeon today, why couldn't they have sent along a 'nice guy', a competent surgeon or, better yet, a female surgeon?

But no, they were enjoying a joke at her expense and had dispatched her worst nightmare. A man with magnetic allure, the kind of man she'd learned was toxic to her. A couple of short relationships at uni had made her consider perhaps she lacked judgement in her choice of men but it had been Greg who'd really rammed home the message. With charm and good looks, he'd drawn her into his enticing web and then trapped her. Now she knew to her very core that letting a man in her life was like taking a razor blade to her wrist—an act of self-harm.

So why, knowing all of that, did it only take *one* look from those dark, dark eyes to set off a rampaging trail of undeniable lust inside her, sending her pulse racing and battering every single one of Greg's painful lessons about charismatic men? Battering her belief that the only way to be safe was to live a single life. A belief she hadn't questioned once in three years.

She bit her lip hard against the delicious sensations and loathed her own weakness. But, despite how she felt about her reaction to him, she couldn't deny Leo was the prize piece in today's emergency. Without him, Jenny and the elderly woman would have been immediately airlifted to Melbourne and there would have been a strong chance both of them could have died in transit. Leo had saved Jenny and given Mavis a fighting chance.

Fatigue pummelled her sitting body and Abbie fought hard to resist closing her eyes. She'd already sent Justin home and she only had to stay awake a little bit longer, do one more round and then, fingers crossed, she could go home too. The squeak of the lounge door interrupted her thoughts and, immediately on alert that a patient had deteriorated, she glanced up, expecting to see the night-nurse.

It wasn't the night-nurse. An intoxicating shimmer raced through her from the tip of her toes to the top of her scalp, leaving her breathless. Had she been blind and not able to recognise the strong brown hand that gripped the edge of the door, she would have known instantly it was Leo from the fresh mint and citrus scent that preceded him. How could a man smell so good after such a long day? 'I thought you'd gone home?'

'I spent some time with Nonna and for the last hour I've been caught up with journalists. Today's crash made it all over the news and it seems that no one could find you.' He shot her a questioning look and then walked straight to the instant hot-water heater unit and made two mugs of tea.

She shrugged, not caring that she'd left him with the press because she was pretty certain it was far more his thing than hers. 'Your patients were evacuated to Melbourne so I figured you had the time and I was still tied up with patients.'

'Well, you owe me because I've done print, radio and television interviews and I'm "mediaed" out.'

The soothing aroma of camomile wafted towards her and, for the first time since she'd walked into work hours ago, she relaxed. 'You'll look good on TV.' The words rolled out of her mouth before her exhausted brain could censor them and she gasped, wanting to grab them back.

Have you lost your mind? Warrior Abbie held her shield high over her heart, her expression incredulous.

Leo grinned—a smile full of the knowledge that not only did he know he'd look bloody fantastic on TV, he'd also heard her gaffe. A gaffe a man like Leo Costa would read as an open invitation. He stared her down. 'I didn't think you'd noticed.'

Establish distance. From the moment she'd met him she'd been cool and it was time to dig deep and find her Zen so she could cope with him and keep herself safe. She tossed her head, hating the way her curls tangled into her eyes, ruining the attempted nonchalant look. 'Let me put it this way. I noticed, and perhaps even enjoyed noticing, but not even your glossy magazine good-looks quite make up for the disrespect you showed me last night.'

She expected a tremor of anger or at the very least repressed indignation but instead he walked over to her and extended his hand.

'Hello, I'm Leo Costa, general surgeon and grandson of Maria Rossi. Pleased to meet you.'

She frowned as she swung her legs off the table and slowly raised her hand to his, all the time wondering what was actually going on. 'Abbie McFarlane.'

His firm grip wrapped around hers, underpinned with a gentle softness that had peril written all over it. 'I hear you're the doctor who's been looking after my grandmother and you've had a few problems with one of the relatives?'

She studied his face, trying to read beyond the charm and the pretend first greeting. 'He hit ten on the difficult scale.'

His eyes widened fractionally but he didn't disagree as he sat down on the coffee table, directly opposite her. 'Looking back, I think he let fear for his grandmother interfere with his medical judgement.'

She hadn't expected that answer—the man had just verbalised his dread and that wasn't something charismatic men usually did. 'I can understand the fright.'

'Well, it caught me by complete surprise. Nonna's always been so fit and well and…' He puffed out a short breath before giving a wry and apologetic smile. 'I'm sorry for what I said; I was out of line. If it makes you feel any better, my family berated me at breakfast.'

Breakfast? The word clanged in her head like a fire bell. 'Hang on; you were still insisting at nine a.m. that Maria be cared for by someone else.'

His shoulders rose as his head tilted slightly like a kid

who'd been presented with the prosecuting evidence of an empty biscuit barrel. 'Stubbornness is one of my less fortunate attributes.'

Her lips twitched. 'One? So there are more?'

He captured her gaze, his eyes twinkling. 'All I will confess to is that I'm not planning on being difficult about this again. Nonna's lucky to have you; indeed Bandarra's fortunate to have a GP of your calibre, Abbie.'

She saw the captivating smile, heard the warm praise, but the bells still pealed loud in her head. 'So what you're really saying is I'm still Maria's doctor because you've realised there's no one else.'

'No. That's not what I'm saying at all.' Dismay extinguished the twinkle in his eyes and for the second time today she glimpsed a hint of the real man behind the smooth façade. 'I admit to making a snap judgement last night and I've apologised for that.'

The tic in his jaw said apologies were not something he did very often. 'But I worked alongside you today and there's no doubt you know your medicine.'

The sincerity in his voice finally satisfied her. 'Thank you.'

'You're welcome.' He moved back to the bench and carried over the tea before sitting down next to her. His firm lips curved upwards into a conspiratorial smile full of shared experiences. 'It was one hell of a day, wasn't it?'

His words matched her thoughts, which totally unnerved her. First there'd been the unexpected apology and now he appeared to want to sit and chat. That alone was enough to cope with, but added on top was his scent and aura swirling around her like an incoming tide, creating rafts of delicious sensation tickling along her veins.

He shifted his weight and the couch moved, tilting her

closer to him. Silver spots danced in her head. *No, no, no.* It took every exhausted molecule to force herself to stay upright and not give in to his magnetic pull—the one that called for her to lean against his arm and lay her head on his broad shoulder. But she knew only too well that men like Leo Costa were like the foxglove plant. Pretty to look at but potentially life-threatening, and the last thing her heart needed again was life-support.

She sipped her tea, trying hard to ignore the delicious tingling on her skin and the fluttering in her stomach that sitting so close to him had activated. Warrior Abbie raised her sword across the shield. She could do this. She could sit here for a few minutes and make polite conversation because, come midnight, Leo Costa would leave her hospital. The emergency was over and they'd resolved the issue of Maria's care. She couldn't imagine him staying in Bandarra very long before Melbourne called him home, and with his departure the status quo of Bandarra Base and her much-coveted quiet life would be restored. Yes, everything would return to normal. She smiled and breathed out a long, slow, satisfying breath.

Leo sipped his tea, watching Abbie holding her cup close to her chest as if it were some sort of protective guard. An unusual cosy feeling of well-being floated through him—something he never experienced when he was in Bandarra. Could an apology really have that effect? Apparently so. He'd always prided himself on being fair and he hadn't given Abbie the same consideration. He let the odd feeling settle over him. Today had been incredible. Not just the excitement of the 'seat-of-your-pants' surgery but working alongside Abbie. She had an air of self-containment that intrigued him. *Those eyes intrigued him.*

She stared at her shapely ankles, which rested again on the

coffee table, and sighed. 'I could live without the todays of this world. We were lucky to have your expertise. Thanks.'

He was used to gushing praise but the plain appreciation had an unambiguous authenticity which he appreciated. 'I'm just glad I was here. These days I mostly do elective surgery, although I'm on the trauma roster at Melbourne City. Thankfully, I'm not always needed.'

She turned her head to look at him and understanding wove across her face, joining her cute sun-kissed freckles. 'But there's nothing quite like the buzz of a good save.'

He grinned. 'Yeah, but you can't actually go around wishing accidents on people or saying stuff like that or you sound macabre.'

She chuckled. 'You're a surgeon; it's a given.'

He tried to look affronted but instead he joined in with her tinkling laughter. Abbie McFarlane had a straight-shooting delivery style that was as refreshing as it was unusual. He realised with a thud that apart from his immediate family, not many people spoke their mind to him any more.

She returned her gaze to her feet and he fought the urge to caress her jaw with his fingers and tilt her head back towards him so he could look into her eyes. He wanted to dive into those eyes which had stared back at him so many times today from over the top of a surgical mask, expressing everything from fear to joy.

Instead, he breathed in deeply, letting her intoxicating scent of fresh berries roll through him.

'So is this a flying visit to Bandarra?'

His libido crashed and burned as the familiar Bandarra-induced agitation spiralled through him. 'Yesterday I would have said yes. I usually fly in and fly out because I'm frantic in Melbourne.'

You keep telling yourself that's the reason. It's served you well for years. He shut his mind against the eminently reasonable voice he'd been silencing for almost as long. 'Nonna's CVA gave me a wake-up call and I want to spend a bit of time with her.'

As if in slow motion, she moved her gaze from her feet to his face, her irises widening into a reflective pool. 'Meaning?'

'I've asked my secretary to set back my patient list for the month.'

A shadow passed through her amazing eyes and her usually well-modulated voice rose slightly. 'So you're here for a few weeks?'

'Yep. Family time.' A jet of edgy unease tangoed with the flow of imposed duty. Spending time with Nonna was the right thing to do but the fact it meant spending a few weeks in Bandarra sent a shot of acid into his gut, eating at the lining. How the hell was he going to fill his days and stay sane?

He leaned back and breathed in deeply, trying to relax his chest as he stretched his arms across the back of the couch. Immediately, his fingers itched to curl around Abbie's alabaster neck and feel her softness against his skin.

Getting to know Abbie would keep the Bandarra demons at bay.

There was nothing quite like the thrill of the chase and the idea offered him the first ray of hope he'd felt since his father had demanded he stay. It would be the perfect distraction. 'I'm looking forward to spending some time with you too, now we're friends.'

Her torso shot abruptly away from the back of the couch as if she'd been electrocuted and her eyebrows shot skyward. 'Friends?' The word sounded strangled. 'That's probably going a bit far.'

Stunned surprise dumped on him like the cold and clammy

touch of slime. He couldn't even think of a time when someone had rejected his overtures and the feeling stung like a wasp—sharp and painful. His jaw tensed as he tried to hold on to his good humour. 'Colleagues, then.'

She gave a tight laugh. 'We're hardly colleagues.'

Her words bit, devaluing his interpretation of the last four-teen hours and stripping bare the memory of the camaraderie and professionalism they'd shared. 'What the hell do you call today, then?'

'Long.' She lurched to her feet, her gaze wavering until it finally rested on his left shoulder. 'I have to do a final round, Leo, so I'll say goodnight. Thanks for your help today and enjoy your holiday in Bandarra.' She turned her back and walked away from him and towards the door.

His jaw fell open at her abrupt dismissal of him and a curse rose to his lips, but it stalled at the sight of her baggy scrubs moving against a curvaceous butt. Lust collided with aggravation and shuddered through him. His palm tingled, his blood roared hot and he wanted to haul her back by those caramel curls, wrap her in his arms and demolish her prickly reserve with a kiss.

For the first time in months his body came alive—every colour seemed brighter, every feeling more intense and he buzzed with the wonder of it. He didn't know if it was the after-math of the sheer rush of the emergency or the challenge of the very brisk Abbie McFarlane but, either way, if he had to stay in Bandarra he had to keep busy. Seducing Abbie McFarlane would be the perfect distraction. He clapped his hands as the seeds of a plan started to shoot. This was going to be too much fun and Abbie McFarlane didn't stand a chance.

CHAPTER FOUR

ABBIE let Murphy, her Border collie, pull her along the path, totally oblivious to the usually soothing gnarled river red-gums with their silver and grey bark. Not even the majestic sight of fifteen pelicans coming in to land on the blue-brown river water could haul her mind away from the fact that Leo Costa was staying in Bandarra.

She gave a half-laugh tinged with madness that had Murphy looking up at her, his tawny-gold eyes quizzical. She'd been dreading Justin leaving, knowing that her workload would double. Now that seemed like a saving grace because she'd be so flat out virtually living at the clinic and the hospital that she'd never have any time in town to run into Leo. Who knew work would save her?

The magpies' early morning call drifted towards her and she heard a message in the flute-like song. Work had saved her before. Greg might have stripped her of everything else, but he hadn't been able to take away her job. She'd survived and rebuilt her independence. Never again would she confuse lust with love, charm for affection, or control for care. Now she had the unconditional love of a dog, which she'd choose every single time over the pile of broken promises men left in their wake.

'Come on, Murph, time for breakfast at the clinic.' She broke into a jog, channelling all her energies into the run, driving away every unsettling thought of an onyx-eyed man with broad shoulders that hinted at being able to shelter those he loved from the world.

The clinic was in the hospital grounds and housed in the original Bandarra hospital which had been lovingly restored in its centennial year. With its high gabled roof, tall chimneys and cream-painted decorative timber, it welcomed patients with its sweeping veranda and kangaroo motifs worked lovingly into the mosaic floor. Abbie had seen an old photo from 1908 where a hammock hung on the veranda so she'd bought a brightly coloured hammock and had slung it between the last two posts on the front veranda. One day she planned to have time to lie in it for more than the brief 'test' she'd taken when she'd installed it. Meanwhile Murphy enjoyed lying underneath it, using it as shade.

The thick brick walls always offered a respite from the heat. 'Morning, Debbie,' Abbie called to her practice nurse as she made her way into the cool kitchen, her stomach rumbling at the thought of fresh grapes just off the vine combined with locally made yoghurt drizzled with honey. 'Where's Jessica?'

Debbie followed her into the kitchen. 'She's come down with a filthy cold so I'm afraid we're juggling reception and patients today.'

Abbie groaned. 'That's a great start to being one doctor down. Has anything come from the board about a new appointee?' She dropped thick slices of crusty bakery bread into the toaster.

'Robert Gleeson said he's had applications from Egypt, India and Kenya and he'd be catching up with you soon for interview times.'

Abbie sighed. Rural medicine seemed to only attract

doctors with the 'short-term' in mind and then they left just as she'd trained them up. The thought reminded her that yesterday's emergency had got in the way of a farewell. 'Is Justin able to have his party tonight?'

Debbie shook her head sadly. 'He's set to leave this morning but I'm sure he'll call by first. Meanwhile, I got in early and pulled the histories for the first patients and my diabetic clinic doesn't start until ten so I can woman the phones.'

She smiled. 'Thanks, Debbie, and thanks for keeping things ticking over here yesterday while I was tied up at the hospital all day. You have no idea what a load you take off me with your clinics, which reminds me, the funding came through for your "travelling pap test" clinic, so well done on that too.'

Debbie beamed with the praise before dashing out to answer the phone, leaving Abbie alone to eat her breakfast. The next time she was alone was four hours later when the morning session finally wrapped up. 'Debbie, I'm grabbing lunch from Tony's; do you want me to get you anything?'

The practice nurse stuck her head out of the treatment room. 'I'm set, thanks, and Eli Jenkins is here for his ulcer treatment. Can you check the fax? I just heard it beep at reception.'

Abbie's head was already spinning from hunger. She had a huge afternoon ahead of her and all she could think of right now was one of Tony's focaccias and a mug of his creamy latte—he refused to serve it in a glass, saying it was a travesty to good coffee. 'It won't be anything urgent. I'll read it when I get back.'

The heat hit her the moment she opened the heavy red-gum door and she automatically reached for her sunhat, which she always hung on the coat-stand. She loved making sure the clinic had an 'at home' welcoming feel to it and the hat-stand was part of that, as was the umbrella stand with its stash of umbrellas. Not that they got used very often as it had been ages since Bandarra had seen rain. Moths would probably fly out if a patient opened one.

Usually Murphy raced to the door to meet her, ever hopeful of a walk, no matter how short, but his smiling face wasn't waiting for her. She glanced down the long veranda, ready to call her dog, but Murphy's name died on her lips as her mouth dried to a crisp.

Lying in her hammock, and looking for all the world as if he belonged there, was Leo. His long and tanned shorts-clad legs stretched out in front of him, and one arm was crooked behind the back of his head, the angle moulding his soft cotton designer T-shirt tight to the well defined muscles of his chest and shoulders. Aviator sunglasses covered his onyx eyes while his other long-fingered surgeon's hand dangled lazily over the hammock's side, stroking Murphy's head.

The Border collie looked up adoringly while his tail thumped out an enthusiastic tattoo.

Turncoat!

Hot and cold streaked through Abbie, making her tremble and sending her already spinning head into a vortex spiral where hunger, lust and fast-fading common sense got sucked in together. *Danger—stay strong.* She dragged in a deep and steadying breath. If she ignored him, she could pretend he wasn't here. She slapped her thigh and called her dog. 'Murphy, here, boy.'

The dog turned his black and white head and smiled at her as if to say, *Look who I found; come meet him too.*

Leo rose elegantly from the hammock, in total contrast to the inelegant way Abbie had fallen out of it the day she'd tried, and he walked up the veranda towards her with her dog trotting besottedly by his side. She wanted to hate him but really she only hated her reaction to him. A reaction she must master.

His smile lit up the air around him, although the slight aura of tension she'd occasionally glimpsed hovered. 'Hello, Abbie. Great dog; is he yours?'

She nodded and, knowing she couldn't ignore him, she chose the direct approach—the one that usually made her sound brisk and officious and had very occasionally sent interns scurrying. 'What are you doing here, Leo?'

He didn't even blink at the bald words. Instead, he tilted his head and met her gaze with a friendly and open expression. 'I thought we could have lunch together.'

No way. 'I don't think so. I'm just grabbing a quick focaccia before afternoon clinic.' She turned away from him and staring straight ahead, determined not to look at him, she started walking towards town.

'Me too.' Leo fell easily into step beside her.

The scent of laundry powder mixed in with healthy masculine sweat encircled her, fuzzing her brain. 'Why do you need a quick lunch when surely the point of being on holiday is being able to have a long lunch?'

'Afternoon clinic starts at two, right?'

Her head snapped sideways so fast she felt something rip. 'It does, but why does that concern you?'

His friendly smile suddenly became wide and knowing. 'I hate being late.'

She felt her brows draw down towards the bridge of her nose and heard her mother's warning voice shriek, *wrinkles*. She batted the voice away, needing all her concentration to stay on top of what was going on. He surely didn't look sick; in fact he looked decadently healthy, and yesterday's fatigue which had played around his eyes had completely vanished.

Today he looked relaxed and gorgeous. Dangerously gorgeous. 'Do you have an appointment?'

A ripple of unexpected confusion skated across his usually confident face. 'Robert Gleeson should have told you this morning.'

Her throat tightened at the hospital CEO's name and every nerve-ending fired off a mass alert. 'Told me what?'

'That I'm doing half days to help out until the new doctor is appointed.'

Silver spots danced in front of her eyes. *Leo working in the clinic.* Oh, God, that was probably what the fax she'd so cheerfully ignored had been about. Jumbled thoughts tumbled off her lips. 'But you're on holiday to spend time with your family.' She heard her rising voice, the words tinged with slight hysteria. 'Surely you don't want a busman's holiday?'

He shrugged, but it seemed overly casual, as if he'd had to try hard to achieve the effect. 'I can do both. Robert contacted me this morning after getting yesterday's report and seeing all the media attention. He thought it would help you out and it suits me. I like to keep busy.'

She grasped at straws but they seemed lined with slippery mud. 'But you're a surgeon.'

Intelligent eyes fixed her with a piercing look. 'So what are you saying? That I can't cut it as a GP?'

The mud threatened to dump right on top of her and she opted for the easy jibe. 'There's a lot of listening and not much cutting. You'll be bored rigid after one session.'

Two jet-black brows rose, disappearing under a thatch of thick hair. 'That's a big statement based on nothing much at all. Are you always this quick to judge?'

His words hit with painful accuracy and sliced open guilt. Yesterday he'd been great with his patients and she couldn't fault that but she didn't trust herself working with him. 'I just meant that the work won't be the high-powered stuff you're used to.'

He crossed his arms across a powerful chest. 'Maybe I can make a dent in the waiting list Robert was talking about, seeing as you only get a visiting surgeon once a month. Like I said, I like to keep busy.'

The reality of the waiting list duelled with the sheer panic that bubbled furiously inside her at the thought of working with Leo. Of staying safe and not being tempted to go down a self-destructive path. *Remember Greg.* But the waiting list issue was bigger than her and the hardworking people of Bandarra had enough to contend with from the tough climatic and economic conditions of the area. They deserved the unexpected advantage of a surgeon in their midst for a few weeks, even if Leo Costa's charisma scared her witless.

She swallowed hard and forced up the words that needed to be said. 'I'll take you up on that.'

He clapped his hands. 'On lunch? Excellent.'

Charm played on his high cheekbones, both enticing and inviting, and deep inside Abbie a tiny crack widened. How much danger could there possibly be in sitting down for a quick focaccia?

Plenty. Warrior Abbie raised her shield. *This is work.*

She cleared her throat and shored up her determination to keep Leo Costa a solid distance away from her, both physically and emotionally. She pasted on her professional smile. 'I'll take you up on the offer of reducing the waiting list. In fact I'll pull out the files and we can prioritise a list. How does that sound?'

He nodded agreeably. 'It sounds fine.'

But there was something about the timbre of his voice and the easy smile that played on his lips that had Abbie regretting the whole idea. Leo Costa working in Bandarra might be good medicine for the town but it was a health hazard for her.

Leo strode from the clinic towards the hospital on his way to visit Nonna before his planning meeting with Abbie. With Debbie's able assistance, Leo's first session had been re-markably smooth and, although he'd seen a lot of patients, he hadn't seen anything of Abbie. It had been on the tip of his tongue to suggest they take their meeting over dinner but that would only give her another excuse to say no and she was ex-tremely good at that. He couldn't remember the last time he'd had to work so hard at getting a date but her 'no's' just made him more determined and inventive. He'd rung Anna's restau-rant and ordered an antipasti platter and a bottle of wine so they could meet and eat at the clinic, and he might just be able to break down that intriguing wall of aloofness she was so good at building.

'*Ciao,* Nonna, *com stai?*'

Nonna raised her hand and smiled. 'Leopoldo. When am I going home?'

'You have to ask Abbie that, Nonna. I promised her I wouldn't interfere.'

Nonna's perceptive gaze instantly turned curious but that didn't hide the lining of reproach. 'You've broken promises to women before.'

He sighed and rubbed his chin, realising he'd just unwit-tingly stepped into a topic he usually did his best to avoid. Nonna had taken his divorce from Christina personally and it was the only thing about him and his life where she actively voiced disappointment. It amazed him that she should be so angry with him over a failed marriage and yet never blame him for Dom's death when the cause lay so squarely at his feet. But perhaps she did blame him because Dom and Christina were inextricably linked and always would be.

'So, Maria, I've got good new—' Abbie breezed into the ward, a white coat covering a crumpled pair of knee-length khaki shorts and a white blouse that begged for the touch of a hot iron. Her green eyes widened as if she'd taken a jolt of electricity.

'Leo.' A ripple of tension wove through her from the top of her sun-kissed caramel curls, down and around pert breasts, across a nipped-in waist, before spinning around curvaceous legs and disappearing into the floor. 'I thought you were still at the clinic.'

Leo deciphered the code as, *If I'd known you were here I wouldn't have come,* and annoyance fizzed in his veins. He'd apologised for his behaviour and she'd accepted so surely their rugged start was now water under the bridge. So why did she want to avoid him so much? It fuelled his determination to cut a swathe through her reserve. He gave her a slow smile. 'I finished the list and cut out early to visit Nonna so I wouldn't be late for our meeting.'

'Oh, right, of course.' Her hands seemed to flutter as she reached for the chart, the action unusually flustered.

Then he caught a flash of something flare in her eyes before being quickly replaced by her professional doctor look—the one she always gave to him. He stifled his grin and mentally high-fived. Abbie McFarlane was working seriously hard to stay aloof. Wine and antipasti might just do the trick.

'Actually, Leo, it's good you're here.' With studied casualness she turned back to Maria. 'I know you want to go home and you've been recovering well but I want you to have some time in rehab, and a bed's just come up. Leo can transfer you now and that way you're ready for physio and OT first thing tomorrow.'

Maria beamed and patted Abbie's hand. 'I will walk there.'

Abbie shook her head. 'Sorry, Maria, but you have to go in a wheelchair; it's hospital policy. But once you're in the rehab ward you'll be able to use your frame.'

The old woman gave a snort of derision and Leo expected a tirade of rapid-fire Italian to follow but his grandmother surprised him. 'Leopoldo, pack my things. *Dottore*, get my dress.'

Abbie looked startled for a moment and Leo wondered if she'd refuse the request or call a nurse but, as his hand opened a drawer, she walked to the wardrobe. Three dresses hung neatly and, without giving Maria a choice, she plucked one off the rack. 'This will do nicely.'

Leo hid his smile. He'd learned early that he did things Nonna wanted but in his own way. Abbie had worked that out fast.

Ten minutes later, with Maria seated in the wheelchair, Leo pushing and Abbie carrying the small suitcase, they crossed the courtyard to the rehab wing.

'When I am home, *dottore*, you need to come again and make bread.'

'Maria, my last attempt was a disaster. It was so rock-hard that if it was thrown it could knock a man unconscious.'

Leo laughed. 'Remind me never to upset you in a kitchen.'

Abbie crooked a challenging eyebrow and lights sparked in her eyes. 'No chance of that ever happening.' She bent her head towards Maria. 'Kitchens and I have never been a match and never will be. I know enough to feed myself and that's all I need to know.'

'Pfft.' Maria threw her hands out in front of her as if Abbie had just uttered a cardinal sin. 'Food is not just for a hungry belly. It feeds the soul.'

Abbie's expression clouded for a moment before her shoulders rolled back and she picked up her pace.

Leo's gaze swept over Abbie's slight but shapely body that had curves in all the right places. Abbie wasn't underfed but he'd noticed occasional shadows peeking from those amazing eyes, and his observant *nonna* had noticed too. Abbie hadn't realised that Nonna wasn't trying to teach her to cook but was trying to teach her the joy of food.

Abbie opened the rehab ward door. 'Here we are.'

Maria's orders started flowing again in a combination of English and Italian and she didn't pause until they'd settled her into the dining room. They left her happily chatting with the other residents and her final words to their retreating backs were, 'Hang my clothes.'

Leo strode into Nonna's new room. Shaking his head in a combination of half laughter and half apology, he opened the wardrobe door. 'And that was Nonna in full flight.'

'True, she organises us mere mortals.' Abbie passed him clothes from the suitcase, a wicked laugh twitching her plump lips. 'But who knew that the hotshot city surgeon is a complete pushover when it comes to his grandmother?'

He slid the coat hanger over the metal rail and grinned. 'Not many people know that. It's classified information.'

Sea-green eyes, devoid of any shadows or clouds, twinkled brightly with teasing in their depths. 'Classified information? How so?'

He winked at her. 'I've got a reputation to protect.'

Her belly laugh brought a delicious pink to her cheeks. 'Are you worried that if the information got out it might put a dent in your macho surgeon image?'

He hung up the last dress and turned to face her, a streak of fun pouring through him unlike anything he'd felt in months. 'Let me put it this way—if word got out I might not be responsible for my actions.'

She chuckled as she leaned against the wardrobe door, her arms crossed firmly against her chest. 'Oh, right, and if I talk, what are you going to do to me? Hit me with that high wattage charm that works for you so well? I hate to tell you, Romeo, but it won't ever work on me.'

Her words laid down a challenge he couldn't refuse. Raising his left arm, he pressed it against the door, leaving plenty of space for her to duck out underneath, should she choose that option. Leaning in closer, he kept his gaze fixed firmly on her face as her strawberry and liquorice scent swirled around him, filling his lungs before pouring through him and leaving a trail of banked heat.

He caught a flicker of movement—the twitch of a muscle in her cheek. A chink in her professed armour? Perhaps she wasn't as impervious to him as she made out. Slowly he brought his right hand up to her face, twirling a tight curl around his finger as he spoke softly. 'And what makes you so sure?'

She tilted her chin, the action all defiance. 'I've been charmed by experts and I know every trick in the book.'

He'd expected her to spin out under his arm and stalk away but instead she stood her ground, so he edged in closer until he could feel the heat of her body radiating out to meet him and the tickle of her sweet breath on his face. 'But you don't know all my tricks.'

She swallowed hard and heat unfurled inside him so fast he thought he'd ignite. A pulse quivered against the pale skin of her throat, completely undoing him, and with a groan he gave in and lowered his mouth to hers.

Plump lips of pillow-softness met his with complete stillness, but the hint of sweet sultana grapes and summer sunshine hovered, pleading to be tasted. He flicked his tongue, stealing the tang, wanting the full taste.

Her arms stayed crossed against her chest like an unyielding barrier and her eyes were squeezed shut as if she was battling herself. He almost pulled back but then she gave a moan-like sigh and opened her lips to him.

His tongue tumbled over the precipice and the taste of summer fruits flooded his mouth. Their sweetness bubbled through his veins like champagne—intoxicating and demanding—and he angled his mouth, seeking more.

Her tongue met his with a jolt and immediately darted away, only to return a moment later, all hesitancy gone. With the experienced mouth of a temptress, she took her full taste of him and at the same time branded him with her own unique essence.

White lights exploded in his head and his blood pounded to his groin with an urgency he hadn't known in months. Pure lust poured through him, driving all of his actions as every cell in his body screamed to touch her, feel her, taste her and fill her with himself. Frustratingly, her arms still stayed rigidly between them, acting like a blockade and preventing him from lining his body against hers. Instead, he slid his free hand up into her hair, the silky strands caressing his palms and releasing their heady scent of floral fragrance.

She tilted her head back and her throaty groan rocked through him. The realisation that buried under those chainstore clothes lay the body and soul of an incredibly sexual woman socked him so hard it threatened to undo him on the spot in a way that hadn't happened since he was fifteen. He gently nipped her lip and she replied in kind and the last vestiges of reason floated away. Sound vanished, light wavered and he lost himself to everything except the overwhelming need to have that amazing mouth on and in his.

Abbie floated on layers of glorious sensation, totally disconnected to her real world and lost in the wondrous touch of

Leo's mouth on hers, trailing along her jaw and down into the sweet hollow of her throat. His mouth suckled, nipped, tasted and branded her, filling her with swirling light and colour. Colour that built upon itself until it detonated inside her, sending a surging torrent of unmitigated lust rolling through her, leaving no part of her untouched.

Her body took over—seeking pleasure, needing it like it needed oxygen. Her breasts strained at the lace of her bra, her hips tilted forward and her protective arms fell to her sides, their barrier utterly vanquished.

The gap between them vanished. His legs pressed against the length of hers, her hips melded with his, her breasts flattened against his solid chest and their combined heat roared into a fire ball of heat-seeking bliss. He absorbed her moan of spiralling need with his mouth, as her hand tugged its way under his shirt, desperate to touch him. Her palm hit the corded musculature of his back, his skin burning hers, and her fingers went exploring, trailing the length of his spine before burying themselves in his thick hair.

The scent of desire cloaked them, tongues duelled, neither able to get enough of the other and then his hand cupped her breast, his thumb skimming across the utilitarian cotton of her blouse, caressing the erect nub so desperate for his touch.

'*Sei magnifica.*'

Leo's usually velvet voice rasped out the words with the grazing sound of gravel, instantly slicing through Abbie's lust-fuelled haze. The hard corner of the wardrobe door bit sharply into her back, Leo's weight pressed heavily against her, as did his arousal, and the shock snapped her eyes wide open.

Everything came into sharp focus. The windows of the rehab ward, the two neatly made patients' beds with their smart green covers and the white porcelain of the hand basin.

Deep inside her, a wobbly Warrior Abbie stumbled to her feet, picked up her sword and shield and screamed in horror. *What the hell are you doing? Remember your pact. Staying single is the only safe way.*

Reality dumped so hard on Abbie she could hardly move her ribcage to breathe and her legs struggled to hold her up. She was wrapped around Leo like a sex-starved teenager, a hair's breadth away from locking her legs up high around his waist and impaling herself against him, letting him have sex with her against a wardrobe door in his grandmother's room at the rehab ward.

Oh, God, how had she let this happen? Since Greg she'd decided to take a totally different path in her life and she wasn't going backwards, yet look what she'd just done. Horrified, she pulled her hands out from under his shirt and dragged her mouth away from his. Somehow, despite her panting chest, she managed to force out, 'That kiss is never happening again.'

Dark eyes filled with the fog of lust stared back at her. 'No, you're right.'

'I am?' Bewilderment lost out to relief. Thank God he knew it was a mistake as well. She tugged at her blouse, straightening it. 'I mean good. I'm glad we agree.'

His finger reached out and tucked a curl behind her ear. 'That kiss has passed and can never be repeated because no kiss is ever the same twice.' Impossibly, his eyes darkened even more. 'Still, it will be fun to test that theory in a more appropriate place.'

Panic lurched through her. 'No. What I meant was *we* are never kissing again.'

He looked at her with a gaze of incredulity. 'Abbie, given what just went down between us, not kissing again would be an absolute tragedy.'

She pushed past him, needing to put a bigger space between them, needing to do everything in her power to remove the temptation that was Leo Costa. 'Famine, disease and death are a tragedy, Leo. Lust is just a nuisance that can be controlled.'

His black brows hit his hair line. 'A nuisance?'

But she wasn't being drawn back into dangerous Leo-filled waters that involved discussing anything other than work. 'Yes, a nuisance. We're colleagues for the next few weeks, Leo. As professionals, I'm sure we can keep our hands off each other and focus on the health of Bandarra.'

Leo's palm slapped the wardrobe door closed and he turned towards her with a lazy smile but shadows lurked in his eyes. 'I have every intention of focusing on the health of Bandarra.'

His words should have reassured her but it was what he didn't say that worried her.

CHAPTER FIVE

LEO walked into the kitchen to find Anna standing at the coffee machine frothing milk for the breakfast cappuccinos. He was grumpy and out of sorts after a night spent fighting the sheets more than sleeping in them. His sleep had been a tangled mess of the usual demon dreams but added in was Abbie's mouth, so hot and delicious against his own one minute and gone the next. 'This morning I need espresso.'

His sister's dark brown eyes gazed at him with a speculative look. 'Too much Cab Sav last night, big brother?'

'I was working late, not drinking.' Leo grimaced and slid into the chair remembering how Abbie had changed the venue of their meeting from the clinic to the hospital and had deliberately sat at the furthest end of the very long hospital boardroom table. They'd discussed possible surgery cases over the travesty that was instant coffee, while the food and wine he'd ordered lay untouched at the clinic.

He'd spent the first two cases struggling to reconcile the distant cool professional opposite him with the exciting and uninhibited woman who'd kissed him so wholeheartedly and without restraint in his grandmother's ward. He hadn't been that turned on since— His mind blanked. He couldn't recall the last time he'd been so aroused. Then she'd coolly stepped back from him and hit him with her calm and uncompromising gaze. It was as if she'd flicked an internal switch and had locked down every single one of her sexual feelings. The fact she'd called the most wondrous of life's sensations 'a nuisance' had totally floored him.

Anna slid an espresso cup under the machine. 'Work? Is that what you call it now? I saw your order at the restaurant and it screamed "seduction plan". Which nurse was it this time?'

He grunted. 'I told you, I was working and it took forever. Abbie McFarlane must have pulled out the files of every possible candidate for surgery between here and Budjerree.' If he had to stay in Bandarra then at least he'd be busy.

Anna laughed. 'I told you, Abbie's a dynamo doctor.'

She's a dynamo kisser.

The wire door thwacked back on its hinges and thundering feet sounded on the floorboards, interrupting his thoughts. Leo turned to see Anna's eleven-year-old twin girls—broad brimmed hats on their heads and green school bags on their backs—charge into the room. The same age when he and Dom had been inseparable.

'Uncle Leo.' The girls threw themselves at him, their eyes wide with wonder. 'Nonna Rosa said you're staying for a long holiday.'

Leo opened his arms, hugging them harder than he should as he forced memories down. 'Well, for a little while.'

Donna, the eldest by five minutes and who'd tried to be first at everything ever since, begged, 'Can you play tennis with me after school?'

It will keep you busy.

Lauren snuggled in closer. 'I need you to pitch softballs to me so I can get really good at hitting home runs.'

'*Stelline mie*, I can do both. In fact I can even come and see you play in your competitions on Saturday.'

They squealed in delight and hugged him hard.

Anna clapped her hands. 'Girls, outside now or you'll miss the bus. Go.'

They kissed their mother on the cheek and, with calls of 'bye' and 'ciao', the door slammed shut behind them.

Anna passed Leo his coffee and sat down with hers, her face filled with surprise.

Her expression ate into him, along with his general agitation. 'What?'

'Sorry, I'm just astounded that you offered to watch the girls play.'

'Why wouldn't I?' He heard the aggravation in his voice and took in a deep breath.

She shrugged. 'Because you're always tense and distracted when you're here.'

He ran his hand across the back of his neck, wanting to deny her accusation, but he could not. 'I'm usually only here for a day or two but this trip I have the time.' *Way too much time.*

'Well, it's good you're staying longer. Mamma's beside herself. You should have seen her in town yesterday. She must have stopped every second person to tell them you were working here for a month. Do you realise you haven't spent more than two days at a time in Bandarra since you left for uni years ago?'

He knew that was exactly how it had been because it was a deliberate decision on his part. Being in Bandarra ate at him like acid, reminding him of Christina and Dom and taunting him with his success in life when Dom hadn't had a chance to excel. Reminding him that he'd stuffed up two lives. He matched her casual shrug. 'I'm a specialist surgeon and it keeps me in Melbourne.'

Anna reached out her hand and in an uncharacteristic gesture she patted his arm. 'It means a lot to Mamma and Papà. It's not often all four of their kids are under the same roof.'

Five kids. He bit off the comment he so wanted to shout but instead he forced a wry smile to his lips. 'Oh, yeah, just like growing up, except for the three sons-in-law and eight grandchildren.'

'At least your sisters have given Mamma and Nonna the family crowd they love.' Her hand touched his in sisterly concern. 'What happened with Christina was a long time ago. I heard she's remarried and teaching school now in Italy. But what about you, bro? It's time you tried again.'

You only married me to hold on to Dom. I won't put up with your resentment any more. Christina's bitter words boomed in his head as if it had only been yesterday. As his mouth opened to say, *No way am I trying again,* Abbie's caramel curls and plump red lips suddenly beamed across his brain in brilliant 3D. *What the hell?* Abbie McFarlane was one sexy woman but he didn't do 'forever' with any woman. He'd tried and let Christina down badly. Just like he'd let Dom down. He wasn't ever doing that to anyone again and that was why he excelled in short-term superficial relationships. Fun, uncomplicated good times and then he moved on, but he always made sure every woman knew the ground rules before the first date.

He drained his coffee, not wanting to have this conversation. 'I'm leaving all the family stuff to you, Chiara and Bianca because you do it so much better than me.' He pushed back his chair and grabbed a brioche off the plate. 'I better not be late for clinic. Ciao.'

He ignored the sigh of frustration that came from his sister's lips and headed out the door into a clear and hot day. A normal February day with the early morning song of the magpies floating across the warm air. The kids of the vineyard's employees shot past on bikes, a plume of red dust rising behind their wheels as they raced towards the main road, late for school. He and Dom had done the same thing every morning, racing each other to the gate.

A sudden pain burned hot under his sternum and he rubbed it with his left hand. Damn it. Day three in Bandarra and already it was too hard. Spinning on his heel, he marched towards his rental car, thankful that clinic started in ten minutes and he had a surgical list to prioritise. Not to mention his pursuit of Abbie McFarlane. A ticking sexual time bomb lay under her frumpy clothes and he intended to be the man to detonate it.

Abbie tried unsuccessfully to out-stride Leo as their paths intersected on the way to the operating theatre but he easily caught her up.

'Abbie, you can walk with me; I promise I won't bite.' He grinned. 'That is, unless you want me to.'

His deep voice streamed over her like rich, dark melted chocolate and it took every ounce of strength not to lick her lips and replay their kiss. Her body wanted him so badly it constantly hummed with need but her head and heart knew better, so she kept walking and answered briskly, 'I had no idea surgeons had such a sense of humour.'

'More than some GPs, it seems.' He shoved his hands deep into his pockets. 'Come on, Abbie, we're colleagues; let's eat lunch together.'

She shook her head emphatically. 'No.'

'Dinner at the best table in my sister's award-winning restaurant?'

The idea tempted her. She'd wanted to eat at Mia Casa for ages. 'No, thank you.'

'Coffee at Tony's under a market umbrella?'

'Uh-uh.'

Leo didn't miss a beat. 'OK, then, popcorn and chocolate at the latest chick-flick blockbuster?'

She laughed. 'Now you're getting desperate.'

His eyes had the temerity to twinkle, making her stomach lurch. He gave a fluid shrug as if all her 'no's' just slid off his broad, broad shoulders. 'I appreciate all genres of film.'

She wanted to scoff but sincerity lined the edges of his eyes and bracketed his mouth, and that disarmed her. She wanted to put Leo Costa into a predictable box but more often than not he just didn't fit.

'If you want to be more active, then how about a bike ride and a picnic?'

'In this heat? Are you insane?'

'Not that I'm aware of, no.' The scar on his chin seemed to suddenly whiten as his jaw stiffened for a fraction of a second. 'We could do it early in the morning or at sunset.'

'I walk Murphy then.' Even to her ears that excuse sounded lame.

'I suppose I should be thankful you didn't say "washing my hair".' He crossed his arms. 'So, basically, no matter what I suggest you're going to say no?'

She nodded. 'Now you're getting the idea.'

'That's hardly in the collegiate spirit.' His voice held not unreasonable criticism.

She sighed. Her body tingled and was busy yelling 'yes' to every invitation but fear kept her saying 'no'. After yesterday's major lapse, she knew exactly what would happen if she said yes to any invitation that threw the two of them together on their own—she'd end up in his arms and probably in his bed, hating herself and hating him. Saying no was her only option.

Leo suddenly stopped in front of the OR doors, effectively blocking them. 'Do you want me to stop asking you out?'

'Thank you.' The words shot out on a breath of relief.

'Hang on, I asked you if you wanted me to stop; I didn't actually agree to it.' His smile was all charm and appeal. 'How's this for an idea? You invite *me* to something and then I'll quit asking you out.'

She rushed to say, *But that's still you getting your own way,* when her brain actually engaged and she clamped her lips shut. This was perfect. She could invite him out to something where there'd be no chance of them being alone—in fact they'd be surrounded by ten kids from the shelter. This was the ideal solution because, not only would it stop him asking her out, she actually needed an extra adult to help run the programme.

Warrior Abbie armed her sword across her shield and Abbie stared straight into his handsome face—staring down danger because now she had the protection she needed. 'So you'll come along to whatever I ask you to?'

'Sure, why not? I'm up for anything.'

She tilted her head, her gaze sweeping his gorgeous and toned body. 'It might involve your designer clothes getting dirty.'

'No problem. I grew up in the country, remember. I can get down and dirty with the best of them.'

He winked at her and his face creased into deep, warm laughter lines. The combination of his dark eyes and black stubble radiated a wave of pure, unadulterated sex appeal that rocked into Abbie so hard she broke out into a hot and tingling sweat. Warrior Abbie fanned herself with her shield.

Oh come on, we can withstand sex appeal and cheap innuendo.

'Tell me what it is, then.' His words sounded impatient and his urbane charm slipped slightly.

She caught a flash—a remnant—of an enthusiastic and guileless, excited little boy. No sex appeal at all. Her heart hiccoughed. *No, no, no.* She tossed her head and rearmed. 'Well, it involves a sense of adventure, a good sense of humour and working with kids. Do you think you qualify?'

'*Sì.* Absolutely. I love kids.'

Her heart lurched again. She loved kids too and had wanted a child of her own but that dream had been discarded, along with her tattered dreams of happy families. Now she worked with kids from the shelter, completely understanding their bewilderment at how their family life had suddenly been turned upside down.

'Great. Then meet me tomorrow night at the old jetty for canoeing on the river.'

Like water connecting with flames, the twinkling light in his eyes doused. The hovering tension that often surrounded him zoomed back in, firmly front and centre, and all traces of the charismatic man vanished. 'I can't do that.'

Abbie blinked in surprise at his steely tone as an irrational and unwanted streak of disappointment shot through her. 'But you just said you're up for anything.'

His tanned skin tightened across his high cheekbones as his left hand brushed the scar on his chin. 'I have to scrub.' Without another word, he disappeared through the door.

Abbie's feet stayed still as if glued to the floor while her head spun, dizzy with unanswered questions. What had just happened? She couldn't match up the flirting charm with the man who'd just walked away from her. She'd seen Leo in action wearing many guises—the determined grandson, the calm professional and talented surgeon, the super-smooth playboy—but she'd never imagined he'd be a man who'd just walk away from something.

It's no big deal, it's just canoeing. Perhaps he had a prior engagement and the timing clashed? What did it matter that he'd said no? She should be relieved and happy. She'd kept her side of the bargain and issued the invitation, which meant he had to honour his promise of not asking her out. This was a totally win-win situation for her.

But the relief she knew she should feel didn't come. If his 'no' was to do with not being available then surely he would have said so instead of walking away. And he had walked away.

He'd said he loved kids so it wasn't that. A gazillion questions zoomed around in her head as she tried to work out his uncharacteristic behaviour but she couldn't fathom any reason for it. It made no sense and yet something about canoeing had made him turn pale and turn on his heel.

Her beeper sounded and she snapped her attention back to work. A patient was waiting for her to administer a general anaesthetic and that came ahead of an enigmatic surgeon. At least it did for now.

Leo stripped off his gloves and dropped them into the bin. The cholecystectomy he'd just performed had been straightforward and uneventful and now the patient was in recovery. As the surgeon, he should be filled with a sense of satisfaction at a job well done. Instead, he kept thinking about how he'd almost lost the plot when Abbie had invited him canoeing.

Several times during the course of the operation he'd caught her staring at him over the top of her mask. Usually he welcomed the gaze of a beautiful woman, loving how much flirting could take place with eyes alone when the rest of the face was hidden. But today there'd been no flirting and he'd found himself ducking her penetrating and insightful stare, hating the fact that his guard had not merely slipped but had plummeted and smashed to pieces at the mention of the river.

Being in Bandarra was bad enough but using the river— that was something he'd never do.

He'd been thankful that as the surgeon he could leave the theatre earlier than the anaesthetist, which meant Abbie was still tied up in Recovery and not able to verbalise all the questions he'd seen flashing in her eyes. But, no matter how many questions she had, he didn't talk about Dom to anyone—not even Nonna—and he had no plans to start talking now.

Damn it, why had he even suggested she ask him out on a promise he'd stop asking her out? He'd thought it such a clever idea, a way to spend time with Abbie on her own turf, gambling on a bigger chance that she'd relax some of those barriers she held up so hard and high. Relax them and lower them so they could resume that kiss. That mind-blowing, blood-pounding kiss that had planted a craving deep inside him which burned like an eternal flame seeking more fuel. But the idea had bitten him hard, leaving his game plan frayed and exposing a part of his life he kept very deeply buried.

He pushed his way out through the double doors, needing to concentrate on doing his final job as the surgeon and keep all thoughts of the past at bay.

'*Buon giorno,* Sofia. The operation went very well and Lorenzo will be back eating your wonderful *zuppa* in no time.'

'*Grazie*, Leo.' Sofia, a younger friend of his Nonna's, pinched his cheek. 'You are a good boy and a talented man. You must come soon and eat with us in the Cantina while you are home.'

Home. He knew there was no advantage in pointing out he'd lived in Melbourne for a year longer than he'd ever lived in Bandarra. Country towns never completely let their favourite sons go, no matter how much they wanted to be gone. He also knew there was no point in refusing the invitation because a 'no' would not be accepted.

'That would be lovely, Sofia.'

'Good. My granddaughter, she is a good cook; I think you should meet her.'

Good cook or not, Leo didn't want to be matched up. 'I'll bring a friend who can enjoy her cooking as well.' He spoke the protective words with no friend in mind but he immediately heard Abbie's voice in his head. *I know enough to feed myself and that's all I need to know.*

The thought of watching Abbie's lush lips close around a slice of the delectable wood-fire pizza that Sofia was famous for, and being next to her the moment she made the connection that food wasn't just for sating hunger, jolted him with heat.

'Bene.' Sofia tried not to look too disappointed as she walked towards the ward to wait for Lorenzo.

Leo puffed out a breath, his duty done. Unless the nursing staff paged him, he wasn't required at the hospital or the clinic until tomorrow. The afternoon stretched before him— him and Bandarra—the thought sent a restlessness to him. He could go home but his parents' house would be empty and he wanted to avoid a quiet and censorious house.

La Bella winery thrived because of hard work. His father would be in the vineyard but, ever since Stefano's decree that Leo stay for the vintage, Leo had made sure he was never alone with his father because he anticipated a conversation he didn't want to have. A tour bus was booked in and his mother and younger sisters would be busy at the cellar door and Anna would be directing lunch at the restaurant. No problem, he'd visit Nonna and then he'd— He had no clue what to do.

He ran his hand through his hair. He supposed he could help

at the cellar door but his sisters would either moan he was in the way or organise him and neither scenario appealed. He could play tennis but his nieces wouldn't be home to partner him until four. The prickling unease he always experienced in Bandarra had, over the last few days, formed into a tight burr that had embedded itself hard and fast. Too many memories made it impossible to relax and he felt like a caged lion, pacing back and forth.

Talk to Abbie.

He rejected the thought immediately. There were plenty of things he wanted to do with Abbie but talking wasn't one of them. As he crossed the car park he heard a whirring sound and a peloton of cyclists in bright green, white and red Bandarra hospital jerseys shot past him with a wave, and he recognised the physiotherapist and the radiologist. Lunchtime cycling? There was a thought. He'd buy a bike and go riding. A long hard ride in the summer heat was just what he needed to keep the Bandarra demons at bay and to banish a pair of fine green eyes that saw too much.

CHAPTER SIX

ABBIE checked the liquid display on the ear thermometer. 'Mate, you've got a fever, that's for sure.' She gently palpated the boy's glands. All up. 'Have you vomited?'

Alec sniffed and rubbed his watery eyes. 'I chucked after breakfast and now my throat hurts a bit but I'll be OK. Mum needs me to go to the shops. The baby's making her tired.'

Abbie bit her lip. Usually getting information out of an eleven-year-old was like pulling teeth and in most situations with children this age the mother of the child hovered, answering any questions before the child could open his or her mouth. She glanced over at Penny, Alec's pregnant mum, who sat staring out of the window with blank eyes.

When had Alec realised he was the carer in this relationship? She remembered at ten having to make toasted cheese sandwiches for dinner and trying to get her mother to eat. This sort of parent-child role reversal was all too common at the refuge and it ripped at her heart every single time.

She'd called into the refuge just to confirm numbers for tonight's canoeing but Rebecca, the case worker, was out. Another resident had called her aside, voicing her concern for Alec. Penny had silently agreed to the examination with barely a glance when Abbie had knocked on the door of their room.

'Sorry, Alec, but you've got a virus and you won't be going to the shops today or for a few days.' She poured a dose of cherry-flavoured paracetamol syrup. 'You drink this and I'll talk to your mum.'

Alec frowned as if he wanted to object but Abbie put one hand on the boy's shoulder and gave a firm nod. 'You need to get better and then you can help your mum, OK?'

The flushed and feverish child drank the antipyretic, relief burning on his face as hot as the fever. Then he curled up against the pillows and closed his eyes, his body needing the restorative balm of sleep.

Abbie opened her prescription pad and scrawled down an order for an antiviral influenza drug. If Alec had been at home in a settled environment she would have gone the recommended route for a flu-like virus and advised fluids, bed rest and paracetamol. But Alec's life was far from settled and living in a communal house changed all the rules. She walked over to Penny and gently touched her shoulder. Her palm met fiery-hot skin.

Penny flinched at the touch.

Abbie silently cursed at her uncharacteristic lapse. Too many women who came to the refuge associated touch with pain. 'Penny, do you have a fever too?'

Baby-blue eyes glazed with a pyretic stare turned towards her. Dusky black shadows marked her pale face and bright red fever spots burned on her cheeks. She coughed—a shuddering wet sound—and immediately brought her arm close to her ribs in a guarding action.

Abbie's diagnostic radar went on full alert. 'How long have you had pain when you cough?'

Penny shrugged. 'I dunno. Since Adam hit me.'

Abbie's stomach clenched as memories threatened her.

She gave herself a shake and refocused on the woman in front of her. Alec had said they'd lived in Victoria until two days ago. 'Did you see Justin and have an X-ray?'

The mother shook her head as her hand caressed her belly. 'X-rays aren't good for the baby.'

'Neither are broken ribs good for you.' But Abbie was equally worried about the cough and the fever. Put together they meant pneumonia. Pregnancy and pneumonia were a shocking combination, especially in someone so emotionally and physically drained as Penny. Not to mention that they were in the middle of an H1N1 virus pandemic.

Abbie kicked herself. She'd been so focused on Alec when she'd first arrived that she'd associated Penny's blank look with depression but now she was seeing the real picture. 'Can I please examine you?'

Penny shrugged again and Abbie took that as a 'yes'.

Gently lifting her blouse, Abbie stifled a gasp at the purple and yellow bruises on the woman's thin body. There was every chance she had bruised or fractured ribs, which would account for the guarding. Abbie mentally crossed her fingers that the cough was nothing too severe but Warrior Abbie did a massive eye-roll and mouthed, *Get real.*

'I'm going to listen to your chest. Can you please breathe in and out when I say?' Slowly she moved her stethoscope around her patient's back as she listened to the lung sounds. The stark sound of fine crackles in the lower lobes was unmistakable. She tapped the area, hearing the dull percussion sounds. Penny had double pneumonia and probable rib fractures.

'Penny, given Alec's symptoms and your fever and cough, I need you both to come to hospital.'

The sick woman could hardly focus on Abbie. 'It's just a cough.'

'No, Penny, it's more than a cough.' She recognised the malaise of depression and illness where any effort was just too hard. She bent down so she was at eye-level. 'I need to take care of you so you can take care of Alec and the baby.'

Penny stared and then slowly nodded. 'OK.' But she remained seated.

'I'll arrange everything and be back in a few minutes.' Abbie picked up her medical bag and walked out of the house to her car. She didn't need anyone to overhear her phone conversations and panic. She punched in a familiar number.

'Paul Jenkins.' The commanding voice of the senior paramedic answered her call.

'Paul, it's Abbie. I need an ambulance at seventeen Creamery Lane and I'll be here when your officers arrive.'

'No problem, Abbie. We're on our way.'

The call terminated and she rang Rebecca, leaving a message on her service asking her to return to the refuge as soon as possible. Then she scrolled down her contact list and, finding the unfamiliar number she needed, she pressed 'call'. The ringtone sounded long and loud in her ear. 'Come on, come on, pick up.' She paced up and down, the tough buffalo grass of the nature strip springing under her feet. She was about to cut the call when the ringing stopped.

'Leo…Costa.'

The whooshing and rushing sound of exhaled air swept down the phone. Instantly, the image of his broad chest with muscles rippling surfaced in her mind and liquid heat poured through her. She gripped the phone too hard. What was he doing?

Stop it. She didn't want to know. Well, she did want to know but now wasn't the time to be thinking about anything except work. 'Leo, it's Abbie.'

'I'll meet you…in EMD in…ten minutes.' His words,

although gasped out, carried one hundred per cent professionalism without a trace of the flirting banter that had tinged their more recent conversations.

Not that she'd seen him since he'd left Theatre after Lorenzo Galbardi's surgery but the fact that he seemed to know instinctively that she needed him for patients gave her supportive reassurance. 'Thanks, Leo, but it's a bit more complicated than that.'

'Where are you?'

'Creamery Lane.'

'That runs parallel with Dorcas Street, right?'

'Yes.' The buffeting noise of wind crackled down the line, making it hard to hear and she didn't want to talk directions. 'Listen, I've got a mother and son with flu and therefore suspected H1N1 virus.'

'How…sick?'

Again with the panting. Was he jogging? The trees waved gently in the breeze, which was completely out of sync with the roaring sound coming down the phone. 'One patient is pregnant and has bilateral consolidation of the lower lobes of the lungs.'

'Hell, that's not good. Do we have a bed in ICU?'

The words sounded clearer and confusingly in stereo. She twirled around to see Leo swinging off a shiny black and red road bike, the hands-free device of his phone still in his ear.

Her jaw dropped of its own accord and she openly gaped as rafts of shivering delight shot through her before pooling deeply inside her and heating into simmering need. He stood before her, his taut, fit body clad in the distinctive green, white and red cycling Lycra leaving very little to the imagination. Every sinew, tendon and ligament was delineated by the clinging material like the chiselled detail on a Michelangelo sculpture.

She fought for a coherent sentence and cleared her throat. 'You're training for the Giro d'Italia?'

He gave her a long, lazy grin. 'Maybe the Murray to Moyne. The Allied Health blokes want to take on Mildura hospital this year so I thought I might join them. This is my first training ride and I was around the corner when you called.' He removed his helmet and his smile flattened out, with deep lines bracketing his mouth. 'So we hospitalise the pregnant woman and we home quarantine the boy. How is that complicated?'

His no-nonsense surgeon's tone immediately centred her, thankfully banishing every inappropriate sensation. 'The complication is this house is a women's refuge and there are five other women with their children living here at the moment.'

'Can we hospitalise the boy too?'

'Yes, we can but–' She ran a statement through her head, practising how to introduce the tricky topic.

He stared at her, deep lines creasing his forehead and then realisation dawned in his eyes. 'I'm male.'

Oh, yeah, all male. Every single gorgeous millimetre.

He rubbed his hand through his hair, raising glossy jet-black spikes. 'So what's the best way to play it? Do you think the pregnant woman will let me look after her in hospital if I have Erin with me the whole time? That leaves you to examine the rest of the women here at the house and organise education and possible quarantine.'

Surprise fizzed in her stomach. *He gets it.* She clenched her hands to keep them firmly by her sides instead of letting them fly around his neck in a hug of thanks. So often her male colleagues were offended by the fact that in this type of situation their gender immediately put them at a disadvantage as the refuge preferred a female doctor. But Leo didn't appear to be at all threatened by this. Damn it, once again he'd broken out of the charm-use-and-abuse-box she so desperately wanted him to stay in.

'Thanks, Leo.'

He shrugged as if he was confused as to why he needed her thanks.

'Abbie, Abbie, come quick!' A pale and feverish Alec came running out of the house. 'Mum's fallen over and she's not waking up.'

Abbie ran, hearing the clatter of Leo's cycling shoes close behind her. She found Penny on the floor by the chair she'd been sitting on and with Leo's help rolled her into coma position. She checked her airway and then slid in the plastic airway guard Leo handed her which would prevent Penny's tongue from rolling back. Then she counted her respirations while Leo's long fingers located Penny's carotid pulse.

He pulled his hand away. 'She's tachypnoeic.'

'And tachycardic. I'll insert an IV.' Abbie pulled an IV set out of her bag and rummaged around until her fingers felt the tourniquet. She didn't need to voice her fears that swine flu and pregnancy were a potentially life-threatening combination—she could see that very thought reflected back at her in Leo's inky eyes.

'Will she be all right?' Alec's scared voice broke over them.

Leo stayed bent down and turned so his face was at Alec's eye level. 'Your mum's very sick but Abbie and I are both doctors and we're doing our absolute best to take care of her.'

'And the baby?'

Leo hesitated for half a beat. 'And the baby.'

'Are you sure you're a doctor? You don't look like one.' Alec sounded extremely suspicious.

Leo didn't even blink at the accusatory tone. 'I'm on holiday and I was having a bike ride when Abbie phoned me. Most of the time I wear a suit or baggy green pants and a matching top when I'm in the operating theatre.'

The boy blanched. 'Does Mum need an operation?'

Leo shook his head. 'No, mate, but she needs antibiotics and she needs to be in hospital.'

'I was looking after her.' The words came out on a wail.

Leo gave him a man-to-man squeeze of the shoulder. 'And you've done a great job but now it's time to let us look after you and Mum.'

'Why is her mouth purple?'

Abbie opened her mouth to explain but Leo continued to talk to Alec in an honest and open way without any sign of condescension that some adults used with kids. She begrudgingly conceded it was great stuff for a guy who usually dealt with patients that were asleep.

'Her lungs have got fluid in them and that makes it harder to breathe. See this?' He held up a clear oxygen mask. 'This will help her breathe and in a few minutes you, me and your mum are going for a ride in an ambulance to the hospital.'

The boy's eyes momentarily widened against his fear. 'Really? Awesome.'

Abbie glanced up and, for the first time since meeting Alec, she glimpsed the child that he was. Too often the child got lost in the emotional maelstrom of their parents' chaotic lives. She'd lived that scenario. She taped the IV in place as the ambulance officers arrived.

'Perfect timing, guys. We need her connected up to the Lifepak.' Leo accepted the ECG dots from Paul and immediately attached them to the unconscious woman's chest.

A moment later the ECG display traced across the screen along with Penny's rapid pulse rate, diminishing oxygen saturation and rising blood pressure. Leo spoke sharply. 'We need to leave now.'

'Oh, God, what happened?' Rebecca, the case worker, rushed into the room, her face white with shock.

Leo exchanged a look with Abbie that said, *You go sort that out; I've got this under control.*

Abbie rose, relief surging through her that she had Leo working with her today. Penny was in good hands and she was going to need every ounce of medical skill they had. 'Paul, Alec and Leo are going back with you.'

The paramedic readied Penny to be loaded onto the stretcher. 'No worries, Abbie. We'll look after everyone.'

She caught Rebecca by the arm, shepherded her out of the room and answered the unasked questions that clung to her face. 'Penny and Alec have flu-like symptoms and, given that we're in the grip of a swine-flu epidemic, we're pretty certain that's what they've got.'

Bec's hand flew to her throat. 'Oh, no. I heard that's really bad for pregnant women.'

Abbie grimaced. 'Penny's extremely ill and we might need to evacuate her to Melbourne if her condition deteriorates any further. I'm also worried about the other residents so I need you to contact everyone and get them back here so I can examine them.'

Bec nodded. 'OK. Most of them went on a picnic but they're due back because of the canoeing, which I guess you'll be cancelling?'

'Postponing, at any rate.' She smiled a half smile. 'Let's have a quick cup of tea and a biscuit and I'll brief you so you can answer the residents' questions. Then we'll turn one of the bedrooms into a clinic and get to work. We're going to be flat out for a couple of hours at least.'

She heard the siren of the ambulance fading into the distance. Leo would be flat out working too.

Leo squinted into the glare of the early evening summer sun and watched the air-ambulance helicopter lift off, the down-draught of the blades swirling the red outback dust into the air. It had been a hellish three hours—every second testing all of his medical knowledge. As a surgeon he was at the top of his field but surgery wasn't what Penny needed.

Murphy, who'd been pressed up against his legs, barked as a familiar white four-wheel-drive turned into the car park and came to an abrupt stop. Abbie jumped out of the vehicle and ran over, her curls bouncing and the wind whipping her plain T-shirt close against her chest.

Leo groaned as his body immediately reacted to her per-fectly outlined breasts and perky nipples. The woman was a fashion disaster but if she thought those clothes hid her deli-cious curves then she was living in la-la land.

'Is that Penny?' Abbie yelled the words over the roar of the engine.

The helicopter banked and headed south, the noise de-creasing.

He plunged his hands into the pockets of his white coat, the lapping waters of despair threatening to spill over. 'Yeah.'

'Oh, hell.' Abbie caught his gaze, her mild expletive under-playing the anguish on her face.

The same anguish that filled him. 'Erin and I did every-thing we could but she didn't regain consciousness. Her breathing became increasingly laboured and we were worried she'd arrest, so we ventilated her.' He ran his hand through his hair. 'God, I haven't done that since I was a resident. She didn't need a surgeon; she needed a respiratory physician and an obstetrician.'

Abbie shook her head sharply. 'She needed a doctor and she was lucky to have you. Did you consult using the Virtual Trauma and Critical Care Service?'

Her hand touched his arm, her skin warm against his own and her assurance floated through him. 'It was odd talking to my colleagues in Melbourne on a screen but thank goodness for broadband technology. With her pregnancy and the risk of multi-system organ failure, Penny's best chance is in their level one ICU.'

Abbie bit her lip. 'And the baby?'

A familiar hot pain burned under his ribs at his powerlessness in the situation. 'She'd started having contractions so we administered Nifedipine but at twenty-six weeks you know as well as I do that it'll be touch and go.'

Abbie's sigh visibly trembled through her body. 'Poor Alec.'

He automatically slung his arm around her shoulder in a gesture of support. 'Alec's doing well. He's got an IV in, he's rehydrating and his nausea's under control. We'll monitor him but I think after twenty-four hours of Tamiflu he'll be a different kid.'

'But his world is already upside down and now his mother is fighting for her life.' The doctor had vanished. Instead, a hurting woman stood in front of him with the vestiges of a child clinging to her like cobwebs. The familiar shadows that sometimes haunted her eyes had scudded neatly back into place like the dark clouds that heralded bad weather. Then her shoulders sagged and her head swayed, until it finally lost the battle to stay upright and her forehead brushed his shoulder.

An overwhelming surge of protection unlike anything he'd

known in years exploded inside him and his hand reached to touch her soft curls. A touch devoid of lust and totally removed from desire. He only wanted to reassure her, murmur into her ear that things would be OK, but most of all he wanted to send those shadows scattering. But this was real life and none of those things were possible. Instead, he held her tight and lowered his face into her hair, breathing in her strawberry scent, soaking up her softness, her spirit and her strength.

Murphy's wet nose nuzzled between them, followed by a bark of, *Hey, what about me?*

Abbie stepped back and Leo dropped his hand, still struggling with the unexpected mix of emotions and glad that Abbie was distracted with her dog rather than turning her all-seeing gaze onto him.

She put her hand on Murphy's head. 'Hey, boy. It's OK; Leo's not all bad.' Then she raised her questioning green eyes to Leo. 'Why is Murphy here?'

He confessed, 'I borrowed him.'

'Why?'

'I thought Alec could use a friend.'

A slow smile wove across her smattering of freckles, lighting up her face, and then she started to move her head from side to side in a disbelieving yet resigned way. 'And let me guess? You called Jennifer Danforth in paediatrics *cara*, produced a box of Baci Italian chocolate kisses, told her that you knew she'd understand that, given the circumstances, Alec needed a buddy and then she let you bring a dog into her pristine ward.'

What the–? He tried hard not to look as stunned as he felt. How could she possibly have known? Yet Abbie had just outlined in perfect detail exactly what he'd done to get Murphy past Demon Danforth. He shrugged and grinned. 'Hey, it worked.'

Her forefinger shot into his chest. 'Well, you owe me, Casanova. I've been trying to get a companion dog into the hospital for months and that woman has blocked it on every turn.'

He gave her a smug look. 'Did you try chocolate?'

She raised one brow. 'No, but without a sex-change operation and fluency in Italian, I doubt that one would have worked for me.' Her finger jabbed him hard in the sternum. 'So, before you leave, I want an approved companion pet programme policy with Jennifer's signature on it.'

He gave her a mock salute and a wink. 'Yes, ma'am.'

'Good.' But her sergeant major voice had faded to a warm and friendly tone and she dropped her hand to her pager. 'Everything's quiet at the moment so does Murphy have time for a "W" before he has to report for duty?'

The dog's golden-brown eyes moved back and forth between the two of them saying, *I recognise euphemisms, you fools,* and his tail started wagging enthusiastically.

He fondled the dog's ears. 'Sure.'

She hesitated and then cleared her throat before asking, 'Do you want to come too? It's been a hellish afternoon and we could exercise and debrief at the same time.'

The completely unexpected invitation made him smile. 'That's probably a good idea.'

'Great. Let's go, then.' She turned to cross the car park, Murphy pulling on the lead as he headed towards the river path.

The river path. Leo's muscles tensed and his hand shot to his chin. Every part of him screamed to stay put. But he'd already refused the canoeing and if he refused this walk after he'd already committed to it, he knew Abbie would start asking questions. Questions he didn't want to answer.

He made a fast decision. He'd go on the walk and he'd ask questions to keep hers at bay. With every ounce of determination that had got him into medical school and had pushed him up the gruelling surgical career ladder, he fell into step beside her, resolving to find out why an eleven-year-old boy's plight had brought the shadows back into her eyes when other patients had not.

The walking path was as popular and as crowded as the river. Houseboats chugged along overtaken by water-skiers criss-crossing behind speedboats. The high-pitched 'toot' of the horn of a paddle steamer could be heard in the distance, a far more pleasant sound than the buzz of the closer and louder jet-ski. On the path, tourists walked with their families, locals with or without dogs strolled and a gaggle of giggling teenage girls eyed a group of teenage boys. Everyone was out just as they were in Italy for *passeggiata* and catching the cool breeze off the river on a hot summer evening.

The first part of the walk was spent nodding and smiling to people as they passed, commenting on the weather, chatting about dogs, until they got beyond the main part of town where the path narrowed and the bush thickened.

A flash of memory—mallee scrub, dark water and ancient trees—flickered unfocused in his mind and he steeled himself to keep the image sealed away. He felt Abbie's gaze on him and he dug deep, forcing the muscles of his mouth to lift in a smile. 'Remind me never to come along here if I want time to myself.'

'It's pretty popular and why not? It's so pretty.' She gazed across the brown sparkling water and then licked her lips, the moisture clinging to them making a rosy red.

'Yeah, it's pretty.'

But she missed the real meaning of his words and just smiled at him as a co-conspirator of two people enjoying the view. A view that sliced into him deeply every time he saw it, remind-ing him of what he'd lost and the trauma that had followed.

She turned back from the river, a genuine smile on her lips that raced straight to her amazingly expressive eyes. 'I know I just gave you a hard time about charming Jennifer Danforth so Murphy could visit the ward, but thanks. It was a lovely idea and you were really great with Alec when Penny collapsed.'

The praise warmed him, pushing the memories away. 'It must be pretty terrifying for him with his mother so ill and I'm gathering his father's out of the picture?'

Abbie tugged on Murphy's lead as he strained forward wanting to chase some little pied cormorants. 'I only met Penny and Alec for the first time today but generally the fact a woman and her child are staying at the refuge means the father's not in the picture.'

He shoved his hands in his pockets, working hard to sound casual as the lapping of the water ate into him. 'Because of violence?'

'Perhaps. Not always. Sometimes women are abandoned or left destitute and they need the support of the refuge to get on their feet again.' This time it was her turn to stare straight ahead and her mouth flattened into a grim line. '*Some* men can be bastards.'

The guttural vitriol in her voice surprised him. Although she'd refused every invitation he'd offered, they'd worked together well and he'd only ever observed respect from her towards Justin and the male paramedics so he didn't have her pegged as a man-hater. And damn it, but the kiss they'd shared made a mockery out of that thought. She'd melted into his arms and kissed him with the expertise of a woman who knew what she wanted out of a kiss and how to get it. 'Perhaps you're getting a skewed view from working at the refuge.'

'Hah!'

The harsh sound echoed back on the breeze and Leo heard the pain. Pain and shadows.

Her voice rose, agitation clearly edging the words. 'You saw the bruising on Penny's chest and you heard how Alec behaved more like he was the parent than the child. That poor kid has needed to grow up way too fast under a roof of uncertainty.'

The shadows in her eyes darkened as she gripped Murphy's lead hard, her knuckles turning white. 'Some men treat women and children like chattels instead of people, disposing of them when they've had enough. They destroy women's lives and leave kids in terrible situations, putting them at risk of it happening all over again.'

The trembling pain in her voice was unmistakable and again he wanted to hold her tight but he instinctively knew that would be the wrong thing to do. What he did know was this reaction was no longer about Alec—it was all about her. He'd bet money on it that it was connected in some way to why she mostly tried to hold herself aloof from him.

'Who left you, Abbie?'

CHAPTER SEVEN

ABBIE'S breath stalled in her throat as Warrior Abbie, who'd been caught napping, frantically pulled on her armour and tried to get her act together. *Who left you, Abbie?* His words hailed down on her with unerring accuracy. How did he know? How had he worked out that everything that had happened this afternoon had brought back in horrifying waves the painful memories of her time with Greg and the insecurity of her childhood?

Still, just because that had happened was no reason to talk about it. If she'd learned anything it was that it was best to just 'get on' with things. She tilted her chin skyward and pursed her lips. 'We're talking about Penny and Alec, and refuge clients in general, not me.'

Mensa-bright eyes looked sceptical. 'Except there's something about their situation that's got to you.'

Denial shot to her lips as her heart thundered hard against her ribs. 'No, it hasn't.'

'I think it has. You're pretty upset and it might help to talk about it.'

Guileless care and concern sat on his handsome face, tempting her to spill her guts and yet terrifying her at the same time. 'I'm so not having a heart-to-heart with *you*.'

'Why not?' He smiled a warm and friendly captivating smile. 'I've been told I'm a very good listener.'

'I'm sure you have.' The moment the cheap shot left her mouth she regretted it.

His jaw tightened, pulling the edges of his mouth downward. 'Abbie, if that comment's to do with me dating a lot of women then let's get something straight—I'm always honest and up front with them. I'm after fun and good times and I never make a promise I can't keep. So don't confuse me with badly behaved men.'

His clear dark gaze seared her as his honesty and integrity circled him, making a mockery of her determination to cast him in the same light as her father. As Greg. She bit her lip, realising she'd just been grossly unfair. Taking out her hurt on him was unwarranted. He was only trying to be a supportive colleague and, hell, she'd been the one who had said, *Let's debrief*. She clearly hadn't thought *that one* through.

She let Murphy lead her down onto a sandy beach. It continued to surprise her that there was golden sand like this so far inland but she wasn't complaining. Murphy barked and she released him from the lead, watching him tear off into the shallows, ever hopeful of catching an ibis. She turned and, with a start, she realised Leo hadn't followed her. He remained standing on the higher bank, his hand rubbing the scar on his chin—something she'd seen him do on and off since she'd met him and usually when he was tense. Damn, but she'd really hurt his feelings.

She trudged back towards him and stood looking up at him, catching his gaze. She'd expected to see anger but it wasn't there. Instead, a mix of undecipherable emotions seemed to be tumbling over each other with no clear delineation but she caught pain. She called out, 'I'm sorry. You're right; today hasn't been easy.'

He held her gaze for a moment longer and a part of her ached. Then, like sunlight breaking through clouds, his eyes cleared and in three strides he was by her side and she was left wondering if she'd imagined the whole thing.

'I shouldn't have lashed out at you; it's just there's too much of my story in Alec's and Penny's and I hate it when I see that it's still happening.' She sat down on the sand and leaned back against a fallen red-gum bough.

Leo lowered himself down next to her in a stiff and uncoordinated way before finally stretching his legs out in front of him.

Funny how all his movements were usually so fluid and he could glide out of a hammock but he couldn't lower himself onto the sand without looking as if all his limbs were overly long.

'Do you and Alec share a father leaving?'

He was far too perceptive and, as much as she wanted to stay silent on the entire topic, she knew she'd lost the battle to keep her story to herself. She'd already had to apologise and if they were to continue to work together as a cohesive team she needed to tell him, otherwise it would hang around like an elephant in the room, affecting their working relationship.

Her palm dug into the sand and then she raised her hand, letting the tiny particles run through her fingers as her mind released her memories. 'My father was a charming but controlling man and he dropped in and out of my life. My mother finally left him when I was ten but the legacy of him never left us.'

A restrained kind of tension lined Leo's shoulders but his expression was one of sympathy duelling with interest. 'How much of it do you remember?'

She stared straight ahead. 'I remember the fear. I remember

the routine my mother had before he came home every night, a sort of ritual. She believed if she followed it to the letter it would mean the evening would be pleasant. She'd make dinner and I'd set the table. Then she'd go to her room, reapply her make-up, change into a pretty dress and insist on brushing my hair. After that we'd wait.'

'Wait for what?' Two lines furrowed down at the bridge of his nose.

We have to look pretty for Daddy so he loves us. She tugged at her now short hair as the memory of the plastic brush snagging through her long hair made her scalp prickle. 'We'd wait for my father. On a good night he'd barrel through the door, twirl me around and call me his princess. He'd compliment my mother's cooking and after dinner he'd crank up the music, grab my mother around her waist and they'd dance through the house.'

'And on a bad night?' Leo's hand spilled sand close to hers.

She glanced at him, expecting to see the prying look that people got when they heard a story so at odds with their preconceived ideas of who she was and where she'd come from, but the only thing she saw was understanding. 'A storm cloud would enter the house and we'd be on high alert cyclone watch, just like Port Headland was last week. Will it hit or will it blow past and miss us? It was terrifying even when he didn't hit us because the fear was always there.'

'I can't even imagine what that would be like.' He spoke quietly. 'We're Italian and, believe me, my parents can yell and argue with the best of them, but there was never any fear in the house.' His eyes lit up with a memory. 'Usually Anna did something crazy which distracted them and it blew over very quickly. Did you have a brother or sister to share this with?'

She shook her head. 'Just me.'

'Sorry.' His fingers skated across the back of her hand in the lightest caress before falling back to the sand.

Heat roared through her and self-loathing filled her. His touch was one of understanding and friendship. Only she could put a sexual tinge on it and, heaven help her, hadn't she learned anything from her life? From Greg? She blew out a breath and fixed her gaze on the peeling bark of a tree on the opposite bank and forced the words to keep coming.

'One night he hit Mum so badly he fractured her ribs. The next day when I was at school a taxi arrived with Mum in it. She'd packed one bag for the both of us and we went into supported accommodation.'

Her eyes burned from staring at the tree but she didn't dare look at Leo. She didn't want to see pity in his eyes—she'd seen that too often over the years from too many people, which was why she kept her story buried deep.

'And you took care of your mother. Just like Alec was doing today.'

She gave a silent nod, letting his deep voice wash over her with its startling insight. She turned towards him, suddenly needing to see his face. Not a trace of pity marked his cheeks, only admiration and respect. *He gets it*. The realisation jolted her and Warrior Abbie laid down her shield, although her fingers stayed close to it. The tightness in her chest slowly slackened and an unexpected peace rolled through her, seeping into places that hadn't experienced calm in a long time. Yet again, Abbie had just glimpsed another side to Leo Costa. He confused her so much with his multi-facets, making her question what she believed, but most of all it made her wonder why was he hiding behind all that superficial charm when there was so much more to him.

'So did things settle down for you and your mother?'

She shrugged. 'Not really. We got out of the refuge and got set up again. Mum got a job and had a few boyfriends who always seemed to arrive with presents and leave us with debt. I craved stability but, by sixteen, I realised Mum wasn't able to give me that. I knew then I had to find it for myself and make a life so I was never dependent on anyone ever again. I got a scholarship to university and studied medicine. People always need doctors, right?' She smiled, trying to lighten the mood. She'd had enough talking about herself.

Leo watched her eyes and tried to read them. His own childhood had been carefree in comparison to hers and at that precise moment he totally understood her self-containment. Anyone who'd lived a roller coaster childhood of over-indulgence followed by abandonment would be very wary of people. Of men.

But she kissed you. The memory of their kiss hadn't dimmed at all. It stayed so strong and clear inside him—a kiss that told the story of an incredibly sensual woman, someone who'd had some experience. The women he most enjoyed being with were totally independent and relationship-free but still staked their claim for a healthy sex life. But in the last few days he'd dropped enough hints to Abbie that he was open to some fun and good times that there was no way she could have missed them. Nothing he had said or done had lowered her major 'road block' signs; in fact she'd done everything she possibly could do to shut him out. And it wasn't because she wasn't attracted to him—tangible lust close to the point of combustion burned between them at every meeting and, had their kiss been anywhere else, sex would have followed.

Lust is just a nuisance that can be controlled.

So I was never dependent on anyone ever again.

Her sweet voice replayed in his head and it was like someone switching on a lamp and illuminating a dark corner. Right then he knew exactly what he had to ask. 'And have you been?'

She glanced up from the sand, confusion creasing her brow into a row of deep lines. 'Been what?'

'Dependent on anyone again?'

She rolled her plump lips inward and a shudder ricocheted across her shoulders, down her torso and into the sand. Without thinking, his fingers moved to slide between hers, needing to give her some support, needing to feel connected to her in some way.

She pulled her hand away and fisted it into her lap. 'Let me put it this way; I had the usual casual and fun uni flings everyone has in the first and second year before they grow up. Then I had a relationship that ran off the rails at six months. But it was well after that I had one serious lapse in judgement which cured me for life.'

I hate what you've done to me. Memories of Christina bubbled up inside him and he spoke before thinking. 'Don't be too hard on yourself. I had one of those.'

Her head jerked up. 'I can't imagine you being dependent on anyone.'

Her accurate words whipped him. She was right; he'd never been dependent on anyone but people had been dependent on him. Dom. Christina. He'd failed them both. 'I meant a relationship that cured me for life. I got married at nineteen.'

Her eyes shot open so wide it was like looking into a tropical pool. 'You…I…you're divorced?'

Regret at telling her clawed him because it opened him up to questions like why he'd married his brother's girlfriend. Questions he didn't want to answer. 'Yep.'

Her astonishment slowly faded, replaced with a knowing look. 'I bet Maria wasn't happy about that.'

The corner of his mouth jerked and he took the segue with open arms. 'That would be the understatement of the century, but we all make mistakes.'

She nodded in agreement. 'Oh, yeah, and Greg was my ultimate. I'd got through the gruelling years, I'd qualified and was working in Adelaide.'

Relief flooded him. He'd managed to divert her. 'Financially and emotionally independent?'

'For a short time, yes. I think I'd been working so hard since third year that I'd forgotten how to have fun. When I finally raised my head up to look around at the world, there was Greg, a silver-tongued actor who told me what I wanted to hear.'

For some unknown reason, Leo really wanted to reassure her. 'We're all susceptible to that.'

'Yeah?' Sceptical green eyes flashed at him. 'Well, given how I'd seen all my security disappear again and again as a kid, I should have known better but I stupidly fell hard for the cliché of the happy-ever-after dream. He moved in, I chose china patterns. We shopped and nested and I was the happiest I'd ever been in my life.'

'So what happened?' Half of him wanted to know; the other half didn't want her to relive what he knew would be painful.

'Piece by tiny piece over two years and under the guise of love, he dismantled my independence and, dear God, I let him.' Her ragged sigh reverberated between them. 'After what "the experts" would call the "honeymoon period" his charm started fading and the insidious controlling behaviour came out. He needed me to be with him when I wasn't at work, he didn't pass on messages, he chose my clothes, and he decided where we went and who we visited. Every time

I started to question this he'd revert to the man I'd first met and convince me I was over-tired from working too hard, that after a good night's sleep I'd understand I was being unreasonable. He had me second-guessing myself to the point of going crazy.'

'*Bastardo.*' Pure white anger surged through Leo.

She mustered a small wry smile. 'Exactly. The day he hit me I told him to leave. I went to work and when I came home that night the apartment was empty. Utterly empty. He'd taken everything, including the mothballs in the linen press.'

'He took your clothes?' Leo wanted to commit murder. How could someone do that to a person?

She nodded and her shoulders straightened with what he was starting to recognise as her trademark strength. 'Everything. Thankfully, I had work and slowly I paid off my debts and the moment I finished my GP training I came up here.'

'Good for you. New start?'

'Totally.'

'And since then?'

Her brow creased. 'And since then, what?'

'Have you had another go? Tried a healthy relationship?'

She shook her head. 'God, no. I choose the wrong men so I'm leaving all that for the people who know how to do it and do it well.'

'Fair enough.' He could understand that line of thinking because he had no intention of ever again entering the black pit of despair that was a long-term relationship. 'What about dating?'

'Nope, nothing.'

'Nothing at all?' He couldn't keep the incredulity out of his voice. An amazingly sensual woman sat calmly telling him she was actively avoiding any sort of liaison. It was just plain wrong.

Her lips twitched. 'It's not a tragedy, Leo. I'm happily single and I plan to stay that way.'

Lust is just a nuisance that can be controlled.

'*Dio mio!* Yes, it is a tragedy. I'm happily single too but I'm here to tell you that it doesn't mean you have to lock down every sexual emotion that you have.'

Her mouth tightened. 'Don't be over-dramatic. What's important here is that it's my choice and it works for me.'

He didn't believe that for a minute. 'Really? A lifetime of no sex works for you?'

Everything inside her stilled. *Get out now!* Like the terrifying spray of wild-fire burning embers, his words scorched and burned into her. Warrior Abbie grabbed her shield and ran for a bolt-hole. Abbie stood up abruptly, determined to end this conversation right now. 'Murphy, here, boy.'

The wet and soggy Border collie shot straight to her, shaking sand everywhere.

Leo brought his arms up to protect his face from the sand and then shot to his feet, his eyes blazing with a mixture of pity and desire. 'If we'd been somewhere more private when we'd kissed you know we would have ended up having sex.'

She knew that too but no way was she going to admit it. With shaking hands she reattached the dog's lead and gave Leo her best disdainful glare. 'In your dreams, mate.'

'Oh, but it is.' His usually smooth voice cracked slightly as he stepped in close. 'You can't deny this incredible thing that boils between us every time we're together.'

Her mouth dried. 'I can and I will.' *I have to so I stay safe.*

'Abbie, neither of us is looking for a relationship and we're both very clear on that.' He tilted his head forward so his forehead touched hers. His aroma of mint and citrus overlaid with an all-masculine scent stormed her nostrils. Her heart pounded fast, driving hot blood through her veins, sending her nipples into tight buds of anticipation and pooling moisture between her trembling legs. Every part of her wanted him so badly she thought she'd explode from the bliss.

But she clenched her fists against every tempting sensation and desperately tried to block him out.

He slowly lifted his head and stared down into her eyes, his expression deadly serious. 'Please know that I'm not any of the men who've marched through your life demanding your love with controlling conditions.'

And on one level she really did know that but it didn't stop the fear about herself from battering her.

His expression morphed from serious to a wicked gleam. 'Abbie, remember those casual flings at uni? The ones you told me were fun?'

Panic fluttered so fast in her chest she thought she'd faint. Dear God, he'd really listened to her. Warrior Abbie stamped her foot. *How could you have been so dumb to say something like that to him?*

His voice rumbled around her, warm and enticing. 'We have four weeks where we could have a lot of fun and some amazing sex, enjoy it all and then say goodbye. Use me to banish that bastard's memory with some fun.' His finger trailed down her cheek. 'The invitation's on the table and the RSVP is up to you. Think about it.'

He stepped back, gave Murphy a scratch behind the ears and with four long strides he reached the bank, jumped up onto the path and walked away.

Abbie's legs gave way and she sat down hard on the sand with Murphy licking her face, his expression confused. Bright spots danced in front of her eyes and her body tried to get some blood back to her brain but all her pleasure centres refused to give it up. She steeled her mind to close down every single sensation. Greg's charisma had been her downfall. The day she'd kicked him out, Abbie had gathered her emotions, reclaimed her heart, jammed the lot into a padlocked box and thrown away the key. Warrior Abbie had stood guard over the box ever since—an easy job as there'd never been a single attempt to pick the lock. Until Leo.

Leo, who, when you navigated past the superficial charm, had more facets to him than a radiant-cut diamond. Confusing and contradictory sides, sides that whispered to her that he was a good guy, an honourable man. Whispers she wanted to trust. Whispers that terrified her.

Remember those casual flings at uni? We have four weeks where we could have a lot of fun and some amazing sex, enjoy it all and then say goodbye.

Tingling sensations ripped through her, shaking her to her very marrow and tempting her so strongly she felt weak all over. She blew out a long slow breath. Forget the facets, it was time to regroup. She mentally ran over her 'life is good' list. She had a good job, lovely friends, a dog who adored her and she was safe. She'd spent years working to keep safe, making sure she kept safe.

Use me to banish that bastard's memory with some fun.

Nothing about Leo was safe.

And so help her; that was the one thing that called so strongly to her and threatened her the most.

'*Dottore*, you need sleep.'

Abbie sat sharing lunch with Maria. She hated to admit it, but she was also hiding from Leo. He'd already visited Maria so she knew she was safe. Maria was right, she needed sleep, but sleep had refused to need her last night. She'd tried watching TV, reading, a long warm soak in the bath, yoga, deep breathing and relaxation but nothing had kept her mind from constantly re-hearing Leo's invitation. *Fun, amazing sex, good times and then goodbye.*

Every time those words rolled over in her head, images of rolling over with Leo wrapped around her had followed, leaving her skittish and completely wound up. Could she really have an affair and keep safe? Could she pretend she was eighteen again and have fun? The thought kept taunting her, calling her and driving her insane.

'You're right, Maria, I need sleep but yesterday was a difficult day.'

'My grandson, he no sleep either.' The old woman put her work-worn hand over Abbie's. 'This woman and her baby, they are sick, yes?'

'Very sick.' Leo had met her at the clinic this morning with the news that Penny's baby had been stillborn and Penny was in multi-organ failure, fighting for her life. Murphy was spending the day with Alec.

Maria grunted. 'A crazy world this is when an old woman lives and the young they die.' She tapped her finger imperiously on the table. 'I want to go home for the vintage.'

Abbie sighed, knowing that when Maria made up her mind it was hard to dissuade her of anything but the family had agreed that Abbie was the doctor in charge and that Maria was only to be discharged when Abbie considered it appropriate. Maria's walking was improving each day but it was still a bit too early for her to go home. 'When's the vintage?'

'When the grapes are ready.'

'Yes, but what date is that?'

Maria rolled her eyes. 'When the sugar is right. Could be

tomorrow, could be next week, could be longer, but I must be home for the twenty-seventh.'

Abbie calculated how many days until the specified date, wondering why Rosa and Anna hadn't mentioned its significance to her if Maria was going to get so het up about it. 'Is that a special day?'

Rheumy eyes usually so full of gritty determination suddenly filled with a resigned sadness and an unusual melancholy circled her shoulders. 'It is a day not to forget.'

Abbie tried not to frown at the cryptic answer. 'Well, if you keep working hard on the physio and the occupational therapist can install the necessary rails and bars in time, then there's a chance you could be home for the twenty-seventh.'

'I *will* be home.'

Abbie leaned forward. 'Maria, I can't make a precise promise but I can discuss it with your family and Leo—'

Maria's fist came down on the table, her eyes glinting as stormy black as her grandson's. 'Leo knows why and he has to be there too.'

A shiver ran down Abbie's spine, leaving behind a sense of unease. *Don't be a drama queen; you just need a good night's sleep.* But one thing she did know—nothing she could say would stop Maria from being where she had to be on that date. But why did Leo need to be there too?

CHAPTER EIGHT

'ABBIE, got a minute?'

Leo's deep velvet voice washed over her, immediately sending her tightly wound body into an overdrive of delicious tingling sensations. Her hand clenched hard against the pencil in her fingers, almost breaking it in half, but still the streaks of unfulfilled need burned hot inside her, tugging at every hard-held resolution. Warrior Abbie lay weak and wounded as the invaders yelled, *Just say yes, get naked and get him out of your system. Have some no-strings fun; how dangerous can it be?*

For two days she'd only seen Leo at work and he hadn't made any attempt to bring up the neither accepted nor declined invitation that lay between them. He'd surprised her again. The fact that he'd really meant that the RSVP was completely up to her and strings-free should have given her some relief, but just thinking about him sent her body into meltdown and her brain into a tailspin.

'Sure.' She carefully put her pencil down, willing her hand not to shake, and she glanced up. Leo and a woman, equally as dark and attractive as him, stood on the other side of the nurses' station. His wide smile raced to his eyes as he slung his arm around the woman's shoulders with the air of a man in very familiar territory.

A bright green flash streaked through her, spiralling around all her good intentions and shocking her to her toes. *No, no, no.* She couldn't possibly be jealous because she didn't care enough. The flash morphed into a face and thumbed its nose at her.

'Abbie, I'd like to introduce you to my sister, Chiara.'

Sister. Abbie hated the relief that settled through her as she stood up and walked around the station. 'Pleased to meet you, Chiara. Leo didn't mention he had more than one sister.'

Chiara extended her hand with a laugh and a smile. 'I think he likes to pretend he only has one but there are three of us.'

'Three bossy, opinionated women.' But Leo didn't sound at all disgruntled and his eyes twinkled like the night star.

Chiara elbowed him. 'Three sisters whose friends provided you with a limitless supply of dates in high school.'

Abbie laughed. 'Poor Leo; it must have been tough growing up in a household of strong women. I bet you dreamed of having a brother.'

His ready smile vanished, replaced by a grim tightness around his mouth that seemed to whiten the scar on his chin. A sharp pain unexpectedly jabbed Abbie in the chest before dissolving into a dull ache that lingered. She instinctively rubbed her sternum.

Leo cleared his throat. 'Chiara, her husband, Edoardo, and their sons are a registered foster family so I spoke to the social worker and Alec's going to be discharged into their care.'

Surprise at the idea gave way to comforting warmth that wove through Abbie at Leo's thoughtfulness. 'Oh, that's wonderful. What a great idea.'

The woman nodded, understanding clear on her face. 'We live at the vineyard too so, with Anna's girls, my boys plus the other cousins who live on the adjoining property, there're plenty of kids and lots of distractions.' She sighed. 'My heart is sick just thinking about Alec. Leo says his mother is frighteningly ill and fighting for her life.'

Abbie bit her lip and caught Leo's tense gaze. 'I just got an update from Melbourne City and Penny's now on extra-corporeal membrane oxygenation.'

'Hell.' His eyes closed for a fraction of a second before opening again, his anguish for Penny's battle mirroring her own.

Chiara turned to Leo, questions clear on her face. 'Is that bad?'

Leo nodded. 'It's the last defence against swine flu. It's a machine where the blood is drawn out of the patient by a pump which acts like a replacement heart, and then it's pumped through this strange diamond-shaped device which adds oxygen into the blood and removes the carbon dioxide before the blood's returned to the patient.'

'So a machine is being her heart and lungs?' Disbelief rang in the words.

'That's right.' Abbie wrung her hands. 'Right now her lungs are so badly affected by the H1N1 virus they can't do their job. We need to hope that she'll recover but it's going to be a long, hard road.'

Chiara rolled her shoulders back. 'We'll look after Alec for her. When can I take him home?'

'In a couple of days.' Abbie and Leo spoke together, their voices contrasting like a melody. Leo winked at Abbie, his smile now firmly back in place, and her stomach went into free fall.

'Great.' Chiara pressed her bag to her shoulder. 'I'll go and spend a bit of time with him now and then visit again tomorrow with the boys.' She spun on her heel and then turned back. 'Oh, Abbie, I forgot to say but Mamma wanted to invite you to the blessing of the grapes and the vintage picnic. Of course the date's still up in the air but it's getting really close and you've been so great with Nonna that we'd love you to be there.'

Abbie's cheeks burned hot as Leo's penetrative and questioning gaze bored into her over the top of Chiara's head. One that said, *Now, this will be interesting. I dare you to come.*

Leo would be at the picnic and avoiding him would be impossible. But refusing an invitation like this would be social suicide in the small Bandarra community and she had to live here long after Leo had returned to his city life. *Fun, amazing sex and then goodbye,* the whispers taunted. *He will leave and that will keep you safe.*

The words hammered her and she closed them down by focusing on Chiara's expectant face and pushing her mouth into a smile. She hedged her bets. 'As long as there's no emergency, I can be there.'

'Fingers crossed, then.' Chiara smiled.

Her fingers rolled in against her palm. 'Fingers crossed.'

'Ciao.' Chiara presented her cheeks to Leo, who kissed her quickly in a European farewell, and then she walked briskly towards Alec's ward.

Abbie's stomach rumbled, reminding her it was lunchtime, and she headed towards the front entrance of the hospital. Leo fell into step beside her. 'Are you going for a training ride today?'

As they reached the automatic doors he stood back, allowing her to proceed first. 'I thought I—'

'Abbie!'

She pulled her attention from Leo and swung quickly around at the strangled sound of her name.

Morgan Dalhensen ran towards them, dripping wet, clutching an equally wet child against his chest. 'Help me.'

Abbie and Leo sprinted across the car park.

The man stumbled as they reached him and he almost threw the child into Abbie's arms. 'He's not breathing.'

The child felt as floppy as a rag doll in her arms, and the telltale sign of blue lips had her kneeling immediately and laying the child on the ground. She checked his airway, hoping for something as easy as a physical obstruction that had choked him but knowing the high probability was he had water in his lungs. Her fingers met no obstruction. She checked for a pulse. Nothing. She moved her fingers, trying again.

'One minute he was on the riverbank and the next I couldn't see him and I turned my back for a minute and, oh, God, help him.' The anguished father's voice rained down on her.

'Starting CPR.' Abbie rolled the toddler over and realised Leo was still standing stock still next to her, his gaze hauntingly bleak and empty and fixed fast on the child. She'd expected him to have already run to ED for the emergency resuscitation kit and a trolley. 'Leo.' Her elbow knocked his leg hard. 'Get the resuss kit. Go.'

As she pinched the child's nose and lowered her mouth to make a seal, Leo finally broke into a run. She puffed in two breaths and started compressions, counting out loud with each one.'

'Come on, Zac,' Morgan's voice pleaded into the hot summer air.

Come on, Zac. The sound of running footsteps and the more distant sound of rattling trolley wheels reassured Abbie as she puffed in two more breaths and started the next round of thirty compressions.

A wailing moan filled with distress broke from Morgan's lips.

'We need to get him inside and warm him up.' Leo's voice wavered as he scooped Zac up and put him on the trolley.

Abbie climbed up next to the child, continuing her compressions as Leo and Erin ran the trolley into ED.

The moment they were in the resuscitation room and Abbie's feet were back on the ground, Leo moved in next to her, attaching the boy to the monitor. 'Erin, get him out of his wet clothes and wrap him in a space blanket. We need to warm him up.'

'Doing it now.' Erin deftly cut away the boy's small shorts and T-shirt.

The monitor started beeping and Leo gripped his chin as he stared at the green tracing. 'We've got a heartbeat but he's extremely bradycardic and needs CPR to maintain his circulation.'

Abbie's arms kept compressing Zac's chest to keep his blood moving. 'Leo, intubate him.'

Leo whitened under his golden tan, the scar on his chin almost luminous. 'Your arms will be tired. You tube him and I'll take over compressions. On my count of five.' His voice, usually so firm and sure, creaked over the numbers. 'Three, four, five, change.'

What? Her arms were fine but Abbie didn't question the change because every second counted. She couldn't understand why Leo wanted her to tube the child when they probably both had the same amount of experience in tubing a toddler—virtually none.

Erin wrapped the boy in a space blanket.

Abbie opened up the paediatric laryngoscope and tilted back Zac's head. The tiny light cast a glow and she visualised the vocal cords, which was always a good start.

Erin handed her the small ETT tube.

Holding her breath, Abbie slid the tube carefully along the silver blade of the 'scope, between the tiny cords and into place. She immediately withdrew the scope.

Erin ripped off lengths of tape. 'I'll tape, you suction.'

With fine tubing, Abbie suctioned the ETT tube, clearing some brown-coloured fluid that squirted into the holding container.

'God, his lungs are probably filled with bloody brown river water.' Leo's ragged voice scraped against her like cut glass.

Erin attached the air-viva and connected the oxygen before rhythmically squeezing the bag, forcing air into the child's damp lungs.

Leo's hands looked ludicrously large against the small child's chest. 'He needs atropine to bring up his heart rate.'

Abbie picked up the tourniquet. 'I'm putting in a line.'

Leo nodded curtly, his face full of sharp angles and taut cheeks.

A shiver chilled Abbie. She'd never seen him look so tense or grim, not even in Theatre when Jenny was close to dying under his hands on the operating table. Zac was one sick child but Jenny had been just as ill so his reaction puzzled her.

She snapped the tourniquet onto Zac's tiny arm, her fingers fluttering over his skin, trying to find a vein. Nothing. She moved the tourniquet to his leg and started over. 'He's shut down, I'll have to–'

'Stop stuffing around.' Leo's eyes blazed with fear. 'Just put the damn adrenaline and atropine down the ETT tube, Abbie. Now!'

Erin's large brown eyes widened at Leo's edgy and frantic tone and her hands shook slightly as she prepared to disconnect the air-viva.

Abbie drew up the drugs, the uncharacteristic tension cloaking them like thick fog. What was going on? She'd never seen Leo lose his cool before but right now his normal and easy control of situations was unravelling like a skein of wool.

Erin removed the air-viva and Abbie dispensed the drugs. 'Atropine and adrenaline administered.'

Leo kept compressing Zac's heart and Erin pressed air into his lungs and Abbie stared at the monitor, silently counting. The beeping sound slowly increased as the drugs took effect. Abbie breathed a sigh of relief for Zac. They were winning.

She wanted to high-five but one look at Leo's pinched face had her feeling as if they'd just lost. What was going on with him? He should be as relieved as she was. She smiled at him, willing him to smile back with his trademark grin, the one he used with effortless ease, but his tense jaw and tight mouth stayed in their grim line as he stopped CPR and stepped back now that Zac's heart was pumping fast enough on its own.

She knew Zac wasn't totally out of the woods yet, given he had river-water-induced pulmonary oedema and a massive risk of infection. 'I'll be happier with Zac at the Royal Children's under specialist paediatric care.' She stared straight at Leo, somehow knowing he needed to be out of the room. 'Erin and I have got this covered. Now he's better perfused I'll be able to get the IV in, so you go ring the air ambulance and then bring Morgan back so I can explain everything.'

Leo's dark brows pulled down as if he was about to object but he stayed silent, his face etched with sorrow. His fingers rubbed the scar on his chin before falling away and caressing the child's hair. Wordlessly, he turned and walked out of the room.

Abbie's heart clenched and she had to stifle a gasp. From the moment Leo had laid eyes on Zac he'd changed. It was as if she'd just truly seen the real Leo for the first time. A man stripped bare of his social props and now totally exposed. Everything about him that she'd feared—his charm and charisma—had vanished. Even the things she admired like his care and professional control had taken a beating and all that was left was a hurting and tortured man. The real Leo.

The realisation stunned her. Every barrier she'd erected to keep him at a distance fell to the ground. Right then she knew that, the moment she could, she had to go to him. She had to find him and do whatever it took to help him.

Leo's thighs burned as he powerfully pressed and pulled the pedals of his bike around, each revolution taking him further away from the hospital, further away from the helipad and everything connected with the now-resolved emergency. But the Bandarra demons sat hard and heavy on his shoulders, digging in deep. Christina's screaming voice and Dom's total silence had bored into him from the moment he'd seen Zac, keeping him back in the past when he'd needed to be in the present.

A child had needed his help and he'd totally frozen.

Blinking against the flashes of red soil, green vines, black road and blue sky, he watched the numbers on the bike computer climb to thirty-five kilometres an hour. He had no destination in mind—he just had to ride. Ride until he could feel nothing and forget everything.

His chest muscles strained as he used every atom of oxygen in the hot torpid air and still he pushed harder, taking himself as close to the edge of what his body could bear. He didn't want comfort; he wanted pain. He drove himself until his body turned inward, completely consumed by the overwhelming physical demands. Until all extraneous thoughts, noises, sounds and scents were blocked from his consciousness.

Ten kilometres later he slowed and the tightness in his chest eased, his leg muscles ceased to burn and relief flowed through him. He opened a water bottle and chugged down half the contents, his body soaking up the fluid like a dry crinkled sponge, and then he poured the rest over himself. Pulling off his helmet, he wiped his brow with his bandana and, as his body gradually uncoiled from its exercise-survival mode, his eyes progressively focused on his surroundings.

The distinctive wiry leaves and furrowed bark of the bull-oak came into view, followed by the blue-green leaves of the river red gums with their peeling bark of green, grey and red. His chest tightened as his head swung around, taking in the muddy edges of brown water, and then his gaze zeroed in on the distinctive carving on one of the trees. *Dom and Christina 4 Eva.*

Wadjera billabong.

His heart pounded hard in his chest, pushing a dull and un-relenting ache into every part of him. Why the hell had he ridden here? A place he'd avoided for years. The ride was supposed to help him forget because he sure as hell didn't want to remember.

Every part of him urged him to leave. Buckling his helmet with numb fingers, he prepared to click his left foot into the pedal before swinging his right leg over the seat and riding away fast. Very fast.

The crackling noise of tyres on gravel made him pause. He turned to see a very familiar white four-wheel drive pull into the clearing. Like a film in slow motion, he heard the engine die, the click of the door opening and saw a pair of shapely legs jump down before the owner appeared from behind the door clutching an enormous basket. A pair of questioning green eyes hit him like a king-punch.

'Leo.'

'Abbie.' How had she known he was here when he had no clue he would be?

His heart sped up. She'd want to talk about what happened with Zac. Women always wanted to talk. *Get on your bike. Leave now.*

Her sweet scent wafted towards him and part of him hesitated. Every cell in his body urged him to flee and his hands gripped his racing handlebars. *Just keep running.*

'I have to get back.'

She stepped closer and a flicker of disappointment flared against banked heat, followed by something vague, half-formed and undefined. She chewed her lip. 'Really? I thought you could do with some time away from the hospital. I brought food and drink.' She lowered the basket onto the ground.

The pull to leave couldn't stop his gaze from following her every movement. The sway of her hips, the way her no-nonsense navy-blue straight skirt moulded to her pert behind and the fact that her plain T-shirt fell forward when she bent over, exposing creamy mounds of flesh peeking out of pink lace. His groin tightened. *Go anyway.*

He opened his mouth to use his time-honoured excuse that had served him so very well for many years—work. But his words stalled. He wasn't needed at the hospital or the clinic and Abbie knew it. If he used that excuse, the questions he didn't want to answer would start immediately.

She straightened up and stepped in close. His hand released the bike, letting it slip back to rest on the tree. Reaching up, she cupped his cheek with her hand, her smooth palm deliciously cold against his stubbled cheek. She tilted her head back until he was staring deep into luscious pools of rainforest-green that invited him to dive right in. 'I'm here for you, Leo. Please stay.'

He was instantly hard. Her voice caressed him like the cool and welcoming softness of silk trailing against hot skin, and a deep crevice opened up inside him, desperately seeking that softness and urging him to lose himself in it. Offering him another way to escape. He lowered his mouth towards hers, searching for the haven he so desperately needed.

Abbie recognised the moment Leo decided to stay. Recognised the fading of whatever it was that terrorised him and saw the burning lust move in to replace it. Lust that she recognised intimately—hot, burning, driving desire that stole every rational thought and absolutely nothing could slake except raw, primal sex.

'I need you, Abbie.' The tormented and hoarse words filled the space between them as his gaze burned for her.

'I know.'

His lips slid across hers, enticing, demanding and giving. All thought evaporated. She was past thinking, past analysing and way, way past resisting. He needed her and she wanted him. Call it comfort, call it sex. She'd given up resisting him the moment she'd seen his façade crumble. Wrapping her arms tightly around Leo's neck, she didn't care he was sopping wet. Nothing mattered except he was in her arms and his mouth was hard against hers.

She met his kiss with one of her own as every firmly suppressed molecule of longing ripped out of its box, splintering its now flimsy enclosure and exploding inside her in a maelstrom of sheer seeking pleasure. Nothing existed except her driving need for him. She plunged her tongue inside his mouth but nothing had prepared her for the assault of his flavour, filling her so hot and fast that her knees sagged and she fell against him.

Without moving his mouth, Leo instantly clamped one arm against her back, pulling her hard against him. His arousal pressed hard up against her belly, his fingers delved in her hair and his other hand found her breast.

White stars exploded in her head as his thumb caressed her through her T-shirt, her nipples pebbling into hard, sensuous buds straining against the exquisite touch. A moan rose to her lips as she panted against his mouth, frantic to have more of his touch on her and at the same time desperate to touch him.

'Got…to…feel…you.' Leo swung her around until her back rested against the bark of a tree and his hands pulled at her T-shirt, hauling it over her head. With a flick of his fingers, the bra clasp came undone and her breasts thankfully tumbled out of her bra and into his waiting hands. She cried out from the wonder of the skin-on-skin caress.

His hand stalled. 'Too fast?'

'No.' She grabbed his hand and, with a frenzied push, pressed it back on her quivering and heavy breasts. She could hardly speak, she couldn't think at all, she just had a primal drive to feel every part of him on her. She knocked his helmet off his head and tugged at his shirt, splaying her fingers against rock-solid muscle as she traced his spine, vertebrae to vertebrae from his neck all the way down to his hips, memorising every tendon, bone, swell and crevice.

'You're beautiful.' He rasped the words out as he moved his lips from her mouth and up along her jaw. His tongue delicately traced the curve of her ear before his teeth nipped her ear lobe.

Pleasure shock waves rocked through her and she gasped, bucking her hips towards him. She heard a growl and then felt his arms under hers and suddenly her feet left the ground.

'Leo.' It came out on a wail of need. She could only force out one word as her body completely took over. One word to represent all that she wanted. She wrapped her legs around his waist and her chest rose and fell with short shallow breaths. Every part of her yelled to have him and she gripped his upper arms and threw herself back against the tree, totally consumed by her desire to have his mouth against her breast.

His mouth suckled her as his hand slid along the soft skin of her inner thigh. She gripped his head as whirls of colour swirled and joined like paint on an artist's palette. Then his fingers brushed the damp, silky crotch of her panties.

Exquisite pleasure rocked her.

His thumb traced tiny circles and then pressed firmly but gently against her.

She sobbed as shafts of wonder built to breaking point.

His fingers stilled.

Her fingernails gripped his back. 'No, don't stop.'

With his thumb still pressed against her, he curved a finger around the edge of the silk and slipped it inside her. She shattered and pure bliss poured through her.

But it wasn't enough. Her body now completely ignited, roared for more. Frantic to feel him, her hands shot down his back, fingers clawing against the waistband of his bike shorts as gut-wrenching frustration hit her. She couldn't reach any further.

'You're sure?' His ragged voice breathed against her ear.

'I'm way past sure.'

His arms cupped her buttocks and she rose slightly for a moment before leaning back. Her hands found their target. Leo shuddered against her before raising her up again.

This time he lowered her gently. Her body screamed for him but it had been a long time and he took it slowly, moving in a little, out a little, which drove her crazy.

'Just do it.'

'Wait.' His growl quivered with hard-held restraint.

She didn't want to wait. She wanted him buried deep inside so he was as close to her as possible. With a cry she pushed down and her muscles almost sobbed in relief as they wrapped themselves tightly around him in a caress they'd ached to give him for so long.

She lost herself in him as they rose together. A scream left her throat as her body flung her into orbit far, far away from him, and as she returned she held him as he shuddered and sagged against her.

A moment later she felt the sharp prickle of bark against her bare back, felt the ripple of a hot breeze against her bare breasts and she gazed down into glittering black eyes. Reality thundered back in brilliant Technicolor. The shadowy image of her mother surfaced. Oh, dear God, what had she just done? She dropped her head into her hands and groaned, 'Well, that was embarrassing.'

Leo gently tugged her hands away from her cheeks. 'No, it wasn't; it was fantastic.'

She shook her head. 'We just had sex in less than four minutes and outside in the open air as if we were animals on heat instead of respectable pillars of the community.'

'Yeah.' He grinned like a kid who'd just got away with stealing lollies. 'I kept telling you what lay between us was explosive. Plus, let's face it—' a wicked grin lit across his face '—you were a ticking time bomb.'

She groaned again and let her head drop onto his shoulder. 'I was so easy.'

His finger caressed her chin and then tilted it upwards so she had to look into his eyes that glowed with desire and appreciation. 'You were amazing and if you're so worried about the frenetic speed, I promise to make long, slow, languid love to you. Just give me a few more minutes.' His grin suddenly faded as if he'd been zapped by electricity. 'We didn't use protection.'

Her voice rose on the back of her agitation. 'That's what I mean. We should have known better; we're doctors!'

He lowered her down so her feet hit the ground and then he bent and picked up her T-shirt. As he handed it to her, frown lines scored his brow and a horror-struck look loomed large in his eyes. 'Hell.' His hand raked his hair. 'OK, well, emergency contraception is eighty per cent effective so the stats are on our side, right?'

She tugged her shirt over her head, stunned that pregnancy was his first concern. 'Leo, it's not pregnancy I'm worried about. I've still got an IUD in from…' She stopped, refusing to think about her past.

The frown faded and he wrapped his arms around her and dropped a kiss into her hair. 'Abbie, stop worrying. You're the only woman I haven't used a condom with and, as you've been celibate, am I right in thinking we're both healthy and there's nothing to worry about?'

His arms urged her to snuggle in against his chest and seek refuge in his reassurance. 'I guess so.'

'So stop worrying.' He trailed kisses along her forehead and down to the bridge of her nose and her blood immediately fired off rafts of tingling and an overwhelming need for him consumed her.

'But if you want long and languid in a bed we need to leave right now.'

Laughing, they grabbed their belongings and ran to the truck.

CHAPTER NINE

ABBIE lay in her bed, propped up on one elbow, while her other arm lay across Leo's chest, her fingers absently tracing along his ribs while her gaze stayed fixed on his face. Part of her couldn't believe she had a man in her bed but Leo had needed her. His pain had called to her so strongly it had hurt, and she didn't regret the sex at all.

His heavy-lidded eyes smiled up at her. 'We're not very good at long and languid yet but I think we could improve if we keep practising.'

She laughed, thinking about the wild, almost uncontrolled coupling in the shower before they'd hit the bed and managed to slow things down slightly. Even so, the sex hadn't been a one-way thing. Since coming home he'd been a generous lover, giving as much back to her as she had offered to him.

Leo wound a curl around his finger and pulled her head down to his. 'If you want, we've got a month to get it right.'

'A month?' Could she do that? It was a period of time with a firm end-date so it came with built-in protection.

He nodded. 'You can make up for lost time and we can have four weeks of fun. You can't deny the sex so far has been amazing.'

And she couldn't deny it. She couldn't deny that her body

had craved him from the moment she'd first seen him. She wanted him and she didn't want to fight herself any more. She lowered her mouth, grazing his lips with hers. Her traitorous heart hiccoughed but Warrior Abbie was too busy reclining with a cigarette in her hand to provide any sort of protection. *One month, one month, one month.*

'A month it is, then.' She stared down into black eyes filled with tenderness but she could still glimpse the lingering and lurking shadows. The time had come to find out what had put those shadows so firmly in place.

Leo lay back on the pillow, not able to remember when his body had been this relaxed or content. For days his dreams had been filled with Abbie but the reality of having her in his arms and the explosive sex they'd shared blew the dreams out of the water. Abbie would make these few weeks in Bandarra bearable. Nonna was improving and Abbie was the perfect distraction from everything else. He just had to hold it together for a bit longer and then he could leave Bandarra still in one piece.

Her fingers drew tiny circles across his chest, slowly creeping up his torso, and his breathing slowed as he enjoyed her touch, his mind spinning out on all the ways they could enjoy each other over the next few weeks.

'What's the story behind this one blemish on an otherwise perfect face?' Her forefinger caressed his chin, neatly tracing the outline of the now-white-with-time scar.

His hand shot out, his fingers clenching around hers as his sense of peace vanished and every muscle tensed under the assault of adrenaline. 'No story.'

Knowing green eyes bored into him. 'Then why do you have the same look on your face that you had when you saw Zac?'

His breath jerked in his chest. 'Don't exaggerate. How can

you compare me lying here after mind-blowing sex with the life-and-death situation we had this afternoon?'

But, like a dog with a bone, she wouldn't give it up. 'Leo, I've never seen you lose your cool, even when Jenny almost exsanguinated on the table, but you did today.'

And he knew it. His temples throbbed and he shifted into damage control, using a politician's ploy of diverting a question with a question. 'What? You don't get that extra tug when it's a kid that might die?'

Two deep lines carved into the skin at the bridge of her nose. 'Of course I do but it was more than that with you.'

The jarring sound of a hammer against metal clanged in his head. She was getting too close. 'Just leave it alone.'

Her lips pursed and her brows shot up under a tangle of curls. 'Like you left me alone after Penny and Alec?'

Her words sliced into him, carving straight down to his moral compass. He sat up, swinging his feet over the side of the bed, intending to get up and walk away, not caring that his only clothing option was sweat-soiled cycling gear.

'Stop running, Leo.'

Her voice punched him from behind. 'I'm *not* running.'

'Yeah, you are. Just like you did this afternoon.'

Her hand touched his shoulder and a part of him wanted to throw off her touch but most of him wanted to hold on to it. Hold it tightly. He shrugged his shoulder and spoke through clenched teeth. 'I went on a bike ride, Abbie.'

Her soft palm stayed put. 'With something chasing you. When you left Theatre you looked like you'd seen a ghost and I was so worried about you.'

Building panic dug in. 'Well, you didn't have to. I'm a grown man and I didn't need you chasing after me. Anyway, how did you know where I was?'

'I asked Maria where you might have gone and that's how I found you.'

Fury and betrayal burst inside him as grief pummelled him, and he refused to turn around and look at her. 'Nonna shouldn't have told you anything.'

She blinked in surprise at his tone. 'She didn't say anything other than you might be at the waterhole. But I'm stringing snapshots together, Leo—today with Zac, you walking away from canoeing, your grandmother's need to be home by the twenty-seventh.'

Her words cloaked him and right then he knew he'd just hit the dead-end of a very long road. He slowly turned around to see her sitting cross-legged on the bed, beautiful and serene. Something so strong and kind pulled at him, unlike anything he'd ever experienced from anyone. Two decades of holding everything at bay collapsed around him. He pulled her down and lay with her, his arms tight around her as if he feared she'd disappear, but if he was going to bare his soul he needed her as close as possible. 'You know this morning you said you bet I'd wished I had a brother... Well, I have one. Dom.'

His throat tightened and he forced out the words he hated to say. 'He drowned in front of me when I was nineteen.'

His pain hit Abbie so violently she shuddered for the youth who'd suffered that trauma and for the adult that still held it so close. She rested her forehead on his. 'I can't imagine how awful that must have been.'

'I've pretty much tried to forget.'

'Doesn't work, though, does it?'

His jaw clenched. 'I was doing OK until today.'

She didn't believe him but she let the comment pass, not wanting to interrupt his story.

His arms tightened around her again. 'Growing up, we

were inseparable. We shared a room, we rode our bikes everywhere, and the only time we spent apart was at school. I was a year ahead.'

'The twins that weren't?'

He huffed out a breath. 'Something like that, at least right up until I left for uni, anyway.' He buried his face in her hair for a moment and then continued. 'When I came home in the mid-year holidays, we met Christina. She was a cousin of one of the local families and she'd just arrived from Italy for a year in Australia. She was a country girl, pretty naïve and a bit overawed by how different things are here, so my parents insisted we do the right thing and invite her to picnics and introduce her to our friends. We had a lot of laughs and she had a bit of a crush on me but my focus was on uni and I headed back and didn't really give her another thought. By the time I came home for the long summer break, Dom and Christina were very much a couple in the intense way only almost eighteen-year-olds in their first relationships can be.'

Abbie remembered. 'No one else in the world exists?'

He grunted. 'That's right and I got a shock. The last time I'd been home, Christina had been more my friend than Dom's and I guess I expected things at home to stay the same. Not that I loved her more than a friend but it was odd seeing my younger brother with a girlfriend. Dom had always looked up to me, even though I was only a year older than him, and whenever he had a problem he'd talk to me about it. Now Christina was his confidante and my brother didn't seem to need me any more.'

Abbie frowned in concern. 'But he would have.'

His voice became hoarse. 'Yeah, he did, but when he came to me for help I let him down.'

His agony reverberated through her and she held him tightly.

'It was a stinking hot day and we were at the waterhole just before I headed back to uni. After a summer of him avoiding me, it was Dom who suggested we go. We'd been swinging off the old rope we'd put in a giant river red gum years before and talking about all sorts of stuff and I realised how much I'd missed his company. And then he told me Christina was pregnant. He'd knocked up an Italian girl whose traditional family wouldn't take her back unless she was married.'

Abbie could picture two teenage youths, not quite men, trying to deal with one of life's biggest dilemmas. 'That would have been pretty scary.'

Leo's eyes burned with unbearable memories. 'I was so furious with him for putting himself in this position where he had no choice, and stalling his life before it had even started, that I yelled at him. I called him a jerk, a moron and plenty of other unspeakable things. He yelled back and told me if he'd wanted to hear crap like that he would have told Papa. He stormed off towards the water, preparing to bomb into it and shut me out.'

His words slowed and he shuddered. 'My rage had me picking up my towel to leave and then Christina arrived. I couldn't speak to her so I strode past her and, as I did, I heard a terrifying crack. Christina screamed and I turned around to see a huge tree limb crash into the billabong, taking Dom down with it. I remember shouting his name, running into the water, diving under, but you can't see a thing in that freaking muddy water. I ripped myself on snags but I kept diving. On the third attempt my hands touched his legs and I pulled but he was wedged tight under the tree. I couldn't move him.' His eyes darkened into bleak black discs. 'I let him down, I let him die.'

Abbie's stomach rolled and acid burned her throat. Shocked by his words, she gripped his arm hard. 'Leo, it was a tragic accident. You didn't let him die. The red gum limb probably killed him before he went under the water.'

He wouldn't meet her gaze. 'Dom was under that tree because I drove him away instead of helping him. I let him die.'

Her palm pressed his cheek, gently pulling his face to meet hers, needing him to understand. 'Leo, I'm sorry the last words you had with your brother were harsh but you know gums just drop limbs without warning in extreme heat. This was bad timing but it wasn't your fault.'

He shrugged, his jaw tense and his cheeks hollow. She knew her words hadn't touched him, hadn't even grazed what he believed and she blinked back the urge to cry.

In an emotionless tone Leo continued. 'He died on February the twenty-seventh and you're right, that's why Nonna wants to be home. She visits the billabong every year on that day.'

The Costas had lost their child, Leo had lost his brother and a young woman had lost her first love. Abbie's thoughts went to her, pregnant and grieving in a foreign country. She did a quick calculation and worked out the baby would now be almost the same age as his father was when he died. 'Does Christina visit?'

He shuddered. 'No. When we got divorced she went back to Italy.'

'*You* married Christina?' Her shocked voice sounded unsteady to her own ears.

A steely rigidity entered his body. 'I had to. I had to make it right. Dom would have married her and because of me he died. I took her to Melbourne and married her quietly there. She miscarried soon after and I lost the last part of Dom I had.'

She could hardly take it all in. Duty, honour and heart-wrenching pain lay deeply hidden inside this complex man.

'And what about you?' Abbie asked the question but she had a strong idea she already knew the answer.

He ploughed his hand through his hair. 'I haven't been back to the waterhole since the accident. At least not until today and God knows why I went—I sure as hell wasn't planning to. Hell, I hardly visit Bandarra unless I have to. This trip is the longest I've stayed in years.'

'Perhaps it was time.'

He gave her a look that seared her. 'I didn't take you for a New Age guru.'

He was picking a fight but she refused to give him one. She'd seen past the image he wanted the world to see—the successful surgeon and charming man. She now knew how much it was costing him to stay in Bandarra, to spend time with his beloved grandmother. With his family. With the memories that plagued him.

She realised with startling clarity why he'd pursued her so relentlessly. Why he'd been as desperate as her this afternoon out at the billabong. Why they'd literally self-combusted with need, but for very different reasons.

Her heart cramped and she crossly ignored it. So what that he wanted to use her to forget. She was using him for fun, sex, good times and then goodbye.

You had sex with him because you saw a hurting man who needed you.

She slammed the voice out of her head. No. She had sex with him so she could get this bubbling desire out of her system and then find her even keel again. The one that had served her well for three years. Neither of them wanted a relationship. They could both use each other for a month and then walk away. Safe in that knowledge, she gently pushed him onto his back, slid her body over his and kissed him.

* * *

'Good wines are made in the vineyard and nothing can be rushed. A bit like life, eh?'

Leo felt his father's hand grip his shoulder and knew the part of his father who was the backyard philosopher had finally caught up with him. They were walking through the vines with the rich irrigated soil sticking to their feet. Stefano had caught Leo alone in the house and had insisted he inspect the grapes with him.

'So how is your life, Leo? It's been a long time that you've been on your own. I think you're too much like the winery right now—busy holding your breath.'

The last few weeks before harvest was like a long-held breath. A breath of hoping and waiting. Hoping the weather would conspire to provide ideal conditions for the fruit to flourish to perfection. Waiting for the moment the grapes reached idyllic ripeness. Once that happened, the winery inhaled like a long-distance sprinter ramping up for the final assault, embracing the fast pace that the harvest dictated. The harvest took weeks because the moment one varietal of grape was harvested and crushed, another variety would ripen and the process would start again. But right now the winery held its breath.

Leo shrugged and tried not to feel ruffled by his father's question. 'Papà, my life is fine and filled with work and friends.'

'And beautiful women who fill your bed but not your soul.'

Stunned, Leo stared at his father. Not since his divorce from Christina had his father ever passed comment on his personal life and, as Leo lived in Melbourne, it was easy to hide the parade of women who marched through his life. 'I'm happy, OK. I'm a respected surgeon at the top of my profession and that's enough for me.' But his voice sounded overly defensive and the need to silence his father shot through him. 'Most parents would be proud of that.'

'Being proud is not the issue.' His father's mouth flattened into disapproval. 'You might just be surprised at what you find if you looked at women with your heart instead of your mi—'

'Papà!' He stopped his father, knowing full well what he was about to say. 'I'm thirty-five, not—' The chime of his phone interrupted him. 'I have to take this.'

'Of course you do.' Stefano nodded sagely and walked away.

Leo barked down the phone as irritation and exasperation with his father churned inside him. 'Leo Costa.'

'Oh, you sound like that scary Mr Costa, the surgeon. I was after the Leo Costa who enjoys kicking back over a complex red wine, loves a really good argument about the pros and cons of federal funding for the state's public hospital system, and who might just be up for a night-time picnic in the moonlight out by Cameron's junction?'

The sound of Abbie's voice instantly drained away his frustration. The last few weeks had been amazing. They'd argued long and hard about all sorts of things, ranging from politics and town-planning to films and books, and she'd challenged him on just about everything. Half the time he wasn't certain if she really disagreed with him or if she was just taking the contrary view to stir him up, but either way he thrived on the intellectual stimulation. And then there was the sex.

'A picnic?' Knowing her appalling lack of culinary talents, he teased her. 'What's on the menu?'

'Me.'

Her husky voice had him hard in a heartbeat. 'I'm on my way.'

Abbie smiled. She'd been smiling a lot over the last few weeks. Spontaneous grinning was probably a more apt description. Work filled her days but Leo filled her nights. He was an inventive and considerate lover and the sex was amazing but, as much as she craved his body, she craved his mind. He made her laugh until her sides ached and tears poured down her cheeks. He argued passionately for what he believed in and, even if their ideas didn't coincide, he didn't freeze her out or put her down. That was a completely new experience and it frequently disconcerted her.

'*Dottore*, you are happy today. This is good. Like Leo, you need to smile more.' Maria sat in her chair, her hand on her stick and her suitcase by her side.

Abbie laughed as she signed and wrote 'February twenty-sixth' on the discharge papers, which were clipped to the chart. 'Maria, Leo smiles all the time, especially at pretty women.'

The grandmother tilted her head and gave her a hard stare. 'But it is not the smile of real happiness.'

The old woman's insight slugged her but, before Abbie could form a reply, Maria was on her feet. 'So I beat the calendar, yes, and today I go home.'

'You're one determined woman, Maria, but don't get too tired or you risk falling.'

'Pfft.' Maria kept walking, heading towards the exit. 'I will sit when I need to. And you—' she pointed a gnarled finger at Abbie '—I will see you in my kitchen soon.'

A flushed and running Rosa met them at the entrance, her car parked under the canopy. 'We'll do our best to make sure she takes it easy.' She opened the car door and settled Maria into the front seat before closing the door and turning back to Abbie. 'Sorry I'm late, but finally Stefano has declared the vintage starts tonight in the cool of the evening. Leo did tell you, we'd very much like it if you could come to La Bella for the pre-vintage picnic and blessing of the grapes.'

'I'd love to, Rosa, thank you.' For the last week or so

Abbie had experienced this niggling urge to see Leo in the heart of his family. She'd tried to ignore it because the idea was just crazy. They'd agreed to casual and fun, nothing more and nothing less. But he sprinkled his conversations with stories of his sisters, and being an only child made her want to experience—even if only vicariously—family life.

The older woman smiled and squeezed her hand. 'We're thanking you for all you've done for Nonna and for putting up with Leo's antics when he first arrived.' She sighed. 'He finds it hard to be home.'

Abbie bit her lip and made a split-second decision. 'Especially at this time of year. He told me about Dom.'

Rosa closed her eyes for a moment and then opened them, her gaze clear. 'My boy was in the wrong place at the wrong time and I miss the man he would have been.' Her face clouded. 'Each year I light a candle and give thanks for the vintage that keeps us all busy.'

Abbie wasn't sure keeping busy was helping Leo. 'I think Leo blames himself.'

Rosa's mouth flattened and her words became clipped. 'He is the only one who does.' She jangled her keys and rounded the car. 'I'll see you tonight.'

Abbie waved absently, deep in thought.

Abbie pulled into the vineyard and both she and Murphy jumped down from the four-wheel drive. Kids were charging around, kicking a soccer ball, and right in the middle of the melee was Leo, holding a squealing five-year-old girl on his shoulders and taking a shot at the ball.

He'd make a great father. She bit her lip hard to jolt away the errant and unwanted thought. Connecting Leo with children was madness. He'd been totally up front about what he wanted and so had she. The plan didn't involve anything beyond a few weeks.

Murphy barked. Alec emerged from the pack and ran towards the dog. Leo turned, a long, slow, potent smile weaving across his face.

A tingle of desire shot through her, draining her brain of every coherent thought, just like it did every time she saw him.

'Abbie, can Murphy come and play soccer too?'

She pulled her concentration back and saw that Alec had his hand buried in the dog's thick black and white coat. Three days ago Leo and Chiara had flown Alec to Melbourne for a day to see Penny, who remained in ICU but was now thankfully breathing on her own. She had a long road of recovery ahead of her and, as soon as she was more stable, she'd be transferred to Bandarra, which would be much better for Alec. Since the trip, he'd lost the pinched and worried look that had understandably tagged him as he dealt with the fact that his mother was desperately ill.

Abbie smiled at him, knowing how much he loved the dog and how much Murphy was helping him get through all the upheaval in his life. 'Sure, but he'll probably just want to charge around the outside trying to round you all up.'

'That's OK.' Alec ran back to the game with Murphy bounding after him.

Leo jogged over, the little girl still on his shoulders, giggling joyfully. 'Giddy up, horsey.' The child slapped her hand against Leo's dark hair.

'*Cara*, this horse needs a break.' He lowered the girl down. 'Adriana, this is my friend, Abbie.'

The little girl yelled, 'Hello,' and then raced back towards the soccer game.

Leo grinned. 'So much energy.'

Abbie laughed. 'You poor old thing.'

'Hey, who are you calling old?' He snaked his arm around her waist and pulled her close, his lips grazing her cheek. 'You're looking gorgeous.'

I expect you to dress well, Abbie, because what you wear reflects on me. She tried to shut down Greg's voice, but still unwanted embarrassment knocked against years of not caring how she dressed. She dressed for herself these days and never for a man. Being with Leo didn't change that but, despite knowing it, her hand moved on its own accord, brushing the red dust from her khaki shorts.

She tilted her chin, a combination of crossness at herself and defiance on the rise. 'So I'm a bit untidy but I got held up at the Aboriginal clinic. I'm sorry I missed the blessing of the grapes but if I'd changed I would have been even later.'

A light frown creased his brow and concern flickered in his eyes as he stroked a curl behind her ear. 'Abbie, I'm not being facetious; you look just like you always do, which is beautiful.'

She searched his voice for a hint of hypocrisy, for the tinge of emotional blackmail she associated with Greg, but all she could hear was sincerity. Her heart rolled over. *No, no, no.* She breathed out a long slow breath, determined to let the compliment wash over her without leaving a mark, but just as the final caress was receding, part of her hooked into it, holding it tight, like an addict clutching at their drug of choice. *Don't be so weak; you don't need any man's approval.*

'Come on, let's eat.' Leo grabbed her hand and they followed the sound of a concertina, laughing and chattering voices. Italian and English intermingled seamlessly, floating on the warm air and creating a sound full of joy and anticipation.

Excitement at being part of this event bubbled in Abbie's stomach. She walked through the gate into a large courtyard bordered by the smoky grey-green foliage of olive trees which were strung with tiny white bud-lights. Between the trees, citronella flares burned, giving off their pleasant aroma and keeping the mosquitoes away, and a large sail overhead cast much-needed shade from the low evening sun. About fifty people crowded into the area, all dressed in heavy-duty work clothes. Abbie felt right at home.

'*Dottore, buona sera, com sta?*' Maria enveloped her in an out-of-character hug and kissed both her cheeks.

'*Grazie, va bene.*' Abbie's tongue clumsily wound its way around the Italian response of 'good, thanks,' much to the amused laughter of Maria, who kissed her a second time.

Leo's parents greeted her warmly, as did his sisters and brothers-in-law, as well as many other people she barely knew. Her own family had been so tiny, she was almost overwhelmed by the enthusiastic greetings and she found herself gripping Leo's hand overly hard.

Leo was kissed by everyone, and with remarkable good nature he accepted his sisters' teasing, unsolicited opinions and instructions until they breached his tolerance. He silenced them with a gruff, 'Abbie's been flat out all day and needs food.'

It was like the parting of the Red Sea. They fell back, full of apologies, and urged her forward to eat.

'Sorry about that; they mean well, but…' His voice trailed off for a moment before he swept an arm out. 'So what takes your fancy?'

Five long tables groaned with more food than Abbie had ever seen in her life. The centrepiece of each table was a large bunch of plump green grapes—the reason for the gathering—but they fought hard for space with huge platters of salami, prosciutto and mortadella which sat beside Maria's delicious bread.

Bowls of glossy black marinated olives, fire-engine-red

sundried tomatoes and roasted capsicum and eggplant all
called to be stuffed into bread. Dazzling green asparagus
nestled with egg and fine slices of parmesan and that was
just the first table. Salads of tomato, basil and red onion
tangoed with balsamic vinegar, deep bowls of peppery
rocket waited to be matched with freshly cooked yabbies,
and tangy pesto dip harmonised perfectly with a large dish
of schnitzels.

'What's inside those simmering pots?'

'Bolognese.' His black eyes twinkled as he gave her a wink.
'You didn't think we could feast without pasta?'

She smiled up at him. 'What about pizza? I'm still
dreaming about that *quattro formaggi* that Sofia made for us.'

His voice dropped low and stroked her like velvet. 'I'm still
dreaming about what happened afterwards.'

Her cheeks burned at the memory and Leo roared laughing.
'Tesoro, don't even think of being embarrassed. You're an in-
credibly sexual woman so be proud of that.'

Proud? She felt her brows pull down and she glanced at
him for the second time in a short period to see if he was being
ironic but the sincerity in his voice and eyes was unmistakable. She urged her heart to stay aloof from this complex man
who didn't often behave the way she expected, but it rolled
anyway, adding to the mix of confusion and uncertainty that
churned inside her. Frantic to change the topic, she asked for
a drink.

His expression turned serious. 'I'm sorry, but wine and
pizza are served at the post-harvest picnic when the grapes are
all in. This meal is really for the workers—a sign of our faith
in them to bring in the crop quickly and carefully so the grapes
are in perfect condition for Papà to turn them into more prize-
winning wine.'

Abbie shook her head in bewilderment. 'Wow. It's hard to believe that this isn't a party.'

'This is work but wait until you come to the launch of the latest sauvignon blanc; now *that's* a party.'

His easy inclusion of her in his family's plans caught her by surprise and added to her already see-sawing emotions. Weren't affairs hidden away? Kept private? They'd agreed to a month together and yet here she was in the heart of his family, with Leo standing next to her, his arm slung easily around her shoulders and pulling her in close, as if she belonged.

Don't even go there.

'Hey, Uncle Leo!'

A group of girls led by identical twins headed straight towards them and Abbie, needing some space to round up her wayward daydreams, slipped away and let the group surround him. She piled a plate high with food, filled a glass with refreshing *limonata* and sat down to eat, her eyes never far from Leo.

From what she could work out, he'd organised the girls into groups and appeared to be setting up some sort of game. Whatever it was, he had their complete attention and cooperation. The relaxed expression on his face was apparent through his entire body and there was no sign of any resentment that the kids had ambushed him and interrupted him. She thought about how he'd gone out of his way for Alec and she realised with a jolt that he was a man who genuinely liked kids.

So what; it changes nothing. And it didn't. She'd given up on her dreams of motherhood when she'd realised she couldn't trust her judgement in men and no child should have the instability she'd had. As much as she knew she could make arrangements to have a child on her own, she hadn't quite been able to work through the chestnut that her child would never know his or her father. She ripped open the bread roll and shoved in roasted capsicums and eggplant. So what if Leo was great with kids? Why had her mind even gone there? He was adamant he didn't want any permanency in relationships so that meant he didn't want children and neither did she.

The increasingly niggling questions about his marriage to Christina reared their heads again and she tried to bat them away but they stayed, demanding answers.

Anna slid into a chair next to her and tilted her head towards her brother. 'King of the kids is my big brother. It's a shame he doesn't have any of his own.'

Abbie sipped her lemon drink. 'Everyone makes their own life choices. Marriage and family doesn't suit everyone.'

'It works when you choose the right partner.' Anna's keen gaze zeroed in on Abbie. 'He's been remarkably relaxed these last few weeks.'

Abbie knew dangerous territory when she saw it so she bit into her crusty bread but Anna kept her speculative stare firmly on her. 'Perhaps he just needed a holiday.'

Anna laughed. 'Is that what you're both calling it?' But her face immediately sobered. 'Abbie, I love Leo with all my heart but ever since his divorce he's run from commitment like it was the plague. Please be careful.'

Abbie squeezed the woman's arm. 'Anna, there's nothing to be careful of. Leo and I are having fun, nothing more and nothing less.' But as every hour she spent with Leo ticked by it was harder and harder to convince herself that fun was all it was.

The huge white lights lit up the vineyard like a night match at the Melbourne Cricket Ground and the grape pickers moved along the rows like locusts. Leo finished his row and turned to see Abbie, the tip of her tongue peeking out between her lips in concentration as she snipped bunches of grapes from the vine.

Her eyes shone brightly and her curls seemed even wilder than usual in the cool air of the night. God, he loved her hair. He loved its sweet scent, the silky way it stroked his skin when they had sex, and the sense of peace that filled him when he buried his face in it. He couldn't get enough of Abbie and usually at eleven o'clock at night he was wrapped around her in her bed, forcing himself to leave her so he didn't have to face a million questions from Anna in the morning if he missed breakfast.

He walked up behind Abbie, plucked the secateurs from her hand and dropped his face into her hair, resisting the urge to tell her how gorgeous she was. Unlike most women, compliments seemed to make her edgy, which was probably a legacy from that controlling bastard, Greg. A legacy he wished he could wipe away. 'I've fulfilled the tradition of each family member harvesting a row.'

She turned in his arms. 'I have a new respect for fruit pickers. It's really hard work.'

'So is being a doctor, so come on, we've got to be at work in eight hours.'

'Thank goodness; my shoulders are killing me.'

He stared down at her and smiled. 'I'll give you a massage before you go to sleep.'

Abbie tried unsuccessfully to stifle a yawn. 'Ah, sleep, what a glorious thought.'

Disproportionate disappointment rammed him.

She laughed and kissed him. 'Don't ever play cards, Leo; you'll lose.'

She pressed in close to him as they walked the two-kilometre distance back to the house. The further away they got from the bright lights, the more the Milky Way appeared, a carpet of stars twinkling high above them in the clear, dark sky. 'I had no idea picking grapes at night meant less split-ting and a lower risk of oxidation.'

He loved the enthusiasm she had for all sorts of things. 'What else did you learn tonight?'

'That Anna knows we're having sex.'

He stopped short and slapped his hand against his fore-head, knowing exactly what his sister was like. 'What did she say to you?'

Abbie's mouth quirked up at the corners. 'Nothing to panic about. It wasn't anything I didn't already know. She just said that since your divorce you were a commitment-phobe.' She looked up at him. 'Does your family know why you married Christina?'

His gut tightened and he realised with a shock that Abbie was the first person he'd ever told the truth about his marriage. 'They thought I was trying to hold on to Dom and if they had their suspicions about a child they didn't ask and they were too numb with grief to question anything. They weren't happy but what could they do; we were adults in law.' He bit his lip. 'I never told them about the baby—they had enough to deal with.'

Abbie's arm tightened around his waist. 'You did an in-credibly selfless thing.' *Misguided but selfless.*

He pulled away as the memories roared back. '*No*, I didn't. All I ended up doing was hurting the woman my brother loved and doing a pretty good job on damaging her life as well. We'd had the expectation of a baby, something that was part of Dom, and then we were left with nothing.' He started walking, needing to move. 'She was distraught and needy and wanted to try for another baby. I was strug-gling to study and working to keep us solvent and a child wasn't something I could deal with right then. I buried myself in study and work and she took solace in medication until one night she took too much. After they'd pumped her stomach she asked me for a divorce. She told me the shame of returning to her village as a divorcée was better than the living hell of being married to me. I thought marrying her was the right thing to do but all I did was drive her mad and exacerbate her grief.'

Sadness loomed large in Abbie's eyes and her hand touched his arm, her fingers gripping him. 'I'm sorry. I doubt you made her depression worse. It would have been hard for both of you.'

He stopped walking and dropped his face into her hair, needing to breathe in her soothing scent and trying to push away the part of his life he usually kept under control. 'All I know is that no relationship is worth the hurt and when kids are involved it's even worse.'

She leaned back slightly, a small frown line forming across the bridge of her nose. 'But what about now? Do you regret not having kids of your own?'

The tightness in his gut unexpectedly extended to his chest and his words shot out overly loud and defensive. 'I've got a heap of nieces and nephews.'

She patted his arm. 'That's what I told Anna.'

She understands. The insight rocked through him, seeping into places untouched for so long by any hint of a real connection with someone. No one in his family understood why he hadn't remarried or had children, especially his sisters. Women usually wanted babies and the thought snagged him. 'What about you, though? Most women I meet want to have children.'

She stiffened against him and her tension ringed him. 'I'm not most women, Léo, you know that.' A tremble ran through her voice. 'I don't want to have a child on my own and with my track record I don't trust myself enough to choose the type of man who'd value me and a child more than himself.'

A finger of sadness crept through him at how much Greg had scarred her, despite him understanding her choice.

A joyous bark pierced the night air and Murphy bounded to the gate as they reached the home paddock garden. Her body slackened against his and she laughed. 'Besides, I've got Murphy and I'm involved with kids at work and at the shelter so I get plenty of kid time. Just like you get with your nieces and nephews when you visit.' She rose up on her tiptoes and kissed him, her eyes filled with the simmering glow he recognised so well. 'All care and no responsibility, right?'

'Absolutely. All care and no responsibility.' He grinned down at her, loving that she thought along the same lines as him. Sex, fun and good times. Meeting Abbie had been the saving grace of being back in Bandarra. Leaning forward, he returned her kiss, melding his mouth to hers and completely ignoring the ache that throbbed under his ribs.

CHAPTER TEN

THE beeping of the alarm slowly penetrated through the many layers of Abbie's deep and peaceful sleep. Consciousness came at a leisurely pace—her body, cocooned in warmth and comfort, was not willing to give up its slumberous tranquillity easily and it held out until the vague and annoying noise became harsh and incessant.

Leo's chest was spooned into her back and his arm curled around her with his hand gently cupping a breast. A very tender breast which ached from the light touch. She moved his hand slightly.

He groaned as the beeping continued. 'Turn the damn thing off.'

Now fully awake, she reached out and shut off the noise as a shower of delight rushed through her. Leo had stayed the whole night for the first time, having declared that if Anna knew they were sleeping together there was no point in pretending otherwise and turning up for breakfast.

Abbie rolled over and stretched her arms above her head, feeling renewed and energised in a way that only restful sleep could deliver. She hadn't slept like that in— Her brain stalled. She couldn't even remember. She kissed him on the nose. 'We have to get up.'

One black eye opened and glared at her before closing again.

She ran a finger down his spine. 'I gather you're not a morning person.'

He raised himself on an elbow and gave her a wide smile. 'I think you'll agree I do my best work at night.'

She wriggled her nose. 'Well, I can't possibly agree with that statement until I have all the numbers, and morning statistics are definitely lacking.'

An imaginative glint streaked through his eyes. 'I love a challenge.'

She kissed him and then pushed at his shoulders. 'Take it on notice then, Mr Costa, because it's Wednesday. You've got a full Theatre list this morning.'

He ran his hand through his thick hair with the remnants of sleep still lingering around his eyes. 'A full list? I usually do half days.'

'Don't ask me; you were the one who suggested it at our first planning meeting and you need to get going because the visiting anaesthetist from Melbourne gets grumpy if he misses his evening flight back to Melbourne.'

A look of disgust crossed his face. 'People need to pull their heads out of their closeted world. The days of not being able to get decent food outside of Melbourne are long gone. We should delay him and take him to Anna's restaurant, which is equal to anything in Melbourne.'

Surprise slugged her and a tiny seed of hope unexpectedly sprouted. She didn't even bother to quash it. 'Sounds like you're reconnecting with Bandarra?'

He shrugged. 'I just choose not to visit very often but that doesn't make me disconnected.'

But she knew that was a lie. Bandarra had too many ghosts for him. *It's Wednesday.* The words crashed into her brain like an out-of-control semi-trailer and she froze. Wednesday the twenty-seventh. The anniversary of his brother's death. Suddenly the reason for his full list become stunningly clear—he planned to ignore the anniversary, just as he'd always done.

Frustration and concern tumbled in her gut. Leo needed to grieve for his brother in a healthy way so he could see that he wasn't responsible for his death and that his misguided atonement hadn't been the sole reason for Christina's depression.

Leave it alone; don't get involved. Warrior Abbie snapped her book shut with a bang and, for the first time in a long time, concern hovered on her face. Abbie stared her down and extended her hand, demanding her warrior's sword. *He needs me to fight for him.*

He won't want you to; he won't thank you.

I have to. I love him.

She gasped as the last of her protective blinkers crashed to the ground and her heart broke free of the now frayed restraints. Restraints that had been worn away over the last few weeks by the essence of a man who hid his real self from the world.

'You OK?' Care and concern flared in Leo's eyes.

No! Panic doused her, making every muscle twitch and jump. She was as far from OK as she could possibly be but she couldn't let him know that. 'Look at the time!' She threw back the sheets and ran to the bathroom, closing the door behind her. Sinking to the floor, she laid her head in her hands. Bile scalded her throat, her stomach roiled and churned, and despair dumped over her like a towering wave.

She loved Leo.

Her heart spasmed. Dear God, how stupid had she been? From the moment he'd looked into her eyes at the waterhole and told her he needed her, she'd been a goner. She'd been kidding herself ever since. From that moment, along with the picnics, the conversations that went long into the night and meeting his family, her desire for him had only continued to grow but in a totally different way. A bone-deep way that made lust look sad and superficial.

She'd fallen in love with a man who only wanted the superficial. *Stupid, stupid, stupid!*

She dragged in a breath, trying to find calm. Leo was only here for another week and then he would be gone. Nothing had to change with their plan just because she'd broken her side of the bargain. Her heart cramped so hard she caught her breath and then she flinched as her excruciatingly tender breasts touched her knees. She stretched her legs out in front of her, welcoming the coolness of the tiles.

She'd never thought love could be such a physical pain.

'Abbie? Are you sure you're OK? Can I use the shower?'

Leo's voice sounded muffled through the closed door.

Alarm zinged through her. She couldn't let him see her like this because he'd start asking questions. She just needed a few more minutes to pull herself together. 'Use the back bathroom. There are towels and soap all there.'

Hauling herself to her feet, she turned on her own shower, catching the slow-to-warm water in a bucket until the hot finally came through. As she moved the bucket she saw there was no soap in the holder so she bobbed down and opened the vanity. A shampoo bottle fell out of the overcrowded cupboard and she made a mental note to clean out the clutter. As she replaced the shampoo her fingers brushed a box of tampons. A thought snagged her. It seemed a long time since she'd used one. When had she last had a period? Her mind creaked backwards. *Before Leo arrived.*

All her blood drained to her feet and she swayed as her brain melted. 'I have an IUD.' She muttered the words in an attempt to slow the panic that tore through her. 'They have a ninety-nine per cent success rate. Periods are late when life is different. Breasts are tender when cycles are longer.'

But even when her life had been totally chaotic when she was a teenager and when she'd been strung-out living in the minefield that had been her relationship with Greg, she'd never missed a period. A wave of nausea hit her and she kept muttering, trying to hold on to faltering control. 'Stop it. You're stressed, so of course you feel sick. It's just an association of ideas.' She tried to put a stop to the rising mountain of evidence in her head. She was a doctor, a scientist and she operated on facts, not supposition. An HCG urine test was the only definitive diagnosis and an early morning urine sample the most reliable.

Whipping a towel off the rail, she clumsily tied it around her and dashed into the hall, grabbing her medical bag, and giving thanks that Leo was in the other shower and not able to question her.

She ran back, locking the bathroom door behind her and somehow with trembling hands managed to open the packaging, tearing frantically at the thick plastic cover. Passing urine was the easy part. Waiting the three minutes was an eternity. So she didn't go crazy; she had a shower, dried herself and then closed her eyes and breathed in and out three times. *You're overreacting. It's going to be one blue line.*

She opened her eyes and the stick shot into focus.

Two blue lines.

She put her head over the toilet and vomited.

'Leo, your *nonna* has rung the switchboard every hour this morning; your mother called twice, Anna called and Chiara left a message.' Erin walked into the doctor's lounge waving a sheaf of yellow pieces of paper.

Leo was grabbing a quick bite to eat before he headed back to Theatre. He knew exactly what the messages were about. Nonna wanted him to go with her to the billabong and had sent in the troops as extra backup. He didn't want to speak to any of them. Just because he was in Bandarra today didn't mean he was changing his behaviour. No way was he going out to Wadjera billabong.

You went with Abbie.

An image of Abbie in his arms with her head thrown back against the tree and her eyes wide with the wonder of an orgasm slammed into him and his breath jammed in his throat, causing him to cough.

Go back today with Abbie. The thought circulated, gathering momentum.

He clenched his teeth. *I'm never going back.* Going back wouldn't achieve a thing, and he abruptly extinguished the thought. He'd let his brother down the day he died, he'd let Christina down, and revisiting the scene wouldn't absolve him of that. Instead, he had his day all planned out and his night as well, and all of it added up to work. He might be 'home' but he was an adult and not subject to being told what to do—not by his father, mother or grandmother.

'Is it your birthday?' Erin winked at him as she handed him the messages. 'You better buy us cake if it is.'

He dragged up a smile. 'If I bring in tiramisu tomorrow do you think Helen on the switchboard would ring them all and say I got the messages but I'm tied up in Theatre for the whole day?' It was easier to lie by omission than go into the truth.

Erin laughed. 'For cake and for you, I'm sure that can be arranged. See you in ten.'

She walked out and the visiting anaesthetist looked up from his paper. 'Now that's a change.'

Leo hadn't warmed to his colleague but working harmony deemed he be polite. 'Sorry, I don't follow?'

The other doctor folded the paper in half. 'You have to admit, compared to frumpy McFarlane, that bit of skirt's worth looking at.'

A cold anger chilled Leo to his marrow. 'Abbie McFarlane is a fine doctor.'

'Sure she is, but you have to admit she's nothing to write home about.'

Somehow he managed not to lunge at the self-satisfied bastard's throat. 'Look at her eyes next time you see her and try calling her plain after that.'

'Mate, you surprise me.' He gave Leo a man-to-man leer. 'It's not the window to the soul that interests me about a woman.'

Revulsion filled him. Surely he'd never been that shallow but his father's voice mocked him. *Beautiful women who fill your bed but not your soul*. He downed his coffee. 'We need to get back to it.'

The anaesthetist rose to his feet. 'What the hell were you thinking when you drew up this list?'

Leo managed to grind the words out. 'I like to keep busy.'

'We're going to be here until well after dark,' the anaesthetist grumbled.

'That's the general idea.'

But his colleague didn't hear the muttered words, having already left the room.

Abbie stared into space. Thirty hours had passed since the two blue lines on her pregnancy test had burned into her retinas. Ever since that moment, everything she looked at was framed by those lines. Two uncompromising lines.

Pregnant.

A baby.

Motherhood.

It was the best and worst possible news.

She re-spun the pregnancy wheel and chewed her lip. By her reckoning, she was four weeks pregnant and she'd worked that out so often she'd worn the date off the wheel. Just pregnant but pregnant enough to know her life had irrevocably changed. The doctor in her knew she had to see an obstetrician as soon as possible to have the IUD removed. Those sorts of practical decisions were the easy ones. Telling Leo—that came under the banner of way too hard. He'd already married one woman out of a misguided sense of duty and that was still eating him alive.

I love kids... No relationship is worth the hurt and when kids are involved it's even worse.

She put her head down on her desk and dragged her fingers through her hair. She loved a man who didn't want a relationship or children, and she was pregnant with his child. A man who would feel honour bound to do the right thing, no matter how much he hated the thought. How much more of a disaster could she have possibly plunged herself into?

She sat up and drank a glass of water. She hadn't seen or spoken to Leo since yesterday morning because he'd gone into self-imposed hiding to get through the anniversary of Dom's death. It hadn't surprised her at all when his text had come through saying, *Delayed at work. Tomorrow night, I promise. Leo X.*

Leo, the man she loved. The father of her baby.

Her phone beeped and she read the screen. *We'll cook gnocchi together at your place. L X*

She smiled and a warm cosy feeling pushed aside all her anxieties. *Food is not just for a hungry belly. It feeds the soul.*

She hadn't understood what Maria had meant when she'd told her that but now she did. When you cooked with someone or for someone you loved then the love transferred to the food.

Leo wanted to cook with her. Leo wanted to stay the whole night with her. He wanted to be with her. The hope that had sprouted yesterday grew taller and, like the grapevine, tendrils curled around her heart, anchoring fast. Would he want to stay for ever because he wanted to?

She bit her lip again, this time tasting blood. During the early hours of the morning, with his masculine scent still on her sheets from the previous night, and with his tender voice in her head, she'd conjured up fairy tales of them together as a couple, together as parents of a black-haired, black-eyed baby and surrounded by the love of his family. A family so unlike her own, a family who adored children. The urge to ring him right then and blurt out the news had almost overpowered her.

But she'd held back. She wanted to do this the right way. She'd have the ultrasound first, check if the IUD was going to cause a problem and get all the facts before she spoke to him face to face. She had a plan and it was important to stick to it. The plan was the only thing she had.

She picked up the phone and dialled Mildura hospital's obstetric department. 'Hello, it's Abbie McFarlane, GP from Bandarra speaking. I need an urgent appointment with Alistair Macklin.'

Leo couldn't settle. He'd had the worst night's sleep in a long time, tossing and turning with snatches of dreams where Abbie lay in his arms one minute and had vanished in the next. He'd searched everywhere for her—running and calling, but he hadn't been able to find her. He'd woken with a start, his heart pounding and with a rushing return of the same unease he'd had when he'd first arrived back in Bandarra. He hadn't even realised he'd been living without it for the last few weeks until this morning.

He'd left home before the family were up and completed his rounds early. All his patients from yesterday were stable, which was great for them but left him with nothing much to do. He'd tossed a few balls to Alec, who'd now joined the Bandarra under-thirteens cricket team and was completely focused on improving his game. Then he'd gone for a long, hard bike ride with the Murray-to-Moyne crew. Hell, he'd even gone grocery shopping for tonight's dinner with Abbie, but nothing had completely banished the simmering sense of unease that bubbled inside him.

He checked his watch again. Abbie wasn't due to finish at the clinic for a few hours and he wasn't rostered on today but he had an increasing need to see her. He needed to breathe in her scent, lose himself in her clear rainforest-green eyes, wrap his arms around her and let her voice wash over him. Her voice, which could be soft and soothing one minute and deep and husky the next, and he couldn't get enough of it.

As he walked towards the clinic's front door, ominous black clouds gathered in the west. Leo frowned, his years in the city never completely removing the country's preoccupation with the weather. Bandarra always needed water but rain during harvest was never welcome. His hand turned the large door handle and he stepped inside the cool and welcoming clinic.

He was immediately struck by the quiet. The front desk, or 'command centre' as Abbie jokingly called it, was empty and Jessica, the receptionist who kept command, was nowhere to be seen. No patients waited in the comfortable chairs and the toys that usually lay scattered were stacked neatly into a box. Had he got the roster wrong? He glanced at the movement board and saw Abbie was signed in and a zip of delight shot through him. As there were no patients, perhaps he could convince her to cut out early.

He walked down the corridor to her office and knocked on the door. After a moment's silence he pressed his ear to the door and, as he couldn't hear the murmuring of voices, he opened the door. 'Surprise.'

But the room was empty, although the computer purred away, so he decided to wait for Abbie and deal with his email on a big screen rather than his phone. With only a few days before he returned to Melbourne, his receptionist was firing emails to him every hour as she adeptly juggled his schedule between his rooms and Melbourne City.

'Abbie, Alistair Macklin's—oh, Leo.' Jessica stalled in the doorway, her hand on her watch. 'Sorry, I thought Abbie was here doing paperwork.'

He smiled at the flustered receptionist. 'I'm looking for her too so I thought I'd check my emails while I waited. Do you want me to give her the message?'

Jessica hesitated as if she was in two minds and then she rechecked her watch. 'Do you mind? It's just I was supposed to have left half an hour ago. Abbie can't be far away because she didn't sign out with me.' She slid a fax onto the desk. 'Just make sure she gets this message about Alistair Macklin changing the date and time. I've moved all her patients over to your clinic in the morning so she's got the whole day off.'

'Can do.' He grinned at Jess, who was usually so efficient and well organised. 'Does that mean I have to start at eight tomorrow?'

'Oh, yes, sorry.' The words floated on a wail. 'I know I should have asked you first but all of this happened so quickly and—'

The sound of an impatient horn beeped three times. 'And Gavin's waiting for you. It's fine, Jess, just go.'

'Thanks, Leo, I owe you one, but make sure you give Abbie the paper.'

He waved her out of the door. 'Consider it done.' He was glad to help out while he was here so Abbie could attend one of the professional development seminars at the Mildura Base hospital. As he picked up the paper to place it under his phone so he didn't forget about it, his gaze caught the word *Obstetric*. Was Abbie brushing up on her baby-catching skills? He looked more closely and read, *Obstetric Clinic, patient Abbie McFarlane #71892.*

His mouth dried as his throat constricted, and the paper crumpled in his hand.

Abbie was pregnant.

His hand jerked up to his head as dread skittered through him, screaming. Pregnant.

No way, not possible.

Somehow his brain managed to kick in, all rational and matter-of-fact. Abbie had an IUD and there'd only been that *one* time they hadn't used a condom. One time. Once. What were the odds?

But, despite the reassurances, his eyes stayed glued on the words *Obstetric Clinic*. It didn't say 'gynaecology', meaning an annual check-up and pap test; it said *Obstetrics*. That meant pregnancy.

A baby.

His blood pounded so hard and fast it roared in his ears. He heard Dom's voice, Christina's grief and his chest seized. *I hate you.* The past hauled him down, back to black and bleak days. He couldn't do this again. He dragged in a ragged breath, desperately trying to push away the voices.

A baby.

His baby.

An image of a plump, round-faced baby with curly hair and large round eyes rose in his mind and the panic eased slightly. *His* baby. For a second, an incredible feeling of warmth spread through him before the fear returned, along with Christina's bleak and miserable expression.

A clap of thunder broke overhead, making him jump. He turned towards the window as huge drops of rain pelted against the glass, quickly joining together to form wide rivulets of water. The rumble of more thunder sounded in the distance.

I don't want to have a child on my own. Abbie's words rumbled in his mind before striking him like lightning and burning into him. She'd been adamant she didn't want a child. He could clearly see the straight set of her shoulders and the legacy of Greg's treatment of her still hovering around her. He could hear her firm voice as she spoke about her miserable childhood, and her determination that no kid would go through what she'd been through.

Never dependent on anyone ever again. His breathing sped up, coming in hard and fast runs, and he was barely able to force air down into his tight chest. There could only be *one* reason for this appointment. Only one reason for the urgency and reorganisation of the clinic and patients.

He dry retched. The thought of a baby terrified him, the thought of even trying to have a future with Abbie scared him rigid, but the realisation of what Abbie planned to do completely gutted him.

Abbie walked through the door. 'Oh, hello. Isn't the rain wonderful?'

Leo dragged his gaze upwards, his knuckles white, still clutching the paper. Her trademark glossy caramel curls framed her face as usual but he caught the vestiges of strain in the creases around her generous mouth. 'Not for the grapes.'

Her brow creased slightly. 'Oh, right, I didn't think about that. Still, you're a lovely surprise.' She sounded distracted and rounded the desk, putting her arms around his neck, kissing him lightly. Almost absently. 'I didn't expect to see you until dinner.'

Leo's brain struggled to function. Part of him wanted to haul her against him and kiss her hard and part of him didn't want to touch her. Somewhere in the 'common sense' zone of his mind he knew he should just let things play out as they would have done if he hadn't come into the office. But the reverberating words 'Obstetric Clinic' boomed in his head, driving out every coherent thought.

'Are you pregnant?'

Leo's black eyes glittered with anger as his scorching and accusatory words burned into her. Memories of Greg stormed in and she started to shake. *How do you know?* Her breath picked up, fast and shallow. This wasn't how she'd planned to tell him. Not like this, when she could hear and see his acrimony. See the terrors of his past so clearly on his face. She bit her lip and faced him down. 'What sort of question is that?'

'One that deserves an answer.' He shoved a piece of paper at her, his hand rigid with a vibrating fury that clung to every part of him.

A flash of lightning lit up the room and with trembling hands she saw the familiar logo of the Mildura Base hospital, read her name and the details of her appointment at the obstetric clinic. A jet of self-righteous resentment surged through her. 'This is private. How did you get this?'

He met her glare with one of his own, completely devoid of any contrition. 'Jess had to leave and I took the message.

But that's irrelevant.' He shot out of his chair and towered over her. 'Why didn't you tell me?'

The oxygen in the air vanished, immediately replaced by fear. *Because of this reaction.* 'It's my problem.'

Leo roared. 'It's a baby.'

The deafening sound of the rain on the tin roof seemed to amplify his anger. She shuddered at his rage, pushing down the memories that threatened to swamp her and forcing herself to stand firm. 'I know it's a baby.' *Against all odds, it's the gift of a baby.* 'A baby who, given the fact I have an IUD, shouldn't even exist but does.'

'*Dio mio*, so your solution is a termination?' He slammed his fist into his palm, his eyes wild and his gaze filled with disgust.

Her stomach dropped to the floor, nausea swamping her, and she gripped the edge of the desk as her head spun. Her chest burned at his betrayal, turning four glorious weeks into bitter dust. 'That's what you think I'd do?'

His arms flew into the air, gesticulating passionately. 'Your secrecy, the urgency of the appointment; what else was I to think?' But for the first time a hint of uncertainty ringed him.

Cloaking sadness made her gag and she dragged in a breath. 'You really don't know me at all, do you.'

'Of course I don't. We only met a month ago.'

His words knocked all the air out of her lungs, leaving nothing but aching cramp.

His defiant stance matched his words. 'You told me you didn't want to have children.'

'And, just like that, you tried and judged me.' She crossed her arms over her chest, trying to stop herself from shaking. 'Leo, I know this is a shock. I'm still reeling too but listen to me. I'm seeing Alistair to have a scan. The IUD could cause problems and I wanted to have all the information first-hand so you and I could discuss it.' A sigh shuddered out of her. 'So we know exactly what we're dealing with.'

'We're dealing with our baby.'

She nodded in silence. At least they agreed on that much. For a moment his face softened and she thought he'd extend his arms out towards her like he did so often, and then pull her gently against his chest before burying his face in her hair and whispering, *tesoro*. But he didn't.

'Right.' He dragged a hand through his hair and started to pace, the surgeon-in-charge. 'And if everything's fine then you'll come to Melbourne.'

She started and hope spluttered. 'You *want me* to come to Melbourne with you?'

He rubbed the scar on his chin. 'It's not really a choice now, is it?'

Resignation and anger simmered through his stark words, hurling hurt at her. Abbie braced herself. 'We have a choice, Leo; I'm not like Christina, I'm not an unskilled eighteen-year-old from a tiny town in rural Italy.'

He stiffened and spoke through tight lips. 'But you're pregnant with my child so we have to do what's right by the child.'

She'd expected this and her legs trembled and she locked her knees. 'And what's that?'

'We give it a go.'

She stared into his eyes, trying to read them, but got nothing. *Give it a go*. What was that code for? 'Give what a go?'

'Us.' His mouth flattened into a resentful line full of past hurt. 'You never know; this time the odds might fall my way.'

Might. Her heart thundered hard against her chest, each beat excruciatingly painful as he seemingly ignored all the wonderful moments they'd shared in the last few weeks. 'And if it doesn't work out, what then?'

He frowned. 'Abbie, we've only known each other a month. You understand what that means? Believe me, I know that's not long enough to predict anything.'

You understand. Like rose thorns tearing through skin, his words ripped through her. The same words her father had used against her. The same words Greg had flung at her. *He doesn't love you.* The agony of that realisation bore down on her so hard she could feel herself crumpling under the weight.

He didn't love her. Just like he hadn't loved Christina. His sense of put-upon duty would eventually make their life a misery. Just like with Greg. She refused to put a child in the middle of a toxic relationship where fear and uncertainty ruled their lives. Warrior Abbie stormed to the languishing box that had been opened for a month, dusted it off and oiled the hinges. Abbie knew exactly what she had to do.

Leo's gut cramped as Abbie's face suddenly hardened and images of Christina and Dom crashed in on him. Two people he'd let down so badly. 'Hell, Abbie, I'm trying to be adult about this.'

Abbie's hands clenched. 'What I understand is that you think you have to "do the right thing" but you really don't want to.'

'Come on, Abbie. Be fair. This was a fling. Neither of us expected this to go beyond next week.'

'So it's all about the brevity of our time together and not the substance?' She crossed her arms tightly. 'I'm not Christina, Leo. We laugh together, we share common interests but you've reduced all that to long odds.'

Living with you is worse than hell. Leo dragged his hand across the back of his neck, trying to think when he really wanted to run. 'Look, I'm willing to give it a good shot.'

'A good shot?' Her voice rose, the tone sheer incredulity. 'But if it doesn't work you can just leave any time. Thanks for the vote of confidence in us; that's a really committed start.'

Her words bit but he had right on his side. 'Look, I once stood in a church and promised to love a woman I barely knew and I let her down badly. I'm not doing that again.'

Her face blanched and she spoke flatly. 'I'm not asking for marriage, Leo.'

Shock ricocheted through him and his heart stumbled on the unspoken request in her soft voice. A request he couldn't honour. *She loves you.* Abbie loved him and wanted his love in return. *Dio mio*; he couldn't give her that.

His jaw ached. 'I'm sorry, Abbie, but I can't promise you anything because life isn't like that.' *I can't promise anyone anything because I just let them down.*

'Because you might fail?' Blazing green eyes speared him, pinning him against an invisible wall. 'So you won't even really start? You just told me you were being an *adult*.'

Exasperation whipped him. 'Of course I'm starting. We need to live together to see if it can work.'

'You already have us failed because of what happened with Christina. I think you're letting the teenage "you" make really bad decisions about your life now.' She stepped away from him and around the desk, putting distance and an obstacle between them.

He ignored the ripple of anxiety that crept through him. 'You have no idea what you're talking about.'

She shook her head. 'No, that's where you're wrong. You married Christina because she connected you with Dom. But guilt, grief and misguided duty are not the foundations for a marriage. Is it any wonder it didn't work?'

Her words pounded him with the truth, harsh and real, and he held on to his control by a thread, trying not to yell at her, hating her expression when he did. 'And we probably won't work either but there's a baby so we should at least try.'

'Well, at least you've openly said it.' Pity swirled in her eyes and sat firmly on her cheeks. 'There's no point then, is there? I will not be the victim of your over-developed sense of duty that will eventually destroy us.'

Her hands spread out in front of her in entreaty. 'I'm sorry that your brother died but it wasn't your fault. It was appalling timing following an argument but it could have happened to anyone. Unfortunately, it happened to Dom. Now you've embedded blame into your heart, not just for his death but for Christina's depression as well and it's stopping you from living your life.'

He wanted to put his hands over his ears but instead he heard himself yelling, 'I'm a rich and successful surgeon.'

Abbie didn't flinch at his bluster. All he could see on her face was sorrow. Sorrow for him.

'It's not a fulfilled life, though, is it?'

Her quiet words lashed him with their honesty and he fought back, wanting to hurt her. 'This from a woman whose approach to life was to lock herself away and deny herself any pleasure. At least I'm out there and not hiding.'

This time she flinched and her voice trembled. 'Against every part of my better judgement, I gave in to pure hedonism with you, did things your way, and I can't see it making either of us very happy right now.'

She spun away, wrapping her arms tightly around her before turning back. She breathed out a long, slow breath.

When she opened her eyes, compassion and affection stood side by side, edged with grief. 'I love you, Leo, but I can't compete with your guilt because it's eating away at you and holding you apart from everyone who loves you.'

He didn't want to hear her telling him she loved him. He didn't want to hear anything more about himself so he rolled his eyes, needing to deflect her words. 'Here we go, more navel-gazing pop-psychology. I'm sorry I don't love you, Abbie, but let's get real, we only agreed to sex.' He ignored the appalled and horrified charmer deep within who always kept him civil.

A flicker of something he couldn't name raced across her face before she spoke slowly and clearly, her words devoid of all emotion. 'You used me and work to try and forget and I let you.'

For a nanosecond, every part of him stilled. Then bile scalded his throat, his chest burned so tight he couldn't breathe and every muscle in his body tensed, ready to run. She saw right through him. Saw his fears, saw clear down to his bruised and battered soul and it terrified him. No one had ever got that close before. No one.

He brushed all her words aside with the sweep of his hand. 'None of this is relevant to the baby and that's what we're supposed to be talking about.'

Utter sadness lined her face. 'You really don't get it, do you?'

His hand tugged at his hair. 'I get I'm going to be a father and, with my workload, both of you need to be with me in Melbourne.'

She nailed him with a flinty glare. 'Go back to Melbourne so you can bury yourself in work and see the baby when it fits in with your schedule?' The scoff was bitter and anger laced every word. 'You can get a nanny for that, Leo, and I reject your offer. I deserve better than that. Our baby deserves better than that and if you can't love us then we're not going to sit on the sidelines, biding our time while you pretend to try and then leave us anyway. I won't live under that threat.'

He couldn't fathom her thinking. 'It's a plan, not a threat!'

'It's a threat.'

Abbie turned towards the door and something inside him tore apart but he couldn't give in to that pain. Instead, he fought for the child. 'How can you walk away from a chance to give this baby the family it deserves?'

She twirled back, a mixture of love and contempt swirling in her eyes. 'I'm staying in Bandarra and this baby will be surrounded by family, Leo. Your family. The one you choose to hide from most of the time.' She pushed her hair out of her eyes, the action decisive. 'I'll get Alistair to send a copy of the ultrasound to you. Goodbye, Leo.'

Resentment poured through him. 'You can't just walk out in the middle of this; we haven't made any decisions.'

'I've made mine.' She stepped through the doorway and disappeared from sight.

CHAPTER ELEVEN

ABBIE stared at the rain. The heavy and cascading type of rain usually found in tropical far north Queensland, not outback New South Wales. Rain that hadn't eased in three days. The town's initial delight at the much-needed water had turned to unease and foreboding. Flood warnings had been issued and the SES had launched into action, sandbagging the river to protect the town. Not since 1970 had the town been faced with a peaking river that threatened to break its banks and spread its damage far and wide.

Low-lying orchards, still struggling to recover from the shocking heat two years ago, now lay flooded with their crops unable to be harvested. The wine industry faced a shortage of grapes to turn into premium wine and the farmers had taken another hit, lurching from drought to flood within seventy-two hours.

Abbie tried to care. Her town, her house, the hospital, her patients' livelihoods—all were under threat and she'd been busy going through the motions of preparing for the flood but, as she packed up equipment and backed up computers, her thoughts were centred elsewhere. On the baby. On Leo. Her hand brushed her lower abdomen. *New life.*

Yesterday, Alistair Macklin had successfully removed her

IUD and reassured her that, as it was so early in the pregnancy, the risk of a miscarriage was no greater than with any other pregnancy. The fact that this embryo had successfully embedded in the first place made her think it was very determined and unlikely to change its mind.

Determined like its father.

She blinked back the tears that had moved in the moment she'd walked out on Leo and now hovered permanently. Walking away had been the hardest thing she'd ever done in her life, but where was the choice? Had he loved her, things could have been different. Could have been wonderful. But the appalled look on his face when she'd told him she loved him had left her in no doubt. That and his duty-bound idea of 'giving it a good shot', which only meant delayed heartbreak because his heart wasn't in it. His resentment would turn into anger and she and the baby would endure the fallout.

As desperately hard as it was, she wouldn't stay with a man who didn't love her. She'd fought for her right to be loved and she'd lost. No way was she ever going to beg for love. She had a child to raise and she had to be strong for that child. The one-month fling was over and an affair was all it had meant to Leo. Life moved on and somehow she had to as well.

But knowing all that didn't stop her heart from bleeding. Bleeding for Leo. He'd accused her of hiding from life and yet he was doing exactly the same thing, only in a different way. Her phone rang, interrupting her unwanted thoughts. 'Abbie McFarlane.'

'Abbie, it's Jackie Casterton, from Riverflats.' The experienced mother's voice sounded extremely anxious. 'Hugh's got a really high fever and extreme pain in his left ear. I wanted to bring him in to you but my car won't start.'

Doctor Abbie immediately surfaced through the quagmire

of Abbie's personal life, happy to have something concrete to concentrate on. 'No problem, Jackie. The clinic's really quiet due to the rain and my four-wheel drive will go anywhere. How's the road out to your place?'

'It's still open.'

'Great. I'll bring the medication with me to make things easier all round.'

'Oh, Abbie, thank you so much. Honk when you get to the gate.'

'Will do.' She rang off, picked up her bag and walked out to see Jess. 'Murphy and I are going to the Castertons'. I'll be in range so call me if there's anything urgent; otherwise I'll be back in an hour.'

Jess nodded. 'If anything comes up I can always ring Leo. He's in town until Saturday, right?'

Abbie forced herself to sound normal. 'That's my understanding.' Not wanting to further the conversation, she grabbed her Driza-bone jacket off the coat-stand and walked out into the rain.

Leo stared at the image on his phone for the trillionth time in twenty-four hours. Yesterday he'd worked a full day in the clinic, burying himself in work so he had no time to think of anything other than a myriad of signs, symptoms and diagnoses. It hadn't really worked. His blazing outrage at Abbie for not only walking out on him but disregarding his plan for them still burned hot.

He should be relieved she didn't want to move in with him. Be relieved that she'd rejected his honour-generated offer that had terrified him and thrown up images of his marriage. But there'd been no relief to the crushing maelstrom of emotions that simmered inside him.

Abbie of all people should know that a child needed both parents around.

He re-read the text that had come from Alistair Macklin with the ultrasound picture. *All looks fine.* He gazed at the peanut-shaped blob that was his offspring and gave thanks because nothing else in his life was fine. Everything else pretty much sucked.

'Leo, come!' Stefano hailed him from the winery door.

Leo pocketed his phone and strode towards his father as they made their way down to the vines. Muddy water eddied around their feet as they headed towards the other workers sandbagging the levee and shoring up what they could against the likelihood of a flood. Fortunately, all the buildings of the winery were on higher ground but many of the vines grew on the fertile flood plains of a river than hadn't flooded in decades.

Leo glanced at the clusters of dark purple grapes. 'What's the chance of Downey mildew?'

Stefano grimaced. 'If we get the usual March heat after this rain, the Petit Verdot are at risk.' His boots slurped in the mud. 'That's if the vineyard doesn't flood and we lose the vines as well.'

Leo hated seeing his father's life's work at risk from omnipotent weather. 'At least you've harvested the whites.'

'True. We give thanks for that.' He sighed and clapped his hand on Leo's shoulder. 'But we've weathered worse than this, your *mamma* and me. Vines can be replanted but lives cannot.'

Leo stiffened as still shots of memory flashed in sequence—the terrifying crack of the falling tree branch, Christina's screams, the image of his brother disappearing— all reverberating through him. Whether it was the touch of his father's hand or the fact that Stefano had mentioned Dom or even the mess of the last few days, but long-unspoken words rushed out. 'I still miss him.'

Stefano nodded, his face lined with understanding. '*Figlio mio*, we all do. Your *nonna* visits the billabong, your *mamma* lights candles, and my love for him goes into every bottle of wine I make. But you—I worry for you.'

His chest constricted. 'No one needs to worry about me.' The staccato ring of his words couldn't block Abbie's voice that rang loud in his head. *You've embedded blame into your heart...and it's stopping you from living your life.*

'You've stayed away too long. You need to come home more often and use your family to find a way to feel closer to Dom.' Stefano placed his fist against his heart. 'There is no fault, Leo, just sadness. Let go of the regret. It's time to honour your brother by being at peace with yourself.'

Peace. Leo didn't know what the hell that was or how to even start to find it. His father had never spoken this directly to him but, try as he might, he couldn't find the words to explain the chaos in his heart. Instead, he ramped up the pace of his shovelling, blocking out the current mess that was his life. As the rain trickled down his back, it sparked the memory of the silky touch of Abbie's hair against his skin, and the scent of it flared in his nostrils. A sensation rolled through him, trickling down into the dark places that usually remained untouched. Was that peace?

I reject your offer.

The sensation vanished and he gritted his teeth. He and his father worked in silence, both busy with their own thoughts. Time ticked by and it was Stefano who finally broke the quiet.

'I think this time coming home isn't all bad, eh? I see you took my advice.' Stefano shovelled sand into hessian bags and gave a deep belly laugh at Leo's blank expression. 'I know; it surprised me and your *mamma* too. Abbie McFarlane.'

A prickle of apprehension ran through him. 'What about her?'

Stefano winked. 'She's a real woman with heart and soul. Not like Christina who you thought would fill the gap your brother had left. Not like the plastic types you've chased since. Now, Abbie McFarlane is a woman who could make you happy.'

I reject your offer. Leo grunted as bitterness boiled inside him. 'Really, Papà? Well, she doesn't think I can make her happy.'

His father frowned at his tone. 'I'm sorry. I saw the love on her face for you and I thought she'd accept your proposal.'

Leo hefted another bag onto the levee. 'I didn't propose. I asked her to come to Melbourne and live with me.'

'Ah!' The sound said it all. 'Leo, women want marriage, commitment and the promise of babies.'

The pent-up emotions of the last two days poured out of him as the wind whipped him. 'You think I don't know that? I've had one nightmare marriage and that's why I've avoided serious relationships for years.' He ran his hand through his rain-drenched hair. 'Both Abbie and I agreed that neither of us wanted marriage or babies, which is why it was a perfect holiday thing.'

Stefano leaned on his shovel, confusion and concern clear on his face. 'If it was just sex, why did you ask her to go back with you to Melbourne?'

Just sex. Indignation swooped through Leo, irritating and shocking him in equal parts. He opened his mouth to object to his father's statement, to say it was more than just sex, but different words tumbled out instead. Words he hadn't spoken to anyone. 'Because she's pregnant.'

Stefano sat down hard on the bags. '*Dio mio.* A baby?'

He shook his head and muttered what sounded like,

'Doctors should know better.' Censure rode on his face and threaded through his words. 'She's pregnant with your child and you ask her to live with you? I thought I'd raised you to do the honourable thing. Now I understand why she refused your tawdry offer.'

Leo threw up his hands, regretting his disclosure. 'She doesn't want marriage, Papà. That isn't the issue.'

'What does she want?'

'Something I can't give her.'

His father's dark eyes glinted harshly. 'Do you love her?'

Leo's gaze slid away. 'I've known her a month! Hell, I knew Christina for longer and look how that ended up.'

'Time is irrelevant and that's not what I asked. Do you love her?'

Leo filled another bag. 'I admire her.'

'Admire her?' His father trembled with anger but he didn't roar. His controlled voice was ten times worse. 'This from the man who's been in her bed for weeks?'

'Don't censure me on this, Papà. We're two consenting, mature adults who knew what we were doing.'

'Obviously.' Stefano's hands rose high in the air. 'And now there is a child. A Costa! Family.'

Leo matched his father's glare. 'And I'm willing to give it a good shot to see if I can make something that was never planned work, but she refuses.'

'You told Abbie this? Can you hear yourself?'

I can't promise you anything. His own bald words deafened him and he fought against them. 'I offered her the opportunity to try. What's love, anyway, but an overrated word?'

'If that's what you believe, then I have let you down badly.' A sigh shuddered through Stefano. 'For years I've accepted you are a man and I've let you make your own way, hoping you would learn, but you've stayed away, replaced real connections with superficial ones and locked the family and love out of your life. It is lonely, *sì?*'

Leo wanted to scream, *No*, but he heard Abbie's voice echoing in his head. *Your guilt...it's holding you apart from everyone who loves you.*

His father pressed on. 'So I tell you now what I should have told you years ago. Loving someone isn't comfortable or easy, but she's the last person you think of when you fall asleep, the first person you think of when you wake up, and she's the person you want to share your day with, good or bad. She's the woman who annoys you to the point where you don't know if you want to yell at her or kiss her until the earth moves.'

Images and voices hammered him. Abbie in his arms, the intellectual arguments, the passionate sex and the snatches of contentment he'd never known before. Was that love?

Stefano fixed Leo with a look filled with the wisdom of life's hard lessons. 'But, most importantly, love is the woman who doesn't tell you what you want to hear but what you need to hear. With a woman like that by your side, then you know you are truly loved.'

You used me and work to try and forget.

It's not a fulfilled life, though, is it?

He broke out in a sweat. From the moment they'd met, Abbie hadn't let him get away with anything. She'd seen through every excuse and challenged him on everything he believed about himself. And she'd been right. He'd been hiding behind an accomplished career, believing that gave him a fulfilled life. But it gave him half a life and the rest was a thin veneer of perceived success that covered a giant empty cavern.

It had taken coming home and meeting her to finally face the truth. He needed her.

I love her. Oh, God, he loved her. What sort of fool was he that he'd loved a woman for weeks and had no clue?

And he'd thrown her precious love for him back at her in the worst way possible.

I deserve better than that. I won't live under that threat.

His heart broke open. Abbie, with her tilted chin, her caramel curls and her generous heart had stood her ground against his fears and her own and yet at the same time had tried valiantly to fight for him. For his messed-up, damaged heart.

And he hadn't fought for her.

He'd acted just like the bastards who'd passed through her life, taking what he wanted from her and then pushing her away with his half-baked attempt at duty. The words, 'give it a good shot' rang in his head. His gut clenched. No wonder she'd walked out on him. He'd forced her to go, pushing away the best thing that had ever happened to him.

The love of his life.

He ran his hands through his hair, the past still holding him hostage. 'What if I stuff it up again?'

His father gave him a cryptic smile. 'Adults take risks, Leo. Make peace with yourself and open yourself up to the love of a good woman.'

'If she'll have me.'

Stefano nodded. 'That I can't answer. All I can say is—go now and build bridges to her heart.'

Leo didn't have to be told twice.

'What do you think, Murph?' Abbie had the windscreen wipers on full pelt and even then she could hardly see through the rain. 'This is our only choice now Old Man Creek's flooded.' She was on her way back from the Castertons, having started Hugh on antibiotics for a perforated eardrum.

Poor kid; he'd been in a lot of pain. 'I guess we just keep going, taking it slowly.'

She changed into low gear, giving thanks she had the full tread of four-wheel drive wheels giving her traction against the slippery gravel that resembled a river of red mud more than a road. She wished she was home. Or already back at the clinic. It wasn't just that the road conditions were treacherous but, given a choice, she wouldn't be on this road today because it put her within five hundred metres of the Costas' front gate and even closer to the vines. No way was she ready to face Leo. Not yet. She needed to be completely on top of things next time they met—emotionally strong—and right now she was a very long way from that.

Most of her hoped he'd return to Melbourne and that it would be weeks before they had to talk again to sort out money and access. The whole situation had a surreal feel to it and she was happy to delay any decisions as long as possible. Delay everything until she'd worked out how to stop loving the father of her child. A child that would bind them together for ever. The irony that the baby now connected her with a family she couldn't be part of wasn't lost on her—their loyalties would lie with Leo. Did life have to be this hard?

The old wooden single-lane bridge came into view and, although the river ran high and fast, the bridge was still above the water line. 'We just need to get across the bridge and then we're on bitumen.'

Murphy barked his approval. Abbie knew how he felt. She wasn't keen on this bridge, even in good weather. Its narrowness and low sides always made her edgy. She hauled on the handbrake and wound down her window, leaning out of the vehicle to double-check there wasn't a car coming in the

opposite direction. Across the river she could vaguely make
out the silhouette of men—Costa employees—building a
levee bank to protect the vines. Her heart tore as her eyes dis-
regarded her instructions and scanned the group for height—
Leo stood out in any group. But the rain obscured details and
she couldn't see much at all. She dragged her gaze to the
other side of the bridge.

No cars.

Leaving her window open so she could see the side of the
bridge, she slowly pressed the accelerator down. Rain drove
into the cabin but it was better to be wet than misjudge things
and end up over the side. Halfway over, she glanced up into
the white glare of headlights. A car had pulled up and was
waiting for her to cross. The lights dimmed and her mouth
dried as an unmistakably tall man emerged from the car. Leo.

Her hand froze on the gear-stick and every part of her
wanted to throw the truck into reverse and retreat but that
wasn't possible. Even in dry conditions she wouldn't trust
herself to manoeuvre a vehicle this size backwards over such
a narrow bridge. Her heart hammered as she ran limited
options through her head. She could just drive past him when
she reached the other side but that would only antagonise him
more. She knew he'd been bitterly furious at her for walking
out on him and she didn't want to add to that. Somehow they
had to find a way through this nightmare so they could be civil
for the baby's sake.

Oh, dear God, but she wasn't quite ready to start now. She
maintained her slow speed, purposely delaying the moment
she'd have to greet him, knowing her heart would die just a
little bit more when she spoke the words, *Hello, Leo*.

Between the pounding of the rain on the roof and the
engine noise, nothing much else could be heard, although

Abbie thought she heard a low drawn-out groan. It had probably come from her own lips as she crept inexorably closer to Leo and another difficult conversation.

The groan grew deeper and louder and then an almighty roar of splitting timber erupted around her and, before she could do a thing, the four-wheel drive rolled. Deafening noise bellowed as water rushed at her through the open window, filling her nose, her eyes and her mouth. Everything was black. Dazed and disoriented, she had no idea if she was up or down. *Get out!* All she knew was that if she stayed strapped in her seat she would die.

Fear both paralysed and galvanized her. Numb fingers pried at the seat belt as Murphy fell against her. The weight of the dog pinned her to the seat and, with an almighty heave, she pushed Murphy out of the window against the tide of water.

She gasped for air as she felt the seat belt come away and she tried to move through the open window but the pressure of the water pushed her back. She could see grey sky and kept her eyes glued to that as she tried again to move. To get out. To live. Suddenly she was flung sideways and the ripping noise of crumpling metal filled her ears.

Water covered her. She pushed upwards and broke the surface, coughing violently. Air. Sweet air. Her chest burned. *Get out, get out, get out.* She pulled up again, forcing her body out through the window. Red-hot pain seared her but her legs stayed put. Trapped.

Panic sucked at her and she fought against it as muddy water swirled up around her neck. Holding on to the car, she tilted her chin and sucked in air. Air for herself, air for the baby. Twisting around, she tried again to free herself but she was pinned tight by the steering wheel and the dashboard. She breathed again. Water ran down her throat.

Coughing, she pushed her head back as far as she could and managed a breath. Darkness ate at the edges of her mind. Was this what her life had come to? First denied the man she loved and now the chance to raise his child.

No. She craned her head, trying to gain vital yet almost infinitesimal height to keep the water away from her nose. She heard Murphy's bark, the faint yell of voices. Help was coming. *Just keep going.* Her hands cramped, her fingers weakened, her legs screamed and every muscle burned as her body strained to stay above the water.

Then fire turned to ice and chilling pain dragged at her as she battled the morbid darkness that crushed her chest. Her energy drained away, completely consumed in the fight to escape, in the immense effort to breathe. A bright white light illuminated the darkness, promising blessed relief.

CHAPTER TWELVE

'NOOOOOOOOOO.' Leo's scream rent the air, slicing through the rain as the old timber bridge collapsed without warning, torn aside by the raging river as if it was as feeble as a matchstick model.

Build a bridge to her heart.

But the bridge had gone, taking Abbie with it, her four-wheel drive impotent against the surging flood waters that tossed it onto its roof and swept it downstream.

Move! He acted on instinct, driven forward by adrenaline and abject terror. He ripped back the tarp on the Ute and grabbed rope and then ran along the riverbank, through mud, through marsh, his eyes never moving from the four-wheel drive, which was being tossed around like a crisp packet. Did everyone he loved drown? Had he finally realised he loved Abbie, only to lose her? The thought struck him so hard he almost stopped breathing.

He saw a black and white flash and then Murphy appeared above water, valiantly swimming across the current. Hope burst through him. If the dog had got out then Abbie could too. *Let her live. Please, God, let her live.* His eyes strained through the rain, desperately searching for Abbie. For caramel hair. For a tilted and determined chin.

Nothing.

The levee bank builders, including his father, hearing the bridge collapse had rushed to the bank, their expressions frozen with shock.

The noise of crushing metal boomed around them. The vehicle slammed against a fallen red gum, its trajectory momentarily stopped as it became trapped between the tree and the bank.

Thank God. 'Call 000,' Leo yelled to the men. Lassoing a rope around his waist, he tied it firmly so it couldn't slide off. Floodwater currents could sweep a man away in a heartbeat so the rope was his only option.

He handed the other end of the tie to his father, forcing out the words against a constricted throat. 'It's Abbie.'

His father's dark eyes glowed with fear and memories. 'Go. Be careful.' His gloved hands gripped the rope as the other men gathered to help.

Leo waded into the water. Images of diving under murky water, images of Dom spurred him on. Water pulled at him, pushed him, eddying around him like a whirlpool, trying to suck him down into its muddy depths and keep him away from the driver's side of the truck. Vital seconds ticked past.

You can do this. He heard the voice of his brother, silent to him for so many years. *She's got a chance.*

'Abbie, I'm coming.' The wind caught his bellow and he struck out across the current.

The first sight he saw was her hair floating around her head like a halo. Her body was half out of the car and her face was underwater.

Dread sent its icy-cold fingers through him, squeezing his heart so tightly he thought it would cease beating. 'Abbie!'

He heard his disembodied wail as he tried to lift her head well clear of the water. Her eyes had rolled back. His fingers fought to find her carotid pulse.

A flutter of a beat. Faint. Weak.

He had to get her out. With his arms around her chest, he gave an almighty pull, but her body refused to yield. *No!* Memories choked him and he tried again, refusing to give up another person he loved to this bloody river.

The water lashed them against the car, threatening to swamp Abbie again. He rechecked her pulse.

Barely there.

He struggled to hold her head above the water. How the hell could he hold her clear and give her mouth-to-mouth at the same time? He was losing her.

You can do this, Leo.

How? *Think.* He yelled to the men on the bank. 'She's trapped; get me an irrigation pipe.'

'We're getting it.' Voices relayed the message.

Water flowed across her chin. He needed the pipe now. Two minutes ago.

Was she breathing? He couldn't see her chest under the murky water. Had he got this close, only to lose her?

Anguish and terror tore through him.

'Abbie! I love you.' He shook her flaccid body. 'Come back to me. Don't ever leave me.'

I love you. The bright light that had promised Abbie relief from pain faded and she was plunged back into inky darkness and burning pain. Her chest screamed as her diaphragm moved up. Air hit her wet and aching lungs. She gasped, then gagged, vomiting into the river.

'Breathe, *tesoro*, breathe. Please just keep breathing.'

She breathed. She didn't have the energy to do anything else. Leo held her. Leo tilted her chin just above the water line; Leo's ragged voice surrounded her, soothing her as she battled the horrifying fear that she'd slip back under to that dark, dark place.

Leo. Her next breath came more easily.

'Abbie.' Leo's hand patted her on the cheek but she couldn't focus on him. She could only focus on her next breath. 'Abbie, the water is too high and you need to breathe through this pipe. Stefano's going to hold you and talk to you and I'm going to try and free your legs. Keep breathing, sweetheart; that's all you have to do. I'll do the rest.'

She felt the pipe against her lips and then another pair of arms wrapped around her.

'Like a snorkel, *sì*? Think of tropical fish. We're right here. Breathe in, breathe out.' Stefano's work-strong arms held her tightly. 'Leo's diving under.'

A moment later Leo's hands touched her on her body, trailing down her legs. Then the touch vanished.

'Abbie.' She heard the surgeon speaking to her, the tone almost vanquishing all traces of the petrified man. 'I have to break your leg to get you out.'

I don't care—just get me out. She couldn't speak and she had no energy to move but somehow she managed a nod.

'Bite the tube against the pain but don't scream. Just breathe through the pipe.'

She closed her mind to everything except the breath and then her body twisted violently and searing pain tore through her leg. Strong arms pulled her clear. The water receded to her chest and she let go of the tube. More arms hauled her up out of the water and dragged her over a log as excruciating pain the colour of fire—red, burnt orange and scorching yellow—tore through her.

Then she felt the soft mud of the bank against her back and rain on her face.

Safety. Blackness followed.

Abbie opened her eyes to flowers. Bright pink gerberas, purple lithianthus, fragrant white lilies, cheery yellow daisies and white roses. Three vases of white roses. She stared at them.

I love you. Had she imagined Leo saying that? Who knew what your brain did when it was being starved of oxygen?

She'd drifted in and out of consciousness and only had snatches of memory but she'd been certain Leo was with her when she'd been in the ambulance, gone into Theatre and been transferred to the ward.

He wasn't with her now.

'Hey, you're awake.' Anna put down her magazine. 'Are you hungry? I've got the chef on standby for whatever you want.'

Abbie gave her a wan smile, the idea of food curdling her stomach. 'I think a cup of tea with toast and Vegemite is all I really feel like.'

Anna stood up. 'Consider it done.' She squeezed her arm and walked out of the room as Stefano and Rosa walked in, bringing care and concern along with a large brown paper bag.

'My irrigation pipe has never been used as a snorkel before.' Stefano kissed her on both cheeks.

'Let's hope it never has to be again.' Abbie reached for his hand. 'Thank you for talking me through it.' She gave thanks she was alive but she really didn't want to think about how terrified she'd been so she changed the topic. 'How are the vines?'

'The rain has stopped and the levee bank is holding so we hold our breath for a few more days. Floods come and go, but it's the people we love who are important. You worry about yourself, OK?'

The people we love.

Rosa nodded in agreement. 'Maria sends her love and her bread. She's been in the kitchen since dawn, making you her special *zuppa* to make you strong again for the—'

Stefano's hand closed over Rosa's and she paused for half a beat before commenting on the flowers and greeting Chiara, who'd just arrived.

The baby. Leo had told them about the baby. The baby that may or may not still be alive after possible oxygen deprivation.

She let their conversation float around her, dutifully answered questions when asked and accepted Anna's tea and toast. Leo's family surrounded her with love and chatter but the one person she desperately needed to talk to wasn't here.

I love you. Perhaps it had been anoxia-induced imaginings after all.

She stared at her toes that peeked out of a bright white plaster cast. The staff had been checking her circulation all night and her foot was toasty warm. She didn't really have much pain from her leg but, then again, perhaps pain was relative after yesterday's experience.

'*Dio mio.*' Leo strode into the room in green theatre scrubs, clutching a chart in his broad strong hand. The quintessential surgeon in charge. 'What are you all doing here? Abbie needs rest.' His arm swept out towards the door. 'I don't know how you all got past Erin, but you have to go. Now.'

Stefano winked at Abbie and walked towards the door. Rosa stiffened and stalked towards the exit, giving her son a look that would reduce a lesser man to a gibbering mess and Chiara and Anna grumbled, telling Leo to never try using that tone at home, but they left anyway.

Silence crept into the room. A heavy, brooding silence that

billowed into every corner, filled with a myriad of unresolved issues. Abbie bit her lip.

Leo finally spoke, throwing his hands up into the air. 'My family.'

'They mean well.'

He stood at the end of the bed, frowning and staring at her—a doctor attending to his patient. 'How are you?'

I don't know. She hated how they'd gone from such an easy camaraderie to this strained and torturous silence.

'Are you in pain?' He strode to the IV pump and checked the analgesia setting. 'I can boot it up.'

'No.' Her hand shot out and caught his arm. She needed to protect her baby and she needed a clear head to deal with Mr Costa, the surgeon. 'Leo, is the baby going to be OK?'

He stilled at her touch and it was like a knife slicing through her heart. She dropped her hand, certain that her near-death experience had tricked her mind into hearing words he hadn't spoken.

Leo ran his hand through his hair and it stood up in black spikes. 'I spoke with Alistair Macklin and he said, "Wait and see." You're fine so we have to assume that the baby got enough oxygen too.'

Panic fluttered through her. 'I was anoxic, though. I saw the white light; I heard things I don't think were said.' She gripped the edge of the top sheet. 'We're doctors; we both know about the chemical changes in the brain just before death and I had that moment of euphoria which means I was oxygen starved.'

He kept staring at her, his eyes boring into hers, filled with swirling emotions that her fuzzy brain failed to decipher.

He dropped his gaze and wrung his hands. 'I heard Dom.'

'You heard your brother?' Confusion tugged at her. Why would he have heard voices? 'But you weren't drowning.'

He flinched. 'When I was in the river, I heard Dom's voice—as clear as if he was standing next to me—telling me you had a chance. It was like he was guiding me to you. I know it sounds crazy but I know it really happened.' He let out a long breath. 'So you can tell me because it can't be more out-there than that. What did you hear?'

What I wanted to hear.

'Abbie?' He sat down next to her, worry carved deeply around his eyes. 'Tell me.'

She swallowed and shook her head, not wanting to see the same expression on his face she'd seen two days ago when he'd told her he didn't love her. 'It's not something you're going to want to hear.'

With a jerky movement, he picked up her hand. 'Abbie, you've always given it to me straight. It's part of what I love about you, so don't go all wussie on me now. Tell me.'

Her heart picked up as blood hammered loudly in her ears. 'You love me?'

He dropped his head forward, his broad shoulders shuddering before he lifted his gaze back to hers, his face drawn and haggard. 'I think I've loved you from the moment you told me in no uncertain terms it was up to Nonna to decide who her doctor was. It just took me until yesterday to realise.'

She wanted to throw herself into his love but she needed more. 'I had to almost drown before you knew you loved me?'

'No.' He clutched her hand with a desperate touch. 'I realised before that. I was on my way to tell you that you're my heart and soul when the bridge washed out. And I do love you, Abbie; you have to believe me. When I held you in my arms yesterday, so close to death, everything I'd valued about my life was reduced to worthless rubble.'

I love you. Don't ever leave me. Come back to me.

Joy exploded inside her, ricocheting through her and lighting up all the darkness. 'You called me back.' Her hand stroked his cheek. 'I'd given up, it was all too hard and then I heard your voice, telling me you loved me.'

'And I do.' His deep voice quivered with emotion. 'I love you with every part of me.'

He truly loved her. Her heart opened wide and she wrapped her arms around his neck.

Very carefully, he lay down next to her, gathering her close and burying his face in her hair. 'I'm so sorry I've been the biggest jerk on the planet. You were right. I'd been keeping everyone at arm's length for so long and it took your love to show me how wrong I'd been. I need you, Abbie.'

She held him tightly. 'I need you too.'

'With you, I've made peace with my past and now you and our baby are my future. Will you marry me?'

She stared at him, loving that he would offer her that, but not needing it. 'I know how you feel about marriage, Leo, and I told you, I don't need to get married. Your love is commitment enough.'

He shook his head, his expression as serious as she'd ever seen. 'No, it isn't. I want to stand up in front of my family and pledge my love for you. For our child. I want it on the public record that I will do everything and give my all to you, the love of my life. You deserve this and anything less isn't enough.'

His love surrounded her and she knew down to her soul she'd finally chosen a man who put her ahead of himself. A man who would stay with her, no matter what, but the need to test that lingered. 'So you'll love me even when I disagree with you?'

He kissed her hard. 'Especially when you disagree with me. I'll even try my best not to yell.'

She smiled at him. 'You're Italian; it's a given.' Resting her head on his shoulder, she gloried in the way his arms sheltered her. 'And you'll love me even though I'll never be able to wear clothes with your style and flair?'

He grinned. 'I'm Italian; it's a given.'

She laughed, embracing the sheer wonder of being loved unconditionally. 'In that case, I accept.'

His answering kiss was all she needed.

EPILOGUE

THE launch of La Bella's Petit Verdot was in full swing. The press had declared it a 'sweet, spicy and appealing red with immense cellaring capabilities', which was sweet news indeed. It meant the wine could become a collector's item as it was one of only a handful of red wines produced two years ago due to the crop losses of the floods.

Family and friends gathered in the shady courtyard of the restaurant, gorging themselves on the bountiful amounts of food, all made from local produce. Abbie snuck more than one slice of her favourite *quattro formaggi* wood-fired pizza, justifying to herself that the calcium in cheese was important for healthy bones.

She wandered over to the courtyard gate and stepped into the garden. Murphy immediately trotted up to her followed by a bouncing and enthusiastic puppy that ran circles around him. Murphy gave her a look as if to say, "Do I really have to put up with this?"

Laughing, she patted both dogs. 'Hey, Alec, you got a border collie. Good choice.'

The teenager grinned. 'They're the best dogs, Abbie. Murph taught me that.'

She'd kept in contact with the boy and Murphy had stayed

with him occasionally when Alec needed him or when Murphy had needed to escape the city. 'How's mum?'

'I'm great.' Penny scooped up the puppy and cuddled it.

Her face glowed with health and an air of contentment circled her. Unless someone took a close look and saw the faint scar of a tracheostomy, no one would know that she'd faced down death and won. She hooked a lead onto the puppy's bright red collar. 'Alec, if you want the top pick of Chiara's mingleberry jam you better come now because a tour bus just pulled in.'

With a wave they walked back inside. What had started out as a kitchen-table enterprise using the Cellar Door as an outlet had grown into a thriving business for Chiara that saw her products in delicatessens far away from Bandarra.

'Abbie.' A deep voice made her turn.

Stefano kissed her on both cheeks and handed her a glass of wine.

She tilted her glass toward him before she took a sip. 'It's a great party and a sensational wine.'

Her father-in-law smiled in his quiet way. 'My love for Dom and all my family is always there in my wine, but this one, I dedicate to you.'

'Really?' A bone-deep thrill rushed through her. 'I don't know what to say except, thank you.' The Costas had enveloped her into their family without a moment's hesitation and for that she loved them dearly. After years of not having family, she now had one in abundance.

'No, I'm thanking you. You brought Leo back to us.'

She shook her head. 'I think he was ready.'

Stefano put his hand on her shoulder, his expression serious. 'Never underestimate the power of love, Abbie.'

'Papà, are you philosophising again?'

They both turned and dark twinkling eyes winked at Abbie. Eyes filled with love and commitment. Eyes that made her knees go weak every time she saw them.

'*Nonno.*' A dark-eyed, curly-headed toddler leaned off Leo's shoulders, his arms outstretched toward his grandfather.

Leo reached up and lifted the child free. 'Papà, your grandson wants you.'

Stefano put out his arms to receive the child. 'Dante, let's go and look at the vines.'

'Grapes.' Dante extended a pudgy finger toward the vineyard.

'Smart boy.' His grandfather grinned as he strode toward his beloved vines.

Abbie waved to her son as he happily went with his beloved grandfather. Motherhood had exceeded all her dreams and she often had to pinch herself that this really was her life. Leo's arms circled her waist and he dropped his face into her hair. Love surrounded her and she leaned back into him, never tiring of his touch or the shelter of his arms. 'Where have you been hiding?'

'I took Dante and Nonna to the water-hole.'

She turned in his arms and smiled. For the last two years, Leo had accompanied his Nonna on her visits to the water-hole and whenever they visited Bandarra, which was about six times a year, he rode his bike out there. 'I'm glad. Dante loves it out there.'

Leo grinned. 'Well, he started life out there so perhaps he has a strong connection to the place like we do but for a different reason.' He wound a finger around one of her curls. 'The twins are busy earning money for a trip to Italy.'

Anna's daughters, at fourteen, were growing into beautiful and determined young women. 'Lauren was telling me all about an exchange program she wants to do next year.'

He nodded, trailing his finger down her cheek. 'The problem is they're underage so they can't work at the cellar door so they've started a babysitting club.'

His touch sent a tingle skating through her, a sensation that their time together had only heightened. 'That sounds like a good idea.'

'I thought so. In fact, they suggested they mind Dante for an hour so we can enjoy ourselves.'

His finger barely touched her chin but every part of her hummed with anticipation. 'Enjoy ourselves at the party?'

His smile carved a dimple into his cheek and his eyes danced with wicked intent. 'They didn't specify *where* we enjoy ourselves. I was thinking more along the lines of the cottage.'

She rose up on her toes and put her arms around his neck, loving that his desire for her was as potent as the day they'd met. 'I love the way you think.'

'I love you.'

And of that she had no doubt.

A FATHER
FOR BABY ROSE

BY
MARGARET BARKER

MILLS & BOON

All the characters in this book have no existence outside the imagination of the author, and have no relation whatsoever to anyone bearing the same name or names. They are not even distantly inspired by any individual known or unknown to the author, and all the incidents are pure invention.

First published in Great Britain 2010
Harlequin Mills & Boon Limited,
Eton House, 18-24 Paradise Road, Richmond, Surrey TW9 1SR

© Margaret Barker 2010

ISBN: 978 0 263 87903 2

Harlequin Mills & Boon policy is to use papers that are natural, renewable and recyclable products and made from wood grown in sustainable forests. The logging and manufacturing process conform to the legal environmental regulations of the country of origin.

Printed and bound in Spain
by Litografia Rosés, S.A., Barcelona

Margaret Barker has enjoyed a variety of interesting careers. A State Registered Nurse and qualified teacher, she holds a degree in French and Linguistics, and is a Licentiate of the Royal Academy of Music. As a full-time writer, Margaret says, 'Writing is my most interesting career, because it fits perfectly into family life. Sadly, my husband died of cancer in 2006, but I still live in our idyllic sixteenth-century house near the East Anglian coast. Our grown-up children have flown the nest, but they often fly back again, bringing their own young families with them for wonderful weekend and holiday reunions.'

A recent title by the same author:

GREEK DOCTOR CLAIMS HIS BRIDE

CHAPTER ONE

CATHY pushed the buggy past the vibrant tavernas edging the harbour, which hummed and buzzed with early evening revellers. Little Rose, squashed against her pillows in the buggy, was leaning forward now so she could point out something of interest that she wanted Mummy to see.

Cathy put her foot on the brake and went round to the front of the buggy, smiling down at her daughter.

"What is it, darling?"

Ah, yes, now she saw it. Rose loved cats. The black and white cat was now mingling with a group of people strolling along the harbour. The nearest woman to Rose's buggy bent down to look at the small girl.

"*Kali spera*," she said to Cathy as she smiled down at her daughter. "*Posseleni?*"

Rose chuckled but didn't reply to the woman who was asking her name.

"My daughter is only ten months old," Cathy explained in Greek. "She's called Rose."

"*Horaya!*"

As the woman hurried away to catch up with her friends Cathy repeated the compliment under her breath. "*Horaya!*" She didn't know whether the woman considered the name or her daughter to be beautiful but whatever it was she was right on both counts.

She paused to look up at the beautiful evening sky, not a sign of a cloud, the golden shades of the advancing twilight mingling with the seemingly endless blue that merged with the lighter colour of the sea. What a difference eighteen months had made! The last time she'd been here on the island she hadn't even known that she was actually going to be a mother. And then when she'd found out!

She drew in her breath as she remembered the shock, horror, her awful, mixed, muddled emotional reactions. How could she have had such dreadful ideas? She swallowed hard. How different her life would be now without Rose, the centre of her universe. There would be no meaning to it at all, apart from her medical career. But even that paled into insignificance now that she was a mother.

Eighteen months ago she'd come out to Ceres to attend her cousin Tanya's wedding, so happy to get away for a while, still licking her wounds and feeling the awful despair of another failed relationship. When Tanya had suggested she apply for the temporary appointment of doctor that would be available when she and her husband Manolis went on honeymoon, she'd jumped at the chance.

But two weeks later, back at home in Leeds, discovering she was pregnant had changed everything. She still had to suffer the awful pangs of despair at the fact that Dave had gone back to a wife she hadn't known existed. Coupled with the morning sickness that had set in with a vengeance, she'd withdrawn her application for the temporary post at Ceres hospital.

When Rose had been a few months old Tanya had phoned to say she and Manolis were taking a six-month sabbatical from Ceres hospital to work in Australia and there would be a vacant post for her if she wanted to apply. She'd got a second chance! Tanya had asked if she would like to stay in their house and she'd even arranged child care for Rose. She could make a fresh start at last and concentrate on her number one priority, Rose.

Looking down at her beautiful daughter, she could feel her heart lifting at the thought that they were going to be fine out here. Life was beginning to take shape again.

Involuntarily, she increased her stride, now desperate to get away from the evening crowds by the harbour, yearning for the peace and calm of the next bay where all would be quiet and she could sit down at a table outside the final taverna, which she remembered from the times her mother had taken her there as a child was always quiet.

She needed to watch the sun setting whilst chatting to Rose in Greek or English as her own mother had done with her. It didn't matter which. Rose was learning both languages as she had when her mother had brought her here every holiday to "pick up Greek" from her cousins and the children she played with.

Later, while at medical school, she'd taken Greek lessons with a private tutor who'd helped her sort out the grammar and linguistic rules. He had also been a retired Greek doctor, which had been a help when she'd made sure she was conversant with Greek medical terminology. She'd always hoped she might have a chance to use it. Never had she thought things would turn out as they had!

The buggy was rattling alarmingly now and not just the gentle groaning of an ancient model that should have been scrapped long ago. She tried to ignore it as she pushed hard against the rough cobblestones. Seconds later it ground to a jolting halt. What now?

She hadn't wanted to borrow it from Grandma Anna's vast array of baby equipment because it had obviously seen years of service. But Anna had been very persuasive, telling her that it would be difficult to get a taxi down from Chorio, the upper town, to Yialos, the area around the harbour. The hourly bus would be overcrowded and with standing room only. Much better to push Rose in the buggy down the *Kali Strata*.

Cathy knelt down to take a look at the loose wheel that was now firmly stuck in a deep crevice in the cobblestones. Rose leaned over the side and stroked Cathy's long blond hair as she struggled to extricate the wheel, gurgling all the while, obviously desperate to communicate her own thoughts on the situation!

"Can I help you?"

The deep masculine voice startled her. She adjusted her sunglasses as she squinted up at the tall figure outlined in the dying rays of the low-lying sun.

"Oh, it's you! For a moment I hadn't recognised you in…in your er…casual gear, Dr Karavolis."

"Please call me Yannis."

That wasn't what he'd said that afteroon when she'd disturbed him whilst he'd been operating in Theatre! His eyes above the mask had carried a definite expression of irritation as she'd pushed open the swing door, taken a peek and then hurried away.

Holding onto the buggy handle, she stood up so as not to feel inferior to Dr Karavolis for the second time in one day. Tanya had told her when she'd been contemplating coming out to work at the Ceres hospital that she might find Yannis Karavolis difficult to understand on a personal level. She'd explained that his wife had died in a tragic accident over three years ago and he didn't seem to have yet recovered. He was an excellent doctor, apparently, but made no effort to socialise.

"Let me take a look at that wheel."

He bent down just as she was standing up and she felt his arm accidentally brush the side of her breast as she attempted to rise from her crouching position as elegantly as possible. For a second it startled her, the feel of a man's arm against her body. The hint of masculine scent as he crouched down. She had thought she was now totally immune to instant attraction. But she couldn't ignore the heightening of her senses, the excitement of being in close contact with a man, the probably imagined increase in her pulse rate.

Heavens above! She would have to get out more so that she could apply her new rules to every encounter with the opposite sex. She'd had her fingers burned so many times before that she wasn't going to ever—repeat, ever—take another chance with a man. However handsome—and Dr Karavolis was decidedly handsome from where she was now standing. If she wasn't now so world weary and experienced she might have considered a little dalliance with this man who'd literally just dropped by so suddenly.

Rose was now giggling, having stuck out a chubby, dimpled hand to grasp a clump of the helpful doctor's thick black hair.

Cathy, glanced anxiously down at the crouching Yannis. Their eyes met. For a moment she felt a definite flutter of excitement. Yes, that's what it was. Just a simple flutter but enough to make her think that this man must have been quite something in his younger days; before tragedy had turned him into a working zombie.

It was a good thing that she'd given up on the difficult male species or she might at that fleeting moment have found herself advancing her embryonic ideas into something exciting.

His eyes were dark brown, sultry, vulnerable. She'd had time to notice that before he bent down once more to his task.

"Gently, Rose," Cathy said in Greek. "You must be careful not to hurt Dr Karavolis"

Rose giggled on, completely ignoring her mother's instructions.

"You're teaching your daughter Greek? That's good."

"Oh, she'll pick it up like I had to when I came out here for holidays and my cousin Tanya and all the other children used to make fun of me. I soon learned out of self-preservation, I can tell you."

Yannis gave one more tug at the wheel and removed it from the deeply sunken crevice between the cobblestones.

"Here's the wheel, but unfortunately it's come unstuck from the buggy," he said, gravely. He pulled himself to his full height, holding the wheel in one hand and making sure the buggy remained upright with the other.

Cathy looked up at him. "Well, er…thank you, anyway. I suppose…"

"Look, I was just going to have a drink and watch the sunset so…"

"Great minds think alike. I mean, we were just…"

"Please, why don't you join me?"

He couldn't imagine why he'd just said that! Company was the last thing he needed after his long, tiring day at the hospital. Especially another doctor…and a child…

"Both of us?"

He took a deep breath. "Well, we can hardly ask Rose to sit it out in her broken pushchair."

He was already unbuckling the seat belt and lifting the delighted baby up into his arms. Something about the way he held her daughter told Cathy he adored babies, children in general.

She wondered, fleetingly, if he had children being looked after by a doting grandmother back in Athens, which Tanya had told her had been where he'd been working before he'd come here. Better not ask. She didn't want to upset the fragile ambience that was building up between them.

Carefully holding Rose, whose fingers, had now transferred from his hair to his ears, he pushed the wrecked pushchair to the side of the path and led the way to the taverna that occupied the rocky peninsula at the beginning of this quiet bay.

The owner came out to the table Yannis had selected, beaming all over his face. He was carrying two glasses half-full of colourless liquid.

"I saw you struggling with that buggy," he said in Greek. "You need a drink, *ghiatro.*"

So, the owner knew Yannis was a doctor. Probably this was Yannis's hideaway when he was off duty, searching for solitude.

"*Efharisto, Michaeli.*" Yannis proceeded to introduce Cathy as Dr Catherine Meredith.

So Yannis had found the time between operations to check that she'd signed in with the admin department today. Otherwise she doubted whether her arrival on the island had registered with him. Certainly, no one had been expecting her to turn up unannounced today. The staff in the small admin department had told her she was expected to start work tomorrow but she could have a look around if she wanted to. That had been when she'd made her solitary tour of the hospital and barged into Theatre.

She picked up her glass. Realising the clear liquid was ouzo, Cathy decided to ask Michaelis for some water to dilute it. "*Nero, parakalor.*"

"You're sure you're happy with ouzo?" Yannis asked as Michaelis disappeared inside the taverna to get the water.

She smiled. "When in Rome...or rather on Ceres...it's best to go with the flow. I prefer wine but I don't want to hurt Michaelis's feelings. He obviously knows you very well."

"Oh, yes, we go back a long way. I've got a house further along this bay, on the shoreline near Nimborio. This is my bolt hole at the end of the day."

"I thought it might be."

Michaelis brought a bottle of water. Yannis, expertly holding the tired child against his shoulder, leaned across and topped up Cathy's glass.

"Thank you."

He raised his glass towards her. *"Yamas!"*

"Yamas!"

Rose's eyes were closing now. In another few seconds she would be asleep. Maybe she should relieve him of the burden on his shoulder. But something told her he was quite comfortable with the arrangement and she didn't want to speak until Rose was asleep.

They sat together in companionable silence that was broken only by the sound of the sea close beside them below the rocky promontory. Cathy found her eyes, protected by her sunglasses, drawn towards the sun that was slipping slowly behind the mountain, casting a shadow over their table. She moved her gaze to her daughter, who was now peacefully sleeping with her small head cradled against Yannis's shoulder.

Yannis saw Cathy looking anxiously at her daughter. Gently he eased the child down to a more comfortable position, cradled in the crook of his left arm. He smiled across the table, wondering why he felt so comfortable here with this mother and baby. It was a whole new experience and not something he'd expected to enjoy like this. He could feel it soothing his jangled nerves.

This was what life would have been like if…if only he… No! He mustn't torment himself by going down that road again. Just enjoy this simple, pleasurable feeling that was stealing over him—if he would let it.

He forced himself to relax again. "Rose is sound asleep now, Cathy, so don't worry about her. Would you prefer a glass of wine?"

"Well, only if…"

He tipped his ouzo glass and finished the fiery liquid in one swift gulp. "So would I."

Usually he sat, watching the sunset, sipping his ouzo slowly before ordering supper and a glass of wine, always reminding himself that he needed a clear head for his work the following morning. He'd no idea where this reckless feeling had come from but he was suddenly feeling in party mood. It had been a long time since he'd felt like this.

Michaelis, who was obviously watching from his seat just inside the door, came hurrying across and after a discussion about whether the wine was to be red or white he disappeared again, bringing out a tray with a selection of mezes and a bottle of white wine.

"We Greeks usually like to eat something if we're drinking wine," Yannis explained, pointing out the different small dishes of taramasalata, squid, calamari and olives. "But, then, you've obviously spent a lot of time in the Greek community so I don't need to tell you all this. I vaguely remember meeting you at Tanya and Manolis's wedding. So you're Tanya's cousin?"

"Yes, our mothers were sisters. My mother was keen to bring me over to Ceres after her sister married Dr Sotiris and came to live out here. Every holiday she would bring me here so that I could learn the language and absorb the Greek culture. I'd always hoped that one day I would have the opportunity to come and work out here."

Yannis leaned across the table and poured more wine into Cathy's glass. She'd hardly touched the ouzo but seemed to be enjoying the wine.

"I didn't know you were planning to start a family when I last saw you."

Cathy raised an eyebrow. "Neither did I! I'd just ended a relationship and didn't know I was pregnant. Tanya had just suggested I apply for the temporary four-week post they needed to fill at the hospital while she and Manolis were away on honeymoon. I'd decided I'd go for it, but when I found I was pregnant I withdrew my application."

"Difficult, I imagine. I'm sorry the relationship ended."

"I'm not! It was far too complicated. But I can't imagine life without my wonderful daughter. She's the most special thing that's ever happened to me. Did you…?"

She stopped herself just in time to avoid the question she'd wanted to ask. Looking across at Yannis now, with her daughter cradled in the crook of his arm, he looked like the perfect father.

He filled the awkward silence that ensued. "You were going to ask if my wife and I had children, weren't you?"

She cringed inwardly. "Well…"

"The answer is no. It…it wasn't to be."

He'd managed to refer to that most poignant period of his life without faltering and that was a step in the right direction. He hadn't told the whole truth but that would be a step too far. He couldn't bring himself to even think about it.

Taking a sip of his wine, he tried to blot out everything that had happened on that fateful day when his life had changed for ever. He put the glass down on the table. Looking across at the sympathetic expression on Cathy's face, he suddenly found his tongue loosening as if he was in an involuntary state of relaxation.

"My wife was killed in a car crash." He didn't need to say anything more but the guilt that always rose up inside him when he thought about the circumstances surrounding her death—which was often—was nagging him to confess more to this obviously sympathetic colleague.

"I often wonder…" He paused. He didn't need to go on. He didn't need to torment himself further. "I often wonder if I could have prevented it."

There, he'd said it out loud; revealed the horrible nightmare that returned over and over again when he reviewed what had happened.

The child stirred against him. In some ways he found the small body tucked against the crook of his arm very comforting. His thoughts returned to the present situation. He waited for the agony of his confession to make him feel awful but he felt strangely comforted to have shared this with Cathy—and the sleeping baby, although, thank goodness, the little mite couldn't hear him.

Cathy was simply looking across the table with a bewildered expression on her lovely face as she stretched out her hand towards him. With his free hand he took hold of Cathy's and felt a sympathetic, most welcome squeeze of her fingers. Something like an electric shock—a pleasant one—travelled up his arm.

For a few seconds they remained like that, simply looking at each other. She thought she could discern the tears that threatened behind his eyes but doubted that he'd ever allowed them to fall since whatever dreadful tragedy had taken place. She could tell this man was made of stern stuff. Strong backbone, wouldn't give in to self-pity but also found it hard to communicate the grief that was holding him back from getting on with a normal life.

Yannis took his hand away and leaned back in his chair, taking care not to disturb Rose. "I'm sorry to talk about the car crash like this. I've never discussed it with anybody before. I can't think why…"

"Maybe you should."

"Should what?" He looked alarmed.

"Discuss it with somebody. Me, for a start. It always helps if you talk a problem over with somebody."

He was silent as he thought of all the aspects of the tragedy surrounding Maroula's death. No, he couldn't discuss it openly with this woman he hardly knew. He shouldn't even have got so close to her that he felt he could trust her with his feelings. He couldn't think what had come over him. In a way it was a betrayal of trust to Maroula's memory. What had happened was part of his life with his wife and no one else. And yet…

"You don't have to discuss it with me," Cathy said. "It's entirely up to you. I would, however, be the soul of discretion so if you ever think it would help you to…"

"Thanks, I'll remember that."

His tone was firm, final, signifying they should move on. He was already regretting the fact that he'd allowed himself to talk about his beloved Maroula with someone he hardly knew. Discussing his feelings of guilt—something he'd never spoken about out loud before—wasn't going to bring her back.

Anyway, he was settled in his bachelor ways now. The future was mapped out and he didn't want to become close enough to any other person to allow them to break through the emotional barrier he'd erected around himself. He needed to retreat behind his safe barrier again. Back to Maroula. He was being unfaithful to her memory, something he'd vowed would never happen.

Little Rose wriggled in Yannis's arms, rubbing her chubby fists against her eyes before she opened them and stared up at him. A big smile spread across her face.

Cathy stood up and moved round the table, holding out her arms towards her daughter.

Rose lifted her arms towards Cathy.

Yannis couldn't help smiling as he handed over the little girl. "There you go, Rose. What a good little girl you've been."

Michaelis came out of the taverna to see if he could get something for the baby.

"I've got some fruit juice in her baby cup," Cathy said, sitting down once more on her seat, baby on one arm as she searched through her shoulder-bag. "Here it is."

Rose was already halfway across the table, reaching for a piece of calamari and dunking it into the taramasalata.

"Bravo!" Yannis said. "Rose is hungry."

"She loves calamari, as you can see." Cathy wiped a paper napkin round her daughter's face to remove some of the taramasalata. Rose pushed her mother's hand away as she savoured the delicious taste in her mouth.

"I've prepared some lamb souvlaki on the barbecue," Michaelis said, looking enquiringly from Yannis to Cathy. "Shall I bring them now?"

The lamb kebabs were delicious. Rose sucked on a tiny piece of tender meat then gummed it for a little while before depositing it on Cathy's plate.

"She likes to try everything."

Yannis smiled. "That's good. By the time you've been here— remind me, how long is it you're working at the hospital?"

"Six months. Tanya and Manolis have been offered a six-month sabbatical, if you remember."

"Yes, yes. I remember signing your contract now. You were interviewed in London, I remember. Manolis has put me in charge of the day-to-day running of the medical and surgical side of the hospital while he's away but I leave the paperwork to our efficient administration team. I knew you were coming in to work tomorrow but when you arrived briefly in Theatre this morning I couldn't think who you were. Sorry if I was less than welcoming. I was in the middle of a difficult operation and—'

"Oh, please. I hadn't realised that the theatre was in use. My fault."

"I'll take time to show you around tomorrow."

"Thank you."

Rose was now crushing a potato chip against her mouth before opening it and demolishing it with her four tiny white teeth. She wiped her hands over her blond curly hair and grinned happily.

"I think it's time for me to take Rose home," Cathy said, reaching for another paper napkin. "I've got the numbers of the taxi drivers in my mobile so I'll see who's free to come and get us."

The brief twilight had faded already, she noticed as she punched in the first number on her list. That number was engaged. She tried the next on the list and was lucky this time.

"Theo will be with us in ten minutes," she said as she closed her mobile.

"Good. I'm glad you're not going to attempt to walk back. I'll take your buggy home with me and ask Petros, the man who helps me in the garden, to see if he can mend it. He can mend most things."

Except broken hearts, Cathy thought as she smiled her thanks. It was so obvious to her that Yannis's heart would need a lot of tender loving care from a good woman. She certainly wasn't the person to do it because she needed to keep her own life on track. Whoever took on the mending of Yannis's heart would have a difficult job breaking down the barriers he'd built around himself.

She reminded herself firmly that whatever it was that that Yannis needed, she shouldn't feel obliged to try and provide it. After all, she was always the one left wanting when she was barrelled into trying to smooth things along for people. Besides which, she wasn't here to get too involved with another man, let alone a colleague she was going to have to work intimately with for the next six months.

Out loud she told Yannis that she didn't think Grandma Anna would need the pushchair for a while.

"Rose is her youngest baby at the moment. Tanya told me she was getting withdrawal symptoms now that they were taking baby Jack over to Australia. Anna told me today she's lost count of how many babies she's cared for over the years."

"She's an amazing woman. But you must still find it hard, being a single parent and working full time as a doctor."

"I'm very lucky. In England, my mother takes care of Rose when I'm working and here I've got Anna. I wanted to spend a short time away from Rose today to see how she would get on with Anna. She absolutely adores her already so I won't have to worry about her when I'm working."

"So why did you want to bring Rose out with you this evening?"

"I wanted to spend some quality time with her. Every mother's guilt trip, I suppose. Working away from home and leaving her baby in the care of someone else."

Yannis swallowed hard. "Guilt is a terrible affliction. We all suffer from it at times."

She saw the worried look on his handsome face and wished she could conjure up that wonderful smile he'd had just a short time ago. She'd noticed the flash of his strong white teeth, the curve of his full, sensuous lips, the vulnerable expression in his dark, brooding, brown eyes.

She gave herself another mental talking-to. She wasn't in the dating market any more. Neither, it seemed, was Yannis—wise man! Never again! Not after the disastrous relationships she'd suffered over the years. Life was going to be very good if she avoided meaningful relationships.

"I think this is your taxi coming along the coast road."

She gathered Rose up into her arms. *"Kali nichta, Yannis,"*

"Kali nichta, Cathy. I…" He hesitated. "I look forward to seeing you again tomorrow."

CHAPTER TWO

CATHY waited until she could hear Rose breathing that easy, steady rhythmic way that usually indicated her daughter was well and truly out for the count—for a few hours anyway. Barefoot, she walked backwards so she could keep an eye on her daughter, just in case she'd misjudged the situation.

She propped open the door then looked back to make sure she'd put the teddy-bear books that Rose loved so much at the end of her cot, where she would see them if she woke up early. With any luck, as had happened a few times recently back home in England, she just might become entranced by one of the pictures and give her sleeping mother a few more minutes of blissful oblivion.

Was she being over-cautious, over-anxious, over the top in her solitary state as a single parent? If she had a husband or lover waiting in bed for her now, would she be taking so much time? That would depend on the man in question. Sitting down at her dressing table, she confronted the image of an exhausted, sleep-deprived thirty-one-year-old mum with developing crow's feet at the corners of her tired blue eyes.

What an evening! she told herself as she wiped off the bronzer that she'd applied earlier in the evening so as not to frighten the tourists with her unseasonal pallor. It may only be April but out here on Ceres the season was already in full swing following the Easter festivities, and there were lots of healthy-looking people tramping over the hills and lying on the beaches.

She'd never imagined that she would end the day in the company of Yannis Karavolis who, although technically in charge of the hospital, hadn't seemed to know who she was when she'd arrived. She'd obviously been infinitely forgettable when she'd met him eighteen months ago at Tanya's wedding, whereas he… She felt embarrassed now that she'd been attracted to him as soon as she'd seen him skulking—perhaps that wasn't the word, more kind of hiding—in the kitchen so he wouldn't have to mingle with the revellers.

She'd split up with Dave two weeks before, and had already been licking her wounds and vowing never to get interested in a man again. But there had been something appealing about Yannis tonight. His total vulnerability. His obvious unshakeable devotion to his deceased wife. Tanya had just told her about his wife's tragic death, she remembered.

She realised now that if she were to fancy him—which she didn't…well, no, she mustn't! But if she were to even think of him as sexy, which he was, handsome, interesting to be with, yes, but only when he wasn't thinking about his wife.

Now, that would be the obstacle. Yannis's total obsession with the unattainable. His wife was dead, but yet, in his mind, she obviously lived on, set on a pedestal where nothing and nobody could ever replace her. So in a way, if anybody did try to take her down from the pedestal, somebody—not herself, oh, no! But just supposing she were to allow her feelings of attraction towards Yannis to develop into…

But she wasn't going to! However, if she hadn't decided never to have a meaningful relationship or even a fling with another man she just might, having imagined herself to be attracted to Yannis, forget her single-woman plan and have another go at romance.

She picked up the hairbrush and brushed her hair vigorously. It would be a stupid thing to do but she was renowned for making stupid decisions—or rather non-decisions, drifting into disastrous situations that started out as fun and ended in tears.

And this hypothetical idea that she'd just dreamed up would most certainly end in tears! The goddess-like wife would always be there with them. And Cathy had played second fiddle long enough. Dave had told her he was separated from his wife and waiting for the divorce to come through. And idiot that she was, she'd believed him. The long business trips abroad he'd had to make away from her! She hadn't questioned them because she had been in love and, therefore, that meant she trusted him implicitly.

What an idiot she could be! For a whole year she'd believed everything he'd told her. She'd been taken in by every single lie he'd told her.

It was the truth she couldn't believe!

That awful Saturday morning when he'd turned up and announced his divorce wasn't going through as planned. Well…sheepish expression on his face…to be honest, they hadn't got around to planning it. Actually, he was still theoretically living at home. He and his wife had decided they were going to make a go of it. Purely for the sake of the kids, you know. His wife didn't know about Cathy so he'd be truly grateful if she would keep it that way.

Mind you, if it were up to him…blah, blah, blah… She'd stopped listening to him by this time as she remembered the lonely Christmas she'd spent because he'd told her he had to go and stay with his sick mother. The numerous weekends when he'd had to fly away on business.

She put down the hairbrush and stared into the mirror again, this time seeing the face of a very gullible woman who never learned by her mistakes. But at least this time she'd learned. It would be the same kind of scenario if she chose to have any kind of dalliance with Yannis Karavolis. She would play second fiddle again to the perfect wife who could do no wrong. Yannis's wife may not be with them in the flesh but she would certainly be with them in spirit.

She forced herself to grin at the picture of desolation she posed in the mirror. "Don't take yourself so seriously," she told herself. "It's not as if you're remotely attracted to the man so the situation isn't going to arise."

And with that she crawled between the cool sheets and tried to fall asleep. The fact that she tossed and turned for half the night was put down to the fact that she was suffering from jet-lag. Towards dawn she decided to get up and finish unpacking and sorting out her bedroom. At the first squeak from Rose she was in there, smiling welcomingly at her daughter, reaching out her arms for a cuddle.

In his bedroom overlooking the wide inlet of moonlit sea in Nimborio bay, Yannis was also finding it hard to sleep. He hadn't expected to enjoy the evening when he'd invited Cathy and her little daughter Rose to join him for a drink. He'd certainly never envisaged they would all have supper together. And now it was time to admit to himself that he hadn't felt so alive since before Maroula had died.

He flung the sheet away from him. It was too hot to be covered tonight. He ran a hand down the side of his naked body as he experienced a feeling of strength flowing through him. It was a good feeling, but the feeling was also tinged with confusion. Was it guilt, this awful feeling now that he shouldn't be able to enjoy life without Maroula? He supposed it was. He didn't really think he deserved to enjoy himself like that in the company of an unattached young woman.

It wasn't as if he'd flirted with her, because he hadn't. But she might have misinterpreted his friendliness as an ulterior motive, mightn't she? She might have thought he fancied her in a sexual way. Well, actually, if he was truly honest with himself, he did! And that was something he couldn't hide from himself.

That was another thing he'd discovered tonight. Looking across at Cathy, who was undoubtedly very attractive, he'd felt himself almost if not actually, physically moved. And that hadn't happened since Maroula had died. He'd made sure that if he was in the company of an attractive woman he held a tight rein on his sexual emotions.

He'd lived like a monk for over three years. But tonight he'd felt himself drawn towards Cathy in a way that he couldn't dismiss. Was it because he sensed that she was also trying to survive, that she was vulnerable like he was? He was attracted by her beauty, her warmth, her forthrightness and the fact that because she was a stranger she had the distance needed to be able to ask direct questions.

Whatever it was, he hadn't been able to stop himself from allowing these long-lost feelings deep down inside him to come back.

But should he let them? Hadn't he vowed that Maroula was his lifelong soul-mate? She was no longer here but he was. And what about all the promises he'd made after she'd died? He was going to make it up to her. She'd been cut off unnecessarily in her prime and he'd pledged to spend the rest of his life devoted to her memory.

He found himself beginning to get drowsy at long last. His last thoughts as he drifted off were about how he would love to have Cathy beside him here in his bed. Because his wicked physical longings were becoming unbearable. He doubted he would be able to resist the temptation of her wonderful seductive body. The trouble was that if he gave in he would never be able to forgive himself.

Cathy hurried down the *Kali Strata,* aware that she wouldn't be able to reach the hospital in time. Having hardly slept all night, she'd spent too much time giving Rose breakfast, washing and dressing her, playing with her and finally taking her to Anna's house.

Breathlessly she hurried into the hospital. A flash of recognition registered on the receptionist's face as she leaned forward.

"Dr Karavolis would like to see you in his office, Dr Meredith."

Cathy smiled. At least she was expected today. "Thank you. Which way…?"

The receptionist pointed. "Straight along the corridor. It's the last door you come to."

As she hurried down the long corridor, Cathy wondered if Yannis had chosen to be right at the end so that he would have a quiet bolt hole when he needed it.

"Come in!"

She pushed open the door. Yannis was seated at a large, imposing desk, staring at a computer screen. He stood up and came round the desk, taking one of the two armchairs and indicating she should sit in the other.

She sat down, wondering why she was feeling so awkward now. Was it that she'd fantasised about him so much in the night and now, seeing this tired-looking man with the serious face, she was realising that she'd misjudged the situation completely? They'd simply had a drink together and eaten some food because they'd been hungry. End of story, thank goodness!

"Did you get home all right last night?" he asked gravely.

"Yes, the taxi took me to the end of the street. How about you?"

"I live very near Michaelis's taverna. A short walk. I asked Petros, my gardener, to collect your buggy this morning and see if he could mend it."

Silence, the ticking of a clock in the background, the hum of the computer. Cathy cleared her throat. "Where would you like me to start work today?"

He picked up a file from his desk. "I've mapped out your duties, which will vary from day to day. All the information you should need is in here. Today we have an open clinic in Outpatients. I've alerted the midwife who's working in the obstetrics section that you'll be joining her shortly. She'll be delighted to see you. Women doctors are always popular with our obstetric patients and at the moment one of our ladies is on maternity leave. Don't worry, we've got plenty of medical staff at the moment so there's plenty of back-up. It's later in the tourist season that we begin to find ourselves short-staffed. April is a good month to start—apart from Easter."

"What went wrong at Easter?"

For a moment she saw him relax his tight facial muscles and a hint of a smile appeared on his decidedly sexy lips. She felt a pang of interest once more. Something she shouldn't be feeling as she listened to Dr Karavolis explaining the workings of the hospital.

"What didn't go wrong?" He stretched out his long legs in front of him as he visibly relaxed.

She couldn't help noticing the expensive cut of his lightweight suit. The silk-lined jacket was hung over the back of his desk chair and the trousers he was wearing were just tight enough to make him look sexy even though the suit was of a formal design.

She waited for him to elaborate. "Easter celebrations on Ceres last more than a week. Fireworks are set off at every opportunity, and as you know they can cause havoc. Our casualty department was dealing with injuries on a round-the-clock basis."

He stood up, possibly to signify that it was time to start work. She clutched her file as she moved towards the door.

"I'll come along to see you during the course of the morning," he said as he reached ahead of her to open the door.

She smiled up at him as he held the door open. "Thank you...er...Thank you."

Her hesitation was because she'd no idea what she should call him when they were on duty so she moved swiftly away, back towards Reception.

She could feel a quickening of her pulse rate. Was he going to have this effect on her when they were actually working together? If so, she'd have to get a grip on her emotions.

Yannis remained with the door open, watching Cathy walking away. He'd managed to maintain a professional attitude, which he intended to maintain while on duty. But he had no idea how he was going to handle off-duty situations. He could, of course, make sure that he didn't meet up with her again in an off-duty situation. But having experienced the warmth of an evening spent with Cathy and Rose, he didn't think that was an option. He would just have to be careful when he was with them and not allow the situation to get out of hand.

He closed the door and returned to his computer, staring at the list of surgical operations he had to schedule. It was a long time since he'd felt emotionally confused like this and it was playing havoc with his concentration.

Yannis's decision to be careful came almost at the same time as Cathy got a similar idea firmly fixed in her mind. She was now following the sign above the corridor directing her to Outpatients. Having found the obstetrics section, she was immediately introduced to the midwife in charge.

Sister Maria welcomed her warmly as she went into the treatment room and explained the case history of the patient she was looking after. Cathy smiled down at the patient as she listened.

"Ariadne is a model patient," Maria said in Greek.

The patient smiled. "Only if you say so, Sister."

Cathy looked down at Ariadne. "I hope you don't mind me coming in halfway through the examination. I'm Cathy Meredith, very new here, but I spent a lot of time in Obstetrics when I was working in an English hospital."

"Your Greek is very good, Doctor."

"I've spent a lot of time over here and I have Greek cousins who made fun of me so much when I was a child that I had no option but to pick up as much Greek as I could."

Maria and Ariadne laughed and there was a good, friendly feel between all of them. Cathy always liked to break the ice when she was working. Tense patients were more difficult to take care of.

A young nurse came hurrying into the room, requesting the immediate attention of Sister Maria in the next cubicle. Maria excused herself.

"These are Ariadne's notes, Cathy, and she understands everything that's going on. She used to be a nurse before she started her family."

"Would you like to tell me about your family, Ariadne?" Cathy asked, glancing briefly at the notes.

"These twins will be numbers four and five in the family," Ariadne said, unable to hide the pride she was feeling as she patted her sizeable bump. "We intended to have four children but we were both delighted when I found out we were expecting twins. The more the merrier, my husband says. He wheeled me into hospital and then he went to do some shopping for me. He'll be back soon. I'm not allowed to drive any more and I have to use a wheelchair outside home."

Cathy glanced briefly at the case notes again. "Ariadne, tell me about the day you discovered you had symphysis pubis. It says in the notes that it was a sudden realisation. What actually happened?"

"I'd had a busy day, got the children to bed, cooked supper and then sat at the table with my husband, who'd just got back from a business meeting. He told me to sit still and let him wait on me during the meal. I suppose I was probably sitting for about half an hour. Then, as I stood up and tried to take a step I felt my pelvic bones split open. It was excruciating. Thank goodness, Demetrius was with me! He got me straight into hospital and they gave me strong painkillers."

"It's a condition that's not uncommon in women carrying more than one baby, Ariadne," Cathy said in a sympathetic tone. "Especially among those who've had a number of births in a short period of time like you have with your first three children. So, I see you were referred to our orthopaedic specialist, who made the diagnosis."

"It was such a relief to find out what was happening. I felt as if somebody had put a sword inside me. I will recover, won't I, Cathy?"

"Yes, you will. Your ligaments, which stretch naturally during pregnancy and childbirth, have become too loose to hold the pelvis together. But you were given steroid injections, which tighten everything up, weren't you? And I expect you were told to rest."

"I didn't move! I don't go out any more except for my hospital appointment once a week. My mother lives nearby and my husband tries to work from home as much as possible."

"Well, you seem to be doing all the right things. I see your twins are due in July."

"It can't come quick enough for any of us! I've been told I'll be delivered by Caesarean section."

"Yes. A natural birth would put too much strain on the pelvis. But the policy here at Ceres hospital is for operations of this nature to be transferred to the larger hospital on Rhodes. Minor operations are scheduled in for our hospital but most major ones are taken care of in Rhodes."

"I've already discussed this with Dr Karavolis and requested that I have the Caesarean here, Cathy. I know it's serious but he's going to make an exception in my case. Because I'm a trained nurse and I know the risks, I also know the qualifications Dr Karavolis has in surgery and I'm sure I'll be safe in his hands. This hospital is equipped with everything required, including an excellent surgical team. The specialist I've been seeing over on Rhodes has also agreed to this because he knows just how desperately I want my twins to be born on my beloved island."

Cathy smiled as she secretly admired her patient's positive attitude to her condition. "In that case, I'll try to be with you at the birth."

"Thank you. I'd like that very much."

Sister Maria arrived back, saying she was going to take Ariadne for her scan.

Maria handed Cathy another set of case notes referring to the patient in the next cubicle. Cathy moved on, scanning the notes as she went. Tatiana, her next patient, was being treated by weekly injections of a new anti-miscarriage drug.

Before giving the injection Cathy asked her patient if she'd had any side effects.

Tatiana smiled. "Nothing at all to worry about. I was so pleased when the doctor suggested he would like to try this new drug. I've had three miscarriages and I'm so anxious not to lose this one."

After giving the injection, Cathy turned round to put the kidney dish back on her trolley.

Yannis was standing in the doorway, watching her. "How are you getting on?"

No smile, no sign that they were anything but medical colleagues. Exactly how it should be, Cathy thought, ignoring the confused feelings inside her.

"Fine!"

"I'd like to take you up to Theatre before I start on my list. I may not have time to show you around before I need you to assist me some time in the near future so I've told Sister Maria I'd like to take you away from Outpatients for a short time."

He moved into the cubicle and smiled down at the patient. "Looks like you're going to be fourth time lucky with this baby, Tatiana. I had a word with your obstetrician over on Rhodes after your last appointment there and he's very pleased with your progress."

Tatiana beamed up at the handsome doctor. "I won't have to go over to Rhodes for the birth, will I? I'd much prefer to be here."

"Unless some complication develops, there's no reason why you shouldn't be delivered here."

"My husband's already planning the celebration. You're invited, of course, Dr Yannis. You were the one who suggested I should go over to Rhodes and see this doctor who specialises in women who've miscarried. I understand that he's also a friend of yours."

"Yes, he was at medical school with me…a long time ago." Yannis swung round. "Must go. Take care of yourself and that precious baby, Tatiana."

Cathy increased her speed to keep in step with Yannis as they went down the corridor together. His face was solemn again, but she was glad she'd noticed the easy, friendly manner he adopted with the patients.

Tatiana had been obviously delighted to see him. Patients and staff alike seemed to regard him as a heart-throb, from what Tanya had told her before she'd gone off to Australia. But Yannis seemed totally oblivious to the effect he had on the opposite sex.

"I thought it would be a good idea for you to familiarise yourself with our operating theatres before you're called on to work there. I've checked up on your CV and found you've had considerable experience in surgery."

"Yes, I was fortunate to have a lot of experience in my early career. I toyed with the idea of specialising at one point but decided to gain wider experience so that I could possibly train as a GP after I'd settled down and had a family."

He turned to look down at Cathy, realising for the first time that he was walking too quickly—as often happened when he was nervous. And he was nervous now. Cathy had that effect on him. He'd no idea why—well, he had, but now wasn't a good time to dwell on it.

"So you always intended to settle down and have a family?" He slowed his pace to a halt so that he could take a proper look at the attractive woman beside him.

She smiled up at him, relieved that he'd called a halt. "I

never actually made any firm decisions about anything in my early career. Things just sort of happened and I went along with the flow. I always wanted to be a doctor but…what kind?" She spread out her hands in front of him. "That changed as I went along, always becoming enthusiastic about the project I was on at the moment and…"

"That's good! To be enthusiastic about your job, I mean." He couldn't help admiring the way her clear blue eyes shone when she found a subject that interested her.

"Not unless you end up as a kind of jack of all trades, master of none."

"I think you underestimate your career progress so far," he said quietly as he decided he really should make the effort to move on.

"You've got a wealth of experience, which will come in useful in a hospital like ours. Here on the island we have a certain amount of autonomy. In emergencies we have to take decisions whether to operate on a dangerously ill patient or to have him or her transferred over to the bigger hospital in Rhodes. If time is against us or if, due to adverse weather conditions, the helicopter ambulance is grounded, we have to go ahead with the necessary surgery here."

A couple of nurses had just passed by, giving them inquisitive glances. He didn't want to give any cause for tongues to start wagging. "As far as I can see, you've steered a steady course since you qualified, gaining a great deal of valuable experience. And this was to achieve your aim to become a GP, you say?"

"I figured it would make sense if I were to find my life partner and settle down to have a large family."

"Your life partner?" His brown eyes were searing into hers. She held her breath, mesmerised by being the centre of his attention. "Do you believe there is a designated person who is meant to be your life partner, your soul-mate?"

Oh, heavens! She wished she hadn't started opening up to him like this.

"Possibly," she said softly, her eyes searching his face. "At least, I did when I was much younger, before I became… disillusioned."

"Oh, you must never become disillusioned about love," he said in a husky, deeply sensual voice.

Looking down at Cathy now, he was trying hard to remind himself that he'd already experienced what it was like to have a soul-mate. His hand moved as if by someone else and gently touched her face, her skin so soft, her expression so vulnerable.

"You've just been unlucky," he finished off quietly. "But don't give up hope." He put his hand under her elbow. "We'd better get on. I'm expected to in Theatre shortly."

As they walked along together again, he was telling himself that he would like to see Cathy settled with a life partner. It would suit her. She was obviously a devoted and competent mother, running a career and parenthood at the same time with no help from a partner. He swallowed hard. How ironic it was that he'd lost his partner and his unborn child and here was a young woman with a child and no man to love her.

He was bound to Maroula even though she wasn't there. And Cathy, with her unfortunate, if mysterious, experiences in the past making her wary of forming another liaison certainly wouldn't want to take on a grieving widower.

They were reaching the surgical suite. He gave Cathy a whistle-stop tour of Theatre number three which he knew to be empty. It would be easier to look around without having staff members there.

She was nodding. "It's very well equipped!"

He smiled. "Oh, yes, we're equipped for general surgery and most specialist procedures."

A nurse pushed open one of the swing doors. "We're ready for you now, Dr Yannis."

"Is the anaesthetist here?"

"Yes, he's waiting for your instructions." She paused. "I'm afraid your assistant hasn't arrived yet. The morning boat from Rhodes is late due to the high wind that blew up during the night. Sister is trying to arrange for someone to take his place but—"

"Tell Sister not to worry. I'm sure Dr Meredith would assist me, wouldn't you?" He turned to Cathy. "They're well staffed in Outpatients this morning. You'd be more use up here in Theatre. What do you say?"

"If that's where you'd like me to work," she said evenly.

"Just for the first operation. It's an appendectomy so shouldn't take long. The patient has been having tests to check why she experiences occasional pain in the area of the appendix. After studying the results of the tests and scans, my conclusion is that it would be best to remove it. I put her first on the list and set the wheels in motion after you called in to see me this morning."

He turned to look at the young nurse. "You're sure our patient has been fully prepped? She's been starved long enough, hasn't she?"

"Yes, sir. She's had nothing to eat since midnight, hoping that you would decide to operate this morning."

"Excellent!"

Cathy scrubbed up at the next sink to Yannis. She held her hands out. A nurse was waiting with a sterile gown to Velcro down her back. Gloves were peeled over her hands. Yannis glanced down approvingly. "Let's go."

She followed behind, noting that Theatre one was exactly like the one she'd just checked out. The surgical team looked alert and focused. Yannis raised an eyebrow above his mask as he looked across the inert figure towards Cathy.

"Scalpel, Cathy."

As she handed him the required instrument she was feeling relieved that he'd chosen to call her Cathy. He'd already introduced her as Dr Cathy Meredith to the assembled team. But it made her feel special, that she was some kind of friend with the surgeon. A kind of friend; that was a good description that she should try to remember if she could.

For the next half-hour she was totally committed to the task in hand. Yannis quickly cut through the patient's abdominal muscles to expose the angry-looking appendix. Yes, the patient would certainly feel much better when that infected organ was disposed of. Yannis was checking other organs in the vicinity.

"It's just the appendix that's infected," he told the assembled team. "No other organ has been affected. Have the biopsies checked out, Sister. Let me know the results as soon as you get them back from the lab. I took a biopsy of this ovary as a precaution. It looks healthy enough but it's in very close proximity to the infected area."

The swing doors opened as a young, harassed-looking young man already swathed in surgical gown and mask arrived.

"Ah, Nikolas! Good of you to join us! Problem with the boat, I hear… Thank you, Cathy. You were a great help. You are free to go back to Outpatients now. I'll see you later."

Cathy smiled at the young man as she went out. From the greenish colour of his skin above the mask it looked as if he wasn't such a good sailor. "Sure you don't want me to take over for the morning, Nikolas?" she whispered as they passed each other.

"Better keep in with the boss," he muttered. "I'm new here and—"

"So am I." She pulled down her mask and smiled at the new recruit, who looked terrified of the ordeal ahead.

"When you've finished chatting, Nikolas, you can bring the next patient in," Yannis said evenly.

Cathy turned to take a last look at the boss and was sure he winked at her over the top of his mask.

CHAPTER THREE

CATHY peeled off her surgical gloves and threw them into the bin before washing her hands. A couple of weeks had passed since she'd worked in surgery again with Yannis.

She'd been beginning to wonder if she'd done something he hadn't approved of on her first morning at the hospital. And then she'd remembered the wink he'd given her over the top of his mask as she'd been leaving Theatre one. Totally out of character! What had that been all about? Or maybe she'd imagined it. Yes, that was more like it. Because he'd given her precious little attention since then!

Oh, he'd called her into his office a couple of times but merely to brief her about a new patient or a different treatment that was going to be introduced. Off duty she hadn't seen him at all. Well, he did live near the sea and she was living in the upper town so there was really no reason why they should meet unless one of them arranged something socially. And it certainly wasn't going to be her! She understood the macho Greek mind too well from her holidays here on Ceres.

She'd felt nervous coming to the hospital this morning because Yannis had told her he'd scheduled her to work for the whole morning with him on his surgical list. She had been relieved to be asked, but apprehensive that she might do something to annoy him.

His manner had been totally professional and decidedly cool for the last few days and she had begun to think she'd misjudged the warmth he'd shown her on that first evening. So she was very relieved now that her morning's work in Theatre had gone well.

She glanced up at her reflection in the mirror above the sink in the ante-theatre.

Not a scrap of make-up. She didn't wear it when she knew she was needed in Theatre. In the mirror she saw the door opening as Yannis came in, shedding his theatre gown in the bin by the door.

He stood behind her. She watched his reflection as a broad grin came over his face. "Don't tell me. You were just about to put on your make-up and I've walked in so you don't want me to watch you. It's OK, I'll go out again."

She swung round. "No, you're OK. I wasn't going to put make-up on. Haven't got any with me."

"I'm glad."

He was standing very close. She could feel his hot breath on her face. He seemed to be studying her skin. She wondered if he'd noticed the spot that had developed on her right cheek.

"Yes, I'm really glad you've come into Theatre without make-up. It makes you look younger and I'm sure it's more hygienic."

"I've never worn makeup in Theatre." She was talking very quickly now, intensely aware of his close proximity. "Not since my professor of surgery at Middlefield General Hospital in Yorkshire ticked me off for wearing it. This particular professor claimed that make-up could harbour bacteria on the skin. He was probably right. And I'd found whenever I tried to wear make-up in Theatre it had gone all streaky anyway."

"It's an interesting theory. Turn round again. I'll help you out of your gown."

She put her hands in front of her defensively. "No, don't do that! I'm going to shower first in the female changing room. I…I'm not fully dressed underneath!"

"I wish you hadn't told me that," he said, his voice hoarse and seductively sexy.

He stepped back as he tried to get his hormones under control. He'd tried so hard for the last two weeks to keep control of himself. It was as if he was coming to life again. A wonderful feeling but he'd no idea how to handle it. Whenever he caught a glimpse of Cathy in hospital, walking down the corridor or bending over a patient, he felt like a teenager again.

He turned abruptly, the guilt of the confession he'd just made to himself rising up inside him alongside the disturbing sensations of sexuality and tenderness that he felt when Cathy was around. He'd forced himself to schedule her to assist him for the entire morning to prove that it was possible for him to remain totally professional.

And he had! But here he was, falling at the last hurdle. "Thanks for your help," he said evenly as he strode towards the swing door. He'd already pushed it open before the strong feelings she'd aroused in him became too much for him to ignore. He turned around again, letting the swing door close.

Cathy felt alarmed as she looked at his solemn face. He'd formally thanked her but was he now going to tick her off about the way she'd sutured that last patient? He'd been watching her so intently she was sure he was going to make some criticism.

"Cathy, I wonder if we could spend some time together this evening? I know we're both off duty."

He still wasn't smiling as he struggled to get his emotions under control.

Cathy had a surge of conflicting emotions herself at his suggestion. On the one hand her heart was telling her she'd love an evening out with this handsome Greek doctor. But her head was questioning whether that would that be wise. She had to be more careful than she had in the past. Meeting up casually with him on that first evening had been fun. But this invitation needed more thought.

She'd vowed not to go out with any man she was attracted to in case she made the same mistake she had in the past by falling for his charms only to be let down when she found out what he was really like. And, anyway, she shouldn't be mixing business with pleasure by going out with her boss. However would she manage to work with him if they started dating?

"Yannis, I hardly know you," she blurted out. "Don't you think it's a bit soon to have a date together?"

For a brief moment he looked perplexed before he managed to reply in a composed tone of voice. "I think you've misunderstood the situation, Cathy. I was merely wanting to have a chance for us to discuss how things are going for you here at the hospital in a less formal setting, away from work."

Oh, heavens! She'd put her foot in it again. How embarrassing to jump to conclusions like that! She felt crushed.

She hesitated before replying. His suggestion now seemed harmless enough. This was by no means an average type of man. Not the men she'd known in her life anyway!

"Well, yes, I agree it would be nice to have time to discuss things when we're not busy in hospital. What did you have in mind?"

Yannis was watching her reactions, trying to look composed but feeling utterly foolish for asking her out in the first place. Whatever had he been thinking? He was so rusty he had no idea how to talk to women any more!

Yes, what did he have in mind? If only he knew! He swallowed hard. "Would you like to come and have supper at my place?"

She hesitated once more. Having misinterpreted the situation completely, she knew she should make up for her faux pas. There would be no harm in simply chatting over supper.

She took a deep breath. "Yes, I would enjoy that. Thank you, Yannis," she said politely.

Relief flooded through him!

"Good! My housekeeper will be delighted if I do some entertaining for once. She's a very good cook but I don't give her enough practice. Most evenings I tell Eleni I don't need her so she goes home to her husband in Nimborio."

He was talking very quickly now, anxious to disguise his nervousness and get the preliminaries out of the way. "Oh, and do feel free to bring Rose along. All the taxi drivers know where I live now. About eight o' clock OK?"

"Fine!"

He left the room abruptly without a backward glance. Outside the door he paused for a couple of seconds to gather his breath. There! He'd taken the first step towards…towards what? Was he going in entirely the wrong direction? Would it all be a disaster? The emotional turmoil inside him didn't augur well. But he felt driven on by forces beyond his control. Was he betraying Maroula's memory by contemplating an evening in the company of another woman, someone he found very attractive and wanted to spend time with?

He sighed as he moved off down the corridor in the direction of his office. Only time would tell and at this moment he wished he could see into the future. Best to simply not look too far ahead. Only as far as this evening.

* * *

Cathy was as nervous as if she was going on her first date. She had to keep on reminding herself that this evening wasn't actually a date. She was simply going to her boss's house for supper and his housekeeper would be doing the cooking. It would be a treat to be spoiled like that—and nothing more!

Her face in the mirror certainly looked an improvement on the face that had stared back at her at the end of a morning in Theatre. And so it should after the time she'd spent covering up that spot on her right cheek, blending in the foundation with the light suntan she'd managed to get by playing in the sunshine with Rose whenever she'd had some off-duty time during the day. And she'd changed the shade of her lipstick three times.

She put the third lipstick down. That was fine. By the time she'd drunk a couple of glasses of wine and swallowed a few olives, she'd have licked it all off anyway. She stood up, adjusting the waist tie on her white cotton top. Too much cleavage?

If you've got it flaunt it, as her mother used to say. But what did she know about relationships? She'd had almost as much bad luck as her daughter! And Cathy was determined not to flaunt herself tonight. She was intent on being totally platonic with Yannis who obviously simply wanted to be a friendly and concerned boss by inviting her to supper. She readjusted her top so that it was in no way provocative.

Her mobile rang. It was Anna. Her son, Manolis, had presented her with a mobile phone before he'd gone off to Australia. Cathy was glad she could stay in contact with Anna throughout the day when she was looking after Rose. This evening, on hearing that Cathy had been invited out, Anna had insisted it would be better for Rose to stay at her house and get a good night's sleep.

"I meant what I said earlier," Anna said now, shouting as

she always did when she used her mobile. "Just enjoy yourself this evening, Cathy, and don't worry about Rose. She's already settled down in my children's dormitory room. I've got two of my granddaughters in there too, so when she wakes up she'll have company. I'll call you in the morning. OK?"

"Thanks, Anna. I really…"

But the line had gone dead. What a wonderful woman Anna was! She'd devoted her life to her family and now, at an age when she could have had some time to herself, she'd chosen to look after the next generation and the next.

After much persuasion from Manolis, Anna had allowed him to pay a young woman from the village to help her. Cathy had insisted on being responsible for the wages now that Anna took charge of Rose whenever necessary. She'd also made an arrangement with the bank to have a percentage of her hospital salary put directly into Anna's account.

Her phone rang again almost immediately. It was the taxi she'd ordered. Apparently the driver was waiting for her at the end of the street. She picked up the new clutch bag her mother had given her before she'd left for Ceres. It was just big enough to hold a few euros, a comb, a lipstick and a tissue.

As she started out down the rickety wooden staircase, being careful not to get her heels caught in the gaps between the wooden steps, she couldn't help feeling a sense of apprehension at the evening ahead of her.

Yannis was waiting for her in the drive of his imposing house. She held her breath as she looked up at the impressive façade.

"This is some ancestral pile you've got here!"

Yannis gave her a nervous smile as he reached out to take hold of her hand. "Rose not with you?"

Cathy thought he looked decidedly disappointed that she hadn't brought her.

"Anna was insistent that it would be better for Rose to be put to bed at her house tonight. I don't like to argue with an older and wiser mother and grandmother."

He was still holding her hand. He raised it to his lips briefly.

They stood in front of each other face to face on the firm gravel, both of them almost too apprehensive to continue with this nerve-racking encounter.

"There's nothing ancestral about the house, I'm afraid," Yannis said as he led her inside. "It was a complete ruin when I bought it and the owners were glad to get rid of it. It took a year to rebuild. I got a good builder who suggested ideas and between us we came up with this."

He spread his arms wide as they stood together in the large square entrance hall where the ceiling was the height of the house. Through the vast skylight that formed most of the ceiling Cathy could see the darkening sky, streaked with the crimson and gold of the spectacular sunset.

"It's beautiful! The enormous curved skylight reminds me of a cathedral dome. Much smaller, of course. But however did you…?" She broke off, unable to voice the embarrassing, intrusive question.

As if reading her mind, Yannis enlightened her.

"You're wondering how I could afford this on my hospital salary? Two years before I came back to Ceres, my mother died and left me the family house where I was born over on the other side of the island."

"I'd no idea you came from Ceres. I thought you were born in Athens."

"No, I went to Athens to study medicine. That's where I met Maroula."

He broke off, wishing he hadn't said that. Surely it was time to stop equating everything with his wife, especially when he was entertaining Cathy for the evening and tentatively planning to move on. He swallowed hard as he realised what he'd just admitted to himself. Was it true? Did he dare? How would he cope with the feelings of guilt that were already creeping up on him?

Cathy stared at her host for the evening. He appeared to have been suddenly struck dumb.

She put her hand on his arm. "Are you OK, Yannis? You look…"

He covered her hand with his own and flashed her a grateful smile. "Yes, I'm fine, thank you."

He bent his head and kissed her on the cheek. Surprised, she turned her head towards him and he kissed her on the lips. Mmm, that was better. He savoured the taste of her lips before gently pulling himself away and gazing down into her dazzling blue eyes. It was so long since he'd felt such strong attraction. If he was being wicked now then the buzz he was feeling at this moment was surely worth the agony of guilt that could possibly ensue.

Surprised but struggling to conceal her emotional turmoil, Cathy said, "You were telling me about your family house."

"Yes." He took hold of her hand and led her towards the kitchen at the back of the house. "The family house happened to be on prime land at a time when more and more tourists were taken with the idea of buying a holiday house on Ceres. I instructed my solicitor to sell it and that was how I was able to buy this ruin and turn it into the house I now have."

They were going into the kind of kitchen that would be described in English magazines as a farmhouse kitchen. Cathy looked around her in wonder.

Her feet positively danced across the stone-flagged floor towards the picture window overlooking the inlet of sea and the hills across the other side.

"It's superb! Did you design this, Yannis?"

"Partially," he conceded, wryly. "I had a lot of input from a friend of mine who's an architect. I met him when Maroula and I lived…in our house in Athens. I told him exactly what I wanted here. It's not so different from…from what we had in Athens."

A small plump lady bustled in through the open door that led to the garden. "Yannis, I've got the herbs you need to add to the soup. I'll put them in now so that they've got time to—"

"Eleni, this is Cathy, the new doctor from the hospital."

Cathy held out her hand towards Eleni, who reached forward and grasped it.

"Good to meet you, Doctor. I'm glad you're coming to keep Yannis company this evening. He spends too much time by himself. Not good. A man needs—"

"Thank you, Eleni. I'll put the herbs in if you want to get off now."

"Well, yes, I do. If I'd known you were going to need me this evening I wouldn't have arranged to look after my grand-children. Normally, I—"

"Supper's in the oven so I'm fine, Eleni. Thank you for getting everything ready. I'll see you tomorrow. *Kali nichta.*"

"*Kali nichta*, Yannis, Cathy."

"Absolute treasure, that woman," Yannis said as he moved across to open the fridge. "Would you like a glass of cham-pagne, Cathy?"

"That would be lovely." She perched on the counter beside the oven. "What's in the oven?"

Yannis was holding the top of the bottle, waiting for the

little fizz that would indicate the imminent popping of the cork. "I think Eleni said it was chicken…or it might have been lamb. I've got to take it out at eight-thirty and the vegetables are prepared and waiting to be cooked in the steamer."

"You're right. Eleni is a treasure."

He handed her a glass. "Don't I know it? Maroula was a good cook so…" He broke off. "*Yamas!* Cheers!"

Cathy took a good mouthful as she reflected that she somehow had known that Maroula would have been a good cook. Yannis had got a perfect kitchen. All it lacked was a perfect woman. Good thing she was intent on keeping a totally platonic friendship with Yannis. Her own cooking would never match up! She loved to mess about, throw things into a casserole and leave them to their own devices in the oven.

On the other hand, she could learn! But would that be to impress Yannis? Of course not, she told herself firmly.

"Would you like me to take a look in the oven?" She put her glass down on the counter.

"That might be an idea. I'll put these herbs in the soup while you're doing that."

"I'll do it, Yannis." She picked up the plate and surveyed the green fronds. "Oregano, my favourite." Sprinkling it liberally into the simmering soup, she turned her attention to the other herb. She wasn't at all sure what it was but if Eleni had thought it OK for the dish, who was she to argue?

"What's that you're adding, Cathy?"

It came to her in a flash of desperation. "Rosemary. So I think we might be having lamb." Thank goodness she remembered something from watching her mother deal with the Sunday joint.

She surveyed the work surfaces. "Do you know where Eleni keeps her oven gloves? Ah, there they are." Peering into the oven, she could tell immediately by the mouth-watering smell that it was indeed a leg of lamb in the oven.

She lifted it out carefully and basted it with the juices. Yes, it was all coming back to her. Piece of cake this cooking lark, especially if somebody had prepared everything in advance!

She pulled herself to her full height again, hoping that Yannis had noticed how experienced she was. So she was trying to impress him! No, she was simply trying to help a friend who happened to be a man on his own.

"It's roasting nicely," she told him, as if she did this sort of thing every day. "I can see it's a leg of lamb. Eleni has chosen to slow roast it,which means it should be very tender and taste delicious. Yes, another fifteen minutes will be about right."

He put a hand in the small of her back as he guided her along towards the sitting room. She was immediately drawn to the wide picture windows that were thrown open, protected by a vast insect screen on the outside.

"The view from here is superb!" She sank down on the sofa by the window. Yannis joined her, setting the champagne bottle down on a nearby table.

They were both silent as they looked out across the stretch of water to the other side where the steep sides of the hill plunged into the depths.

"I swim every morning," he said quietly. "It's a good way to start the day."

"Did you…?" She stopped.

"Did I used to swim with Maroula when she was alive? No, she couldn't swim. I tried to teach her but she didn't take to it."

Cathy remained quiet. How had he known that was what she was going to ask? Was it because she felt all the time that they weren't really alone? There was always a third person with them. A perfect, unblemished woman who could do no wrong.

She shouldn't resent that. It was churlish of her to be so petty as to deny Yannis the pleasure of talking about his wonderful wife. If it helped in the healing process then she was glad to be of service.

She stood up and murmured that she would check on the lamb.

It looked fine when she lifted it out and placed it on the serving dish that had been prepared near the oven. Somewhere at the back of her mind she had a vision of her mother hovering over the Sunday joint.

She could hear her voice now. "You've always got to let lamb rest before you serve it," she'd said way back in those days when she'd introduced a new boyfriend to their small family of two people, her father having long ago deserted the domestic bliss that her mother so yearned to create.

The soup smelt delicious and was still simmering along, creating a mouth-watering aroma across the kitchen.

"Shall I set the table?" Cathy motioned towards the large wooden table in the middle of the kitchen.

"Eleni has set the dining-room table. I'll take the soup through." He picked up the soup pan and poured the contents into a tureen that Eleni had placed in a strategic position beside the cooker.

She followed Yannis into the dining room. This was another room with the wow factor everywhere. A crystal chandelier in the centre of the room illuminated the table perfectly and brought dancing lights out from the crystal glasses on the table. Yannis put the soup tureen down on the table and lit the central candelabrum before holding out a chair for her.

He sat down at the head of the table. Cathy was sitting beside him on his right side. He served the soup and watched her take her first taste.

She raised her eyes to his. "Delicious!"

"Eleni makes delicious soup with vegetables from the garden. Courgettes and…er…*melejanes*. How do you say that in English?"

"Aubergines." She took another sip from her spoon.

"Yes, aubergines, beans, carrots—in fact, whatever the gardener tells her is ready to be used."

"I love making soup," she said, surprising both of them.

"Do you?" He smiled. "Somehow, I can visualise you in Theatre but not working over a hot stove. When did you learn to cook?"

"I learned all the simple stuff like soup from my mother when I was a child. Later on she used to tell me to get on with my homework, because she just knew I was destined to be a doctor. So I had to work hard at my schoolwork because I needed scholarships or grants to pay for my expensive education. Money was always scarce at home. But I could easily get back into the swing of cooking again if…if I had to."

"I would imagine you've got enough to do working full time in hospital and looking after your daughter."

Don't underestimate me, she thought as she put down her spoon. I may yet surprise both of us if these home-making vibes continue to grow.

They moved on to the next course. "This lamb is superb," he said. "I'm so glad you supervised it at the end. It made all the difference."

"Don't patronise me," she said, with a grin.

He smiled. "I would never patronise you, Cathy. You never fail to surprise me with your many skills."

He leaned across to pour some red wine from the bottle, which he'd just opened, into her glass.

At the end of the meal she managed to eat a small portion

of the freshly baked apple tart so that Eleni wouldn't be disappointed with their fast-fading appetites.

"Let's take our coffee out to the veranda," Yannis said, standing behind her chair to help her as she stood up.

He guided her through the French windows at the end of the dining room to an insect-proof veranda with another moonlit view of the sea inlet at the end of the garden.

He went out to the kitchen, returning with a glass of Metaxas brandy, which he placed beside her tiny coffee cup. For a few minutes they sat quietly, simply soaking up the nocturnal sounds. An owl hooted from somewhere on the dark side of the house. A gentle breeze was murmuring over the sea. She could almost sense the salty depths beneath it.

He was close beside her now. Alarm bells were ringing in her head. Was she letting down her guard? The trouble was it felt so right to be here together. She'd never enjoyed anything that could remotely have been called domestic bliss in the whole of her life. Neither had she ever seen her parents sitting together like this, simply enjoying each other's company. The little she remembered of her frequently absent father was that in the evenings he'd preferred to go out alone to the pub or whatever took his fancy. When she was four he'd gone out for the evening and never come back.

"You're looking very solemn." He moved closer until his thigh was almost touching hers.

"I was just thinking how nice it is to sit here, doing nothing. Simply listening, thinking, enjoying being with…being with someone you can get on with."

"It's a long time since…" He broke off. "Yes, I'm enjoying having you with me. It's good feeling that I can tell you things and you won't…well, like that first night when we were by the sea at Michaelis's taverna. I felt quite comfortable talking to you about Maroula. I've never told anyone before. It helped."

"I'm glad. I'd like to see you…getting over your loss."

He took a deep breath. "I haven't been entirely honest with you, Cathy. I've never been able to tell anyone exactly what happened the day that…the day that Maroula died."

She waited, feeling that if she spoke she would break the spell that seemed to have descended over them.

"Maroula had gone to stay with her parents for the weekend. It was her mother's birthday. I'd been invited as well, of course, but I was due to give a paper at an important medical conference on the Saturday. I was terribly ambitious in those days. My medical career took precedence—even over the needs of my family."

She could hear the stress in his voice. "Don't beat yourself up," she said gently.

He looked at her with wide staring eyes and the anguish she saw in them was heart-breaking.

"I said I would take a taxi out to her parents' house on the Sunday so that I could drive her back. But Maroula said the birthday celebrations would be over by then. She would drive back during the afternoon. I'm ashamed to say that I felt relieved that I didn't have to leave the hospital on that Sunday because I had ward rounds to make in the morning and preparations for the week ahead. I was in line for a consultant position and anxious to create a good impression."

He brought both his hands up in front of his face almost as if he was praying. She waited. When he took his hands away, he turned towards her again.

"At the back of my mind I was worried about the drive that Maroula had to do down winding roads from her parents' house in the country. She was nearly seven months pregnant."

"She was pregnant?" Cathy echoed softly, immediately wishing she'd kept quiet.

"Yes, you asked me last time we talked together if I'd had children with Maroula and I said it wasn't to be—or something like that." He hesitated. "Well, we were expecting our first child. Scans had proved we had a son on the way."

Cathy could feel the tears welling up behind her eyes. Should she tell him to stop now? She didn't want to know the details of how his wife and their unborn child...

"Maroula was making her way down from her parents' house on that fateful Sunday afternoon. It was raining heavily. The road dipped into a narrow ravine and then climbed steadily to the top before the final descent. I was told by a man who was in a car only metres behind her that a big lorry had come round the hairpin bend near the top on the wrong side of the road and ploughed straight into her. She stood no chance."

It was now so quiet she could hear the clock ticking. She daren't move or speak.

Yannis was sitting bolt upright staring in front of him, trying to deal with the confused emotions coursing throughout his whole body. He wanted to go on speaking until he'd told Cathy everything he knew.

It was almost as if he was talking to the priest in the confessional when he was a teenager. He had to keep going even though he wanted to give in to the tears that were threatening to make him stay silent again for ever, never to have told a living soul the hell he'd gone through, the guilt he carried with him.

"The police rang me at the hospital. They said an ambulance was bringing Maroula into the hospital. I was to stay put and wait for her. I went out to the ambulance. The paramedics had already covered her face with a sheet."

"Oh, no!" She pressed her hands against her lips to stifle the sobs that were welling up in her throat.

"Maroula had been killed outright and our baby with her. In that moment of impact I'd lost both of them."

CHAPTER FOUR

WHEN he'd finished speaking she couldn't stop her arms from reaching out towards him in a completely involuntary gesture. It was if they moved of their own accord regardless of the consequences.

He was drawn towards the expression of compassion in her eyes. As he tried to stifle the tears and then the sobs that choked in his throat, threatening to destroy all his macho credentials, he couldn't help moving into the warm, comforting embrace that, suddenly and bewilderingly, felt so right.

She held him against her as the tears rolled down her face. Listening to his heart-rending sobs only made her own tears increase. She wanted to take his anguish away from him but felt utterly powerless.

Suddenly he became quiet and pulled himself away.

"I'm sorry," he said, his voice hoarse with emotion. "I haven't cried like that since I was a small child. It's not the sort of thing that men do, is it?"

Out of the corner of her eye she noticed some tissues on a nearby table. Gently, she eased herself up, trying not to dispel the undeniable feeling of closeness that now existed between them. Moving across the room, she took a couple of tissues for herself before handing him the box.

"Maybe you should have cried before," she said gently.

"I couldn't. I didn't even cry at the funeral. I've got used to keeping my emotions to myself. Just getting on with whatever life throws at me, I suppose."

He took a deep breath and, squaring his shoulders, he got up and moved towards the window, looking out across the water.

"I hope I haven't upset you tonight, Cathy."

She joined him at the window. "I feel honoured that you chose to tell me about…about the family you lost. I can see now why…"

"Oh, Cathy, you've been such a help tonight," he said, looking down at her, his eyes searching hers as he drew her into his arms.

She felt the vibrancy of his strong athletic body. He was a magnificent, virile man. He shouldn't waste any more time living in the past. It was a wonderful gesture to honour the memory of his wife as he had done, but he needed to move on and start living in the present and for the future again. How could she persuade him that was the path to take? If only she could help him to do this.

But was it her place to try? What were her real motives? Was she being totally altruistic or did she have a vested interest in persuading him to start considering his own needs and the possibility of forming a relationship with…well, someone like herself?

Not with her previous disastrous experiences! She mustn't, simply mustn't get too involved.

He lowered his head and kissed her gently.

"Thank you for being here with me tonight. I feel…I feel for the first time I'm beginning to think about the future again."

She could feel his hard muscular body pressing against hers. In spite of the harrowing events he'd just described, she felt her own body yearning to respond to the nearness of him. But even as the realisation came she knew it wouldn't be appropriate so soon after they'd both shed tears for the two lives that had been taken away and the agony that Yannis had suffered.

She waited, hardly daring to speak as she watched him. Seconds passed before he took a deep breath and released her from his embrace.

"It's too late for you to get a taxi. And as Rose is safely tucked in at Anna's house, I suggest you stay here tonight," he said quietly. "It's been a harrowing end to our evening, hearing about the sadness in my life, so I'll take you to the guest room where you'll be comfortable. Early in the morning I'll drive you home."

He took her hand as they mounted the wide staircase together. The touch of his skin against hers was temptingly sexy. And going up the stairs with Yannis was making her think how wonderful it would be to spend a whole night with him. That's what she might have done in her previous life, before Dave had made her think hard before she gave in to romantic temptation.

He kissed her briefly at the door to the guest room before showing her inside, pressing a switch by the door that illuminated several beautifully shaded lights. Standing in the doorway, he made it quite clear that he was going to leave her alone.

"You'll find everything you need in here. Sleep well." He closed the door.

She heard the muted sound of his footsteps going away from her as she looked around the well-appointed room, the opulent, hand-made silk curtains, held back by swathes of tasselled, embroidered silken swathes. Taking off her shoes, she walked across the thick white carpet towards the bed, gently easing herself onto the white silk coverlet. She turned on her side and pulled the coverlet back to reveal white linen sheets. Nuzzling her face into the pillows, she allowed herself to imagine she wasn't alone.

And then she remembered Dave! The disaster that her affair had been. From meeting him in a Leeds wine bar on a girlie night out with a few friends when he'd singled her out. He'd asked her to have dinner with him the next evening.

He was so handsome, charming, attentive—and she'd fallen for his lies, taken him back to her flat after he'd wined and dined her the next evening, and they'd spent the most romantic night together. Shortly afterwards he'd moved in and they had been together for a whole year.

He'd told her his wife had left him and she'd comforted him—just as she had done with Yannis! But Dave's story had been just that, a story. While she'd opened up her home and her heart to Dave, he'd been dividing his time between her and his wife and two children. He'd told her he hadn't any children—as Yannis had done on that first evening and had then told her later he'd lost a baby son! Oh, but she believed everything Yannis told her. He was not the sort of person who... Hang on! Should she trust her own terrible judgement on anything to do with men? She'd been far too gullible for far too long! Once bitten twice shy, and she'd been bitten more than once!

Dave had told her he was a banker in London when they'd first met. He'd come up to Leeds to see a client. After moving in, he used to stay in London Monday to Friday—at first! After a few months he began to have frequent business trips and sometimes she didn't see him for two or three weeks.

Shouldn't she have suspected something? The words *Love is blind* sprang to mind! Well, she'd certainly been blind to all his faults. In defence of her utter trust in him, she had also been busy working long hours in hospital so she hadn't had time to pine.

But she'd always found time to welcome him back with open arms. She sighed. Much as she was attracted to Yannis now, she had to be careful not to get carried away. He was a good friend. They could have a platonic relationship. Yes, they could, couldn't they?

Neither of them was in a position to commit to a meaningful relationship. Apart from her fear of making another relationship mistake, there was Rose to consider. She mustn't put Rose through what her own mother put her through, bringing men into their lives, only for them to be gone before she knew it.

Her priority was her daughter. She must create and maintain stability for Rose. But that didn't mean she couldn't be Yannis's friend, of course. They could help each other emotionally. Yes, that was how she would deal with the situation, she told herself sternly.

Yannis went into his bathroom, stripped off and went into the shower. The water cascaded over his body as he tried to blot out the new sensations he'd had to contend with all evening. What was happening to him? It was as if he'd become two different people now. Half of him wanted to move forward as a free man who could make new, radical decisions about the future without reference to the past. The other half wanted to stay firmly rooted in the past with Maroula, which he'd felt was his duty since her life had been cut short. She'd had no chance of achieving her allotted lifespan.

But here he was, in good health, with a good career, and had now met a wonderful woman. Cathy made him feel so alive!

He stepped out of the shower and grabbed a towel from the freshly laundered pile near to hand. As he walked naked back into his bedroom he felt the urge to make love with Cathy. It had been so long since he'd felt like this, his body vibrantly pulsating, longing to give all he had and to be welcomed into the paradise of two bodies delighting in sharing themselves with each other.

He'd had several girlfriends before he'd met Maroula but he'd known almost at once that she was the one. The special woman he wanted to be with for the rest of his life. And he'd been completely faithful to her during their marriage and after her death.

He stretched himself out on the bed. But now there was Cathy. This whirlwind who'd come into his life, disrupting all his ideas of how he should conduct himself since he'd chosen to remain a confirmed bachelor. What was it about Cathy that made him think she could replace Maroula? When Maroula had died he'd decided that nobody should replace her. Maroula had been unique. No one could hold a candle to her.

But Cathy was also unique. She was a wonderful, compassionate, sexy, attractive woman and she was only a short distance away down the landing. He sat up. Should he…?

No, he mustn't give in! It was too soon. He must control himself until he felt absolutely sure that he could handle the feelings of guilt that would undoubtedly follow if he were to consummate his desires. He mustn't let his heart rule his head tonight.

Cathy awoke with the dawn sun streaming through the open casement window. The first sound that alerted her to the unfamiliar surroundings was the gentle lapping of the sea on the pebbled shoreline beyond the garden. She stepped out of bed onto the thick carpet, which tickled her toes and muffled the sound of her feet as she moved towards the open window.

She sat down on the cushioned window seat and leaned out, smelling the delicious scent of the frangipani still covered in early dew. Across the stretch of the narrow seawater inlet she could see the steep hillside rising up to be warmed by the sun's rays at the top. She'd always loved this early part of the day when everything was calm and unspoilt. She wouldn't think about the events of last night, the confused thoughts that had kept her awake.

The quiet knock on her door brought her back to reality. The day had begun and she could no longer live in dreamland.

"Come in," she said breathlessly.

"Did you sleep well?" He was standing on the threshold, his mid-thigh-length towelling robe drawn tightly around him, knotted securely round his waist.

"Yes," she lied. "Did you?"

He nodded, not wishing her to know the wicked thoughts that had plagued him all night, the number of times when he'd almost broken his resolutions.

"Come down when you're ready and we'll have breakfast."

"Actually, I ought to get back in case Rose wakes up early and Anna phones me."

"Yes, you must be there for Rose. Such a lovely little girl. You're very lucky to have her," he said, unable to disguise his wistful tone. "I'll drive you home as soon as you're ready."

"Give me five minutes. I'll shower when I get back, then I can change into my day clothes for the hospital."

As Yannis drove her up the side of the hill that led to Chorio, she looked out at the tiny boats bobbing in the water of the harbour. The higher they rose, the smaller the boats seemed to be.

"That's always fascinated me," she said. "The way boats and cars appear to be like little toys the higher you go."

He took one hand from the wheel and placed it on her thigh. "That's one of the things I like about you, Cathy. Your delight in simple things. Maroula was like that."

She could feel herself stiffen up as she heard him speaking his wife's name again. Was Maroula always going to be there with them? Would they ever be able to get away from this iconic woman?

Just as soon as the thought entered her head she chastised herself sternly. Why was she thinking of them as a couple when she'd vowed to herself that they were to be just good friends? And why did she suffer attacks of jealousy whenever Yannis mentioned Maroula's name?

He removed his hand and put it back on the wheel, sensing that he'd somehow offended her. It was difficult to understand women. He hadn't had enough practice recently. Last night she'd listened so intently to everything he'd told her about Maroula but this morning she seemed different.

They reached the end of the street just as her mobile started to shrill. Yannis switched off the engine.

"Yes, Anna?"

"Hope I didn't wake you up, Cathy. Rose is awake and keeps looking for you. Shall I...?"

"I'll come and get her now so she doesn't disturb your granddaughters... Yes, I'm already dressed."

She turned to look at Yannis. She remembered his wistful tone when he'd told her this morning how lucky she was to have Rose. On impulse she asked if he'd like to come in and have breakfast with them. "You were saying you'd like to see Rose again."

He smiled. "I'd enjoy that very much."

She handed him her keys. "Go inside and make yourself at home. I'll go and get Rose."

He was walking around the kitchen when she arrived with

Rose in her arms, still swathed in the blanket Anna had insisted she needed in the early morning air.

His face lit up. "Oh, little Rose is so beautiful!"

"Would you like to hold her while I get breakfast?"

"Of course!" He held out his arms.

Rose turned to look up at her mother questioningly.

"It's OK, darling. Go to Yannis."

Rose turned her head and smiled at him.

She held out her arms towards his hair, suddenly remembering what fun it had been when she'd twirled it in her fingers.

As he took the child in his arms Yannis felt something akin to comfort flooding through him. This little trusting angel seemed to have been sent to take the place of... No, he mustn't think like that. This was Cathy's child. A completely different child from the son he'd lost. But the rush of paternal instinct that came over him was a wonderful experience.

Cathy turned round after switching the kettle on. What a touching picture. The obviously besotted Yannis holding her daughter as if she were a prize he'd just been awarded. She tried to obliterate the flights of fancy that were hovering in her head as she saw how easily Yannis interacted with Rose. For a brief second she allowed herself to imagine how wonderful it would if Yannis became part of their little family.

She gave herself a mental shake. The idea had to stay in fantasy land if she was to keep her resolutions intact.

"I'll get Rose dressed after breakfast but for the moment she can crawl over the floor if you watch her. I'll be putting her in clean pyjamas tonight so she can get as dirty as she likes—and she does enjoy getting dirty."

Yannis grinned. "So I see." He was following Rose as she made her way to the veranda. "It's OK, Cathy, I won't let her fall over the edge into the garden. Don't you think it would be a good idea to put a fence round the veranda now that she's moving so quickly? Would you like me to send someone up to do it today?"

She was putting yesterday's bread rolls under the grill. "That would be great if you could arrange it. I was planning to find a carpenter myself."

He picked up Rose from the floor and came over to stand behind Cathy.

She was acutely aware of him. He'd put aftershave on. She'd enjoyed breathing in the heady aroma as they'd come up the hill in the car but now, having him so close, it was putting her completely off what she was supposed to be doing. Good thing she wasn't in the operating theatre with him! It didn't matter if she burnt the rolls.

She swung round so that she was facing him, breathing in the combination of his natural male scent mixed with the one that came from a bottle.

"Would you really be able to organise the fence for today? I mean…"

He leaned even closer, his sexy lips curving into the most disarming smile that displayed his strong white teeth. His brown eyes were warm, compassionate and fixed on hers as if she was the only person in the world who mattered to him.

Gently, he touched the tip of her nose with a teasing kiss. "Consider the job done." Rose, enjoying the warmth of what felt like a cuddle, reached out her hand and grabbed Cathy's hair.

"OK, Rose, I'll take you… Oh, bother! Yannis, you keep her for a moment while I try to salvage these bread rolls."

Yannis, holding onto Rose with one hand, switched off the grill. "I've got a better idea. Why don't I go to the bakery for some freshly baked ones?"

* * *

Minutes later they were sitting at the table out on the veranda, Rose strapped into her high chair, eating fresh rolls liberally covered in Anna's home-made plum jam.

Yannis picked up the cafetière and poured more coffee into Cathy's cup before refilling his own. "Rose looks as if she's enjoying herself."

Cathy smiled as she looked at her daughter, who was running her jammy fingers through her blond hair while she chewed.

"Who will you get to make a fence around the veranda?"

"Petros, Eleni's husband, who does the garden and takes care of all the house maintenance. He can turn his hand to anything, so a small fence won't be a problem. I phoned him while I was waiting to be served at the bakery. He'll be here soon to assess what he needs for the job."

"Such efficiency, Doctor!"

"Not really. I get spoiled in my domestic situation by Eleni and Petros. Nothing is too much trouble. They know I'm a widower and it's almost as if they're sorry for me being all alone. Do you know what I mean?"

She nodded as she swallowed a piece of roll. Oh, yes, she knew perfectly well what he meant but she wished she didn't have to be constantly reminded of his situation. She looked out across the garden towards the bay of Pedi at the bottom of the hill. Even though the sun was shining on the water and the sky was blue she felt as if a cloud had emerged, threatening her so far idyllic day.

"I'd better get Rose cleaned up and ready for me to take her back to Anna's when I go down to the hospital."

"You seem very comfortable here. This is Tanya's house, I believe?"

"Yes, she inherited it from her grandmother Katerina, who was a dear friend of Anna. Manolis was living in the house next door so when they got married they had a door knocked through—see it there at the side of the kitchen? I've got the key for that house as well but I prefer to stay in this smaller one."

"I remember Tanya telling me about it before she and Manolis went off to Australia. Manolis's house is called Agapi, which means love, doesn't it?"

"Yes, and this house is called Irini, which means peace," she said quietly. "Tanya told me that when she first started working in the hospital with Manolis she couldn't imagine how they could live next door to each other in houses called love and peace. They'd had a previous relationship with each other that hadn't worked out."

He reached across the table and covered her hand with his own. "You have an English saying that the path of true love never runs smoothly. It was certainly true in their case, I believe."

As she looked across into his eyes she wished the turmoil of her emotions would go away. Yannis was a true romantic. She shouldn't allow herself to dwell on the expression in his eyes when...

Rose was whinging, struggling to pull herself out of the straps in her high chair.

"OK, Rose, you've made your point." Cathy stood up briskly and released the straps, gathering up the sticky child into her arms. "We're heading for the bathroom now so if Petros arrives..."

"I'll get him started then I'll go to the hospital. He's bringing the replacement pushchair I had sent over from Rhodes. Petros said the old one you'd borrowed from Anna wasn't worth repairing so I've got a new one."

"That's very kind of you but..."

"I kept meaning to explain what was happening." He stood up, brushing a hand over his trousers.

"I think you've got some dirty marks from playing with Rose, Yannis. I'll get the clothes brush."

"No need. I've got spare clothes down in my shower room. Sometimes when I have a few hours off duty I go out in the boat and come back needing to change."

"You've got a boat?"

"Every man on Ceres likes to have his own boat! It's part of our Greek heritage. You must let me take you out in it when we're both off duty."

Walking down the *Kali Strata* some time later she was alarmed at the high wind that had started to whip up the waves down in the harbour. Further out to sea she could see the white caps on the waves. Men were pulling their boats out of the water up onto the side of the harbour. She knew this was a sure sign that a bad storm was on the way. As a child she remembered being marooned on Ceres for several days. During a bad storm the port authorities forbade any boats to leave or enter the harbour.

She quickened her step, anxious to get inside before the storm arrived.

As she walked into the hospital she was thinking she must make the effort to behave naturally when she met Yannis. The events of yesterday evening and the warmth she'd felt flowing between them this morning had bowled her over. She felt so different from the way she'd felt this time yesterday.

"Dr Meredith!"

Cathy walked briskly across to the reception desk. "Dr Karavolis is asking for you in Casualty. There's been a traffic accident."

"Thank you." As she hurried along the corridor she wondered how serious the accident could be. It seemed strange that traffic accidents could happen on this small island which, until recent times, had only had donkey paths. But traffic was building up now that more and more paved roads were being made. Many of the older roads tended to be too narrow for cars to pass each other. She hurried into the treatment room.

"Good. You're here!"

She didn't know if Yannis's peremptory tone had something to do with the fact that she'd taken too long getting down there.

"Take over from me, please. I've put it in the notes. Mario had this sedative…" he pointed to the notes "…five minutes ago so you can go ahead with fixing the cast. X-rays up there on the wall screen show the scaphoid bone is fractured. They're waiting for me in Theatre where two more of the accident patients require immediate attention."

The middle-aged man on the couch looked up at her beseechingly as Yannis swept out of the treatment room.

"Are you a proper doctor, miss?" he asked in Greek.

She smiled down at him and replied in the same language. "Of course I am. They wouldn't let me loose on you if I wasn't. I'm Dr Meredith from England, but you can call me Cathy."

"It's only that you look so young. I thought perhaps you were a student."

"Bless you! I'm thirty-one but don't tell anybody. Now, let me help you to sit up, carefully, slowly, yes, that's fine. I want you to hold this wooden roll in your hand for me. Now, I'm just going to bring your hand back a little so that the wrist will be in the correct position for the next six weeks."

"Six weeks? I've got a plumbing business to run, miss, sorry, Dr Cathy."

"Have you got an assistant?" she asked as she wound the bandage around his hand and up over the wrist.

"I've got two—my two sons. Twenty and eighteen."

"Well, as long as you give them the heavy work to do and you just supervise, you'll be OK. Once I've set this it will be good physiotherapy for you to keep the fingers moving. There! That's perfect!"

"How can you be so sure?"

She paused for a few moments to check the angle at which she'd set the fractured scaphoid.

"Well, the scaphoid bone is a tricky wrist bone. I've known one or two patients come into the hospital where I was working back home in England with complications usually caused by the wrist bones being set at the wrong angle. But I don't think that will happen in your case."

"Why?"

"You can never be sure of anything in orthopaedics. We're all at the mercy of the bone structure we started out with as children and the problems it's been subjected to over the years. Doctors apply their expertise but it's Mother Nature who has the last word."

"Thanks, Cathy. You've been great. Can I go now?"

"Is anybody with you?"

"Not yet. My wife's gone over to Panormitis to see her mother. She won't be back till this evening. I phoned my sons and they're coming as soon as they've finished putting in the shower rooms at the new hotel. I told them I was OK, just a broken wrist or something. I told them not to leave the job until they'd finished. I can't afford to lose the contract I've got with the hotel. I said I'd phone them when I'd been seen by a doctor."

"What actually happened?"

Outside the treatment room she could hear voices and people moving around. She would have to take on some of the work as soon as she'd finished with Mario.

Her patient frowned as he tried to remember the details of the crash. "I was coming down the hill from Chorio in my lorry, having dropped off my boys at the new hotel. Everything was OK until I reached the corner at the bottom of the hill. The bus loaded with passengers was coming along from the harbour at its usual steady pace when a man in a flash sports car behind me, who'd already hooted at me twice, overtook on the bend."

Cathy put her hand over her mouth. "Oh, no! Not on that narrow bend by the water."

"Exactly so! Well, the bus swerved and demolished the side of the house alongside as the driver slammed on his brakes. The sports car went straight into the water, after he'd clipped the side of my cab and thrown me against the dashboard with my arm outstretched."

"So what happened to the sports car driver?"

"Hopefully he's in hospital here. The last thing I saw as they carted me off in the ambulance was a couple of policemen diving into the water, trying to find him. A crane had arrived to fish out the car. The ambulance was having to do several trips, I believe, because of all the stretchers from the bus."

She could feel the hairs on the back of her neck standing up in horror. However many times she had to attend the aftermath of a serious crash she still couldn't keep herself from feeling shocked. No wonder Yannis had been abrupt with her when she'd arrived.

"Are you OK to call your sons and tell them what's happening or shall I do it?"

"I'm OK. It's only my left arm." He was already fishing in his pocket for his mobile.

"Tell them you're going to rest here until they come for you this evening. I'll find you a bed or a quiet corner." She took a peek outside the treatment room. Hopefully! She called a nearby nurse and asked her to see that Mario was taken care of till his sons arrived.

"Come back to Outpatients in a week's time and ask to see me, Mario."

Her patient smiled. "I'll look forward to that, Cathy."

Another patient was wheeled into the treatment room on a stretcher as Mario was taken away in a wheelchair.

CHAPTER FIVE

"You need to take a break, Yannis," Cathy said gently.

They were both in the anteroom of the theatre, Yannis still in his theatre gown, leaning against the sink as he studied the tail end of the list of the RTA patients who still needed to be dealt with.

"At least we haven't had any fatalities," he said, without looking up from the list. "In another couple of hours I reckon we should have everything under control."

"Yannis." She spoke a little louder. "You have two excellent young surgeons in there, part of a team who've just come on duty. Let them take over where we've left off. I'm exhausted."

"Cathy, I'm not suggesting you stay on any longer." He crossed the room and stood looking down at her in concern. "You've been assisting me since midmorning and it's now…" He stared up at the clock. "I hadn't realised it was so late."

"Exactly! I'm not going off duty unless you do. You're exhausted but you won't admit it. You've got to delegate these two final operations to your staff. You need to rest now so that you'll be fit to deal with all our post-operative patients tomorrow."

He stared at her. Nobody had spoken to him like that for a long time. Maroula had always tried to make him take more care of himself. Was it possible that Cathy really cared for him? Just like Maroula had?

"OK. You're probably right," he said quietly. A wry grin spread across his face. "I'll go and do some delegating. And you must go off duty. Will you come along to my office when you're ready to leave the hospital?"

He gave her no time to answer as he disappeared through the swing doors back into Theatre.

She pushed open the door into the corridor and made her way down to the female medical staff changing and shower room.

"I'm ready to go home now." She stood in the doorway of Yannis's office. He was holding open the door, already looking more refreshed than he had done in the theatre anteroom. She noticed his dark hair still wet from the shower, his casual clothes—jeans and a T-shirt. Nobody seeing him now would think he'd been working all day in Theatre, in some cases saving lives.

She'd made the effort to improve her appearance. But it would take more than showering and putting on the clothes that had been stuffed in her locker since she'd donned theatre greens hours earlier to make her feel presentable. Still, she only had to get herself up the *Kali Strata* and home again where she could relax and look as scruffy as she liked.

Thank goodness the storm had abated for the moment. She'd been aware of the rain lashing on the windows, the wind whistling round the hospital while she'd worked. The helicopter ambulance was grounded and no boats were allowed into or out of the harbour, which had meant they hadn't been able to offload the more serious patients and make their workload easier.

He put a hand on her arm. "Quick drink? Down at the

harbour? The rain's stopped now and the wind has died down.
I presume you've been in touch with Anna about looking
after Rose longer than expected?"

"I phoned this afternoon to tell her about the emergency
situation. She'd heard all about it. News travels fast on Ceres.
She was already planning to take care of Rose until tomorrow
morning. Told me to get a good night's rest when I came off
duty. So I'm going to get back home, Yannis. It would be
lovely to collect Rose if she's still awake—"

He put a hand on the small of her back. "Well, you need a
little relaxation first, Doctor, then I'll put you in a taxi and
send you up the hill to your bed."

Yannis was probably right. She did need to unwind first.
It had been an exhausting day.

"OK. But just one drink and then…"

"Yes, yes, I understand, Cathy."

It was good to feel she was being taken care of as he steered
her along the corridor. This was something she hadn't felt with
any of the men in her life. The emphasis they had insisted on had
usually been pleasure, having a good time and, of course, sex.
As long as they had been happy, that had seemed to be all that
mattered to them. Consideration and caring didn't come into it
and she'd got used to thinking that was the norm. Especially after
witnessing the way her father had treated her mother.

As they went out through the side door of the hospital into
the still warm night she was thinking that this caring attitude
was a two-way affair. She'd felt the need to protect Yannis and
make sure he didn't tire himself out. Had she ever cared
enough for any man to worry like that before?

They were walking side by side down to the harbour now.
His hand was hanging loosely by his side and she knew he
wouldn't try to hold hers. Not here in downtown Ceres where

it would be noticed and gossiped about. They were simply good friends and colleagues relaxing after a hard day.

He chose a table right by the waterside. The plastic chairs were still wet from the rain. A young waiter came out with a cloth and wiped the seats.

"Just look at the white caps out there on the top of the waves," Yannis said, pointing out to the rough sea while the waiter dealt with the water on their chairs and table. "The port authorities were predicting on the radio just now that no boats would sail tomorrow. And the helicopter ambulance isn't allowed to fly either, because the wind may soon start again. It's going to be impossible to transfer any of our patients to Rhodes."

"Oh, well, we're coping OK, don't you think, Yannis?"

He smiled down at her. "We've got a good team at the hospital."

She sat down and ran a hand through her hair. It felt such a mess. She hadn't had time to dry it properly after her shower and it was going all curly.

He put a hand across and touched a strand of hair where it fell onto her shoulders.

"Leave your hair casual like it is now. Looking across the operating table when we'd finished this evening, I thought what a pity it was you had to keep your gorgeous hair locked up under your theatre cap all day."

"It doesn't feel very gorgeous now."

"Believe me, it is." He moved his hand up, allowing his fingers to run through the freshly washed, scented hair before leaning back against his chair where he had a perfect view of this wonderful woman who was bringing him to life again.

A waiter arrived at their table so he ordered a bottle of wine and some mezes. He looked across the table to see if Cathy was in agreement.

She hesitated, wondering how long this was going to take. But she realised she was ravenously hungry. "Probably a good idea to eat something. I haven't had anything to eat since breakfast, have you?"

Yannis shook his head. "Never even thought about it. Food and drink is what you need to help you unwind. I can see you're as tense as a coiled spring."

"Is that your diagnosis, Dr Karavolis?"

"Yes, it certainly is!" He signalled the waiter back and gave their order.

They sat without speaking for a while, simply soaking up the after-work atmosphere by the water's edge. Snippets of Greek conversation could be distinctly heard around them.

"Terrible crash!"

"They got the driver of the sports car out of the harbour."

"Well, of course they'll charge him with dangerous driving!"

"Terrible injuries."

"In the hospital, of course."

Yannis leaned across the table. "It seems everybody knows more about what's happening than we do!"

She smiled and leaned closer so that their heads were almost touching. "We merely patch people up."

"*Signomi, ghiatro*. Excuse me, Doctor, but I just wanted to say thank you for taking care of my husband today."

Cathy looked up at the pleasantly plump middle-aged woman who was standing by her chair. By the woman's side was her patient Mario, sporting his new cast, which was already covered in signatures, looking slightly embarrassed that his wife had insisted on approaching the doctor while she was off duty and trying to relax.

"Mario told me how brilliant you were with him this morning. I can't thank you enough. And you, Dr Karavolis, you must have been working all day as well. We're all talking about the crash down here. Must have been terrible for you at the hospital."

"We're trained for that sort of thing," Yannis said quietly. "I'm glad Dr Cathy was able to help Mario."

Cathy could see that Mario was trying to pull his wife away from the two doctors. After the day they must have had the last thing they needed was a patient's relative bothering them.

"See you next week, Dr Cathy," he said cheerily, as he escorted his wife back to their table.

Yannis looked across at Cathy. "Maybe it was a mistake to come and sit outside such a crowded taverna."

"Not at all! It's good to join in sometimes."

"Meaning I usually prefer to spend my off-duty time by myself?"

"Well, I'm sure you weren't always like that. You've had a difficult few years and now it's time to come out of the hard shell you've built around yourself."

She picked up the glass of wine he'd just poured for her and raised it to her lips.

They began to eat from the plates of delicious mezes, olives, feta cheese, Greek salad, taramasalata, whilst chatting companiably to each other.

"I'm feeling a lot stronger now," she said as she put down her fork. "Hadn't realised just how hungry I was."

He reached across the table to take hold of her hand.

"Cathy, I can feel myself coming to life again. You're right. I had built a shell around me. Maybe it is time to move on. But…the trouble is there's always something inside me that holds me back. I feel guilty to be enjoying myself when…"

She waited, knowing he was thinking about Maroula but

didn't want to say it out loud. Somehow he had to realise it was OK to feel as he did. But again she reminded herself it was Yannis's problem, not hers.

She put down her half-finished glass. She was physically exhausted and knew she couldn't deal with emotional problems tonight, her own or Yannis's.

"I'd like to get back home now before it's too late to get a taxi."

"You must be exhausted so that's probably a good idea," he said, standing up and signalling to the waiter. "There's a taxi coming along the quayside now. I'll get it for you."

Lying in her bed later, she looked out through the moonlit casement. Yes, it was going to be difficult to deal with the emotional problems ahead of her. She had to maintain a platonic relationship with Yannis but it was getting harder every time she was with him. But she had a history of giving her heart away too easily. She must keep on reminding herself that she wasn't going to have another meaningful relationship. Otherwise she would fall into the same trap she had with Dave. He'd had a real living wife always in the background.

She hadn't known about it otherwise she wouldn't have entered into a relationship with him. Yannis had put all his cards on the table. She knew the score, knew what she would be letting herself in for if she didn't stick to her resolutions. This time the wife would always be with them as a much-loved memory. Someone it would be difficult to live up to.

Did she want to put herself through all that? Again? Did she have the emotional strength in her? No, she didn't! No, a thousand times, no! Her head was telling her it would all end in tears again. But her heart was whispering it would be fun to have a romance with him. The trouble was she could feel herself falling for him. And it was so difficult to keep to her resolution not to.

But if she went along with her feelings it would be history repeating itself all over again. She should stay resolved that they were good friends only. They enjoyed being together.

A cloud was crossing over the moon. Was that an omen? She closed her eyes so that she couldn't see it. Sleep would come eventually if she tried to stop thinking…

Yannis was standing on the balcony outside his bedroom, looking across the water at the moon above the hillside on the opposite side of the inlet. His thoughts were all about Cathy tonight, not Maroula, he realised. Since he'd moved into this house he'd found himself out here on so many nights in just this position. It was still the same moon that had somehow soothed him as he thought about Maroula. So why was he now thinking about Cathy? Was she beginning to take Maroula's place in his affections?

He gripped the rail that ran round the balcony. He still loved Maroula but he had deep feelings for Cathy. How did she feel about him? How could he find out unless he became closer to her?

He was longing to become closer to Cathy. Tonight as they'd sat beside the water in that crowded area of the harbour he'd longed to take her away, to be alone with her, just the two of them. But could he bear the feelings of guilt at his betrayal?

He had to take things slowly—for both their sakes. He had to make absolutely certain that he could be with another woman whilst at the same time revering Maroula's memory. Cathy was too precious to have him toy with her affections only to decide he couldn't bear the guilt. For the moment he should simply enjoy being with her.

There was a big cloud occluding the moon now. He shivered as he turned to go inside.

A month later, as Cathy walked down the *Kali Strata*, she realised that the shock waves of the disastrous RTA were still being felt on the island. It had been the main topic of conversation everywhere she'd gone and had affected many lives. In the hospital they'd been extremely busy with inpatients and outpatients. But the main effect on her own life had been that she and Yannis had found very little time to relax together in an off-duty situation.

They'd both been working longer hours on duty. Yannis seemed to be taking his position as temporary director very seriously. When they'd seen each other briefly, usually at the end of the day, it had seemed that they were both treating each other warily.

As she reached the harbour-side she increased her pace. Yannis had sent her a text late last night asking her to meet him in his office early this morning.

When she arrived he opened the door and led her inside, suggesting they should sit in the armchairs over by the window. There was a cafetière of coffee and two cups on the small table.

"This all looks very civilised, Yannis. Not the way I usually start my day in hospital."

She sank down into one of the armchairs and allowed him to pour her a cup of coffee.

"So what are we celebrating?"

He smiled as he put down the cafetière. "I wanted to say thank you for all the extra hard work you've done over the past month and to tell you that we're resuming normal working hours from now on."

"Wow! That's good news!" She took a sip of her coffee. "So, what have you done? Sent all the patients home?"

"The majority of the RTA patients have now been discharged. I had to take on extra temporary staff and we've now reached the stage where we've got a good ratio of staff to patients. The patients with limb fractures still attend our orthopaedic clinics. All in all, I feel we've weathered the storm and we're steering in calmer waters now."

She smiled. "Talking of steering in calmer waters, have you been able to spend any time on that boat you were telling me you had? It must be very therapeutic to go out there on the sea."

He stared at her. Had she been reading his mind about the proposition he was about to put to her? But he had to tread carefully, not simply blurt it out.

"I'm afraid I simply haven't had time. It's still tied up to the jetty at the bottom of my garden. Petros checks it over and even goes out fishing on occasions, always bringing me back something for Eleni to cook for my supper."

He hesitated. "Eleni was asking about you the other day. Wondering when you were going to come round again. I told her we'd both been too busy."

She waited, hardly daring to breathe in case she broke the fragile ambience that was developing once more between them. It was true that during the past month they'd both been frantically busy. But on the rare occasions when they'd got together for a drink at the end of the day she'd felt he was decidedly wary with her.

Something seemed to have changed him since the night they'd had a drink down by the harbour and he'd told her he felt he was coming alive again. Perhaps he'd decided he preferred to stay with the past, to continue to worship at the altar of the iconic Maroula. In that case, she'd had a lucky escape that it was all going to end before she'd made a fool of herself-again!

She put down her coffee cup and stood up. "Thanks for the coffee. There's a patient I need to see before—"

"Cathy!" He moved swiftly to detain her. She hadn't given him time to work out what he was going to say even though he'd been thinking about it for days, ever since the workload in hospital had begun to ease off.

"I've made arrangements for us both to take the weekend off. I wondered if you'd like to go out in the boat with me?"

It had all come out in a breathless rush. Now all he had to do was hope she wouldn't come up with an excuse. After the busy month they'd both had he wouldn't blame her.

She stared at him. How could he suggest such a thing? Just when she was beginning to reach a state of contentment in their seemingly platonic relationship! To be thrown together with him in his boat, spending the whole day in close contact? No, she mustn't! She didn't trust herself to stay focused on keeping her distance. If he made any kind of advances towards her… On the other hand, it would be wonderful to get out on the sea…and she could be careful not to get any silly romantic ideas. She'd been cooped up working in hospital for so long…

"Well, I'll have to check with Anna to see if she can look after Rose," she said carefully, playing for time to get her thoughts together.

"Oh, Rose is invited too, of course. I've really missed seeing her. We'd better get her kitted out in a small life jacket which she can wear when we're actually sailing."

Cathy could feel her interest in the idea increasing. If Rose was with them it would be OK, wouldn't it?

"The sea air would be good for Rose," she conceded, carefully. "Yes, I think we would both enjoy it."

"Good! So, as I said, we'll need to get Rose kitted out."

She took a deep breath. She was well and truly committed now. "There's an excellent sea and beach shop that's just opened at the end of the harbour. I bought some armbands for Rose in there and I've been taking her down to Pedi beach whenever I've had a couple of hours off duty during the day. She simply loves the water. As long as I'm by her side I know she's safe."

"So you'll take the armbands with you, won't you?"

"Of course!"

"How do you think Rose would be if we were to drop anchor in some quiet little bay on the Saturday night and she could sleep on the boat?"

Heavens! Once more she stared at him as she tried to sort out her confused feelings. On the one hand she found herself longing to say yes. The thought of a whole weekend! With her track record, did she dare?

"Give yourself time to think it over," he said amiably as he watched her, realising she was having deep reservations about this. Do you have a portable cot we could take with us for Rose? If not, we could buy one when we get her life jacket."

"Yes, I have a travel cot."

She looked up at him suddenly realising it had taken him a great deal of courage to ask her and Rose out for a whole weekend. They were after all just good friends. She shouldn't misinterpret the situation. It was a kindly, friendly gesture and he would be disappointed if she turned the idea down.

She told herself to stop taking the idea so seriously. Yannis wasn't the sort of man to take advantage of her. Not unless she made it clear she wanted him to—which she was determined not to do!

She smiled and began speaking quickly and enthusiastically before she could change her mind. "Yes, I think Rose would really enjoy a weekend on the boat. The cot doubles as a play pen if we want to let her play on deck without having to hold her all the time and…" She paused to draw breath. "And I think I'm going to enjoy it as well!"

He put out his arms and drew her against him. "And I think I love your enthusiasm for life. It's sort of…infectious."

She could feel herself revelling in the feeling of his muscular body against hers. So much for trying to stay cool! She really should pull herself away. There was nothing platonic about the way he was holding her.

She looked up at him, still feeling, oh, so comfortable in his embrace, not even daring to move in case she broke the magic spell that seemed to be binding them together. His eyes were shining with excitement. She'd never seen him so fired up.

He bent his head and kissed her, gently at first and then with more urgency as if he couldn't get enough of her. She could feel him moving his body closer to hers so that they fitted exactly together.

Someone was knocking on the door.

She tried to break away but he held her tighter for a moment before reluctantly loosening the circle of his arms.

"Dr Karavolis?"

"Yes. I'm coming!"

The door opened. As the newest doctor to have joined the hospital walked in, all he saw was a couple of senior doctors looking less than welcoming at his interruption.

"I'm sorry to interrupt you, sir," he said nervously. "You asked me to come and see you this morning. I didn't know…"

"That's OK, Stamatis. Dr Cathy is just leaving."

Dr Cathy was definitely leaving! Feeling hot and flustered, Cathy tried to stay calm until she was outside the door. It was a long time since she'd actually blushed! But it did make her feel very young again. Almost a teenager.

As she walked down the corridor she was thinking she would have to get her reactions to Yannis under control if she was to spend a whole weekend on the boat with him. And she would most certainly have to strengthen her resolve!

Yannis ran a hand through his hair as he sat down behind his desk, desperately trying to look as if he was in charge of the situation.

"Do sit down, Stamatis."

He motioned to the chair at the other side of the desk.

"I've brought the papers you asked for, Dr Karavolis."

"Please, call me Yannis. We're working together now as colleagues. I've been impressed with the work you've done in the four weeks you've been here. Especially yesterday evening when you took over that orthopaedic operation. I've seen the patient this morning and the post-operative X-rays show you made an excellent job of plating his tibia."

"Thank you…er…Yannis. I'm very interested in orthopaedic surgery and since I qualified I've spent a great deal of time working in orthopaedics."

Yannis glanced down at the personal papers Stamatis had brought him. He'd seen the duplicates when he'd first arrived but he liked to check the originals of all new staff and simply hadn't had the time during the past weeks.

"Yes, we were both trained at the same medical school in Athens," Yannis said, smiling as he looked up at the eager young doctor. "So what made you want to come to work at a hospital on Ceres when you were in line for a good career in Athens?"

"I had already applied to come here when we were alerted to the fact that you needed extra staff. Now that I've been taken on sooner than I'd hoped for, I would very much like to stay on here. You see, I have family connections here. My father died a few months ago and I feel it my duty to take care of my mother. I'm her only son."

"So were you born here?"

"Yes."

"So was I. I think coming back to your roots can be very healing when you've suffered a bereavement. It helps to put life in perspective. You've probably had to sacrifice some of your ambitious ideas but there's certainly a place for you here, Stamatis."

The young man swallowed hard. "You mean you'll give me a contract?"

"I'll certainly recommend you to the board of governors. Your contract should go through as a matter of course."

Yannis stood up and came round the desk, holding out his hand. "Welcome to the team, Stamatis."

"Thank you, Yannis. Thank you very much for all the help you've given me."

Yannis sat silently at his desk after the young doctor left him alone again. Only twenty-eight years old but full of promise. Just as he'd been ten years ago. No girlfriend apparently. He'd soon find someone here on the island. He didn't seem to have any hang-ups in that direction.

Whereas he was starting out on a romantic journey with so many memories from the past to contend with. How would he deal with romance and guilt at the same time? And how could he make sure he didn't hurt Cathy while he was getting himself sorted out?

She'd become very precious to him. Cathy—and little Rose. A mother and a daughter all on their own. And he was a man without a wife. It could be the most perfect combination if only he could find out how to let go of the past and move on.

CHAPTER SIX

By the time they were leaving the jetty in front of Yannis's house Rose had become decidedly fractious. Having been taken down to the shop in the harbour during the morning and slotted into a variety of life jackets, none of which had proved to be ideal for such a small child, she was now in a non-cooperative mood.

"She's tired," Cathy said, as Rose's wailing continued, even though she was being rocked gently in her mother's arms.

"Rose will be fine when we get out on the water and we can let her loose in her play pen," Yannis said confidently, turning round from the wheel to view his two guests huddled at the back of the boat.

He was thinking that he was glad that he'd chosen to buy a motor boat instead of a larger vessel that would have been reliant on sails and the need for an experienced crew. This boat was very easy to manage so he'd be able to concentrate on keeping his inexperienced crew happy. Once they got out of the narrow part of the inlet.

A large ferry was coming across from Rhodes, making its way into Ceres harbour. He slowed so as not to get too near. Even so, he caught the full blast of the wash several seconds later as the waves rippled towards him. He turned into the waves and rode through them. It was a choppy ride!

"Whoops! Nothing I could do about that, Cathy. Is Rose OK?"

"She's nearly asleep. We had an early start today and then that long session in the shop was very tiring. I did take her in a couple of days ago and the man promised to get some smaller sizes in for me. But apparently they didn't have them in stock over in Rhodes."

"Don't worry, I've made sure she's secured into the one we bought. There should be a smaller one in the next delivery and we can get that one."

Cathy moved further into the cabin, cradling the now sleeping Rose in her arms. Yannis had one hand on the wheel and was turning round to talk to her. They were out on a wider stretch of water now, though still hugging the coastline. Rose, having made such a fuss at being made to wear the wretched jacket, had now fallen into a deep sleep, snuffling through her crocodile tears.

Cathy had been impressed with the way Yannis had taken charge of everything when they'd been in the shop. The shop assistant had been profusely apologetic that the expected supplies hadn't turned up. His boss had made a special urgent order. "No, sorry, sir, he's not here at the moment... Yes, I'll tell him you're not pleased about that, sir... Of course... If there's anything else I can help you with..."

They'd come out of the shop with the jacket and several toys that Yannis had insisted on buying for Rose. "To keep her happy in the play pen." He'd taken care of payment and had brushed aside Cathy's efforts to make a contribution. Yannis seemed to be the only person in the shop enjoying himself.

She'd been so looking forward to this weekend that she

realised maybe she'd expected everything to run smoothly. Now that Rose was quiet again, she could begin to relax. And worry!

Worry that she'd brought the wrong clothes for both of them. Too many obviously. She always packed too much, especially when she was nervous of the occasion. But would it matter out here?

She moved to the stern of the boat so that she was just outside the cabin, still holding Rose tightly in her arms. Leaning back, she turned her face up towards the sun. Carefully she allowed one arm to dip over the side of the boat towards the spray that was coming up from the sea as they sped across the water.

Mmm, this was the life! But she'd glimpsed the tiny cabin as Yannis had been stowing their bags away. Hmm, not much room in there! There was a tiny alcove at the end of the cabin where Yannis had said he would erect Rose's cot and he'd explained that the two bunks at either side of the cabin opened out into a full-size double bed.

She'd felt he'd been testing her out when he'd said that. She knew he'd been watching her reaction but she hadn't made any comment or even dared to look at him. Yes, they were both nervous! She would deal with the situation later, keeping her head, not listening to her heart, remembering the past.

"Are you two OK out there, Cathy?"

"I'm fine! Rose is completely out for the count. And how about you?"

"Excellent! We'll be stopping for lunch soon."

The sea was now completely calm again. She watched as Yannis steered the boat into a small bay with steep hillsides falling down into the deep water. No one in sight. Bliss!

"I feel we're playing Robinson Crusoe," she said as Yannis cut the engine so that they could glide alongside the small stone jetty. "I remember coming here with my mother when I was younger. There's a small deserted chapel up on the side of the hill, as I recall. There was a sheep that had got locked inside it by mistake and Mum persuaded it to come outside and drink some water."

"Childhood memories are so precious. Here, let me take Rose while you get yourself ashore. Do you want to change on board for swimming first?"

She handed over the sleeping Rose and slipped into the cabin, searching out her bag and struggling into the new bikini she'd bought as soon as she'd agreed to this weekend. Black and white, couldn't go wrong with that. At least the marine shop had come up trumps in that respect.

By the time she got to the shore, Yannis was sitting on the sand, talking quietly to her daughter who was staring up at him in half-awake fascination with this man she'd begun to like enormously.

"Yaya," she said, stroking her fingers through his hair.

"She's trying so hard to say Yannis," Cathy said, spreading a couple of towels on the beach as she joined them. "Yaya is her approximation."

"It's a difficult name to say for one so young. It's the Y sound at the beginning that gets her. Wow!" He was looking at her new bikini now, admiration gleaming in his eyes. "I like that! But I like the look of who's wearing it even better."

How long had it been since he'd paid a compliment to a woman? she wondered as she felt a glow of pleasure spreading over her.

"Are you going to swim in your new bikini or is it too precious?"

"Of course I'm going to swim in it." She stood up. "I'll put Rose's armbands on and she can come in with me."

"She's only just waking up. Why not let her come round slowly? We'll have a nice little chat while you swim. And I can admire you from here, looking like a sea nymph."

She laughed. "You've got a good imagination. OK, if you're happy holding Rose…"

It was an offer she couldn't refuse, she thought as she ran to the outcrop of rocks at the corner of the bay. She remembered it so well from the times she'd been here as a child. Her mother had taught her to dive here.

"It's quite safe from here, Cathy," she'd told her as she'd explained how to put her arms in the correct diving shape above her head. "Now, bend forward and I'll tip you in when you're ready… There we go!"

As she stood on the rock and looked down into the deep water she could hear her mother's voice again, urging her on and then gently tipping her over.

She dived now, down, down into the cold depths, so refreshing, so energising. She rose to the surface and lay on her back, looking up at the blue sky, with not a cloud in sight. Turning towards the shore, she could see two pairs of eyes glued on her.

Yannis waved. "Spectacular display! Are you training for the Olympics?"

"Of course! Come on in, the pair of you. It's wonderful! Rose's armbands are in my bag there beside you."

Soon Yannis was swimming out on his back with the armbanded Rose on his chest. Cathy swam to meet them.

"Mama!"

Rose could hardly contain her excitement at meeting her mother in the sea like this.

They had a picnic lunch when they were all back on the shore. Cathy had been to the bakery on the corner of the Ceres harbour by the bridge and bought spanakopita, spinach pies and teropita, cheese pies. Yannis had bought far too many tomatoes at the fruit and veg shop.

"Just in case we get marooned out there for the summer," he'd told Cathy.

And, of course, Cathy had got too many freshly baked bread rolls simply because she loved the smell and had got carried away.

They were huddled together on two towels, eating as if they were starving. Rose had discovered the delights of a ripe misshapen Mediterranean tomato and was enjoying the feeling of the juice dribbling down from her mouth to her chin. She tried without success to bend her tongue down to catch some of the delicious dribble but it escaped down onto her bare chest.

Reaching down, she rubbed it over her skin and smiled as she admired the lovely red colour her chest now had.

She was now babbling happily.

Yannis went down to the sea and lifted the bottle of wine from the pool he was using as a wine cooler. Touching the bottle against the side of his face, he nodded.

"That's better. Anyone for a glass of wine?"

Cathy held out her empty glass. "Yes, please."

He sank down beside her, his sandy body close against hers. "I thought I would cook supper this evening when the sun's gone down."

"You're going to cook?"

"Well, of course I'm going to cook! I'm not just the captain of this ship, you know. I have to double as ship's cook."

"And what am I?"

A wicked grin was hovering on his lips as he leaned forward, kissing her gently on the side of the cheek.

"You, my dear, are the cabaret, brought on board for the captain's pleasure."

"Oh, sir! You'll have to tell me what your pleasure is," Cathy teased him back, trying to keep the mood light.

"I haven't decided yet."

"Mama, mama!" Rose demanded more attention and insisted on putting herself between them.

"I know the role you can play tonight," Yannis whispered to Cathy over the top of Rose's head. "You can be chief nurse-maid and rock the baby to sleep while the cook prepares the food for the captain's table. Then when the baby is sleeping the captain and the cabaret can have the rest of the evening to themselves."

"Sounds good to me. You're on!"

They spent the rest of the day in and out of the water. Rose was beside herself with happiness, having the full attention of her mother and this wonderful man who'd come into their lives, making it so much more interesting.

They all watched the sunset together, Cathy holding small sunglasses over Rose's eyes.

"Rose doesn't really need these," she whispered to Yannis. "Her eyes are already closed."

"I noticed that myself," Yannis said as he snuggled close to the pair of them, his arm surrounding their tight little huddle at the edge of the shore.

The sun was dipping low in the sky, making wide swathes of crimson and gold over the smooth surface of the sea. It seemed to pause for a short time as if contemplating its dive into the deep water, elongating its lower side until it resembled a golden aubergine, before taking the final plunge.

"It's gone!" Cathy breathed, as awestruck as she had

always been when she'd witnessed the uncanny sunset ritual. "As a child I couldn't understand how the sun could go down in one place and come up the next morning in another. However many times my mother explained to me about the earth being round, I still preferred to imagine it sitting at the bottom of the sea, deciding where and when it would emerge and spread its fantastic light again."

He drew her towards him. "Oh, Cathy, don't ever change. I hope you'll always keep your charm. I've become immune to the simple happiness that occurs every day if you look for it. I'm still hoping it will come back again when…when I'm able to forget."

She turned her face upwards towards him and saw the anguish that had reappeared in his eyes as unpleasant memories flooded back. Even after the wonderful day they'd enjoyed together the pain of bereavement was still just under the surface, waiting to erupt and spoil the moment for him.

A cool breeze blew across the shore. His arm tightened around them. He would so like to imagine that this was his family. This beautiful woman who'd come into his life and made such a difference already…and who knew what a great difference she would make in the future? And this gorgeous, magical child who'd arrived with no input from himself, but already he felt as if she was a part of him.

"Let's go on board," he said gently. "You go ahead and start putting Rose to bed. I've erected the cot in the alcove off our cabin. I'll gather up our things from the beach and bring them on board."

She was singing an age-old lullaby as he pulled up the steps that led from the boat down onto the jetty. It was an English song he remembered his mother teaching him when he was a child. The words had sounded foreign when he was small but he'd loved the tune. He hummed along to it now, very quietly because he was sure that Rose would already be asleep and Cathy was simply making sure.

"Rock-a-bye baby on the tree top…"

She smiled up at him as he stood in the doorway of the cabin, putting a finger to her lips so that he wouldn't speak.

He sank down on the bed he'd prepared using the two bunk beds, watching his new miracle family. Their eyes met and locked in a contented gaze, each thinking how they were experiencing one of the rare moments of pure magic that sometimes occurred in life.

Rose's breathing had settled at last into the slow, peaceful sleep of childhood.

"She's off," Cathy said quietly, standing up. He reached out and drew her down beside him.

For a few seconds they both remained still, simply looking into each other's eyes.

Cathy broke the precious silence. "You know, I was thinking just now how wonderful it is to be spending a Saturday evening in such an idyllic situation. Remembering all the times I used to make such an effort to be busy-busy, going out to noisy places, loud music, chattering people…and here we are, nothing but the murmur of the waves lapping against the side of the boat."

She sighed as she lay back in his arms. She knew she was giving in to temptation but her treacherous body was trying to overcome her resistance. Mmm, it had been a long time since…

"Everything depends on who you're with," he said quietly, nuzzling his lips against her hair. "That's nice! Don't wash your hair when you're in the shower. I love the smell of the sea water."

She laughed. "And the jam from Rose's sticky fingers as she ate her supper."

"And you, just you, that wonderful certain, indefinable aura that follows you everywhere."

"Ever thought of becoming a poet?"

He grinned. "Ah, but I couldn't be a poet unless I had a beautiful woman in my arms to write about."

"I don't know about beautiful. I feel in desperate need of a shower. Would you show me how to work that weird and wonderful shower in that tiny wet cubicle?"

"I'll give you a personal demonstration…soon…when you really need it…when…"

He was punctuating his words with kisses. Lingering on the final kiss as he savoured the taste of her salty lips and lost himself entirely in the sensual waves that were coursing through his body. He could feel her reciprocating, moving her wonderful, sexy, delicious body into the momentum that had started up between them.

He knew beyond a shadow of a doubt that there was no going back now. He could no longer contain his desperate longing for her, no longer think about the consequences of his love-making. His heart was telling him that this was, oh, so right for both of them…

She lay back against the rumpled sheets and looked up at the wooden roof of the cabin. Her body felt totally different somehow. Sort of liquid, languid, completely boneless. Just a mass of sensual nerves, heightened and tuned to perfection. Their love-making had been so heavenly, so completely abandoned, totally spur of the moment yet indefinably out of this world.

She sighed with contentment. "I feel utterly ravished!"

He laughed. "Is that good or bad?"

"Mmm, good, I think." She turned on her side to look at him. "What about you?"

"On a scale of one to ten?"

"Yes."

"Eleven."

She grinned. "Me too."

As he held her close in his arms she realised that she was keeping up her light-hearted banter to make sure he didn't start thinking serious thoughts about whether it was right or not. This was a milestone in their relationship. Making love together in a light-hearted way, each giving themselves and holding nothing back. But she didn't want him to read anything too deep into it. Didn't want him to feel the slightest bit guilty.

"About that shower," she said, moving out the circle of his arms. "I definitely need one now."

"Me too!" He put out his hand to help her off the bed and into the tiny cubicle. "It's going to be a squeeze but you'll never be able to cope without my help."

"Oh, I think I could manage by myself." She was now flattened against the side of the shower, unable to move because Yannis's chest was hard against her.

"Spoilsport! Of course you couldn't shower by yourself." He turned on the tap and water was pumped up from the tank with a loud gurgling sound. "Stop wriggling so I can soap your back and make you think I'm totally indispensable in this operation."

She began giggling uncontrollably. "Don't! You're tickling me, you're…"

He silenced her with a long hard kiss as the water coursed over them both and their bodies became totally entwined again…

* * *

Afterwards, enveloped in large fluffy towels, they lay back on the bed, fingers locked together, breathing rhythmically as they both closed their eyes, thinking their separate thoughts about what had just happened.

Cathy was the first to speak. She was anxious to keep up the momentum of their light-hearted togetherness.

"I'm feeling ravenously hungry. Are you still going to cook me supper, Captain?"

"Of course. So long as you'll provide the cabaret."

"That was the cabaret."

"In that case, I'd like some more." He was already gathering her up into his arms again.

"Later," she told him in a playful tone.

He flung a dry towel round his waist and stepped out into the galley. "Don't want to burn my vital organs while I'm cooking."

"Absolutely not!"

She dug deep into the bag she'd brought with her and found a flimsy sarong. Winding it round her body, she secured it so it wouldn't fall down—unless someone pulled it away, which was a definite possibility!

There was no mirror in the cabin. Pointless to try and see in her small hand make-up mirror. She'd no idea how she looked but decided that Yannis seemed to like the natural look. Damp hair, no make-up, salty lips. He'd told her he found that very sexy. Maybe she should have another dip in the sea. But that would mean another shower and who knew where that would lead to?

He turned from the stove as she walked barefoot from the cabin to the galley, three steps in total.

"Hope I'm not late."

"Perfect timing. You look stunning!" He leaned across and kissed the side of her cheek. "I hope you like Chinese food."

She perched on the stool beside the stove. "Chinese food cooked by a Greek doctor while we're marooned in a deserted moonlit bay. Absolutely perfect! Where did you learn to cook Chinese food?"

He tossed some narrow strips of beef into the pan and began stir-frying them with the vegetables already in there.

"Would you pass me that soy sauce by the sink there…? Thanks. My father taught me. He was a sailor before I was born and from the stories he told me he'd been everywhere in the world many times over. He was much older than my mother and family life came to him after many years of travels. So he was a fantastic storyteller and a fantastic cook."

"You told me your mother was a widow when she died. How old were you when your father…?"

"I was twelve. My mother and I were heartbroken but I had to be the strong one. The man of the house from then on. When I got my place at medical school in Athens she closed up the house and came with me, living in a rented flat. After a couple of years she said she was missing Ceres. She didn't like the hustle and bustle of Athens. So I helped her to return and open up the house again. I arranged for her to have a housekeeper to take care of her and I came over to see her as often as I could."

He put down his spatula on the wooden chopping board. "It's ready now. If you sit across the table I'll keep this place nearer the stove."

He poured some wine into their glasses. "Are you OK with chopsticks?"

"Of course! I love Chinese food and it always tastes better with chopsticks. This is absolutely delicious! If you get bored with being a doctor you could always open a restaurant."

He gave her a sexy grin. "Only if you'll do the cabaret."

"Ah, but that's by special arrangement."

She looked across the table at this gorgeous hunk of manhood and felt a sensual stirring deep down inside. His hairy chest, the towel loosely slung around his waist made him look so very desirable.

She just knew there was going to be the most fantastic climax at the end of this evening. It was inevitable. The two of them together in that tiny cabin. Couldn't she allow herself to have just one night of fantasy?

She'd checked on Rose before she'd come into the galley. Her daughter was blissfully asleep and likely to stay that way after the tiring day she'd experienced. So it would be just the two of them all night long.

Suddenly she felt nervous. She took a deep breath as she told herself to keep it light, go with the flow. Yes, she was playing with fire but it was all part of the fantasy.

"Yannis, you've got a bean sprout sticking to your chest."

He laughed as he glanced down and deftly picked it up with his chopsticks. "Good thing I hadn't changed into my dress shirt."

"It would have looked out of place with that towel you're wearing. I love the colour of it."

"Sort of greyish white. Yes, I chose it most carefully."

He sighed contentedly. This was an evening he was going to remember for a long time. It was good to find he was enjoying life to the full again. What a difference Cathy was making to his life. And little Rose, taking the place of…no, not taking the place of his little son but definitely helping the healing process.

He poured more wine, leaning back against the cooker to get a better view of the beautiful woman across the table. This had been the most relaxed meal he'd eaten since he'd been with Maroula. In some ways Cathy was like Maroula, in other ways she was completely different. But in the most important way she filled that awful void that had been with him since Maroula's death.

The candle on the table was flickering. He knew he ought to get up and change it before it went out but he didn't want to break the peaceful ambience that existed between them. The way she was sitting, completely quiet and relaxed, content just to be with him.

She was exactly like Maroula had been on the night when she'd told him he was going to be a father. They'd been sitting in their little kitchen and he'd cooked a stir-fry because she loved Chinese food.

He leaned forward now, reaching towards the beautiful slim hand on the table. "Mar…" He stopped himself, realising he'd just made an unforgivable mistake.

He'd been speaking his wife's name softly. For one brief moment in time he'd thought that Cathy was Maroula. Maybe she hadn't heard him? He swallowed hard as he gazed at her. Had she heard?

Cathy's eyes flickered as she allowed her hand to stay in his grasp. Should she comment on his slip of the tongue? Was that all it was, a slip of the tongue? Or was Yannis wishing that she was Maroula, that he could turn the clock back? When they made love had he been pretending that…?

She stood up quickly, unable to pursue that awful line of thought. "I'll just check on Rose," she said quietly.

He watched her bending her head to go down into the cabin, heard the swish of her sarong as she passed along the side of the bed where they'd made love. Had he blown it with Cathy?

He stood up and snuffed out the end of the candle, reaching

up to the locker above the sink to find a fresh one. He would have it burning brightly by the time Cathy returned.

She seemed to be taking a long time.

Cathy leaned over the side of Rose's cot and tucked the sheet over the baby's plump arm.

"Night-night, my precious," she whispered. "I'll always have you, whatever happens to me."

She gripped the side of the cot.

It was all just too close to home for her. She'd been here before. Dave had called out his wife's name in the night on two occasions. As he'd lain dreaming beside her, she'd distinctly hear him say "Maggie". And she remembered how devastated, how jealous she'd been, even though at that time the lying, cheating Dave had told her his wife had left him.

When Yannis had begun to say Maroula's name she'd had exactly the same reaction. That meant her feelings for Yannis were becoming too strong. She'd vowed not to lose her heart to any man ever again after the way she'd been treated in the past. She was too trusting! Yannis probably just saw her as a diversion to his ordinary life. Ultimately that's all she'd been to Dave.

She should have learned by now that all men would disappoint her in time. Even her own father. So she'd got to be careful not to let Rose get too attached to Yannis. Men came into your lives and left when it suited them. Once again she vowed that she wouldn't put Rose through what she'd been through in her childhood.

No, it was time to rethink their situation and go back to their platonic relationship. Business as usual when they were in hospital working together.

She walked back through the cabin and saw him sitting dejectedly, staring at the new candle.

His face lit up as she stood in the doorway. "Is Rose OK?"

"She's fine. I think she'll sleep all night. She was completely whacked out when I put her down."

"It's all that fresh sea air."

"Yes, I feel tired myself now, so I think I'll turn in, just in case I do have to get up in the night to see to Rose. Goodnight, Yannis."

"Goodnight, Cathy."

He half rose to reach out for her, but she had hurried back into the cabin.

He sank back on his chair and stared into the candlelight.

CHAPTER SEVEN

As she sat waiting for the next patient to arrive, Cathy had a few moments to reflect on the situation between herself and Yannis. Three weeks had passed since they'd spent that weekend on the boat together.

It had been idyllic until the whole atmosphere had changed at suppertime in the tiny galley. She'd finally come to her senses and stopped the role play that had allowed her to be so provocative. She knew she'd gone over the line she'd drawn for herself and was in danger of history repeating itself. When she'd heard Yannis beginning to say his wife's name she'd known she'd been a fool—again!

She remembered how she'd lain awake, feigning sleep when Yannis had finally come to bed. Before he'd arrived she'd heard him going out on the deck, probably staying there until he felt it was safe to come into the cabin.

And when Rose had woken up crying in the middle of the night she'd known that Yannis had almost been relieved that they could focus all their attention on the distraught child. Cathy had checked her daughter's temperature. They'd both agreed it was slightly raised and that they would head back to Ceres harbour in the morning.

Cathy had suspected that the heat of the cabin and the unfamililiarity of the surroundings were causing this slight discomfort to her daughter. And she'd guessed that Yannis had also come to the same conclusion and had been glad of the excuse to get back to the normality of his bachelor freedom.

"*Kali mera*, Cathy."

She smiled as her next patient was wheeled into her small office.

"*Kali mera*, Ariadne. So, how've you been since I last saw you?"

She took Ariadne's notes from the nurse who'd wheeled her in. She knew already from her perusal of the state of Ariadne's health on the computer that there was a further problem with this mother of three. She had symphysis pubis caused by the loosening of the ligaments which held the pubic bones in their correct position.

"I've had a lot of pain, Cathy."

Cathy watched her patient as she clutched the sides of her wheelchair. She didn't look at all well. She glanced at the results of the ultrasound scan she'd had that morning, which had taken longer than expected and was the reason she'd had some time to herself just now.

Cathy took a deep breath as she read the scribbled notes Yannis had put at the bottom of the page. Apparently, he'd been called to look at Ariadne's scan and was on his way to discuss the best course of action.

"Under the circumstances it would be unwise to allow the pregnancy to continue," he'd written.

What did he mean? Was he contemplating….?

"Yannis!" She looked up from the notes as he arrived.

"I was in Theatre when I got called down here to Ariadne's ultrasound. I've got to go back but I thought we should discuss this."

He smiled at their patient. "How's the pain now, Ariadne? Any better since I gave you the painkiller?"

Ariadne shook her head. "I don't know how much more I can take, Yannis. Some days I can't move without my whole body going into spasm. Are my twins OK in there? They're not being harmed, are they?"

"No, they're perfectly safe inside your womb, Ariadne. But all things considered, I think it best we get them out as soon as possible."

The patient's eyes widened. "You mean…?"

"You're thirty-six weeks pregnant, almost full term. The twins are definitely viable if we deliver them today."

"Today?" Ariadne's face registered her relief that the end of the ordeal was in sight.

"In fact, this morning." Yannis looked across at Cathy. "I've arranged for Stamatis, who was assisting me in Theatre, to finish off the suturing. I'll get someone to finish your list here so that you can come with me to the obstetrics department and assist me there. Is that OK with you?"

"Of course."

They'd discussed Ariadne's case several times during the last few weeks and both had already agreed that if there were any complications they would operate immediately. And Yannis had remembered that Cathy had particularly requested she be involved in the birth if possible.

Ariadne raised a feeble hand in the air and touched Yannis's arm. "Will it be painful, Yannis?"

"I'll give you a Caesarean section under general an-aesthetic. It will be much less painful than trying to get you in position to administer an epidural, the surgery will be really quick and I promise you won't feel a thing."

"Will you get somebody to call my husband? He's had to

go off to Rhodes today on business. He's told me all the way through this pregnancy he would try to be at the birth if I went into labour early. But, to be honest, I think he'll be relieved to miss this. He's been with me for the first three and found them pretty harrowing. He fainted for our first, had to leave the room for the next two, so…"

Cathy smiled. "So we'll just get on without him, shall we? I'll give him a call now to let him know what's going on."

They stood either side of the operating table in the obstetrics department. With a gloved hand, she handed Yannis a scalpel and watched as he made an incision across Ariadne's abdomen. As he skilfully cut through the abdominal muscles she was almost holding her breath. It was strange how some patients came to mean such a lot to you. She'd bonded with this plucky mother of three, soon to be mother of five—hopefully.

Yannis's hands were now inside the womb, carefully lifting out the first blood-covered baby. Cathy leaned over to take it from him as Theatre Sister stepped forward to take delivery of the second.

Cathy's baby was the first to utter the desired squawk that signified life. The cord was cut. She handed the baby to the midwife standing beside her.

"A boy and a girl this time," Yannis said, smiling across at Cathy. "Ariadne didn't want to know what they were. She said as long as they were fit and healthy she didn't care. She's already got a boy and two girls so she'll be happy with these little ones."

"Not so little either," Cathy said. "Both a good size for thirty-six weeks. Ariadne will be glad to be relieved of the weight. This should ease the strain on the ligaments and help the pubic bones to get back to their correct position."

Cathy looked down at Ariadne who was still anaesthetised, completely unaware that the operation had been a success. Lucky woman, five children and a loving husband!

Yannis looked across at Cathy. "It's time you were going off duty, Cathy. I scheduled you for a free afternoon. I'm almost finished here and the theatre staff will assist me."

"Thanks. I'm looking forward to spending it with Rose."

"That's what I thought." He bent his head and continued suturing.

She went into the anteroom and peeled off her gloves, staring into the mirror above the sink as she washed her hands. The face in the mirror looked strained. Yes, she definitely needed to spend more time with Rose.

She flung her gown into the bin and set off across the room towards the corridor door. The door from Theatre opened and Yannis came through. She turned in surprise.

"Finished already?"

He gave her a wry grin. "Yes. When I dismissed you just now I didn't say I'd given myself the same afternoon off duty."

Her heartbeat accelerated. "Why?" Oh what a stupid thing to say! "I mean, won't you be required to...?"

"Everything's under control here. The postnatal team is taking over. We'll be back early this evening to check on Ariadne and her new twins when she's fully awake again. Well, at least I will. I haven't checked on what your plans for the afternoon are. I scheduled you to take the outpatient clinic that starts at six so you may wish to come back later than me."

"Well, I was simply going to play with Rose and give her some quality time."

"Could I share in the quality time with you? I've hardly seen the pair of you since that unfortunate flick of temperature Rose had on the boat meant we had to come back early.

Would you like to come out to the house? Eleni will rustle up some lunch for the three of us."

Cathy swallowed hard and reviewed the situation. Having ignored her for three weeks, why was he suddenly inviting her for lunch? This was exactly how Dave had been, except he would disappear completely for a few weeks and then reappear with flowers and chocolates, trying to woo her back again. Well, she wasn't going to be wooed back by the offer of lunch. She'd renewed her vow to stick with their platonic relationship, hadn't she?

As he watched her he could see there was some kind of conflict going on. "Cathy, it's only lunch I'm suggesting. And I'd love to see Rose again. I haven't seen her for ages and we had such a marvellous time swimming in the sea together. What's the problem?"

If he only knew! Did she dare allow Rose to start bonding again with Yannis? A small voice inside her head was now saying it would do her daughter such a lot of good to spend the afternoon with both of them. After all, she was only speculating that Yannis was the same as all the other men who'd passed through her life, wasn't she? She could be wrong about him, couldn't she?

She took a deep breath. "Yes, that would be most enjoyable, Yannis," she said politely.

He smiled with relief. "Good! I've got the car in the car park so we'll go up to Chorio and pick up Rose."

Eleni was delighted to see her again, asking her where she'd been, fussing over Rose, carrying her on one hip while she finished setting the table in the garden room overlooking the shore.

"No, you sit still, Cathy," Eleni insisted as she gave Rose

another biscuit to suck and scatter crumbs around. "You've been working in hospital all morning and I've enjoyed my morning out here.

"I've cooked your favourite vegetable soup, Yannis, as you asked me to. Enough for the two of you. I remember you told me this morning. But I've made enough for Rose just in case she came along as well. I'll put it through the blender and cool it for her. Maybe it would be better if I fed her in the kitchen. It's too hot out here."

"I find it nice and shady under the trees," Cathy said. "And there's a nice breeze from the water.

Yannis was giving her a meaningful look, indicating she leave the decision to Eleni. As soon as they were alone he explained that Eleni liked nothing better than to have sole charge of a baby.

"Eleni rarely gets her chance to have a small baby to herself. Even her grandchildren are growing up too quickly for her. She'll spoil Rose rotten but that's no bad thing. I don't think you can give too much love to children. As long as they feel secure, that's one of the most important things in life."

She leaned against the cushions in the high-backed wicker chair and looked out across the water to the steep hill at the other side of the inlet. It had only been a few weeks since she'd spent the night here but it seemed like a lifetime ago. She had to admit she'd hoped she would be invited back here. But she'd had no idea how complicated it was going to be.

"This is such a lovely garden room," she said, looking around her at the low fence separating this area from the rest of the garden. "You've even got a fridge for the drinks over there."

She took a sip of her fresh lime soda.

"I don't use it often enough. It's a lunchtime sort of place. More ice in your drink?"

He returned from the fridge with a bowl of ice cubes just

as Eleni came out from the kitchen carrying a tureen of soup. She set it down on the table together with some home-baked bread rolls.

"Don't worry about Rose. Petros is taking care of her."

"Thank you, Eleni."

Yannis dipped the soup ladle into the tureen and gave Cathy a generous portion.

"That's far too much!"

"You haven't tasted it yet."

"Mmm! You're right. It's delicious. I can taste courgettes, peppers, carrots, beans and wonderful herbs."

"All from the garden." He looked across the table. He'd been so nervous of setting up this lunch meeting but so far so good.

The ironic thing was that after that weekend together he'd realised that his affections were now totally centred on Cathy. That awful moment when he'd started to call her Maroula had given him just the momentum he'd needed to realise exactly what was now important to him. But Cathy's whole attitude towards him had changed after that.

He hadn't known how to treat her when they'd met in hospital. He'd been polite and professional but he hadn't dared to show any kind of warmth towards her. She'd seemed so cool and withdrawn. He'd even felt nervous of asking her to assist him this morning.

Cathy put down her spoon on the empty soup plate and looked across the table. Yannis was staring at her in such a serious way she was sure he was going to tell her some bad news.

"Is something wrong, Yannis?"

"Wrong? No, quite the reverse. I was just thinking… how…how wonderful it is to have you and Rose here today. I've missed you…both of you."

He reached across the table and took hold of her hand.

"Cathy. Thank you for being so understanding. You've helped me so much to come to terms with my bereavement. I never thought I could move on and have a happy life again...until you came along and changed all that."

Eleni was coming across the lawn with a large wooden bowl of fruit, which she placed on their table.

"Rose is asleep on the kitchen sofa. Petros is sitting beside her so she'll come to no harm. I'll bring her out here when she wakes up."

Cathy smiled. "Thank you, Eleni. I'll come in soon and rouse her gently so that we have time to play on the shore under those trees. Our time together is so precious."

"You're so understanding, Cathy," Yannis said quietly, as soon as they were alone again. "You seem to realise what I'm going through in this transition from grieving widower to...well, how would you describe me now?"

She took a deep breath. "New man?"

He smiled, his eyes crinkling as he gazed at her. "That's what I'm aspiring to be...with your help. I've still got to get rid of the guilt I feel that I'm here getting on with my life and Maroula is no longer alive. Her life was cut short when she was in her prime and I'm happy again."

"Why should you feel guilty about that?"

"Sometimes I feel I could have prevented her death," he said quietly.

"The chances of that are remote," she replied evenly. "Even if you'd been driving the car, and the timing had been exactly the same, you couldn't have prevented a large lorry on a blind bend on the wrong side of the road smashing into you."

He closed his eyes and she could see the tears squeezing out from under his eyelids. He'd told her when she'd first met him that crying was something men didn't do. But she was convinced that it could be therapeutic. She put her arms tightly around him and held him close until his shaking body was still again. All the time she was trying to convince herself that she was just being a good friend but the feel of his strong body in such close contact was having a devastating effect on her confused emotions.

She put her head against his shoulder and lifted her eyes to his.

He looked down at her. "Cathy, how long do you think it will take me to forget entirely and to get rid of the guilt?"

"I don't think you'll ever entirely forget," she said softly. "You don't need to forget. Just try not to dwell on the unpleasant aspects and the guilt."

"Easier said than done." He gave her a wry smile. "But I'll try. Because I would hate to think that this could spoil our relationship."

She remained quiet. It was obvious to her that Yannis's idea of their relationship was different from what she was trying to maintain. If she hadn't been hurt so many times before, this was the point at which she would begin to relax and enjoy thoughts of a future together. But she simply daren't think any further than one day at a time.

She stood up. "I'll go and wake Rose up."

"Cathy." He was on his feet beside her, drawing her against him. "Thank you so much for being here with me, for all the help and comfort you're giving me. You're right. I am a new man!"

He bent his head and kissed her gently on the lips. His kiss deepened. She drank in the sensual waves of passion that spread down from her lips throughout her whole body. Oh, yes, he was a new man all right. There was so much sexy, vibrant vitality in Yannis, not to mention that his hands were now beginning to drive her senses wild with anticipation.

She broke away, telling herself she mustn't give in to temptation. But looking up at him now, she recognised that she wanted him as much as he wanted her.

"Tonight?" he whispered, trying to gain control of himself again. "Could I bring you home after we both come off duty? I presume Rose will be staying at Anna's if you're working this evening."

"Well, yes, it's already arranged, but, Yannis..."

"Yes?"

She was struggling to get a grip on her emotions. But the sensual waves coursing through her body were driving her mad with desire. She remembered the way it had been on the boat when they'd made love before supper. They had been light-hearted, simply role playing, hadn't they? Couldn't she suspend her fears just for one night and enjoy being with Yannis? Have a whole night in which there was no past, no future, simply the present moment?

"Well then... Do we have a date for tonight?" He took hold of her hand and led her across the lawn towards the kitchen door.

"I think we do," she said, feeling too weak to struggle against that tempting voice inside her head.

Rose squealed with delight when Cathy put her down on the sand and allowed her to crawl down towards the sea. She was wearing her armbands and knew very well that this meant swimming and splashing around in the big water.

"It's very deep further out," Yannis said, as he cradled Rose in his arms and trod water. I don't want her to do her doggy paddle out here. "I know she could drown in shallow water but it still seems more dangerous the further out we go. I wouldn't want anything to happen to our precious little one."

Cathy made no comment about Yannis calling her daughter "our precious little one".

She doubted if it had even registered on his mind. All his paternal instinct seemed to be focused on her daughter and that was therapeutic for him. She found herself praying that he wasn't going to disappear from their lives. That he would always be somewhere in the background so that Rose would never get hurt. She'd allowed the bonding of Yannis and Rose to go too far now.

She did a swift turn-around. The dark depths of the water held a fascination for her but they were always dangerous and she knew from studying records that this stretch of water had claimed the lives of tourists who'd thought they'd had the strength to swim to the other side.

"Let's go back," she said. "Will you take Rose or shall I?"

"I'll take her."

He turned on his back and swam towards the shore, his muscular legs kicking strongly against the water. She swam breaststroke alongside but found it hard to keep up with him.

Rose, firmly held by Yannis on his chest, laughed with sheer happiness at the wild adventure she was having. Once again she'd got her mummy and this magical man who made their lives so much more exciting when he turned up occasionally. Not as often as she would like but it was always fun when it happened.

Dried off and de-sanded they had tea in the garden room. Petros brought out the new high chair which had miraculously appeared in the kitchen.

"When did that arrive?" Cathy asked as she strapped her wriggling daughter in.

Yannis pretended to look puzzled. "Oh, we've had it for ages, haven't we, Petros? It belonged—"

"No, Yannis. You asked me to collect it from that shop in Rhodes."

Petros, bewildered, set off back to the kitchen to tell his wife that Yannis was losing his memory.

When the ritual of jam sandwiches and cakes had been performed and Rose had been persuaded to eat something whilst enjoying the fun of crumbling and spreading jam with her fingers, Cathy gave her daughter a banana.

Concentrating hard, Rose, with a very serious expression on her face, unzipped the banana and peeled it halfway down before biting the top off.

"Very good!" Yannis said, with parental-style pride. "What a clever girl!"

Cathy smiled. "Well, I figure if baby monkeys can do it, my daughter should have the intelligence to work it out."

"Yes, but it needs hand-eye co-ordination."

"True. But Rose will be one in two weeks' time so…"

"Oh, Cathy, we must have a party!" Yannis said happily. "Would you like to have it here?"

Decisions! Decisions! Events were moving too quickly for her to keep up. "To be honest, I hadn't thought about a party. I don't know if my boss will give me time off. It's in the middle of the week and I'll have to ask him."

"Ask away and take a whole day off…take two…so will I."

"Hey, steady on, Yannis. Don't go to extremes."

Yannis took hold of her hand.

"Why not? A birthday is something to celebrate—especially the first one. Clever little Rose successfully survived nine months in her mummy's uterus and then navigated herself down the birth canal. And she's learned so much in twelve months, how to sit up, how to crawl… Very soon she'll be walking. Did you see how she was trying to pull herself up from the floor by holding onto that chair?"

Cathy's smile broadened. "Yannis, I do like you when you're in this…mood."

She'd been going to say paternal mood but had decided not to. If Rose was the substitution for the child he'd lost then that was something to be happy about. Anything that helped in the healing process was heaven sent.

Yannis glanced at his watch. "We'll have to go. I'll drive the car again so we can take Rose up to Anna's."

Cathy took a clean cloth from the outdoor sink and wiped the jam and banana bits from around Rose's mouth. Yannis was already thinking ahead to the hospital schedule for the evening. He was trying not to think any further to the time when he would bring Cathy back home with him.

Cathy too, was trying to concentrate on other things, thinking ahead to the clinic she was going to take and trying not to allow herself to think about the night ahead.

"Ready, Cathy?"

Yannis deftly undid the straps on the high chair and took charge of Rose. "We need to go right now if we're going to give ourselves time to spend with Ariadne and her newborn twins."

They reached hospital with a few minutes to spare, having delivered a tired but happy Rose to Anna, who welcomed her as always with a big hug.

Ariadne was propped up in bed, a twin cuddled up on each side of her. The proud father was sitting in a chair, gazing fondly at the latest editions to his family.

"Isn't my wife just the most amazing woman, Yannis? And I understand you were there at the birth as well, Cathy. Pity I couldn't make it. Important business meeting, you know.

Well, somebody has to pay the bills when there are all these mouths to feed."

Ariadne smiled indulgently at her husband.

Cathy and Yannis conferred with the midwife in charge before staying a short time to chat with Ariadne and her husband. Yes, Yannis assured them, they would love to go to the twins' christening party when they received an invitation in due course.

"So where will you be this evening, Yannis?" Cathy asked as they walked together down the corridor outside Obstetrics.

"In my office to begin with, hopefully. I've got a load of paperwork to catch up with and have even got my secretary to stay late to help me. So if you need me, you've only got to give me a call."

Cathy gave him a wry smile. "I'll be too busy to call you. My midweek outpatients clinic is developing into a social club. There are more patients than I can handle usually."

"I'll get you some help," he said, taking out his mobile.

She listened as he spoke briefly.

"There's a trained nurse on her way. She lives around in Vasilios bay and her husband is going to bring her into Ceres town in his boat. She's just waiting for the port authorities to clear them. There's been a strong wind but she assures me she'll be with you in half an hour. Can you manage till then?"

"Of course."

"I'll come and collect you about eight, then."

The outpatient clinic started at six and finished at eight. Patients made appointments at a time that suited them. At least, that was what was supposed to happen. But this being Ceres, the patients wandered in when they felt like it, knowing that the kind lady doctor wasn't the type who would turn them away if they didn't have an appointment and she never watched the clock.

The female population of the island who worked during the day or couldn't get away from the house without the children had learned over the couple of months that Cathy had been doing the evening clinic and that she was a very good doctor. And what was more, she was a female who understood female medical problems and was easy to talk to.

So this midweek outpatient clinic had become very popular with both young girls and older women and had turned into something of a social club. When she arrived just a few minutes before six there were already six women sitting in her waiting room.

"*Kali spera*, Cathy!"

"*Kali spera*." She smiled as she went into her consulting room and turned on the computer. According to the information that appeared on the screen she had only three patients booked this evening and they weren't supposed to be here until after seven. Oh, well, she made a point of putting down names and medical case information after she'd treated a patient so all she had to do was make sure she knew who she was dealing with.

As long as the medical secretaries in the records department had kept up to date with putting the written case histories onto the computer she would be fine. But as she'd come to realise, some of her patients just enjoyed an evening out of the house and a good gossip with women of their own age.

She'd left her door wide open so that her patients could see she was soon going to be available for them to come in and pour out their troubles to her.

She went to the doorway and looked around the assembled ladies. "Who's coming in first this evening?"

"Daniella." By general consensus everyone had agreed that Daniella should be the first.

"So what can I do for you?" Cathy asked, when her young patient was seated in front of her. She'd closed her door now so as to give them some privacy. Her patients might discuss their most intimate problems with each other out there in the waiting room but here in the sanctity of the doctor's consulting room they liked everything to remain private.

"I've missed a period."

Cathy had already noticed the ungainly gait of her patient as she'd waddled in through the door. The loose clothing intended to camouflage her belly was doing nothing to hide the obvious advanced pregnancy.

"Just one, Daniella?"

"Well, probably a few more. I can't remember... Oh, Doctor, my mother's going to kill me when she..."

The tears ran down her cheeks as Daniella tried to stifle her sobs.

Cathy reached for the box of tissues with one hand and with the other she put her arm round her patient's shoulders.

She waited until the sobs subsided. Daniella wiped a tissue over her face and blew her nose vigorously.

"Have you tried to tell your mother?"

"No, I daren't. I think she might have guessed but she hasn't said anything. I live with my dad and his new wife on Rhodes but he's turned me out now he knows I'm going to have a baby.

"He just told me to go back to my mum. But I don't get on with my mum. I just arrived on the ferry this afternoon. I'll have to go to my mum's tonight because I've nowhere else to go. And she'll kill me!"

"I don't think she'll do that, Daniella. She'll be concerned about you but most mums get used to the idea that their daughter is going to have a baby."

"Not mine!"

"Have you seen a doctor on Rhodes?"

"No!"

"Does the father know you're having his baby?"

"I don't know who the father is. It was just one night out in Rhodes. I met him that evening. He was a tourist just staying there for a few nights. I went back to his hotel with him and it just happened."

Cathy took a deep breath. "How old are you, Daniella?"

"Sixteen."

Oh, no. It was getting worse. "How old were you when you spent the night with this man?"

"I was just sixteen. It was my birthday."

Thank goodness for that! Cathy was glad she wouldn't have to make a report to the police. Even so, this was definitely a case for Social Services. But first she must establish how far advanced this pregnancy was.

"I'd like you to lie down on the couch here so I can examine you, Daniella."

As Cathy helped her patient onto the examination couch her apprehension was growing by the second. The young girl was in obvious pain. She groaned as she lifted her legs up and then shrieked as she floundered onto the surface of the couch.

"No, oh, no. Doctor it's been getting worse all day. On the boat the pain was awful. It's in my back now and down my legs. It's everywhere. What's happening to me?"

Cathy had a pretty good idea even before she pulled aside the voluminous camouflage and saw the swollen abdomen. She placed her hands on Daniella and checked the muscular spasms that were causing her so much pain. The poor child was already in labour. No time to scrub up or perform any of the usual preliminaries. This baby was hell-bent on getting out under its own steam.

She pulled Daniella's legs into a lithotomy position so that she could examine the birth canal. Oh, no! The baby's head was crowning already. She needed another pair of hands. Where was that nurse when she needed her?

"Don't push, Daniella. Just pant for the moment." Realising that here was a young girl with no antenatal preparation, she began to show her how to pant. "Like this so that you don't start pushing, bearing down. You have to…"

Too late. The head was out now, Daniella simply giving in to her deep primaeval urge to push. Cathy's eyes widened in concern as she saw the umbilical cord wrapped around the baby's neck. She really needed another pair of hands now because Daniella was refusing to keep still, moving from side to side, trying to get the baby out of her body.

The panic button was across the other side of the room, as was the phone. Holding the cord away from the baby's neck with one hand, she got her mobile from her pocket with the other and punched in Yannis's name on her address book. At least she hoped it was Yannis's number but it was difficult for her to see at this angle.

"Dr Yannis here. How—?"

"Yannis, please come…" She dropped the phone on the couch as she deftly unwrapped the cord, using both hands this time.

She breathed a sigh of relief. "It's OK, you can push now, Daniella."

The door opened and Yannis came in. "What was it that—? Ah!" He looked down at the young girl, her whole body drenched in sweat.

Cathy was carefully wrapping the new baby in a dressing towel, handing her to the new mum.

"There you go, Daniella, you've got a little boy."

"Oh, thank you, Doctor! Oh, he's lovely. Look at his little eyes."

Daniella's groans had turned to shrieks of delight now.

Yannis was already on the phone to Obstetrics. "Yes, the baby has already arrived, Sister, so if you could just send someone down to take the patient and the newborn up to your department for postnatal checks, that would be excellent. She'll be staying in at least overnight. Dr Cathy will give you the case history as soon as she's prepared it."

"That was an unusual start to the evening," Cathy said, as she sank down on her consulting chair, having despatched the happy young mother and child to Obstetrics.

"I'll get the notes written up on the computer as soon as the nurse arrives."

"I've just had a phone call from her. There's a big storm in the north of the island and the port authorities have cancelled all boat movements."

"So she won't be coming?"

"Evidently not. I might be able to pull in a nurse from another department if I rang round or I could help you myself."

"You?"

"Don't look so shocked. I am a qualified doctor, you know."

She smiled. "Well, that's what I mean. You're vastly over-qualified for the things I'm going to delegate to be done this evening."

"Try me. I've given my secretary a load of letters to write. All I've got to do is go back later and sign them and that's the paperwork finished for the day. I could do a further round of the patients but I've already delegated that to young Dr

Stamatis, who's always pleased to fill in for me. So, the more I can help you here the quicker we'll get away this evening. We do have a date, if you remember."

She looked up at him. He was so close. "How could I forget?"

He kissed her gently on the lips. Pulling himself reluctantly away, he looked down into the shining blue eyes that were gazing up adoringly at him. How lucky could a man get?

"OK, Dr Cathy, what would you like me to do first?"

"Go and call the next patient in, please."

"Do you have a list?"

She gave him a wry grin. "A list? Now, there's a novel idea. If you stand in the doorway, the patients will have decided who's next."

CHAPTER EIGHT

YANNIS parked the car in the drive at the front of the house and switched off the engine.

For a few moments they both sat completely still, relishing the peace and quiet of their idyllic surroundings after the noise and non-stop demands of the day.

Yannis turned to look at Cathy, sitting so still with a shaft of moonlight shining through the open car window onto her beautiful face. Cathy turned her head and saw he'd been studying her profile. For an awful moment she wondered if the loving look on his face was really for her.

No! She mustn't think like that! And she must also remember that she wasn't committing herself to a relationship. This was one romantic night together, not looking into the future. No strings attached.

He leaned across and took hold of her hand. "What's the matter? What's troubling you, Cathy? Are you still worried about Daniella? I've told you, she's in good hands up there in Obstetrics. Tomorrow, I'll get in touch with her mother, ask her to come in and see me, explain the situation and take it from there. I'll get in touch with Social Services as well but I'll take the first step to resolving the situation."

Relief flooded through her—on both levels, professional

and personal. He was a fantastic doctor who really cared about all his patients. An honest, caring, wonderful man. How could she possibly continue to doubt whether he would stay with her if she were to commit to a meaningful relationship? She couldn't walk away from everything that was building up between them. Her feelings for this man were deepening in spite of the fears that had grown out of her past experiences, especially with Dave.

"I'm tired, that's all," she said quietly. "It's been a long day."

He gave her a relieved smile. For one awful moment he'd felt she might be having regrets about coming home with him. Last time she'd spent the night here he'd put her in the guest room. He'd spent the night aware of how near she'd been but afraid to spoil their early tenuous friendship. But they'd moved on now and tonight she would be with him, in his bed.

He drew her into his arms. "Let me take you inside and take care of you. You need to relax now. I'll open a bottle of champagne to celebrate."

She looked up into his dark brown searching eyes. "What are we celebrating?"

"The end of the day, the moon, the stars, Rose's birthday, the joy of being together... Come inside and let's get on with the celebrations."

His arm was around her waist as they went into the large entrance hall. The house was still and quiet but Eleni had left lights on to welcome them. There was a piece of paper on the kitchen table instructing Yannis what she'd prepared for their supper.

Cathy sank down on the old wooden armchair beside the wide iron stove and watched Yannis as he opened the champagne he'd taken out of the fridge. Bubbles ran down the side of the glass as he handed it to her.

He moved to the other side of the fireplace, sitting down in the other almost identical chair. Glancing across at Cathy, he felt relieved that she seemed to be gathering her strength again. He cared so much for her now that he couldn't bear to see her looking worried. She was becoming central to his life and he wanted so much to think that she would always be with him. But always was a long time and so much happened along the paths they were both treading, sometimes together, sometimes apart.

He raised his glass. "Here's to us!"

She smiled at his jocular tone. He must be just as physically tired as she was but he was making the effort to appear relaxed and refreshed.

"I'll drink to that!"

She raised her glass to his.

"I brought these chairs over from the house where I was born," Yannis told her. "When I sold the house I put some of the furniture in storage. As soon as I was settled in here, I reclaimed it. There are various pieces dotted all over the house."

"It's good to have memories from the past around you."

"I remember my grandmother sitting in this chair. I think I must have been about six or seven when I listened to her giving my mother a lecture on how my father wasn't good enough for her. My mother! My father! The two people I loved most in all the world."

"Did your grandmother know you were listening in?"

"Not exactly. My mother had sent me out of the room when her mother had started ranting at her. I went out but I stayed the other side of the door and heard everything. Apparently, my grandmother hadn't wanted my mother to marry my father because she didn't trust him to stay faithful. She'd thought he would leave her once I was born. I think she must have been pregnant with me when they got married."

"But your father stayed with your mother till he died, didn't he?"

"Oh, they were really happy, so in love as far as I remember. When I heard my grandmother shouting at my mother I wanted to go back and stick up for her."

He leaned his head against the back of the chair and looked up at the high ceiling. "Strange how memories come flooding back once you trigger them off. Do you find that?"

She nodded. "Often. Happy memories, unhappy memories. Once you set them off they won't stop coming. My mother made the best of everything but it was difficult for her to be left alone to bring me up by herself."

He brought the champagne bottle across and topped up her glass. "Did you have any idea that your father was going to leave your mother?"

"Oh, yes! He often went out and didn't come back for a few days. When he actually went away for good I kept expecting him to come back, but he never did."

"How awful for you!"

"Not really. I'd got used to having my mother to myself. I don't think she missed him either. She missed the small amounts of money he gave towards the housekeeping but that was all."

She broke off, not wanting to dwell any more on the hard times in her past. Was the possibility of real happiness with a good man beckoning her? Could she trust her own judgement? Even if she decided to trust Yannis completely, there was still the permanent presence of the iconic first wife to contend with.

She'd seen the photographs everywhere she'd gone. A beautiful young woman who would stay forever young, forever faultless. Her long dark hair always looked as if it had been styled professionally. Her mouth with the impeccable pearly white teeth smiling at the camera. The beautiful eyes showing such love towards the photographer—which of course, must have been Yannis.

Don't dwell on it, she told herself once more.

She put down her champagne glass on the small table beside her. "You know, every family seems to have its problems. It's how you deal with them that matters. I remember my mother telling me that if something needs changing, you should have the courage to change it. If there's something that you have to put up with, stop moaning and put up with it. But make sure you know the difference between the two situations and act accordingly."

"Wise woman, your mother. Rather like you."

"I'm not wise! I try to learn by my mistakes and..." She broke off, telling herself it was time to lighten the conversation. "What's that wonderful cooking smell that's getting my taste buds excited?"

Yannis laughed and picked up the oven glove from the side of the stove. "According to her note, I think it's Eleni's famous beef cooked in Metaxas brandy."

He opened the oven door and the delicious aroma wafted across towards Cathy. "Mmm. If that tastes half as good as it smells..."

He led her into the dining room and held out a chair before lighting the candelabrum. Returning from the kitchen moments later, he placed the casserole on the table.

She discovered how hungry she was when she took her first mouthful of the delicious dish.

"Mmm. That's absolute heaven. I'm so glad you invited me to your dinner party this evening, Dr Yannis."

Stretching out her hand, she reached across the table to grasp his.

He smiled happily. "I'm glad you were free this evening."

"Oh, I was just having a quiet time to keep myself amused. Delivering a baby, comforting a distraught teenage mum, you know the sort of thing."

"Absolutely! All in a day's work."

She took another mouthful as she watched Yannis opening a bottle of red wine.

"I have to say this is one of my favourite restaurants in the whole of the Greek islands."

"Mine too."

He leaned over her, his hand caressing the back of her shoulders as he poured some wine into her glass.

"I feel strong enough to go back and help the poor night staff, Yannis."

He gave her a wry grin as he sat down again. "Steady on! The poor night staff haven't worked all day. Besides, I need you here so you're not going anywhere. Don't get any ideas about leaving me alone tonight."

"That suits me fine. It's good to be needed."

He swallowed hard as he looked at the beautiful woman across the table from him. He'd been so lucky to have known two perfect women in his life.

Cathy recognised the gleam in his eye and held her breath. His expression was exactly the same as when he'd looked across the table in the cabin of the boat. She sensed instinctively that he was thinking about Maroula.

At the present moment she was feeling happy to be spending an evening like this with this wonderful man. She wasn't going to dwell on the problems of their relationship. Tonight was all that mattered. She would just imagine there had been no yesterday, there was no tomorrow, that only the present mattered.

She smiled as she put down her fork on the empty plate. "That was utterly delicious. Eleni did us proud tonight. Where do you get your mushrooms?"

"Petros brings them from the field behind their house. And the rest of the vegetables come from the kitchen garden here, potatoes, beans, peppers, courgettes. I've never been so spoilt in all my life."

He hesitated. "You know, I feel as if I shouldn't have said that. It somehow reflects badly on Maroula's cooking. She could cook…but…well, not like this."

Cathy remained very still as she watched Yannis frowning. At least the goddess Maroula had been as human as she was!

She allowed her wineglass to be topped up, revelling in the closeness of the wine waiter as he deliberately lingered beside her. She felt utterly replete now and certainly relaxed enough to look forward to the night ahead. When she'd first arrived she'd felt she could have fallen asleep in the car. But now…!

Now she was ready for anything. Maybe it was the champagne, red wine and delicious food. Or perhaps it was spending time with a man she simply enjoyed being with, a man who made her feel relaxed, content and safe. Simply sitting by the fireside, reminiscing about family and past times, good and bad. Being able to say anything she wanted, knowing that Yannis would listen and understand.

She didn't want to change anything about him at all—even if she could. She realised she'd never felt like this about any man in her life before.

He leaned forward. "You're looking very serious. Is something the matter?"

She shook her head. "Everything is…perfect."

He put down the wine bottle and drew her to her feet, enclosing her in his strong, muscular arms.

"I'll bring coffee upstairs…later."

"Good idea." She gazed up at him, unable to get enough of the adoring expression in his eyes.

He turned away for a moment to blow out the candles. Then, before she knew what was happening, he'd swept her up into his arms and was carrying her out towards the wide staircase.

He laid her down on the bed, his fingers deftly undoing the buttons on her blouse. She reached up, desperate to feel his skin against hers.

When they were both naked he lifted her again and carried her into the bathroom. She was barely aware of the opulent surroundings as she stepped into the scented bath he was preparing, revelling in the swish of the water around her body as she sank back against the fragrant foam.

He climbed in beside her and they lay together in a spoon shaped embrace, the contact of skin against skin driving them both wild with anticipation. Then he turned her over to face him and tantalised her body, with his fingers dwelling just long enough in the places where her anticipation was at its highest level.

"Yannis," she moaned as the sensual movements of his fingers became more than she could take. She was now desperate for the ultimate consummation. As she moulded herself against him he thrust inside her, his muscles quivering against her until they became one complete rhythmic body fused in an orgasmic frenzy.

She cried out over and over again as she found herself in an experience so completely unworldly she felt she was floating somewhere in outer space on an ethereal cloud.

For what seemed like an infinity they lay together in this climactic fusion until Yannis moved to one side and put an arm around her quivering shoulders.

She lay back against him and looked up at the tiled ceiling above her. It was only then that she realised how enormous this bath really was.

"Is this a jacuzzi?" she murmured, not wanting to move away from the comfort of Yannis's arms.

"Mmm," he whispered. "Shall I turn it on?"

"Do I have to move?" she asked languidly.

"Absolutely not."

She felt him putting out an arm to flick a switch and then bringing it back to complete their embrace again. She was conscious of the gentle vibration of the water soothing her satiated body.

"Mmm, that's nice. Do you lie in your jacuzzi every night like this?"

"Only when I can catch a mermaid to share it with me. I spotted you in the sea this afternoon and I thought to myself, She'll be okay for tonight."

"Only okay?"

"Actually, much better than I could ever have imagined," he whispered as his lips came down on hers.

She felt her body quivering again, synchronising with the movement of the water as she gave herself up to the continued heaven of their joint passion.

Someone was stroking her wet skin. She was waking up in the strangest place. Had she fallen asleep in the sea? Oh, no. "Rose!"

"Darling, Rose isn't here with us!"

Strong arms were holding her safe as she came back through the haze of her sleep-befuddled brain.

"Yannis! Oh, thank heaven it's you. I thought I was swimming with Rose." She looked around her at the enormous jacuzzi. "How long have I been asleep?"

"Only a few minutes. It seemed a pity to wake you, so I switched off the jacuzzi and cradled you in my arms. I was almost asleep myself when you woke up just now."

He gave her a sexy grin. "Actually, I'd sort of decided to wake you." He leaned forward and placed his lips gently on hers.

"Let's dry off and go to bed," he whispered against her lips.

The next time she awoke she could see the early-morning light stealing through the French windows. Half-remembered visions of last night were jumbled together in her drowsy mind. Yannis was always centre stage in every vision.

What a man! It had been a night to remember, a memory nothing and nobody could ever take away from her in the future, whatever it might hold.

She leaned her head back on the pillow as a niggle of self-doubt tried to impose itself into her brain. How would she feel when the sexual euphoria had evaporated and she had to face the cold dawn of reality?

She crept out of bed, planning to sit on the balcony so that she could watch the sunrise. Through the window she could see the haze hanging over the water and a red glow appearing along the top of the hill opposite the house.

As she moved, she heard Yannis stirring. He reached out towards her just as she was slipping her feet down to the soft lamb's-wool rug at the side of the bed.

"You're not leaving, are you?"

She heard the urgency in his voice. Part of him was joking and yet the insecurity surrounding him was palpable.

She turned and sat down on the edge of the bed. "I'm going to watch the sunrise."

"I'll come with you."

They were just in time to see the tiny triangle of light

peeping out from a cleft in the peak at the top of the hill. Slowly at first and then gathering momentum the round ball of the sun revealed itself in its full morning glory.

"Magic!" she breathed. "Every time I see a sunrise or a sunset it never ceases to amaze me."

"And what a wonderful night we've had," he said huskily, drawing her closer to him.

They stood entwined in their embrace, naked skin against naked skin, in the warming rays of the sun.

"We're like Adam and Eve at the dawning of time," Cathy said, as she pulled herself gently away from his arms. "Time to leave paradise."

"Let's stay longer in paradise before we go back to the real world. I'll get you a robe. The sun is warming up but it's still a bit chilly for you."

"Thanks." He put the fluffy white towelling robe around her shoulders and she slipped into it.

He moved a couple of cushioned wicker chairs to the front of the balcony. "Would you like that coffee now?"

She smiled. "You mean the after-supper coffee you promised to bring upstairs last night?"

He grinned. "I did say later, didn't I? Although I hadn't intended it to be breakfast time."

"I'm not complaining."

She sat very still on the balcony, snuggling into Yannis's enormous robe. The haze on the water hung over parts of the garden as well. The grass that she could see was covered in dew. Somewhere in one of the trees a bird was singing its welcome to the dawn. The same rhythmic repetition she'd heard birds use in England.

He returned carrying a large tray and placed it on the wooden table at the edge of the balcony.

"Toast, apricot jam, fruit, coffee, orange juice. Is there anything else we might need?"

"We've got absolutely everything. I'm starving."

Yannis smiled. "Can't think why!"

She noticed he was wearing a beach towel slung round his waist. It showed off his muscular, athletic legs to perfection, she thought. She was glad he'd given her his robe. It would be a pity to deny her such a stimulating artistic vision to appreciate during breakfast.

Whereas she wasn't so sure what she would look like if she was simply wrapped round with a towel. And she desperately needed a shower—by herself!

Yannis's mobile was making itself heard from the bedroom. He went inside.

"Yes, Sister… No, that's OK. I'm always awake at this early hour."

Cathy smiled at him through the open doors. He pulled a face to indicate it was work he could do without.

He sat down again and picked up a piece of toast.

"Night Sister would like me to get in before she goes off duty this morning. She wasn't happy with the diagnosis that the house surgeon gave her just now for one of her newly admitted female patients. I've told her to starve the patient and I'll take her down to Theatre as soon as I get in. From the symptoms she just described she could be right in her diagnosis of an ectopic pregnancy."

"Is the alternative diagnosis appendicitis?"

Yannis nodded, still chewing thoughtfully.

"It's not an uncommon mistake," Cathy said. "But presumably the house surgeon has ordered the tests that reveal the correct diagnosis."

"Yes. Night Sister wants me to check the results as soon as

I get in. Which I think should be a few minutes from now."
He was standing up. "They're sending a hospital car to collect
me. I'll ask Petros to drive you home later... No, don't rush.
Take your time. Eleni will be in this morning to clear up the
mess we left downstairs so just spend your time getting ready."

She heard the car in the drive, peeped over the balcony and
watched him being driven away. She was queen of the castle
now—and what a castle! As she padded over the thick carpet
towards the bathroom she paused beside the photograph on
the table near the window. Another photo of Maroula she
hadn't seen! They were everywhere in the house.

She blocked off her uncharitable thoughts as soon as they
arose. It didn't do to dwell on them. Moving swiftly over to
the bed, she picked up her mobile from the bedside table.
She'd kept it switched on all night but Anna had obviously
not felt the need to call her.

As she placed her phone on the table beside the shower
cubicle, she reflected that it was far too early to call Anna. She
had time to take that much-needed shower she'd been promising herself.

Arriving at the hospital, she had a feeling of déjà vu when the
receptionist told her that Dr Karavolis would like to see her
when she got in. Apparently, he was in Theatre.

She hurried up, taking the lift, standing to one side so that
a porter could bring in a pre-operative patient.

She went into the theatre anteroom. Yannis was peeling off
his gloves at the sink. He turned round.

"We were right. It was an ectopic. In the left Fallopian tube.
I had to excise it but the other one seems viable and the patient
is young and otherwise healthy. So a future pregnancy should
be possible."

He walked across and stood looking down at her with the confident assurance of someone who felt at ease in their relationship. He was standing very close to her now, but moved back as the swing door into Theatre opened.

"Sister, you'll get those biopsies and tests on the viable Fallopian tube done as soon as possible, won't you?"

"Of course, sir." Theatre Sister went out into the corridor.

"So was everything OK at home when you left?"

"Yes, Eleni is already bustling around clearing up and cleaning. What a treasure!"

"And how was your treasure when you went up home?"

"Do you mean Rose or Anna?"

He smiled. "Rose, actually."

"Happy to see me and equally happy to carry on playing with the other children in the house." She paused. "About her birthday party…"

"Yes?"

"Anna was rather hoping to be involved."

He smiled. "But of course she must be involved. I'll arrange to have everybody brought to my house. Anna, her grandchildren and their friends, the more the merrier, don't you think?"

All things were possible with Yannis when he was in a mood like this. The night they'd spent together seemed to have given him new energy.

She just hoped he wouldn't be plagued with guilt when he returned home this evening and went up to his room alone. Would he pick up that photograph from the table and…?

"Cathy, what's the matter?"

He put his hands on her arms and looked down into her eyes.

"Nothing! Just thinking about the day ahead. I'll go up to Obstetrics and check on Daniella and Ariadne."

He drew her towards him and held her close for a few moments before releasing her so that he could look deep into her eyes.

"You would tell me if there was a problem, wouldn't you?"

She nodded. "I haven't got a problem and, yes, I would tell you."

She moved out of the circle of his arms and hurried away before she could say anything more.

As she went along the corridor she could feel herself coming back down to earth. She'd had her wonderful night with Yannis. Now she must face reality. Their problems were still with them. Yannis's obsession with his beloved wife, his guilt at betraying her memory. Her own fear of committing herself to a meaningful relationship with any man, however sincere he appeared. The real crux of the matter was that she didn't believe she would be enough for Yannis, like she hadn't been enough for Dave, like her mother hadn't been enough for her father.

Was history repeating itself?

CHAPTER NINE

CATHY found Ariadne propped up against her pillows feeding both her newborn twins. With the practised ease of a mother of five, the twins hadn't fazed her. She'd tucked their legs under her arms, allowing them to suckle at her breasts. She smiled with delight when Cathy walked in.

"Cathy! I was hoping you would come in to see me this morning. How was your night over at Nimborio with Yannis?"

Cathy smiled. Ariadne had become a personal friend over the weeks she'd been caring for her. She'd trained as a nurse in England and had spent time as an au pair with an English family before she'd married. So her English was excellent and they usually conversed in that language. But Cathy was usually careful how much she divulged of her personal life. She'd been tired last night when she'd called in to check on her and had probably given away too much information.

"Listen, Ariadne, you positively dragged out of me the fact that I was going out for supper at Yannis's house. What makes you think supper lasted all night?"

Ariadne deftly swapped her twins over so that each could take a different breast. "It's just the way you look this morning. Sort of radiant…in a shattered sort of way. I may be a long-time married woman but I do remember that feeling.

M...

that ...

"Ariadne, I pr... I'm wrong, but it's obvious

not about my private love... how you're feeling,

serious and professional but still una... trying to look

ful warm glow to herself. ...wonder-

At least with her other patients she wouldn't have to sub...

to the third degree!

Ariadne laughed. "Aha! So you admit you're having a love life?"

Cathy smiled. "No comment! I'm here to check you out, not the other way round. I've got to make out a report so…"

"Oh, that young obstetrician came in earlier. The one who looks as if he's just left school but seems to know everything about babies. He gave me a complete examination and put it straight on the computer thing he always carries with him. It's all there for the medical staff to read."

"In that case, why did I come in to see you this morning?"

Ariadne took one hand off her boy twin and patted the side of her bed.

"To have a girly chat, I hope. Can't you see how bored I'm getting in here? These little darlings, although very precious to me, are numbers four and five in my family. Demetrius is always off on business somewhere, trying to keep the wolf from the door of our large family, so I need some intellectual stimulation from time to time."

Cathy sat down on the side of the bed. "I don't know about intellectual but I suppose it's my duty to spend time with a patient who's had a rough time."

"Oh, it wasn't that rough. You and Yannis were wonderful with me. We must keep in touch after you let me out of here. Then I can see if the pair of you have the sense to make a go of it."

A FATHER...

...stage where it could
...e, his first wife died?"

Cathy raised an e... ...bout that soon after he came here,
go either way. Y...alk about it. He seemed so sad when he
"Yes, eve... ...the island but you've certainly brought him
but nobo... ...his shell. So what's the problem? My Demetrius has
first... ...first wife. He was divorced when we first met and look how
ou...
happy we are now. His first marriage only lasted a couple of
years before he found her in bed with his best friend. He's
had no contact with her since. His solicitors dealt with the
divorce. He can't stand the sound of her name!"

"Well, that's slightly different to our situation," Cathy
said quietly.

Ariadne frowned. "You've lost me."

Cathy took a deep breath. "Yannis still adores his wife."

"His deceased wife?"

"Yes, they were idyllically happy apparently and he still
loves her."

They both remained silent. Only the sound of the suckling
babies disturbed the peace and calm of the private room.
Ariadne spoke first to break the awkward silence.

"I can see what you're up against now."

Cathy took a deep breath. "And there's also the fact that he
feels guilty when…when we're together, enjoying ourselves."

"Like last night?"

"I don't know about last night. It was…yes, it was fabulous,
but I don't think he's had time to worry about it yet. Actually…"

The door opened and Yannis came in, his theatre mask
slung underneath his chin.

He smiled. "Don't let me stop your little chat, ladies. I
presume Cathy is telling you how to take care of your newborn babies?"

Ariadne grinned cheekily. "Invaluable advice, Yannis,

but I'm glad you came to answer a few important questions, like—"

"I was just telling Ariadne we were having a birthday party for Rose and I wondered if she and Demetrius could come along, bringing all the children, of course."

"Yes, that's right." Ariadne said, quickly recognising she might make things worse if she tried to interfere with their love life. "I've agreed to check diaries with the boss when he comes in. Where did you say you were holding the party, Cathy?"

"Over at my place," Yannis filled in, wondering why the two women were looking so secretive. "You should be fine by then. Your obstetrician has given me a full report on your condition. I came to say that we think we could let you go home tomorrow if you've managed to arrange for full-time help at home."

"Don't worry about that. It's all taken care of. My mother has moved in temporarily and we're already employing a full-time nurse. I shall be spoiled rotten when I get home. That's not to say I wouldn't like the occasional house call from the pair of you."

Yannis smiled. "We'll see what we can do."

He turned to look at Cathy. "Have you been along to see Daniella yet? She was asking for you earlier."

"She's next on my list."

"OK. Let me know what you arrange with Social Services. I'll see you later."

"He's obviously in a hurry to get back to Theatre," Cathy said, taking the little girl twin who'd now stopped suckling and putting her over her shoulder to release the wind that was bothering her.

"Oh, he's perfect for you," Ariadne said dreamily. "Don't let him slip through your fingers."

"Everything we've said was in confidence," Cathy said quickly.

"Of course it was. Anyway, you didn't tell me anything I didn't know about…except the fact that he's hanging onto his memories. That's a tricky one, but I do wish you both the best of luck. It's obvious there is something between you."

"Thanks." The baby she was holding gave a loud burp. "Good girl! When are you going to give names to your twins?"

"As soon as I can nail my husband down to spending a couple of hours with me. Time is always a problem with him. But we'll get there. I might even persuade him to cancel everything and come to Rose's birthday party."

"Yes, do. Yannis would like some male support amongst all the mothers, grandmothers and children.

"He adores Rose, doesn't he?"

Cathy nodded. "It's almost as if…well, he's almost paternal with her. And she adores him."

"And so do you, so go for it."

The door opened and Obstetrics Sister came in. "Oh, Dr Cathy, I came to find you. I heard you were in here."

"I'm just going, Sister." Cathy finished changing the baby's nappy and laid her down in one of the cribs at the side of the bed.

"Could you go and see Daniella, please? She's been asking for you."

Sister drew her on one side. "Dr Karavolis contacted Social Services this morning but they can't send anyone in today and the poor girl is worrying too much about what her mother will do when she hears from them." She hesitated. "I actually know the family and I could perhaps ease the situation myself."

"That would be a big help if you could, Sister."

"If you'd like to come into my office we can discuss the situation."

* * *

"Daniella's mother is a neighbour of mine," Sister said as soon as they were alone in her office. "I've known Daniella since she was a small child. Her mother's had a hard time with her husband, Daniella's father. He left her last year and went off to Rhodes to live with someone a lot younger than himself. Daniella's a hot-headed individual—a bit like her father—and she kept on having rows with her mother. In the end she simply upped and left. Next thing we heard was that she was living with her father and his girlfriend on Rhodes."

"So her mother didn't turn her out, as she told me?"

"Maria's a good mother. She's bringing up six children on her own. Daniella's the eldest. She'll give her a good talking-to when she knows her predicament but she'll welcome her back—and the new baby. I know she will. Shall I phone her and ask her to come in?"

"I think that could well be the answer to the problem," Cathy said thoughtfully. "Thank you very much, Sister. I'll go and see her now and prepare her for the fact that she's soon going to see her mother. From what she said last night, she may not be too pleased about that."

"I'm sure it's for the best, Doctor."

"Let's hope so."

'So how are you feeling now, Daniella?" Cathy looked down at the sullen young girl stretched out on top of her bed. "I heard you wanted to see me."

"Yes, well, nobody else around here seems to know what to do with me. I need to see if I can go into a hostel or something till I'm feeling a bit stronger. Feel really tired today."

"That's understandable, Daniella."

Cathy pulled up a chair and sat down at the side of the bed. "We're going to keep you in here until we've sorted where you're going to live. I thought it would be best if we let your mother know you're in here and—"

"No, she'll kill me!"

"I'm sure she won't, Daniella. I'll stay with you while she's here."

"She's coming here?"

"Yes, Sister is phoning her now so it shouldn't take long for her to arrive. I understand your house is close by."

"Yes, but she'll have to get somebody to mind the kids and…"

"Yes, Sister?" Cathy looked up enquiringly.

"I've phoned your mother, Daniella, and she's on her way."

"Always poking your nose in," Daniella said under her breath.

"What was that?"

"Nothing, Sister."

"Now, I hope you're going to behave yourself when your mother comes in," Sister said. "I remember you since you were very small and you've always been difficult to handle. But just for once, can you please listen to what your mother has to say? She's been a good mother to you and she needs some respect from you, if nothing else."

"Do you understand, Daniella?" Cathy asked, firmly but kindly, as Sister left them.

She felt so sorry for her patient who, it seemed, had stood little chance in life. But at the same time she would have to grow up quickly and toe the line for the sake of this new life she'd brought into the world and also for her poor long-suffering mother.

Cathy leaned over the crib. The new baby boy's eyes were open and he appeared to be looking around as if wondering what kind of world he'd landed up in. She leaned down, picked him up into her arms and held him against her, relishing the sweet scent of freshly bathed baby, baby powder and cream.

"Who bathed your baby this morning?"

"I did." The sullen expression softened. "I've been bathing my brothers and sisters for ages, ever since I can remember, really. My mother gets so tired, she just likes to sit at the end of the day so I have to get them all ready for bed. And they stink if I put them down dirty. We've only got one bedroom with two double beds in it so we're all squashed up together. Mum sleeps downstairs so she can get a bit of peace."

Cathy felt a wave of compassion sweeping over her. No wonder Daniella had left home. This was one family that definitely needed rehousing and to be given more help.

She looked down at this feisty young mother and hoped she could make a difference to the difficult situation. "You've got a fine son here, Daniella. He's gorgeous, your little boy. Have you got a name for him yet?"

"I thought I might call him after my dad, Elias."

"That's a good name. Your dad would like that."

"Do you think so?"

Sister came in, bringing a visitor. A small plump woman wearing a large flower-patterned apron over her long brown dress that reached almost to her ankles stood near the bedside, staring across at her daughter. She was breathing heavily, as if she'd been hurrying too fast.

Daniella pulled herself up and sat very still, watching her mother.

Cathy was feeling desperately apprehensive as she watched the tense, as yet silent confrontation. She took a deep breath, knowing she would have to act as mediator before the confrontation turned verbal or even physical.

But just as she was about to intervene, Daniella's mother moved quickly over to the bed and put her arms around her daughter. "You naughty, naughty girl! I've been so worried about you. God be praised he's answered my prayers and you've come back home!"

Relief flooded through Cathy as she watched the tears of

mother and daughter mingling together as they clung to each other.

Sister touched Cathy's arm and whispered, "They're going to be all right now, Cathy."

Cathy nodded. "I'll arrange as much help for this family as I can."

Cathy looked out of the window of the tiny office she'd been given and noticed the shadows lengthening down by the harbour. Glancing at the clock, she saw she should have been off duty an hour ago. She switched off her computer with a sense of relief. It had been a busy day, as usual, but a satisfying one.

She'd had a long talk with Social Services, who were going to take over the case of Daniella's family and make sure they had as much help as possible with housing and child care. Apparently, the family network on Ceres, which had been the norm until recently, sometimes broke down.

Daniella's parents had lived on Rhodes before they'd set up house on Ceres. There were no near relatives on the island to help out and now that the father had decamped, the situation had worsened.

But as she looked out of the window at the warm friendly atmosphere down in the harbour Cathy was sure that things could only improve from now on for Daniella's family.

She went along the corridor to tell Yannis she was going off duty. He stood and came round his desk when she walked in.

"I'm just off, Yannis."

"Time for a drink?"

She shook her head. "No, I want to spend some time with Rose. I'm planning she should sleep in her own cot at home with me tonight."

"So I'll be all on my own tonight?" He drew her into his arms.

She heard his wistful tone as she allowed herself to lean against him. "I'm afraid so."

She hesitated for a moment. Ariadne's advice was at the back of her mind, urging her to go for it. But she needed to spend some real quality time with her daughter. If she invited Yannis back to her place, her loyalties would be divided. He wasn't the only one to suffer from a guilt complex!

She looked up into his dark brown eyes. "Being a working mum isn't easy, Yannis. I need to spend time alone with Rose— for both our sakes. We need to strengthen the bond between mother and daughter."

"Of course you do," he said gently, holding her even more closely.

She relaxed against him, tempted to give in to her sensual demands but held back by some inner voice warning her about becoming too complacent.

"It was when I saw Daniella and her mother today, hugging each other in spite of all they'd been through, that I realised I mustn't take my relationship with Rose for granted."

"I don't think you'll ever do that," he said.

He bent his head and kissed her gently. "Last night was wonderful," he whispered.

"Mmm." For a brief moment she snuggled against him, before making a determined effort to move from his embrace.

She had an awful feeling of déjà vu. She'd been here before, hadn't she? Given all her love to a man she'd adored, trusted completely. But he'd betrayed her. Her mother had been betrayed in the same way. Having loved her father, given him a daughter, he'd chosen to take off and leave her.

From the experiences of life she'd had so far she couldn't expect Yannis to be any different, even if he seemed completely perfect now. She'd known him such a short time, but long enough to know that he still loved his wife and there was no way he was ever going to forget the wonderful marriage they'd had. However wonderful her relationship with Yannis felt at the moment, it could crumble away when she least expected it.

But her love for Rose would always be there. Blood was thicker than water. Whatever happened in the future, the bond with her daughter would always be there and she had to continue to strengthen it. For her own sake and for Rose's.

They would need each other for the rest of their lives, no matter what happened in the future.

Yannis was looking down at her with a quizzical expression. "Cathy, I wish you'd tell me what's worrying you so deeply, something you haven't explained to me. You've hardly told me anything about the man who left you. Rose's father. Don't you think it would help if you opened up more and we could discuss it together? I could help you as you've helped me. But not until you explain what—"

"I don't want to discuss it!" She stared up into his dark brown eyes. "My past is so...so complicated and..."

"But if we could talk about together I'm sure it would help! I hate it when you draw away from and start worrying about something that I'm sure I could help you with if only you'd bring it out into the open."

He reached forward and drew her against him. She leaned against him for a few moments before pulling away again.

"I'm sorry, Yannis. I really don't want to talk about it. I'm...I'm not ready to explain. Maybe one day you'll understand why... Look, I've got to go."

CHAPTER TEN

"HAPPY birthday, dear Rose, happy birthday to you!"

Cathy was feeling complete, surrounded by people she loved—Rose, Yannis, Anna. Life was so good at the moment—but how long would this last? Was it just an illusion? Yannis hadn't made them any promises, and as time was passing she ought to make a decision before it was too late and her heart was broken, and Rose's too.

"Mama!"

Cathy smiled as she bent over her daughter.

"Blow out the candle, Rose," she said gently.

Rose looked up at her mummy enquiringly, not sure what was expected of her now.

"Look, like this," Yannis said gently, making a blowing sound and pointing to the candles on top of the cake that Eleni had gone to so much trouble to make.

He was feeling so relieved that Rose's birthday celebrations were going so well. Maybe Cathy would begin to relax soon. He hoped so because she'd seemed a bit strained for the past few days. He'd no idea what the problem was but something was definitely worrying her. Perhaps he could find out what the matter was tonight, if he could only persuade her to stay over when everyone else had gone.

Little Rose was looking up at him now, still confused about what was expected of her.

"Rose, darling," he said, bending over her as he pointed to the all-important candle. "I know you've never had a birthday before but you'll soon get used to having them. You'll get more than you need as time goes on."

Everybody laughed and Rose giggled.

"Rose, blow when I blow, OK?" He pouted his lips forward and blew gently at the edge of the table.

Rose giggled again and copied what Yannis was doing with his lips.

"Do that again," Cathy said, "but make it like that strong wind we sometimes have by the sea."

Hmm. Strong wind? OK, if that was what they all wanted. So long as she got some cake at the end of all this! Rose pouted her lips and instinctively drew in her breath to make a really big strong wind that would blow that candle thingy off the top of the cake.

Everybody was cheering now. Rose clapped her hands together like they were all doing.

"Would you like some cake, Rose?" Cathy asked her daughter.

She removed the smouldering candle and picked up the cake knife, putting her hand over Rose's and guiding her tiny fingers carefully towards the centre of the cake.

"Let's put the knife in here, Rose," Cathy said gently. "Don't worry, Yannis, I'm holding the knife very firmly. It's quite safe."

There was more clapping as Cathy guided the knife that was being loosely held by her daughter's tiny fingers into the cake.

Yannis could feel himself becoming completely sentimental as he watched Cathy and Rose reacting to each other. After Maroula had died he'd never imagined he could be so happy again. Did he deserve all this? Why couldn't he get rid of the feelings of guilt when he enjoyed himself?

"I'll take the cake to the kitchen and let Eleni cut it up with a big sharp knife," he said.

"Good idea," Cathy said.

He picked up the cake and knife and went across the lawn to the kitchen. If only he could completely commit himself to this wonderful surrogate family, deal with the guilt he felt at being so happy, and find out what it was that was troubling Cathy, life would be perfect!

"Is something worrying you, Yannis?" Cathy said, as she cradled the sleeping Rose in her arms.

"I'm fine, but I'm worried about you. I wish you'd tell me what's troubling you," he said, quietly, as he leaned over to hand her a glass of chilled champagne.

She looked up at him as she put the glass to lips. "It's been a fabulous party. Thank you so much for everything you did to make it such a success."

"It's not speeches I want, Cathy," he said evenly, pulling up a chair so that they could be close. "You haven't answered my question."

"I'm not sure how to explain it." She put down her glass on the table and looked around her at the debris left behind after the guests had gone home. Eleni and Petros were in the kitchen, putting away food, washing dishes, but they would be out here soon to clear up.

"Start by telling me what's worrying you. You've been so…preoccupied with your own thoughts for the past couple of weeks, since you stayed here that night and everything between us was so wonderful. You've kept yourself to yourself…almost as if you don't trust me any more."

"I do trust you," she told him adamantly, wanting desperately to believe what she was saying.

Of all the men she'd known in her life there had never been anyone like him. But there was always that nagging voice at the back of her mind telling her that she would never be able to hold onto him, that he would break her heart in the end. He would leave her, as her father had left her mother, as Daniella's father had left Daniella's mother. And like men in so many films she'd seen and books she'd read. It was in their nature. They were simply doing what came naturally. The grass always looked greener on the other side or, in Yannis's case, she suspected his past life when he'd been totally committed to Maroula always seemed perfect.

She remembered how she'd thought her relationship with Dave was going to last for ever but he'd decided to stay with his wife.

When this idyllic period of their life together began to wane, would Yannis's guilt at betraying his perfect wife take over? Would he choose to go back into his safe state of bachelorhood, content to dwell on the idyllic past he'd shared with the first love of his life?

He leaned forward, putting his arms around both of them. "You mean the world to me," he said quietly. "You and Rose. I couldn't bear to lose you."

She looked up from her sleeping child into his trusting eyes. How could she doubt him at a time like this, after the wonderful day they'd had together? Why didn't she stop looking into the future and simply enjoy the present?

"I couldn't bear to lose you either, Yannis," she said softly.

He gave her a relieved smile. "Well, neither of us is going anywhere. Please stay here tonight...both of you. We can put Rose to bed in the small dressing room adjoining my bedroom."

Cathy could feel herself relaxing. Yes, she had been tense today. Probably nobody had noticed it but Yannis. But now the thought of going with the flow was very appealing. What did it matter if she was deluding herself about their relationship? The present moment was all that mattered, wasn't it?

"Yes, I'd like to stay," she said quietly. "I'll take Rose upstairs and put her into her cot."

"You'll find everything you need in the dressing room but give me a shout if you need some help. I'll stay down here and help Eleni and Petros clear up."

Cathy was halfway across the lawn to the kitchen when Eleni came out.

"Are you going to put Rose in the cot in the dressing room now?" she asked in hushed tones so as not to wake the little one. "I'll come up and help you find everything."

"Yannis says there's everything I need up there."

"Of course there is. I got the little room ready myself this morning when I suggested you and Rose might like to stay here tonight."

"That was very thoughtful of you, Eleni."

"Men never think ahead, do they? Everything spur of the moment, whereas we women are always one step ahead."

Rose stirred and opened her eyes as Cathy sat down on the chair by the side of the cot.

"I brought some clean baby clothes from my house yesterday. My grandchildren have all grown too big for them. I thought this little nightdress would fit Rose perfectly. Might still be a bit big but you don't want it too tight, do you? It's thin cotton so she won't get too hot. I remember when my own babies were small..."

Cathy listened to the soothing voice, chatting away in Greek. What a wonderful lifestyle she was having at the moment. Working at the hospital, doing a job she was trained for, skilled at and found so stimulating and satisfying. And then being able to combine that with motherhood in an environment where she got so much help and Rose was so happy.

Rose had submitted to having the cool cotton nightdress put on her before closing her eyes again and sinking contentedly against the mattress.

"I'll cover her with the sheet, Cathy," Eleni said. "It will get cooler when the sun goes down."

Cathy nodded. It was so nice to have the advice of an older woman—even if she didn't agree with it! She would pop back soon and remove the sheet if she thought it wasn't necessary. Although Eleni was more experienced than she was in caring for babies during a hot Greek summer.

"*Efharisto poli*, thank you very much, Eleni," she said as they both tiptoed out.

"*Parakalor*," Eleni replied with a smile.

They were passing through the master bedroom when Eleni paused at the table with Maroula's photo on it. She leaned down and picked it up before turning to look at Cathy.

"I dust this every day and I can't help thinking it's time Yannis put all these photos of his late wife away, don't you?"

For a brief moment Cathy didn't know how to answer. "I'm not sure…" she began cautiously. "I think Yannis finds it comforting to have these reminders of his wife around."

"Well, it's more than three years now since she died and I think it's time he moved on completely," Eleni retorted, holding the picture at arm's length. "Some days when I'm dusting I feel like gathering up the whole lot and putting them in a box."

"Oh, you mustn't do that!"

"I don't think he'd really notice. Men aren't observant about what's sitting around in the house. When he first moved in he used to be always staring at her photos. But I've noticed he never gives them a glance nowadays."

Cathy felt her spirits lifting upwards. She could have hugged Eleni for that piece of comforting information!

"Well, I think we should leave them there until Yannis decides to put them away, Eleni," Cathy said firmly. "It has to be his decision. He will know when the time is right…even if that time never arrives."

Her voice trailed away at the end of her conclusion. She could tell by Eleni's frown that she didn't agree with her.

As they went out on to the landing and began their descent of the wide staircase, Eleni continued to put forward what she thought about the situation.

"I've always told Petros that if I go first he should find himself another wife as soon as he possibly can. Men can't manage without a woman. It's not natural for them. And Yannis has got you to care for him now so why he's hanging onto those old photos I don't know. It doesn't…"

Eleni stopped in mid-sentence as she noticed Yannis standing at the bottom of the staircase, looking up towards them.

"Cathy, I was just coming to see if Rose is OK up there."

"She's fast asleep. Eleni helped me to settle her."

"*Efharisto*, Eleni. Petros is ready to go home now. We've finished clearing up."

Eleni smiled. "*Kali nichta*. Goodnight. I'll see you both in the morning."

Yannis took hold of her hand and led her across the lawn towards the garden room. "I thought we could watch the sunset from here tonight. We're directly outside Rose's room so we'll hear her if she cries."

They sat quietly, holding hands, watching the big red ball

dip down behind the hill at the back of the house. They still remained there in the gathering dusk after the sunset.

"Are you hungry, Cathy? I thought I would make us some supper. You've only been grazing at the party food. I could heat up some soup from the fridge."

"I'll help you."

As they went back into the house, she was thinking about Eleni's words. She was a very wise woman who'd worked out exactly what Yannis had to do to get his life back on track. Come to think of it, so had she! But getting him to see the light was the problem.

They ate their soup sitting at the kitchen table, a Rachmaninov CD in the background. They discussed which of his works they liked best and discovered it was his second piano concerto.

"Not surprising!" Cathy said. "I think it's everybody's favourite."

"Oh, I don't know. His third symphony is another favourite of mine."

"Yes, I like that too," she conceded as the music rolled over them. "Especially the second movement."

Yannis was watching her as she listened.

"You know, it's good to be with someone who appreciates classical music. Maroula constantly changed the music when we had the radio on in the car."

"Really? What kind of music did she prefer?"

"She liked Greek folk songs…but that was all…so…"

He was staring at her with that expression he'd had on the boat when he'd almost called her Maroula. But she was becoming immune to the fact that he thought often about his late wife. At least this time he hadn't said she was a musical genius. Now, that really would have been a pain!

"You know, Cathy, I always feel I have to be careful when I'm speaking about Maroula. I don't like to criticise her because she can't answer back. But the fact that she didn't like the same kind of music as I did was often a bone of contention between us."

"Really?" She found she was holding her breath at the revelation. "That bad, was it?"

"Well, no relationship can be perfect all the time, can it?"

"Of course not."

Well, glory be! Was he beginning to see the light? Was the goddess beginning to slip from her pedestal? She stood up and began to clear the dishes.

"I'll go up and check on Rose," she said.

"I'll join you soon," he said absently, as he changed the CD. "I just want to listen to this new CD I bought last week. Mozart's piano concerto number twenty. It's a new recording by a young Greek pianist which I'd like to hear. I couldn't resist buying it. The internet just makes shopping too easy."

"I'd love to hear it but not tonight."

As she went up the stairs she reflected that the easy relationship they'd had together tonight gave her hope that progress was being made. She would be an idiot to leave all this behind just when they were beginning to really get to know one another.

She was lying in the bath when he came in dressed in his robe. He sat down on the edge of the bath.

"Shall I put the jacuzzi switch on?"

"Not yet. I was just having a time of quiet contemplation."

"Thinking about what?" he asked as he slipped off his robe and joined her.

"Mainly about us."

"Mmm, that's good," he said, snuggling up to her. "I love having you here to stay with me. Maybe…"

He hesitated. He'd been going to suggest she bring Rose and move in with him, but the way she'd been behaving towards him recently meant he didn't think she would consider it a good idea. There was so much about Cathy he didn't understand. That relationship she'd had with the man who'd fathered Rose must have been difficult. What man in his right mind would abandon his girlfriend when she was pregnant? It would be a long time before Cathy was ready to put her trust in someone so that she would make any kind of commitment.

And he needed to make sure he was ready for commitment himself. He still hadn't learned to handle the guilt that nagged him constantly about liaising with a woman other than Maroula. He still had awful flashbacks in his dreams about that fateful weekend. He shouldn't have left her…not straight after their awful row…

Cathy could feel Yannis tensing up. The more she got to know him the more she felt he was holding something back. He'd told her so many intimate truths that he'd never told anyone else but there was still something secret. Something that he daren't divulge to anybody. Maybe that was why he still suffered from guilt.

"You would tell me if something was worrying you, wouldn't you, Yannis?" she whispered.

"Of course." He moved away to press the switch that set off the jacuzzi jets. "Let's have some bubbles to float away our problems."

"If only it were that simple," she said quietly as the jets came on to drown her voice.

He moved back again and took her into his arms. The close contact of his skin, the soothing bubbles relaxed her until she found herself desperate to make love with him. The last time they'd been in here together neither of them could wait to quench their sexual longings for each other.

But tonight they took everything more slowly, savouring every step towards consummation. As she felt herself reaching orgasm she cried out, unable to control the vibrations of passion that had taken over her body. Last time had been out of this world. This time had been completely different, more cerebral, each giving more consideration to the reaction of the other as they moved forward towards their joint climax.

"You know, Yannis," she said breathlessly, as she lay back amongst the bubbles cocooned in his strong muscular arms. "Making love is different every time, isn't it?"

"I should hope so, otherwise couples who'd been together for a long time would get terribly bored."

"Do you think they would?"

"Probably. But we don't need to worry about it. We've only known each other a matter of weeks, haven't we? Which reminds me. I had a phone call from Manolis yesterday. He's been offered a promotion in the hospital in Sydney. He and Tanya are thinking of staying out there for at least another year and he wanted to know if I was interested in applying for permanent post of medical director at the hospital."

"And what did you say?" She shifted herself in his arms and moved to one of the seats in the sides of the jacuzzi.

"I said I'd think about it and let him know. He told me he'd have to advertise the post as a matter of protocol but he wanted me to know that from the reports sent back to him from the chairman of the Ceres hospital board the job would be mine if I applied."

"So what is there to think about? Don't you want to be permanent director?"

He hesitated. "I used to be too ambitious. I've been careful about each step I take since…"

He broke off, thinking once more about that fatal day. He thought he'd changed since then but deep down he was still the same. But he'd learned what was most important in his life.

Cathy was waiting for him to continue. She knew that it wasn't a good idea to enquire too deeply when Yannis was deep in thought. He was obviously thinking about something that had happened in the past. He would tell her in his own good time—or not! She was learning to be patient and fatalistic. What would be would be.

He focused his eyes directly at her as he came out of his reverie. "Are you going to apply for an extension to your contract when it expires at the end of October?"

"Hadn't thought about it yet," she lied.

Of course she'd thought about it! How could she not have? But until she knew whether Yannis wanted to commit to a more permanent relationship she wasn't going to commit herself to anything. She wasn't going to hang around for ever. Either he stopped sitting on the fence and asked her…asked her for what?

She was his number one girlfriend but that wasn't enough. Before Rose got much older she had to be careful who she allowed her daughter to regard as a father figure. And she had to make sure, this time, hat their relationship, fantastic as it was at the moment, wasn't going to collapse when the man in her life decided he wanted to renew his old lifestyle and left her in the lurch.

"Let me know when you've decided what you want to do at the end of October, Cathy."

"Of course."

She pulled herself out of the water and wrapped herself in

one of the huge fluffy towels. She wouldn't make any decision until he'd made his intentions towards her clearer. Once bitten, twice shy! And she'd been bitten more than once or twice so was many times more shy than most women.

She pretended to be asleep when he climbed into bed. She found herself sleeping fitfully, turning over carefully so as not to waken him. As the dawn light began to filter in through the French doors that led to the balcony she came to the decision that she would enjoy her relationship with Yannis until her contract expired at the end of October. But then, if nothing had changed, if he was still clinging to the past, unwilling to move forward and make a permanent commitment with her, she would go back to England. She had to come to terms with things herself.

She sat alone on the balcony, watching the sun come up over the hill on the other side of the water. Yannis was still asleep or feigning sleep, she didn't know which, but she'd had time to herself to make her decision. For the last few weeks of the summer out here she was going to enjoy what they had together and not think too much about whether it was permanent or temporary.

Make the most of every day, she told herself, and don't look too far ahead. Whatever happened, she would be in control this time and well prepared to deal with it.

She was fixing Rose into her high chair down in the kitchen when Yannis came down.

"You shouldn't have let me sleep so long."

He flopped down into the armchair at the side of the stove, running his hands through his ruffled hair. She thought he looked like a truculent boy who was trying to think where he'd put his homework and her heart went out to him as she tried to stifle her longing to go back to bed and make love with him.

"Did you sleep well, Cathy?"

"Yes." She was getting good at saying what she knew he expected to hear.

She handed him a cup of coffee. He put it down on the table so that his hands were free to draw her into his arms.

"Mmm, good morning, darling," he said, as he finished kissing her.

"Mama!" Rose called in a demanding tone from the table.

Cathy went back to the table and kissed her daughter. Rose gurgled with delight and offered her mummy the piece of bread she'd half eaten.

"No, thank you, darling, I'm going to have some toast in a moment."

Yannis sat down beside Rose and kept her plate replenished with bread, honey, yoghurt and fruit.

Cathy was the first to leave the table and take some of the dishes over to the sink. She glanced at the clock.

"Time to make a move, Rose," she said, hauling her daughter out of the high chair and wiping a damp cloth around her face.

Yannis stood up and held out his arms towards Rose. She laughed with delight as Cathy handed her over.

"Rose almost walked yesterday," he told Cathy as he held the little girl against him. "I'm going to take her out onto the lawn and see how she gets on."

"I'll give her a quick shower afterwards," Cathy said, turning away to move some more dishes.

Yannis put out a hand to detain her. "Come with us outside. We can take a few minutes to play with Rose. These early days in a baby's life are so precious, aren't they? We can't get them back again when they're gone."

She took hold of his hand and they went out on to the sunlit grass. She could hear the sound of the gentle waves lapping on the shore. He put Rose gently down on the grass and then offered her his hand. She hauled herself up, holding onto Yannis to steady herself. She took a few tentative steps and giggled with delight. Very gently, Yannis loosened his fingers from her grasp. She looked up questioningly.

"It's OK, Rose. I'm not going to leave you. And the grass is very soft if you fall."

Rose smiled, held out her arms at the sides to balance herself and staggered across the grass for a few seconds before sitting down.

"Clever girl!" Cathy said. "Come to Mummy!"

Rose looked up at Yannis, holding out her little hand for him to help her up.

As soon as he'd set her upright she started off again, staggering back across the grass unaided like a baby foal that had just been born.

"Marvellous!" Cathy said as her daughter reached her and collapsed against her. "Oh, Yannis, I'm so glad we came out here. I'll remember this morning for…for a long time."

Her eyes locked with Yannis's in a heart-rending gaze.

She took a deep breath. Tears were prickling the back of her eyes. If only she could be sure that Yannis would be with her for the rest of her life. But she'd decided not to worry about how long their relationship was going to last, hadn't she? They'd enjoyed this precious moment together. The memory would stay with her for ever.

She turned away before and the precious moment was gone.

She took a deep breath as she composed herself. "Time to go, everybody," she said, gathering up her daughter.

CHAPTER ELEVEN

As Cathy switched off her computer at the end of another busy day at the hospital, her mind was on the phone call she'd just received. The summer weeks were flying by so quickly now. The tourists on holiday on Ceres had made the workload heavy. She was coping with her busy lifestyle, but always felt exhausted at the end of each day—like now. She'd been longing to go back to Anna's and pick up Rose so that the two of them could relax together for the evening.

But Anna's phone call just now had added to her problems. She stood up and was halfway to the door when someone knocked.

She opened the door. "Hi, Yannis. I'm just on my way out."

"You look tired. Let me take you…"

"Not tonight. I've got to go up to Anna's. She's just phoned to say she's got to go over to Rhodes tomorrow to be with her sister who's seriously ill in hospital. Her nearest relatives have been alerted and are gathering there as soon as they can make it. Anna could be there a week or two, so…"

"So you're worrying about Rose," he said, taking hold of her hand as they walked down the corridor towards the side door of the hospital.

"And Anna as well. She sounded so worried when she rang

that I thought something had happened to Rose. It was almost a relief when I realised my only problem was to find child care for Rose. Of course I told her I'm terribly sorry for the distress she's going through at the moment but she assured me she's tough enough to handle it. She said she'd had enough practice in her long life to handle anything. That I can believe!"

"Has Anna got enough help with organising her transfer over to Rhodes tomorrow?"

Cathy nodded. "One of her sons is coming to take her down to the early ferry tomorrow morning. But I need to get up to take Rose off her hands as soon as possible and give her some space to get ready."

He held the outer door open for Cathy to go out first. "I've got the car with me. I'll take you up to Anna's now."

She watched his firm hands on the wheel as he steered the car through the main entrance of the hospital. The porter on the door saluted him. Yannis smiled and saluted him back. The porter grinned happily.

Over the past few weeks she'd come to realise that Yannis had become a very popular temporary director of the hospital. She wondered if she could take any credit for bringing him out of his shell. What was important was that she hoped he was going to make a decision about becoming permanent director.

"Someone to care for Rose is not going to be a problem," Yannis said evenly, as he began the steep ascent up the hillside road.

"Eleni would be delighted to take care of her. You know how she adores her. She's actually got her first great grandchild staying with her at the moment. Little Alissa is two years old and her mother, Eleni's eldest daughter, is expecting her second baby soon, so Eleni asked if she could bring Alissa to work with her sometimes so that her daughter could get some rest."

Cathy was overawed by the proposition, playing for time before she gave a definitive answer.

"It would certainly solve the problem," she said cautiously. "But Eleni is a great-grandmother. She still looks strong, but how old is she?"

Yannis smiled. "She told me she had her first child at seventeen, her first grandchild at thirty-six, and now she's still in her mid-fifties. She's like Anna. Children have been her life's work and she loves it."

"Younger than I thought. Well, if you're sure it wouldn't be too much for her, I would be happy to bring Rose along every day if that's what you're suggesting."

He took a deep breath. "Better still, why don't you move in?"

He found he was holding his breath now, not only because there was a big lorry with a large load of timber coming down towards him on this narrow bend but also because he'd finally got around to saying what he'd wanted to say for the past few weeks of this long hot summer.

"Wow, that was a close shave!" Cathy said as she tried to regain her composure. She'd tensed up as the lorry had rumbled towards them. But the child-care solution that Yannis had just come out with had been so spontaneous, so heartfelt that she was thrown into confusion at the implications of the situation she had to consider.

Yannis took one hand off the wheel as they reached the straight section of the road at the top of the hill and took hold of her hand, waiting for her reply. She looked down at the toy-like boats moored in the harbour for the night as she tried to calm herself. The lights had just come on, twinkling all the way down the road below her. The harbour looked like a toy town.

Everything was moving too fast for her. She needed more

time to think – but under the circumstances she had to come to a quick decision.

"You're very quiet," he said, taking his hand away again in case it was clouding her judgement.

It wasn't a big decision, was it? He still couldn't understand what went on in Cathy's head half the time!

"Surely, it's the obvious solution. I mean, you've often stayed at home with me over the summer, haven't you? Sometimes with Rose, sometimes by yourself like last weekend."

She couldn't help herself smiling at the memory of last weekend. Anna had insisted she needed a complete break because she'd been working so hard. So when Yannis had suggested a weekend at home with him she'd jumped at the chance. And it had been truly paradise, just the two of them!

But one night was different from moving in with all the implications of surrendering her independence. There was absolutely no guarantee that this was what he really wanted. She reasoned that he was such a good-hearted person he'd simply been thrust into a situation where he was feeling it his duty to help her out in an emergency. She shouldn't read anything into it.

His fingers had slid back to grasp hers. She told herself firmly now that she had to stick to the survival plan she'd made weeks ago. Take their relationship day by day. Don't expect anything to be permanent. Just enjoy the present.

"Well?" he asked.

"I think that would be the best solution to the problem," she said carefully. "But we should run it past Eleni and see what she thinks."

"I know already what Eleni will think," he said happily. "She'll be over the moon to have the two of you there all the time."

"Just temporarily," Cathy put in quickly. "One or two weeks, Anna said."

"Whatever," he told her, switching off the engine as they arrived at the end of Cathy's street. "I'll ask Petros to pick up you and Rose in the morning so you don't have a problem with the luggage. I've got an early start in Theatre tomorrow."

He got out of the car and came round to open her door.

"I won't be bringing much luggage," she said as she climbed out. "I won't be there for long."

"Bring what you like," he said easily, sensing that she was still worried about the situation and needed reassurance. "We're kitted out already for Rose, as you know, so it's just a case of a few clothes for the pair of you. Can you be ready by eight? When you've settled Rose in with Eleni, you can come along and start work. You're in Outpatients tomorrow, aren't you? I'll make sure you're covered until you arrived."

"Thanks a lot. You've been so helpful about this."

She looked up at him, wanting so much to be taken into his arms, to know that he wasn't just being dutiful towards her.

"Mama!" Anna had appeared in her doorway, holding Rose's hands so that she could walk a few steps towards her mother.

"Come to Yannis!"

He was holding out his arms towards the small girl, who was beaming with delight at the sight of her mother and her beloved Yanyan. He took a few steps towards her and she reached out to grasp his hands.

"Well done!" He lifted Rose up into his arms. "*Kali spera*, Anna. I'm so sorry to hear about your sister. Cathy and Rose are coming to stay over at my house until you get back."

Anna smiled. "That's good. I won't worry about them if they're over in Nimborio with you, Yannis."

* * *

Lying in the warm sun, stretched out on the shore at the end of Yannis's garden, Cathy was telling herself that however temporary her relationship with Yannis was she was certainly going to make the most of it.

She looked around her at the sparkling sea, the hills with the heat haze rising from them to burn away before it got as far as the blue, blue sky. If this wasn't paradise, what was? And to think, a couple of days earlier when Yannis had suggested she and Rose move in, she'd hesitated before coming to a decision.

After two days of being pampered and cared for she was feeling as if she was a completely different woman to the harassed individual she'd been before she'd moved in with Yannis.

Oh, she'd had to go into hospital and work during the day, but that was what she was trained to do and it always gave her a sense of satisfaction at the end of the day. And she often got whole weekends off, like today.

She turned on her side to look at Yannis stretched out beside her, and found her pulses racing at the sight of his sensual, virile body. Only hours before he'd held her in his arms and they'd made love again. The culmination of a wonderful night together.

"Two weekends in a row, Dr Karavolis," she murmured. "Are you sure you're not giving us preferential treatment?"

"What if I am?" he said huskily. "We've shouldered a heavy load this summer. Things are easing off now and I can afford to be generous with time off duty for deserving doctors like you and me who've toiled through the difficult weeks. You can look forward to more time off than you've had of late."

She gazed through her sunglasses up into the sky where the sunlight was filtering through the dense branches of the olive tree that provided shelter for them. This was surely where she belonged. But for how long? How long before the dream life-style ended? It couldn't go on like this for ever. Not in her experience of real life!

She was right to be cautious, to take life with Yannis one day at a time.

Yannis eased himself up on one elbow and looked down at her. "Do you fancy a swim?"

"Soon. I'm enjoying being lazy, doing nothing for a change."

"What time is Eleni bringing Rose back here?"

"They're having some kind of family lunch at her house. They all adore children in their family, as you know, and I think she wants to introduce Rose to them. It's a good thing Rose is a gregarious little girl. Large gatherings never faze her. I don't expect she'll be back until the end of the afternoon. Why? Were you thinking we could go out in the boat or something?"

He bent his head closer to hers and kissed her gently on the lips. "Actually, I was thinking more along the lines of 'or something'," he murmured against her parted lips.

His kiss deepened and she felt the wonderful waves of renewed passion coursing through her body, tingling, tempting, impossible to resist... And why should she? The timing was perfect, both of them ready to renew the intimacy they'd enjoyed throughout the night.

He sensed her arousal as he gently drew her to her feet, brushing the sand off her arms as he held her closely against him.

"Let's go back to bed," he whispered huskily.

She smiled up into his eyes. There was nothing she would like better than spending a few more blissful hours alone with him.

* * *

They went in through the kitchen door and made their way across the hall to the foot of the stairs. One hand round her waist and the other on the carved oak of the banister, Yannis frowned and pointed across to the ornate highly polished hall table.

"What's the matter?"

She felt a chill of apprehension running through her. Was she about to wake up from the dream? Had it been too good to be true after all?

"Maroula's photograph. It's gone." He paused before staring at Cathy in bewilderment. "Have you moved it?"

She could feel the anger rising up. To be accused of something she hadn't done, something she'd wanted to do but had resisted for so long, was unbearable.

"No, I haven't moved Maroula's photograph!"

She could feel herself trembling. "Not that one on the hall table or any of her other photographs that seem to be everywhere in this house."

"Cathy, I was only asking. It seemed so strange not to have it there in its usual place."

"Well, I think it's strange to have the place full of Maroula's photographs when you've brought me here as your...I don't know what I am when I'm here with you, surrounded by all these reminders of your first love!"

She sank down at the foot of the stairs as tears of frustration poured down her cheeks.

He sat beside her but not too close. Her body was rigid, set in a don't-touch-me attitude.

"I'd no idea you felt like that. I'd simply got used to the photo being there and I noticed that—"

"Eleni must have moved it," she said evenly.

"Why would she do that?"

"She told me she thought it was time all the photographs were put away."

He stood up and began to pace around the hall. "So you discussed me with her, did you?"

"It wasn't a discussion. She simply came out with her opinion."

"And you agreed with her?"

"Actually, I told her you would put the photos away when you were ready to move on."

"Let me get this straight. You think the photos being around signified that I wasn't ready to move on?"

"I don't know what to think any more. It certainly didn't help me to have them here as a constant reminder of your idyllic first marriage."

"It wasn't always idyllic," he said quietly. "In fact, on the day Maroula drove off to her parents' house we had a big row."

He was standing very quietly now, looking down at the space where his wife's photograph had been.

Cathy waited as she saw the look of anguish on his face, knowing she mustn't break the silence or he might never reveal what was troubling him.

"She accused me of being completely selfish, always putting myself first. She said I was too ambitious to take her needs into consideration. I told her I was working hard to make a good life for my family. I had to take part in the conference that weekend. But she wouldn't listen. She slammed out of the house…and I didn't stop her. I was too wrapped up in the work I had to do."

He paused. Cathy could hear the grandfather clock ticking near him. She remained silent, willing him to continue.

He took a deep breath. "The next time I saw her was at the hospital. I never got to say goodbye. I drew the sheet back from her face and told her I was sorry. But the awful guilt remained."

Cathy stood up and moved swiftly across the hall to reach her arms out to him. He drew her against him and they stood, motionless, together.

"Yannis you've got nothing to feel guilty about. You were doing what you thought was right for your family. You had a row about it. All couples have rows. You didn't know Cathy would die the next day. That's why we should…"

She stopped. How could she tell him what she was thinking?

"Please go on, Cathy," he said, holding her even more closely.

"I think all couples should make the most of what they've got," she said cautiously. "We don't know what's around the corner in life."

He drew her closer to him. "Cathy, you're so precious to me I couldn't bear to lose you. I can't imagine life without you any more. But whenever I try to find out what's really worrying you, you hold back on me. You've got to tell me what's making you afraid of being really open with me."

For a few moments she remained absolutely still in his arms, knowing it was make-or-break time. As she raised her eyes to his she saw an expression of such love that she knew she had to tell him everything.

She moved out of his embrace and took hold of his hand, leading him into the sitting room. "Let's sit down together and I'll try to explain."

He looked at her apprehensively as they sat side by side in separate armchairs by the open windows.

She fixed her eyes on the wonderful view across the water, the tops of the gentle waves twinkling in the sunshine. She gazed at Yannis who was waiting for her to open up to him.

"Yannis, I've given my heart to several men and had it broken. It started with my father, my own flesh and blood. I adored him. I thought he would be there for ever with me. But one day he just walked out and never came back. So my heart was broken for the first time."

She drew in her breath, trying to control the tears that were threatening.

Yannis remained absolutely still. He longed to take her in his arms but he sensed she wanted to continue now and tell him the whole story.

"Later, there were boyfriends who seemed charming and attentive, fun to be with. But I was always too trusting. They were never what they'd seemed at first. It always ended in tears. But when Dave came along I really felt I could trust him."

She paused before continuing. These were memories she'd like to forget. "I met him in a wine bar in Leeds. I was relaxing with a few girlfriends for the evening. He came across and asked if he could buy us some drinks. Then he sat down at our table. He singled me out from the start and I was utterly charmed by him. He asked if he could take me out for dinner the next evening.

"Over dinner he told me a pack of lies —and I believed him! He told me his wife had left him the year before, but actually nothing could have been further from the truth. She had no idea that he was seeing me behind her back, their marriage was solid as far as she was concerned. I later discovered that not only was he still married, he also had children."

"Cathy, I can't bear to think how you must have felt when you found out the truth." Yannis moved across and sat on the arm of her chair, reaching down to cradle her in his arms.

"It was a whole year before I did. He'd moved into my flat. He said he was a banker in London so he used to work away Monday to Friday. After a while he started going away on so-called business trips and I wouldn't see him for weeks at a time and…"

He held her close as she began to sob.

"And then, on two occasions he called out his wife's name in the night. Maggie, she was called. So when you started to say Maroula's name on the boat it brought it all back to me and just as I was beginning to trust you I couldn't help thinking you would be like all the other men in my life. I couldn't trust my own judgement where men were concerned. Eventually you would leave me. I was just too afraid to give myself to you completely. I had to hold something back, to plan for a future where there was just Rose and me so that—"

"No, no, that will never happen, my darling. You are the love of my life now. Maroula will always be precious to me, but it doesn't diminish my love for you in any way. My feelings of guilt have absolutely vanished. And while I'll never forget Maroula, you are the centre of my life now. You were saying just now that couples should make the most of every moment together because you never know what's round the corner. Well, that's especially true of couples like us."

He took a deep breath. "Cathy, I've wanted to make the most of every minute of my time with you. But I sensed you were wary of making a commitment to me…and I don't blame you, after all you've been through. But if I wait until I think you might agree to…what I'm trying to say is…will you marry me?"

She lay back against the pillows, wondering if it had all been a dream. In a book she'd read as a child it had said that sometimes people would pinch themselves to make sure.

"Ow!"

"Cathy, what's the matter?" Yannis came into the bedroom and hurried across to the bed.

She smiled up at him. "It definitely works."

"What does?"

"The pinch test to see if you're dreaming or not. Try it on yourself."

He set the bottle of champagne down on the bedside table and still holding the clean glasses in one hand he reached out towards her, stroking the side of her face tenderly.

"I know I'm not dreaming," he said huskily. "The last few hours have been completely real to me. As soon as you gave me the answer to the question I've been wanting to ask you for so long, I knew I'd never felt so alive."

He opened the champagne, handed her a glass and climbed back in beside her.

"Here's to the beginning of our real partnership," he said, linking his arm through hers as they brought their glasses to their lips. "Let's make a pledge that we'll be together as a family for ever."

"A family for ever!" they said as they clinked their glasses.

"You know, Yannis, Rose was one reason why I was holding back. I could see how she loved you and you loved her and I didn't want to put her through what I'd been through. My mother would bring a new boyfriend home, I'd get to know him, become fond of him, then he'd disappear and I was heartbroken."

"Darling, that would never happen with me. I adore Rose. I feel as if she's my own daughter. I can't wait…" He broke off and smiled. "What I'm trying to say is I do hope we're going to add to our family."

Cathy smiled back. "Of course we are. Well, we can try anyway."

"That will be fun!"

Cathy sighed. "To think it took a row to bring us to our senses."

"It certainly cleared the air." He lay back against the pillows, his head close to hers.

"That was our first row. We should have had one sooner."

"How about instead we both speak our minds when there's something worrying us? Then we won't need to have rows when we're married. For instance, if you'd told me sooner that you were fed up with seeing Maroula's photos around the house, I'd have put them away ages ago. I put them on display when I first moved in. They were a source of comfort to me at first but after I met you the photos remained simply because I'd got used to them being in the same places."

His words were taking away any doubts that might have lingered about the sincerity of his proposal. She felt she'd never been so happy in her life as she listened to his husky, emotional voice.

"More and more, during the past few weeks I've come to value my present life more than my past. I haven't dreamed about Maroula for ages…but I've dreamed about you. The first time it happened I woke up to find you weren't there and I was longing to go back to sleep and get back into my dream."

She sighed. "I still feel as if I'm dreaming. I can't actually remember what I said when you asked me to marry you."

"You didn't speak for what seemed such a long time to me. You looked as if you'd been struck dumb. And when you finally put me out of my misery you were whispering so quietly that I had to ask you whether you'd said yes or no."

"For the first time in my life I'd been struck dumb. And don't look at me like that because it was true."

"I never thought you would be at a loss for words, but you really were. I was worried you might faint."

"Was that why you carried me up to your bedroom and—?"

"Our bedroom," he corrected. "I was hoping we could live here after we're married but if you prefer we start off some-where new, I can—'

"I love this place. I'll make a few changes here and there but…"

"Talking of changes, I almost forgot."

"Where are you going?" She watched as he climbed out of bed.

He was opening his wardrobe. "I put them in here when I got back from Rhodes the other day. I was going to show you earlier today. Now, there's a coincidence!"

She was completely mystified. "Yannis, what are you…?"

"What do you think?" He swung round, holding a couple of silver-framed photographs in his hands. "I've been taking photos of you for weeks now. Sometimes you didn't even know, like on the boat with Rose… Look!"

He held out the lovely picture of mother and daughter that he treasured so much.

"I finally got around to having these two photos framed. I've discovered this excellent shop where they will make silver frames for your favourite pictures. I love this one where I asked you to look at the camera. You look so relaxed here."

"Yannis, I'd no idea you'd done anything with them! People take photos and forget about them, leave them in the camera or on their mobile."

"I couldn't forget these. I've got a whole boxful waiting to be framed. Very soon when we get loads of wedding photos we—"

He broke off as he heard voices downstairs.

"Eleni is back with Rose!" Cathy said, putting down her glass and leaping out of bed. She was pulling on her hastily discarded bikini and sarong which was lying on the floor together with Yannis's swimming trunks. "I'll go down and explain we were changing after our swim."

Yannis laughed. "Let's tell them the good news before we explain anything. Eleni will be so excited to be the first person to be invited to the wedding."

They linked hands as they went downstairs. "And Rose will be over the moon when I tell her she's going to be a bridesmaid," Cathy said, happily. "Even though she won't understand she'll realise that something wonderful is happening."

"The most wonderful event in my life."

"Mine too."

EPILOGUE

THEY'D chosen to have the wedding in the spring mainly because of Yannis's deep desire to adopt Rose so that she would be his daughter when they were married. He'd asked Cathy to put him in touch with Dave so they could arrange a meeting with a solicitor in London. It took several weeks to organise this but eventually, in the depths of an English winter, a meeting was arranged.

When Yannis got back from London, Cathy had been relieved to hear that Dave had been so amicable. He'd agreed that Yannis could adopt Rose. He'd explained that his wife still didn't know of the existence of his daughter. However, when Rose reached an age when she could understand that Yannis wasn't her biological father, she should be told the truth. If or when she asked to see Dave he would be happy to meet her. His wife would then learn of the existence of his daughter but he would deal with the consequences of that when it happened.

As Petros drove Yannis, Cathy and Rose back from the church to their house, the narrow road beside the water was lined with people calling out their good wishes to the happy couple.

Rose, firmly ensconced between the two of them, was waving madly. Above her head Yannis leaned across to Cathy.

"Happy?"

"What do you think? The church service was so moving. But I'm longing to get back home."

"Me too. I'll be especially happy when everybody leaves us by ourselves tonight."

Cathy gave a dreamy sigh. "Absolutely! But the feast that Eleni has prepared will be the finest wedding breakfast in the history of the world. Yannis, keep waving! We'll have plenty of time to ourselves tonight."

And tonight she would tell him her wonderful secret! Oh, she'd hugged it to herself ever since the test had confirmed her suspicions that morning. She hadn't dared to tell Yannis when they had to go through that long wedding service together. He would have been just too excited!

He was hoisting Rose onto his lap. "My beautiful daughter is my official waving person. She's doing a great job."

They were pulling into the drive now. Rose was allowed out so she could show off her beautiful bridesmaid dress to anybody who hadn't seen it. She twirled on the step in front of the front door and the photographers snapped madly.

"Bride and groom in front of their home!"

Cathy shook out the creases from her fabulous ivory silk gown, stepping carefully over the gravel in her impossibly high, strappy, elegant shoes. Yannis was holding her arm to make sure they made it to the top step.

They obliged with a couple of photos and then Cathy, catching sight of her mother in the crowd of guests, called out, "Mum! Come and have another photo taken with us."

"You can't be the mother of the bride," one of the photographers said. "You're much too young."

Cathy's slim, glamorous mother, radiant in an oyster satin suit, smiled at her daughter.

Cathy squeezed her mother's hand. "Sorry your new boy-friend couldn't make it. How's it going?"

"Well, as you know, I always live in hope but I'm never sur-prised if it goes wrong. One thing I'm certain of, though, you and Yannis are soul-mates. Nothing will go wrong with this marriage. Absolutely rock solid you are. Take it from me…"

"Smile for the camera, please. Three generations of beau-tiful girls, grandmother, bride, bridesmaid…put the little girl in the centre…"

"Ah!" The guests assembled in front of the house voiced their approval of the lovely family scene.

"And now, bride and groom, just one more time, please!"

"We're going inside after this one," Yannis whispered as they obliged the photographers. "I thought we could perhaps go upstairs and change into something casual like…how about that new negligee you bought?"

"Later…not long now…"

Yannis was nestled against the pillows waiting for her when she came out of the bathroom, loosely fastening the belt of her new silk negligee.

"Wow!"

"Do you like it?" She gave a twirl.

"What?"

"This expensive negligee you bought me."

"Oh, yes. I was talking about what was in it, though. Come a little closer so I can get a better view."

As she reached the side of the bed he reached out and with a deft flick of the hand removed the belt. The negligee hung loosely open now.

"Mmm, that looks much better. Better take it off so you don't crease it."

She smiled as she shrugged it to the floor, her body already tingling with anticipation of the night ahead. Climbing into bed, she snuggled against him.

"Would you like me to tell you a secret?"

"Only if you want to tell me. Is it good news or…?" He'd never seen her look so radiant.

"Cathy, It's not what I think it is…is it?" He was holding his breath as he waited for her answer.

"Well, that depends on what—"

"Are we going to have a baby? Are we…? Tell me, darling."

"We're going to have a baby, a little sister or brother for Rose."

"Oh, that's wonderful! I hadn't dared to hope. You've just made me the happiest man in the world! But, hey, are you sure?" His eyes twinkled mischievously.

"I did a test in the bathroom this morning. I'd bought the most reliable testing kit because I was late with my period. I'm sure."

He drew her closer. "Don't you think we should make absolutely sure?"

She smiled provocatively. "How?"

"I'd hoped you'd ask that! Let me show you…"

MEDICAL™ 2-in-1

Coming next month

WISHING FOR A MIRACLE
by Alison Roberts

Mac MacCulloch and Julia Bennett make the perfect team.
But after an illness left Julia unable to have children, she
stopped wishing for a miracle. Yet Mac's wish is standing right
in front of him – Julia…and whatever the future may hold.

THE MARRY-ME WISH
by Alison Roberts

Nine months pregnant with her sister's twins, paediatric
surgeon Anne Bennett bumps into ex-love Dr David Earnshaw!
When the babies are born, learning to live without them is
harder than Anne expected – and she soon discovers that
she needs David more than ever…

PRINCE CHARMING OF HARLEY STREET
by Anne Fraser

Temporary nurse Rose Taylor is amazed when her playboy
boss, Dr Jonathan Cavendish, expresses an interest! Swept
off her feet, shy Rose realises she's misjudged this caring man,
but when her contract ends she knows she *has* to walk away…

THE HEART DOCTOR AND THE BABY
by Lynne Marshall

When Dr Jon Becker agrees to father his friend René Munro's
baby, he's determined to support her…but his attraction
to the radiantly pregnant René takes him by surprise! Jon's got
used to the idea of becoming a father – is becoming
her husband the next step?

On sale 6th August 2010

MEDICAL™

Single titles coming next month

THE SECRET DOCTOR
by Joanna Neil

Dr Lacey Brewer knows she shouldn't let playboy Jake Randall into her life but her instincts tell her there's more to Jake than meets the eye. Lacey is the only one who can help him and if she can do that, just maybe – she can also win his heart.

THE DOCTOR'S DOUBLE TROUBLE
by Lucy Clark

Abbey Bateman was looking for a fresh start and working alongside her old rival Dr Joshua Ackles wasn't part of the plan! Until she learns that Joshua is now a single father. Abbey longs to be more than just a helping hand – if Josh will let her, she'll be a mother and wife too!

On sale 6th August 2010

2 FREE BOOKS
AND A SURPRISE GIFT

We would like to take this opportunity to thank you for reading this Mills & Boon® book by offering you the chance to take TWO more specially selected books from the Medical™ series absolutely FREE! We're also making this offer to introduce you to the benefits of the Mills & Boon® Book Club™—

- **FREE home delivery**
- **FREE gifts and competitions**
- **FREE monthly Newsletter**
- **Exclusive Mills & Boon Book Club offers**
- **Books available before they're in the shops**

Accepting these FREE books and gift places you under no obligation to buy, you may cancel at any time, even after receiving your free books. Simply complete your details below and return the entire page to the address below. You don't even need a stamp!

YES Please send me 2 free Medical books and a surprise gift. I understand that unless you hear from me, I will receive 5 superb new stories every month including two 2-in-1 books priced at £4.99 each and a single book priced at £3.19, postage and packing free. I am under no obligation to purchase any books and may cancel my subscription at any time. The free books and gift will be mine to keep in any case.

Ms/Mrs/Miss/Mr _____ Initials _____

Surname _____

Address _____

_____ Postcode _____

E-mail _____

Send this whole page to: Mills & Boon Book Club, Free Book Offer, FREEPOST NAT 10298, Richmond, TW9 1BR